# A Shroud for Laertes

# A Shroud For Laertes

## by
## Gerald Wallerstein

Some Notes on Father/Love, Father/Hatred
and the Unraveling of Identity

International Psychoanalytic Books (IPBooks)
New York • http://www.IPBooks.net

**A Shroud for Laertes**

Published by IPBooks, Queens, NY

Online at: www.IPBooks.net



Cover design by Blackthorn Studio

Book formatting by Noel S. Morado

ISBN: 978-1-956864-61-8

*"Why this desire to relate what we recall of the past? Because, just as any race has its mythology, so an individual bears within him his own private myths, which also gradually fade, finally disappearing into the depths of time; and yet things leave their traces, events of the vague and distant past having found their way into the heart, and these things concern us through the years, are a constant preoccupation of the deeper reaches of the mind, lasting until that time when all our actions cease. And suddenly one day this usually unconscious activity may open up for us, become an awakening of sorts; much like a silkworm, as it slowly eats away a mulberry leaf for no reason it can comprehend, becomes conscious of the slight sound its own mastication makes. So it raises its head, unsure, fearful almost as it gazes around its world, experiencing itself as something… whatever that might be."*

— Morio Kita, *Ghosts*


*"When I state myself, as the representative of the verse, it does not mean me, but a supposed person."*

— Emily Dickinson July 1862 letter, qtd Thomas Wentworth Higginson, *Carlyle's Laugh*


*"And things, what is the correct attitude to adopt toward things? And, to begin with, are they necessary?"*

— Beckett, *The Unnamable*


*"… [H]ate would not exist if love were not present."*

~Wilfred Bion,
*Learning from Experience*

*It is natural for a child to become more interested in the larger world as he grows and begins to come into daily contact with it. Waiting for him are school, neighborhood, friends and extended family, all of which merge into a fabric of life to which he becomes accustomed and from which he learns how to be human. [We are born animals; we grow into humans]. But that fabric, for all its value, acts also as a cover which begins to obscure his early years, so that memories he has kept of them, even if he has not understood their import, recede into the unconscious before they can be considered in the light of his later experience. In growth there is also loss, a loss which may certainly be hurried almost automatically if what has been forgotten factually led to pain, confusion or a severe lack of understanding of what was done to him (and his role in it); it is only by chance and the pressing of circumstance that the man who was once that child is led to try to recall the memories of those early years and when it becomes necessary, it must be done by forcing his way through that very fabric which allowed him to grow up but which now hinders him as he strives to recall the past.*

Father was dead. Mother lived alone in the house. Fifty years of smoking two packs of cigarettes a day had killed him. Seven hundred thousand cigarettes. He left no secrets; they never do, really. It's no secret that I didn't know him. It's the natural order of things. Mother cried for a day; she cried in the hearse on the way to the cemetery; then she ordered new living room furniture, had the house repainted and new windows installed. They had been married for forty years. She no longer had to hide the chocolate bars smuggled in by her friends. She smoked her Lucky Strikes (she had smoked as long as had my father; aside from a stroke, she had suffered no permanent damage). They smoked because they were unhappy, because they wanted the nipple, because they knew they would die; it was a game of roulette, in a way. But I don't really know why; I speculate. No matter where we had lived, in an apartment or a house, our living space had always been permeated by two palls: smoke and anger. When people ask me how long I have been a smoker, I tell them, "since I was three days old."

I remember him as short and lean. He began to go bald by the time he was twenty-five. Later he joined the American Communist Party. I wonder if he had political motives or merely thought shortness and baldness were not symbolic of power. He entered the army and finished his tour quickly in Lexington, Kentucky, where the disturbed were sent before going home. No records remain (fire in St. Louis). He refused psychiatric treatment when he returned.

She was a housewife who had been a tootsie. Pictures of her on the beach in pre-War Havana remain. She held one job in her life, as a stocker in the shoe section of a department store. She quit after the first day when she found she had one shoe left over. Attractive, plumpish, curvy. I saw her in the bath, once, and it has stayed with me. Her form is what I sought, later. I seldom think about her now; she must have been a decent mother.

It has suddenly occurred to me that I have begun by calling my parents Mother and Father, whereas I always referred to them as Mom and Dad. Am I trying to distance myself from any intimacy I may have felt for them? Do I want to create a false formalism to our relationship in order to mislead myself about its qualities, its nuances? Formalism, civility are disguises behind which anger lies. I do not know the answers to these questions. Since they occur to me so soon, though, I will take them as a warning: I must try to be accurate in my recollections without bending them toward falseness for my own sake. Otherwise, why put these words to paper? And my anger is obvious from the beginning[1]; it is a bitter beginning, why deny it? But let me consider this story as an attempt, anyway, not to lay aside ghosts, but to bring them forward in a sense of equality, for our natures are the same. Perhaps only our circumstances were different.

I have seen pictures; he in uniform, smiling. Behind him, a squad is marching, giving their leader the finger behind their backs. He always took a good picture, always an interesting *mise-en-scene.* Even when he had his arm

---

1 The first two sentences of these notes seem to me similar to gunfire.

around mother, he was smoking, with trees in full leaf in the background. Mother, smiling, in her Red Cross uniform; she had followed him to his first posting, in California.

I had thought for a long time that they hated each other, but I only saw, I did not observe. After supper (when we had moved to a house) he went down to his basement workshop, where he cursed her over the whirr of the power saw and the electric drill. She sulked in the living room. I went to my bedroom to read; I could hear his cursing through the heating flue. I imagined her sulking. I often went outside to the front lawn, where I lay on the grass and imagined breaking the windows; I thought, too, of making noise. I was not very old, then; it would not have changed anything. I could not have saved them. They did not want to be saved. He had planted azaleas on that lawn; I sometimes spoke to them, or, rather, I muttered as he had; but they only bloomed for three weeks in the spring; they were useless in the remaining seasons.

*This much I know: Mother was one of eight children. The oldest of them was Abe. Abe returned from high school one afternoon, retrieved his bicycle, and went to his job as a Western Union delivery boy. He was never seen again. The family thought he had been Shanghaied; they lived in the River wards of P and such action was possible. All the same, he never reappeared. Her father had already left on a visionary quest to South America. No photographs remain of either parent. My father was the youngest of six. His parents had married in Liverpool; no one has been able to verify the marriage; synagogues did not keep such records. Of the six, he seems to be the one who most worried my grandmother, according to the few relatives with whom I have spoken who were his contemporaries. He suffered from Ricketts as a child. His father ran a bar. None of his siblings have ever mentioned their father in my presence, nor did he. None seem to have any photographs of him, either. I have seen one photograph of my father with his siblings and his mother. A man is also in the photograph who was not my grandfather. One cannot say that these facts supply clues; nevertheless, both grandfathers do not appear to have been loved or respected. They hardly existed in the minds of any of their children.*

*I cannot say that this state of affairs affected my life, but in a sense it has. It is my prehistory, part of the constitution of my predispositions and drives.*

They, my parents, left me a thesis—Communism, action, and an antithesis, sitting, waiting—but no synthesis. And a definition of love–because they remained together—of torture, attack, siege, sulking and the double meaning of every word, every gesture, every silence.

⟫ ⟪

I was gone before he died. It hadn't been easy to leave. I was frightened of him. We'd made a contract, he and I, though I thought he didn't know it. I was wrong about that. I'd twist and contort myself into the shape I thought he wanted; he'd not embarrass me by letting me know he was onto my game. It lasted for a while, too. But he broke it in a huge way. He'd been to an Ivy League university for two years, before he dropped out to join the working class. Taught me the University's fight song, never spoke badly of it, until the same University admitted me. *"You're not going there,"* he said. I was supposed to go to the other university, where the proletarians went. I had no strength to withstand him. I was afraid of myself as well as him. Mother convinced him to change his mind, but I had already sent my rejection. I did not try to withdraw it. I could not have withstood the rancor I'd have expected if I went against his wishes.

I didn't know I'd leave until we had our major blowup. He was cursing in the cellar. Mother went down and begged him to stop. He was enraged; my fright turned to rage, too. I picked up an ashtray from his workbench, full of butts it was, and threw it to the floor as hard as I could. I had never stood up to him before. You'd think he'd have given pause, but he didn't. He cursed me, too. I had made that ashtray in metal shop. It was a bad job, too, full of dents I hadn't hammered out. I suppose I was telling him I wasn't going to be in the trades. I wonder what had happened at the University: anti-Semitism?

Snobbism? It even occurred to me that he may have been a homosexual. I ought to think about it; I owe him that much. Perhaps he did not want me to be born. But I don't think about it with certainty, either. His memory raises an issue: can I remember and revise without forgiving? Is forgiveness necessary? Anyway, it's me who has to atone for what was done to me. Strangulated love is so difficult to unravel.

I may return to them, in time, in more detail, turning them about as if they (and I) were pieces of sculpture that must be examined on every side to comprehend their beauty and its flaws. I will try not to repeat myself too often. After all, there is much I cannot recall, and I may have willingly taken on a role in the house of being a go-between, a child buffer-zone. A child, even a young child, has already created heroic and violent fantasies. I will not absolve myself of that possibility. It is possible that the very attempt to go back is only a heroic fantasy, a revenge fantasy, or a putting-back-together fantasy. It is also possible that I loved my father fiercely before and even after his betrayal. In fact, his death came in the middle of this story, not the beginning. I thought I would begin with it—he played and plays yet such a large role in my life. I will describe his death later; it was a lesson in our family relations. And, if I write only out of revenge, what am I?

That is one beginning. There could be many beginnings, but only one ending. Stay with me. My history and the reading I have done force me to consider two questions: am I justified in going on? Am I qualified to go on? Another beginning must come first.

I have had a professional life with some accomplishments; I married, raised a son to adulthood; I believed I had been able to love one or two people (and a pet cat). A few people may have loved me. When I began to think about them and my relation to them as husband, father, worker (as a necessity), I had first to examine these accomplishments in order to feel comfortable spending years, perhaps the rest of my life, in the undertaking. I had also to consider my own betrayals, to ask whether the very act of becoming an adult hurls one into a world where betrayal is simply self-preservation. I had no views in the matter; I had a moral conscience that judged only others, yet I had loathed myself for years; after I took an inventory of those accomplishments, the loathing seemed illogical. But only after considerable thought did I understand that I had missed an important consideration in looking at those accomplishments, namely, that my reason for doing so had been as a preparation for further work; I still believed I had to *achieve*, and the achievement had to be great, perhaps grandiose. I had already come to believe that all actions have more than one motive; we are fortunate to understand even one motive; but I had discovered that I not only knew little about the way my past (and the pasts of my parents as well) had brought me to where I was, but I had not understood why I wanted to look at events and emotions that had occurred years ago, at a time when I understood almost nothing. To return to a life of incomprehension in order to understand the present seemed almost impossible, a quest to derive the comprehensible from the incomprehensible. In other words, what could I possibly use in the present to make sense of what made no sense when it happened? Accomplishments disappear after a while. What is left is more important. And I grew toward an uncomfortable conclusion, that I may have been a rotten bastard for most of my life. I had no trouble recalling every mean act I had committed. Yet neither did I think I could balance the scales by recalling my few acts of generosity. I took a risk, for better or worse. It was another way of accomplishing, which might fail; all the better if it failed grandly. [I was fortunate in one respect. Having begun to write this manuscript, having begun to listen to the endless stream created by some unknown bundle of neurons, I understood that there was an "I" who listened and a "Me" who thought. That they were not the same allowed me to become—temporarily—an orphan. After that, having no parents, or rather, their lifelong disagreements which I had adopted having become gentler inside me, I had no reason to judge myself or anyone else. I found, later, that I had misconstrued the method I chose. Bringing the past into the present was not the goal; instead, the goal was to *apprehend* the past which was already in the present, which had been there every instant of time and will remain until I am dead].

There were other questions to consider which arose from a certain ethical concern which surprised me and came as a memory of a quote the author of which I cannot recall, but I can paraphrase it as follows: "After Hiroshima no one should write poems." (It turns out that it was Adorno who said that to write poetry after Auschwitz is barbaric). But the dictum applies to all suffering, without equating holocausts with personal suffering. And do not take what I am about to say as pretentiousness—I read recently a book of lectures by Jacques Lacan on psychoanalysis. In the preface, he asks himself whether he is *qualified* to lecture on a subject that he certainly knows more about than anyone. I was impressed. Why should I not take his hesitation with the utmost seriousness? It may be true that I know myself less than anyone and I am the least qualified of all to delve into my own history. And may it also be true that, in a world where we take the most horrible suffering for granted, is it justified for anyone, yes, anyone, to write about himself for the most selfish of reasons, i.e., to wallow in his own history? Perhaps the only explanation I can provide is that no personal history, if an honest attempt is made to be accurate, can show the writer to be anything more than a mixture of good and bad (often more bad than good, sometimes completely vile). And I cannot deny that a desire for personal masturbation accompanies every word here [writing itself may have a sexual component]. So be it. It is also true that analyzing one's life may make one sick of it. One may find that, on the whole, one's existence has been a burden on one's self and others. One's self-loathing may have been completely justified on behalf of others. That is the risk of asking "why."

[As I write, I am thinking of several memoirs I have read, by schizophrenics, one specially impressive by Leonora Carrington. As I read them, I considered the narcissistic mechanism that impels any story, whether it be complete self-concern or a desire to save the world. The latter is as fantastic as the former and equally self-indulgent. I learned however, that every human being has experienced, in his or her life, all of the mental illnesses, from neurosis through schizophrenia, psychotic episodes, compulsions, sexual confusion, and anomie. The pit into which I intend to dive is crowded. I will not be lonely there].[2]

And now, a third beginning.

To examine one's past is a foolish quest. It certainly has nothing of the heroic about it. No glory, no visible purpose. One should never go about it unless he believes he is at the end of his rope, about to be hanged (one can do it in the shortest possible time) or is about to fall into the abyss. The method is never to be prescribed by a physician unless the most serious symptoms become manifest: anomie, loss of one's way, total incomprehension of life and self. A broken love affair hardly qualifies.

It is this way. One walks onto a beach, calm, serene, dragging a small boat behind, to where the sand meets the water. The waves roll in sweetly, thinning to a wide swath of warm water covering one's feet. The wind is also warm, and steady, and you set off in the boat. The bright sun shines on your forehead, the hair on your forearms glistens. After you seesaw over the first few waves, you are in the middle of an endless vastness with no edges and no midpoint. You have always thought geometrically, using the various markers at hand to determine your place (as best you could) on earth. Suddenly, there are no markers. The shore, the present, which now are seen as acceptable, say to you, "Come back," as a lover might who only wants to toy with you a bit more. The image itself reminds one of mother, the great ocean; perhaps remembering is a way of going back to the womb, where we are still partly amphibian, perhaps to die. A wish to be stillborn. One forgets how much strength was necessary to leave the womb; the energy one needs to go back to it is equal to that. Perhaps, in the middle of that ocean, you will talk and talk until there are no more words to speak. And then, you will begin, without geometry. And it is

---

2 Recently I learned of a form of writing called "Disguised Autobiography As Clinical Case" which may seem useful as I procede, as it could reasonably apply to all the characters herein.

mother, not father, who has asked you to go back. You may be doing it for her without knowing the reason.

A child grows and with that growth come words. He listens for 'mama' and 'dada' and is happy when these words reflect back to his parents; it is an opportunity for the child to understand that he can make his parents happy by repeating words back to them. But given the number of events that occur to any child, it is likely that the word *"why"* will become another ghost. I have come to understand what Kita was driving at; I only add the word *"why"* (and many other words) to the category of ghost, for a word, too, constitutes a memory, [and often a person] and it is only by chance or by the innate strength of the word that it remains buried but waiting, patiently, growing stronger with the pressing years, until it, too, rises up. And this rising happens though the grown man may use the word in his conversations every day without sensing its archaic meaning for himself until something happens to draw his attention to it in a new way. It is as if a word, a memory, must be turned this way and that throughout one's life on the off chance that it will find the right place to assert itself in a new way. Words are comparable to sculptures.[3] People also become words. It is for this reason that no one who begins to look to the past in order to apprehend it in the present can say that he is doing so solely out of desperation. It can be considered a. creative act. I cannot say that I have suffered more than any other human being. Timing is everything and we have no control over the rising of a word, a memory, a ghost. Until these find their proper position, we can do little. ["why" may not even be the right word; "no" certainly came before it. I shall make mistakes, without care. "How" is perhaps a better word, scientists begin with it; but I am not a scientist, and it is not the word one begins with.] Though, If "why" is a member of a community of words, then a scream originating in the body has no meaning yet. It needs

---

3 Though there are other points of view. "Words are like us, they're born with one face and what can you do about it." J. Cortazar, *Hopscotch.*

those other words, as if it is not yet part of a sentence. That is why the need to ask "how" eventually becomes important. It is the way we put words before and after "why" to complete its meaning.

Memories wait quietly to be brought forth; they need not hide; they would offer themselves if you asked them to appear. If you cannot summon them they become ghosts; they haunt in acts of surprise; they attach themselves to everyday objects or to faces which pass in the street; they appear in dreams. When you awaken, you feel as if someone has visited you, has watched you sleep. Someone wished perhaps to leave a trace behind, an echo, a scent, but, though you sense these things may be there in the room with you, you can find no signs of the visit. You are left to wonder: did your visitor come to harm you, to warn you, or simply to observe you with the tenderness of one who remembers you from long ago? All day you carry with you a vague unease. You walk about thinking, "But I know my past; haven't I just described it?" In fact you have begun to draw a map without knowing the territory; you describe but do not depict, you cannot place the history of your emotional life on that map, for a map has only two dimensions and you have lived in four. (I learned this mathematics much later). In this sense, you are inexperienced. You are a system, and a system cannot understand itself. You must leave the system behind to view it with the necessary perspective.

I have read recently about a phenomenon called eidetic memory, which children are assumed to have until they reach the age of eight or nine, and which allows them in their earlier years to have a kind of photographic memory, but which disappears as they grow older. I have asked people if they remember any of the events they might recall of their early years, and most have replied that they remember little or nothing before the age of eight or nine. Whenever I described the few events I recalled from my earliest years to anyone, I was laughed at. *"How could you make up such outlandish memories?"* I was asked, *"Your brain isn't capable of recalling such memories."* I find this kind of comment unsettling, because I have vague memories of events that happened when I must have been one or two years old, three at the most, and I cannot understand why they remain. [As I wrote this last paragraph I felt a shiver of dread, and I stopped to ask myself what it had possibly been about. After a few minutes I realized that I had read *Confessions of A Mask,* by Mishima, several years ago, and that his novel began with his narrator's description of how his elders did not believe him when he recalled aloud events which had occurred in the earliest years of his life.[4] That is, I knew pre-consciously that I might already be taking someone else's memory as my own, as if I were borrowing a template from a great writer to begin my own work. I can say only that, when I went back and read the first several pages of *Mask,* I had borrowed the scene but not the memories]. I am left with the knowledge that I have warned myself again; it is difficult to be accurate without such borrowing interfering. What saves me is my belief that my memories are factual, even if they are only screens for earlier, deeper ones; what worries me is that I cannot verify them. No one can verify that your memory is accurate. I'll go on anyway. My warning to myself is also a warning to the reader (if there be one)].[5] I also recalled a comment Joyce is reported to have said about his characters: "The presiding imagination of the book appears more and more distinct from his characters, with purposes to which they are only tributary." *Ulysses On the Liffey,* Ellman, p. 109. There will be characters herein, who I will manipulate to tell a story.

⇒⇒⇒ ⇐⇐⇐

---

4 I must consider whether that shiver may have been about something else—the unspoken homosexual theme in *Mask.*

5 Every story ought to be considered first as a *story* for this very reason. Whether one calls it a story, a novel, a memoir, even an affidavit, it is a *whole* before it is true, false or a mixture of both. But how can I claim that I want to be accurate and yet say that the story is fiction? Am I pretending to accuracy while writing a false story? Or may I claim that the story is *psychologically* accurate? Or are all accounts of a life true and false at the same time? I will consider that as I read this story, I may see the true (as I perceived it) and the false (as I perceive it now), and true and false might meet someday and greet each other in wary friendship.

My earliest memory is being held in my mother's arms in the apartment where we lived. I remember other people standing with us. They must have been visitors. My mother was patting me on the back to produce a burp. I was no more than one year old. The memory brings a sense of comfort, but I cannot trust it fully, for no one would believe me. Another memory, the event of which occurred about a year later, I find to be more accurate. Even if it is a screen memory, it has sharper lines in my mind and seems more in line with the developmental state I had reached.

I was on the potty in the bathroom of our small apartment. My parents were standing in the doorway, and they seemed pleased. I remember looking up at them as if I had performed a great deed. I am sure it is a typical scene for a family, with a young child demonstrating his prowess in the most basic of activities, but I believe I remember it only because it is the one memory I have of the three of us being happy together at the same time. This memory, vague as it is, is the last one. There are no more. I did not consider until recently the act of discovery in that memory, the child comprehending that something *inside* may find its way *outside*. I wonder if the great discoverers of our day began by sitting on the potty, but I would not compare myself to them. I would like such a comparison, but it must be earned, else it is nothing but self-bloviating.

My first clear memory after the previous one is of my mother using a needle to remove a splinter from the sole of my foot. I was four, and we were on my father's bed—they had twin beds. It took place in the afternoon, while my father was at work. I do not remember the pain of being jabbed by the pin, or even if there was any pain. Now that I describe it, though, I wonder *why* it is that I remember it. Could it be because I was on [not in, but on] my father's bed with my mother, while he was away? Did I associate comfort or pleasure with being 'pricked'? It seems insufficient merely to recall the event; it is as important to understand how, of the ten million events that had occurred in my short life, that particular one became the first to implant itself securely, as if to say *"You may need me someday."* And if I place this memory in a sexual context, it means only that I am correct to conclude that I played an active role in the triangular scene of my childhood, for it must be true that the usual complexes that others have worked out were already operating in me. (I recall a conversation I had with Hart, a friend (and writer) who has and will read these notes).

*"You are not really exposing yourself",* said my friend Hart. *"What is written on the page is false."* I know he is quoting someone; still, I do not know what he means. *"You will talk about hiding in view, but you do not come out." "I am exposing my falseness, then." "But that is silly,"* he replies. *"Then I am nowhere." "Yes,"* he says, *"You are nowhere. Begin there." "How can I begin if I don't know where to begin?" "Settle into nowhere and ask yourself what it is like."* I cannot overcome these suggestions, which, because Hart speaks them, become demands. I believe every word said about me. If I overcame him, would I be somewhere? Is he playing with my naivete? Or is he telling me to plead, to beg for understanding so that I may reject that understanding (he seems to know that I would). Yes, to ask for and reject is the definition of nowhere. And nowhere becomes somewhere. So I will plead: understand me though I do not want to be understood. I am immobile; force me to move and I will recoil. I say to myself: I will move when I am ready to move, when conditions are propitious for movement. Now I nourish myself on immobility; it has a bitter taste and I am used to it. I will have to love my immobility; it is so perfect. Only then will I give it up, after I have perfected it. Otherwise, I would be as others are, a thought that repels me. Men often plead for what they do not want and will never accept. I think Hart is telling me to write these pages in four dimensions; otherwise they will ring false. But if I am able to go through with this enterprise, which might undo me, I will have to take my chances with the talent I have, no matter how many dimensions there are. It is more probable that he is telling me *"Don't bury the action."*

There is a great difference, too, between what is remembered and what we are told about our lives as children. The first kind of memory belongs to us;

the second is more a memory of a retelling of an event. It is often difficult to distinguish between the two. I can think of one example. I remember that when I was about three years old I used to look at the mail that was delivered to our apartment. [The memory of a series of actions seems to be different than the memory of a single event]. Letters were always placed on a large mahogany table in the hallway at the top of the stairs, where we lived over the apartment of our landlord. I often crawled under the table; the stability of the thick legs was comforting, a way to hold onto legs when my mother was busy [she had thick calves]. The letters at which I looked had marks on them which I could not understand, but I vaguely remember examining them and being puzzled. That memory belongs to me, though it is not as clear as the memory of the splinter. My mother told me when I was older that by the time I began school, I was able to read. I have seen a photograph taken on my first day of school; I am standing on the porch in front of our apartment, dressed in a blue suit (with shorts rather than trousers) and a blue cap on my head. After the first day of school was over, our teacher pinned notes to the shirts (or, in my case, a suit jacket) or blouses we all wore—(there were probably at least twenty-five children) which were to be read by our parents when we returned to our homes. My mother went on to explain that as she waited in the schoolyard to walk me home, I began to read the notes aloud to my classmates. I am sure she told me this anecdote because she was proud of my ability, for which she deserved some credit, because, with my father away at work all day it was surely she who must have helped me with letters and words, but I cannot claim it as my memory. To remember the story rather than the event itself is not unusual; but if I claim it as my own recollection, I am already bending the past false. [The landlord I just mentioned may be the first person who ever caused me to be afraid. I may have understood, without having the words to explain to myself, that his meanness and avarice—he was rumored to have been a black marketer during the War—played a strong part in our lives. My parents would certainly have been worried about paying rent—their income was variable from week to week. Never again did I live in the same building as a landlord]. [I mentioned him in passing, but I wonder if his meanness contributed to those palls I mentioned earlier. I have carried a hatred for my father for years, but I see, by this one mention, that I am already considering the stresses with which he was burdened when I was a child]. [I may consider later the possibility that it was our landlord, not my father, who was the first person who terrified me; he could well have threatened my father in my presence, but if such an event happened it has been buried so deeply that I cannot recall it].

My mother had begun a few years before my father's death to put together a book of family photographs, which she kept in our living room for aunts and uncles to page through—many of the pictures were, after all, of them with their own children. I never bothered to look through it much; it was only when I had grown and left the house that I browsed the pages on one of my rare visits. Then, I discovered a photograph of me at the age of three, the age at which I believe I had first become my parents' liaison and had taken an unknown [to me] role in our triangular unit; it was also the age at which, I believe, I took on the fantasy role of trying to keep our family together. Their conflicts were already a part of my mind; but a child does not understand that he has taken on the role of referee to save his own life. The date of the photograph had been written on its back. I am standing next to my father's bed (they slept in separate beds). I have no recollection of the event. The sun coming through the window to my right has cut me in half, my right side lit, my left in shadow. A director of 1940's noir films could not have shown me in conflict with more skill than the person who snapped the picture. It must have been mother; father would have been at work. I am holding a toy in my left hand—I am left-handed—but my expression is serious. The photograph has a genius which only became apparent much later: brightness on my right side, sinister shadow on my left. I use the word sinister deliberately; its origin is latin: 'lefthanded'. [My father has always appeared in my dreams on my left side]. I removed the picture from the album, put it in my pocket, and took it back to my flat. It must have been taken about the time of that memory of the splinter, but my look is so severe that it leads me to believe that something permanent had already happened to me, that whatever emotions I was to experience from that point on would be private and almost always painful. It was the look of introspection that affected me the most whenever I glanced at the picture, as if at that age a question had already been born that I would have to solve, but a three-year-old child does not know how to figure out anything. Later, one memory may lead to more; memories exist in constellations. Each one is attached to a string of memories; if you tug on one, you pull on the rest. I suspect that the beginning of that introspection was also the beginning of a sense of brokenness which followed me for years, but in which I had not the courage to immerse myself. [That brokenness expressed itself later in a dream over which I have puzzled for years, along with an image which shot up from the depths of my mind which expressed just the opposite, that is, a clearly sexual image of family unity. The dream and the image were both painful; they expressed a conflict I have never resolved. Kantian or Hegelian synthesis has always been useless to me]. [I may consider here that the bitterness with which I have begun has much to do with the early years of my life; whatever happened in those years has left its indelible mark, but it is difficult to go back that far by remembering. Listening to the internal static of my mind at the odd hour has been the only way to get there, and is subject to much distortion. I keep in mind that bitterness itself is a burden which needs, eventually, to be examined and discarded.]

There were other recollections of which my mother spoke as I grew older. She reminded me many times of the words I mispronounced as a child: 'wascus' for washcloth; 'abodmen' for abdomen (I had read a newspaper account of a man being shot in the abdomen); 'arpiggy' for Arpege perfume, (how would

I have even heard anyone speak the word in our household?) and 'hotipal' for hospital. She took pleasure in these reminders; but the happiness was hers, not mine. If I cannot recall more of these mispronunciations, though, I can at least consider why it was always she who brought them up. I cannot remember my father ever reminding me of any of the peculiarities I exhibited as a child, though I must admit that I spent much more time with her than with him, as we were a typical family of the time; my mother stayed home while my father went off each weekday to earn a living. She, at least, was expressing some pride in me at her recollections.

Do not these three or four memories, whether vague or clear, form an arc from comfort to desire [from oral and anal pleasure] and then to serious puzzlement?[6] Even were the latter memory, of the needle and the bed not explicable in sexual terms, yet it contains the elements of a psychological constellation: my father's bed, my mother sitting on that bed with me, my father away. And the pin? She was sticking me. Perhaps there is a touch of homoeroticism in the memory, or of polymorphic perversity, or of being done to. Certainly there is evident the divergence in me from any reasonably normal development. [I am struck, as I write, by the memories that never quite buried themselves; they are set in my bedroom, the bathroom and the parental bedroom].

The longer I considered this idea, the more I began to wonder if the *way* I thought was abnormal. I suppose the issue at hand was this: is a memory just a memory? Or does it have meaning? But posing these questions seems to me to be close to what a child must begin to ask himself at that age. And if that is so, I am led to ask: what was happening in that household? And why? And did something then create the myths—false myths—I carry today? It is the history of the false myths I have carried that is the subject I will examine if I have the nerve.

---

6 The phallic stage seems never to have begun, or was detained in transit.

Each of us dedicated to one topic: the subject of 'me'. And we feel no shame or hesitancy about it. I do not think we are selfish, no more so than a man who studies cockroaches or fashion for his entire professional life. It is an authentic striving and hurts no one. At least we like to believe so. We want to think of authenticity as maturity, quietude, the Golden Mean, but it is raucous and painful.

Once one identifies a mental disorder, (and I have always believed I had one; immobility is one) one begins a spatial relation to it. That relation takes the same course that any relation does, it changes, is added to or subtracted from, becomes, in a sense, a large table in the living room for which one has to make allowances by not bumping into it before one has turned on the lights. It serves a function, too—one can place things on it, books, drinking glasses, writing instruments. Disorders may even be adorned or decorated.

Every disorder also mutates. What begins as a fear of a single constellation of forces, a single puzzle of opposites that cannot be resolved, adds to itself and stretches its tentacles; it may not be alive, in the strictest sense, but it behaves in a way that strengthens its lifespan.

It is for this reason that we have a proprietary interest in our own memories and our own suffering. As I spoke to Dr. Gold (a middle, not a beginning), it became clear that *the inability to recall the memories is the suffering.* I understood that I was not bitter at the world at large or at the beings by whom it is inhabited. Not for me the narrator of *Notes From Underground.* It is myself I loathe, not others, [because I could not juxtapose the opposites and the memories I could not bring forth]. Self-loathing is a comfortable justification for being alive, I find, and it is only by finding a way to make memory clearer that I can defeat the self-loathing. [Though accomplishment diminishes the loathing if one thinks reasonably about it, one still continues the battle against it]. It is a deadly fight against one's own instincts. One must learn that disturbances of the mind have two functions: to protect and to injure. In other words, we kill ourselves, or, rather, we destroy our minds, for our own protection. Therefore, I justify my self-examination and the danger it represents as well. Though I may destroy myself or commit serious injury to my psyche, how may I learn to experience myself if I do not examine the events which have occurred in my life? I cannot scoop out from my mind the damage I have suffered (nor can anyone); but if such an examination permits me to understand my experiences, to see them with accuracy, I can go on from there into a life I cannot see yet, a life less ice-bound. And I am not brave; I may stop at any moment. My wish is only to discover that these notes are not merely a long tantrum.

*[If you want to become familiar with ghosts, even if words are ghosts, you must parse them. That is why I read these words over and over, to become familiar with the words I use to describe other words. It is a process of learning the ghosts and their descriptions at the same time. First, we describe. Then we describe the description. Then we describe the description of the description. We run away from the story into the safety of words. We cannot describe events that happened before we had words; we can describe only the aftermath. It is the method I have chosen to return to the first cause, or at least, to approach it. And if several causes merge into one effect, how can each cause be separated out? By considering the words we use in our thinking about cause and effect.*

⤙⤚

One morning my father did not get out of bed. I can think of no reason why that should be meaningful; he worked long hours and was usually at his gasoline station when I was already falling asleep. My mother and I went off to shop at the neighborhood stores several blocks away. I remember leaving our apartment in the morning and returning very late, but the several hours we spent away from the apartment are as yet unrecoverable. We did not return until nightfall. We climbed the stairs to find my father still in bed, in his boxer shorts and sleeveless undershirt, an ashtray on his chest filled with cigarette butts. (It was not the same ashtray I hurled to the floor, but I cannot deny the connection between the two, though fifteen years separated the two events; I might someday link ashtrays to the heredity of immobility). The apartment was filled with smoke; it was difficult to breathe, and my mother, who had always claimed to suffer from asthma, must have found it painful to be there. In every room the smoke hugged the ceiling; it did not seem to move, there being no fans or air conditioning. I recalled this day for many years at various times, never understanding why the memory returned at particular times, never considering that on that day something had happened which might have serious consequences for all of us. I wonder now if the greater part of that day cannot be recalled because in some vague, probably unconscious way, I knew that a crisis had occurred or was about to occur and had no means with which to face up to it. I know that this day occurred during those years when I had lost most of that eidetic memory which I learned of later. Yet, if I consider the day logically, I must admit that I was so upset that I put it out of my mind for years, so that when the memory returned, it did so almost as a not-so-subtle reminder. It would have been wise for me to ask myself, when I thought of that day, *Why now?* As if that day was composed of sound rather than sight, the memory has continued its echo up to the present. It was a real day; now it has become a ghost, one of many without substance or emotional content, but nevertheless floating on the surface of my mind. Does an event of this nature persist to remind us to pay attention to its origin? Or will it attain substance if we are able to recall the emotions which accompanied it? Or, in our ignorance, are we yet warning ourselves, at the time we recall the event, *that we are in a similar position?* How difficult it is to discriminate among these possibilities when we are unaware of our own instincts. It seems that each ghost remains in the past and the present at once, beseeching us to substantiate it and, by doing so, ourselves. How frustrating it must be for our ghosts when we are unable to pay attention to them. Perhaps that is why they assume their own desperation and begin to force their way upward (for they have always been within us) toward the surface of our minds.

It may also be that that day has become a touchstone for annihilation, annihilation of my mind, for it must have been accompanied for me by a terror I do not want to recall, which has left its mark on one of the lower tiers of my consciousness and which says 'Come to me' in a way that is more terrifying than the memory of the event itself. I may have been called upon that day to *do* something, without having any idea of what my responsibility was. [Once an event such as this one occurs, one may spend years waiting for that annihilation to return without recalling the original event]. [I have no right to use terms such as annihilation. I will say instead that I may have desired to disappear. Apparently, so did my mother, who kept us out for most of the day].

I learned only after my father died something of the circumstances which occurred at that time. Agents from the Federal Bureau of Investigation had come to our apartment to interrogate my father, who had been allowing his sister, who was a member of the American Communist Party when it was a violation of federal law to be a member, to use our apartment for Communist party meetings. Someone, a neighbor or relative, had notified the FBI that people were coming to our flat late at night. [I wonder now if that was the first betrayal I had experienced, which must have been puzzling because it had no context]. My father had admitted to the agents that he, too, had joined the Party. No one had ever spoken to me of the stresses on my mother and father during that period, but I surely felt the echoes of them in our household. The genesis of a fear of loss that remained as a subconscious aura was finally made clear, but too late. If I were to place this event next to that photograph of me which was taken several years before the day my father stayed in bed all day, it would become clear that *why?* had begun much earlier than the day of his late sleeping, which has remained in my mind for years, and is only a screen memory, though it has power in its own right. Explanations are not sufficient to bring ghosts to the surface of our minds.

I have wondered lately, again, about that day my father stayed in bed. As I turn the memory around, looking at it from one angle and another, turning it upside down and looking at from behind, [again, as one should look at a piece of sculpture], some questions finally arise for the first time: did mother know what was going to happen, and was that why we left early and remained away all day? It seems as if I was removed from a kind of primal scene—which does not need to be sexual in its nature—before I had the chance to be affected by it; I compare it to a mother closing the door to the parental bedroom before the sex act. Yet it becomes clear that even if a child is removed or barred from an emotional scene, it will continue to echo, as if it reached beyond a closed door, or, in our case, beyond our flat to the street, and constitutes a kind of space music, dark matter, unseen, but matter nevertheless. I note that, without intention, I am rewriting my family's history by viewing it as part of the triangle, that is, with a lessening of anger and self-loathing. I shall continue. [And if the triangle of which I speak has been inside me, will it come forward as another ghost?]

A child builds a structured consciousness from events whose importance was not known, and the structure is false because the growing mind selected some events and repressed others, or did not understand them. Perhaps what is not remembered is the aura surrounding the events. When the adult begins to draw his map, it also becomes false; at best, it becomes a map of falsity which possibly can be examined with an adult mind. Perhaps the comprehension of one's self as a thing, or as Martin Buber explains, an *It*, as well as a human, begins to redraw the map. Things are real; they are facts. One sees that one is a fact; the history may be false, but the thing, the person is not; he is a fact. And one is now not merely in history, one *is history (as Paz stated)* [It is difficult to escape the idea of *reification,* another Marxian concept. Even if I am a thing in one construct, I am the product of a Marxist father in another construct]. It is as if the scream that has always been inside me was an acknowledgment of growing into a labyrinth from which no escape would be possible. The infant perceives a horror for which he has no language; by the time he can reason, he has the language but has buried the horror, has taken the best of a bad deal. That is a place to begin. One must know the past before sloughing it off, though it does not go far away. The people I believed I had to overcome went away before I could resolve our relations.[7] (poor Dora!). I never confronted Hart, and only once did I confront my father. I cannot say that I will re-enter that labyrinth to rescue that child, to recognize him in the present, but the task is part of my story. I mean to say that one does not enter the labyrinth; one *reenters* it.

*[A story is a form which attempts to give form to what seems to have been a formless life. One tries to go above the formlessness, not understanding that it, itself, is a form which has never been seen as such. And the form has always changed because it is alive.].*

One more memory has come about, which occurred around the time of the last. I awoke in the depths of night; the door between my bedroom and my parents' was open; our family doctor and my father stood at the foot of my mother's bed. The lateness of the hour, the presence in the bedroom of my father and the doctor talking, may have frightened me. If so, however, I have recalled only the brightness of their room; I could not even see my mother, for she was lying in bed. It is probable that I will never recall the fright which accompanied that night, or the emotions that may have been engendered by my father's immobility; [it is a serious business to ask a doctor to make a home

---

7 In an essay Erik Ericson describes Dora, Freud's early patient, who left Freud in the middle of her treatment for hysteria, but who reappeared years later to tell Freud that she had finally insisted on hearing the truth from her father of the complicated and tawdry milieu in which she had grown up. She seemed quite proud that she had done so. Ericson uses this vignette to discuss the difference between psychological truth and reality-truth, in arguing that psychological truth leads to a greater maturity. If Dora had come to understand through her analysis the family forces that led to her neurosis, Ericson seems to say, she would have felt no need to confront her father. As for me, there is no one left to confront. I face the history, not the persons who populated it. It is better that way. Anyway, I found confrontation brought only temporary relief.

visit in the late hours] but if the memories themselves have returned—or have never really left—they point, perhaps to a time which has remained part of the bedrock of my life. I am not sure about one part of the event: it may be that I felt no terror at all about it. That possibility, in its way, indicates only that by the time it occurred, I had already frozen into immobility.

On another morning I woke to find my father in bed; he had been beaten and robbed at his gasoline station. A huge bandage covered his nose, which the robbers had hit with a monkey wrench. I remember a dream I had afterward, about robbers. I began to sleep with my entire body covered, with a small opening through which I could breathe. I was sure that gorillas were roaming our neighborhood. [Apes would return to me later as symbolic of cosmic fear].

As I recall the above instances, I consider, for the first time, that it may have been the perceived destruction of our family unit that was the cause of my fear. No matter what myths were already operating within me, I may have been most terrified by the possibility, which I never spoke of, that I would not be able to withstand my family's destruction, whether by death or circumstance. [We tend to consider infants and toddlers as weak, but the strength with which they want to bond with their family is stronger than steel, as is the frustration which occurs with the effect of even one negative event!]. [I have also neglected the possibility that I may have been so angry at my parents at the time that I would have felt that it was my fault and my wish if my family fell apart].

⧛⧛⧛ ⧚⧚⧚

I have in mind at this moment three self-descriptions in which the writers discuss their early years. One describes a world of beauty and enjoyment. A second describes a childhood of abuse; a third, a life of drudgery beginning at the age of eight. Each relates, in some specific way, the relation between their early life and what they eventually became. But how to explain that relation? How to feel that it is accurate? And another writer, Genet, who, to my knowledge, avoided the examination completely, preferring to re-create himself in a way that would have no relation to his past. The first of these men is Lampedusa, who wrote *The Leopard.* The second, Stendhal (whose abuse was not physical but had more to do with his dissatisfaction with his family); the third was my uncle, a man named Joe D______, who had become a striker in the Pennsylvania coal mines at the age of eight, and who later became a labor organizer for the American Communist Party during its years of illegality (he married my father's sister who I mentioned earlier). It is easy to consider the adult years of these three men as resulting from their descriptions of how they lived as children; that ease, however, ignores almost everything else that transpired which they did not see fit to include, though they must be given credit for even attempting a relational explanation for what they became. They presented us with the information they believed was available to them; they tried to be accurate and forthcoming; still, they edited, they ignored, they elided. If we have no evidence of these actions, we have only to consider ourselves and how we attempt to explain-and to justify-our lives. We can also, if we choose, consider the motive for looking at how the impression is given that Lampedusa writes for his own amusement; he says this directly; Stendhal worries about all the "I's" and "Me's" he will have to put on the page; D______ has a strong didactic impulse; and Genet ignores his literary impulses. What is not apparent, and perhaps never can be, is whether these writers learned from telling their own stories, and whether we must, in a sense, learn from their written works what they may not have learned themselves; that is, were they enlightened by the exercise? [What would have happened to me if my father had left a statement of his life? I cannot know, but I speculate that it would have contained more dogma than facts. Yet, it might have demonstrated his yearnings, even if he had not intended them to become public].

I wanted to examine my past, if for no other reason than this one: it had become necessary to apprehend my mind. [There was another reason, too, but I was not aware of it. It was necessary to wrest myself from mother and father. I have thought often that my ego belongs to my father, not to me]. I did not know how to experience myself, except as their son, with the fantastic responsibilities I had created regarding them, two unhappy people. I did not know if I was experiencing myself. It was always as a member of my family that I experienced anything. [It may be that the anger I have carried for so long is connected to my refusal to be only a son, and the inability to escape that identity]. I saw everything as from a remove, *as if I was watching the three of us relate, waiting for trouble;* and if I knew what I thought, I did not recognize the way I thought about it, or how I ordered my thoughts. *I did not know what I knew.*[8] The difficulty I saw was that my mind, any mind, is constantly changing into something it was not seconds before. I believed that I would fail unless I found a way to rise above simply paying attention to my thoughts; I would have to pay attention to *how* I thought. [I will discover that I will end by understanding that the structure on which my thinking has been based—the way in which I ordered my thoughts—has been completely wrong; even this attempt will likely be embedded in false presumptions]. Looking at the past without understanding the means with which I might undertake the task seemed a waste of time. I made this idea even more difficult by considering the topics it would be necessary to examine; they were many, and I saw no way to create a narrative [a word I dislike intensely] that would combine them into an organic whole, i.e., a novel with the examination of the past as its basis. (I may not be writing a novel; it might as easily be an essay, a map or an affidavit!, or a set of notes). I believed I was a describer, not a depicter, and I understood from having read many great novels that the most powerful of them depicted internal thought in an atmosphere of external action; they took place in the real world of nature, whether that nature was the countryside, on the ocean or in the city. At most, I went ahead knowing that I might not be writing a

---

8 It is discomforting to realize that in these notes I may answer the question I have posed without understanding that I have done so. I may have to write more notes about this attempt. [I have played chess games without realizing that I won].

novel at all. I was mindful of another one of Hart's warnings: *"Getting a man to cross from one side of a room to the other is the most difficult thing in literature."* I do not think he made up the warning, but he knew it would make it more difficult to focus.

One question I consider is whether a human being has a spatial relation with his mind. That is, since humans can listen to their own thoughts, can a person ever grasp the totality of his mind as if it were a palpable thing? In some types of therapy, one pays attention to particular facts of the mind as it works. The id, ego, superego construct is a valuable tool in the process.[9] But the mind is not only an engine running all the time; its contours are always changing with new information and defenses in agreement or conflict. Is it possible to stand outside the mind sufficiently to see how the whole thing works?[10] Is it possible to have a mind outside one's mind, capable of apprehending the inside mind? Possibly not. The 'outside mind', which is a projection of the inside mind, would work in the same way as the 'inside' mind, also constantly changing, accepting and defending. For all practical purposes, both minds would still be one. And what would occur if one mind actually grasped the other? Probably, the horror of it would eventually lessen, if one has acknowledged all (or most) of the thoughts our culture considers vile. But then, if the spatial relation I have posited actually exists, even as a construct, why shouldn't the inside mind begin to grasp the outside mind? This train of thought sounds outlandish, but it is not outside the scientific method of making guesses about what cannot be seen, and then experimenting to prove or disprove the guesses. It becomes a kind of play, which is what we did as children. We play as adults to understand how we played as children. [Thinking about our behavior can be play, serious play, but nonetheless play, if one understands the risk. Games have winners

---

9  There are many theories to choose from. I chose the one most topographical. It mirrors the family struggle; there are forces involved, effort is expended. As I go on, I expect that other theories will follow in the patchwork manner in which I am preparing these notes.

10  What Freud calls"the mental apparatus."

and losers, though there are also zero-sum games]. [I am reminded that in some Zen Buddhist thought, the mind is one of the ten thousand things, i.e., the worldly forms that meditation is meant to overcome].

The answer to this difficulty came by chance from a time several years ago when I became friends with Hart, whom I had met at the university. Hart is not his real name; I have given him the small honor of assigning him the name of a swift forest deer, (perhaps because I hunted him in a way) but I will speak more of him later (it will be necessary, for he became the one person with whom I argued in a way that allowed me to grow, though the growth was almost against my will). Hart encouraged me—if I wanted to write—to read Balzac, Stendhal, Orwell, even Alfred Kazin, that is, any writer who described *the city* in all its fullness. His idea was that the city's history mirrors that of its inhabitants (I will not call them citizens yet); that the continual destruction and re-creation of the city parallels our own continual reconstituting of our minds and histories, but the one from whom I took the most was Stendhal, specifically, *The Life of Henri Brulard,* which was, in fact, his autobiography couched as fiction. Stendhal began, as I've said, by expressing his concern over all the "I's" and "Me's" that he would have to include in order to explain his life (as Brulard). I glossed over the facts of that life, i.e., that he had been a soldier, a diplomat, had exhibited bravery and had a hand in European history that would certainly justify his writing of his life. It was his concern about how to say what he wanted to say that impressed me. I was further encouraged by finding, in a used bookstore, a slim book by Giuseppe Tomasi di Lampedusa, author of *The Leopard* (which I had partially read even prior to becoming Hart's friend). The book was titled *Places of My Infancy.* Lampedusa writes that, even as he is composing his little remembrance, he is reading *The Life of Henri Brulard.*[11] Lampedusa says that " [W]hen one reaches the decline of life it is imperative to try and gather as many as possible of the sensations which

---

11 An example, perhaps, of the first "disguised autobiography as clinical case."

have passed through our particular organism." He further notes that Stendhal "interprets his childhood at a time when he was bullied and tyrannized." (I believed I was bullied and tyrannized!) After reading these lines I became more comfortable with trying to sketch a sort of map of my own life; I was buoyed by the last sentence of Lampedusa's introduction: "If it bores [the reader] I don't mind." I add here a reference to memory by Leopardi, who states that memories can be counterfeited; he is speaking, I believe, of memories of events in which we played a role but which we take on as our own memories though the event has been described to us by someone else, i.e., we had no recall of the event until we were told of it. One can always find a quote to justify or discourage one's task. I have also found one: *The path to self-knowledge is, in fact, tragic.* It became obvious to Hart, if not myself, that searching for contradictory quotes permits a writer to dither. *"Get on with it!,"* he has said. Our relations were such that he may have wanted me to try first; if I failed, he'd have enjoyed seeing me fail. [As I read over what follows, I will in fact discover the history that accompanies the one I have already written, that is, the underlying history of feces, penises, incest, father-hatred, father-love, masochism, shame, homosexual imagery, repetition, the images that flitted or struggled upward to which I paid little attention over time, but which were always present, all of which, I believe, were the result of a failure to resolve the unresolvable conflict between brokenness and unity. [Though I have said that every human being experiences these images, our refusal to place them in the structure of our minds does us harm]. It is this history that has no arc, because it remains pure and unadulterated, in a sense, not the surface history. It is this history that remains constant yet was never attended to, though it was a companion throughout my life. [It is no consolation to know that all men and women have these things in their minds. Men want to be singular, unique, and they hide these ideas from themselves, which makes it more difficult to admit that they are in this respect no different than early man and modern man]. [I suspect that the apprehension of the underlying history, however terrifying yet exciting it may be, is but a preliminary step, for it stands as a symbol, in contrast to one's perceived everyday mental life, of the distance between love and hatred that has never merged. Perception of that distance has great value].

Later, when Hart spoke to me of the City, I was to understand that the city I chose was the equal of the cities of three thousand years ago. My myths, which I did not want to acknowledge, were no different than the ones the Greeks knew of which grow out of the underlying history I have mentioned above. Ericksen, another friend, said to me once that we live and dream our myths. I rejected the idea immediately, as I reject at first any idea that appears to be true. [He was correct!]. It is for that reason that I have emphasized accuracy, for I evade it much of the time. There is another way of looking at this issue, though, that brings a sort of relief. As one begins to find out how one's unconscious processes have shaped one's life, one finds that those processes have not changed significantly from the beginning of reflective thought in man. Any myths I may uncover have been with man for centuries and I ought not to think I am less human for that.

I found that I yet had much work to do in order even to begin to tell a story, which would certainly have no surface arc, for I did not believe that any life has an arc, [and an accurate story has no arc, because it takes note of the unconscious, which does not know time] not even in hindsight. I had read Petronius and Henry Miller; I thought a story ought to be made primarily of gossip. [As it happens, this story is, too]. But I considered the topics I had been thinking about for many years, which had, I thought at the time, little to do with remembering, or ghosts (a term I borrowed from Moria for my own purposes) because I thought they might be relevant to the past as I attempted to comprehend it. The list began to be almost impossibly long, almost unruly; it seemed to demonstrate to me how unsystematic my thinking had been for a long time. Nevertheless, I had given thought to them and decided to consider them. I tried to define them in my own way before I began, even if I could provide only contingent, inexact definitions. I did not use a dictionary, because

I believed that even if I defined a term or word incorrectly, that definition would lead me somewhere, to a place that ought to be considered. I am a maker of lists, too. It is a saving grace of a banal life. It is ridiculous to make a list in a story; I am getting on with it, though, as directed by Hart.

*[Sometime in the past—I won't say how long ago—I wrote a novel in the form of a journal and several vignettes about living in the city of P. It was a fairly typical story, a child is born, grows up, leaves home for the City, learns the little he is capable of learning there. It ended quietly, with no indication of what might happen to him in the future.[12] I read it recently and was struck by the bitterness I had carried—toward my father—for most of my life that ran through it, a bitterness I had been aware of but had not confronted as I wrote it. More than that, I seemed to have completely ignored it. The rancor I saw in every page upset me. At first, I did not know what to think, though I felt relieved that I had never tried to publish it. After I thought about it, however, I considered that there had been something missing from the story from the very beginning of its telling; there was an absence that had become a presence I had avoided. I had to think about what was missing! To do that, I found that it was necessary to examine, not what I had been thinking as I wrote it, but how I had been thinking. In other words, what threads of thoughts which had concerned me for years had I completely ignored as I wrote? And how had it been possible for me to put them aside so easily. **That is, I had not known what I was saying, nor how incomplete it was!** I saw that if I were to tell an accurate story, I would have to tell it from a different perspective. I'd have to leap into that absence to see the story from its point of view. I know of no one who chooses to do that in any fashion, in writing or life, with one exception—a woman who had leapt into the abyss and rose from its depths. I felt I had no other choice, if for no other reason than to know why I did not know myself. I began to annotate that story, looking for that absence that had made itself felt even while I*

---

12 This statement is certainly false. the novel was the story of an angry bumbler who insisted that the world must come to him and who fought strenuously against self-awareness.

*wrote blithely about* events. *I began to consider the wrong ideas and beliefs which I had brought with me to P along with the furniture I took from home. I knew that I might discover that my rancor toward my father was out of proportion to his actions; if it were, I would have to consider the earliest years. In fact, the pages I have written so far are the beginning of my annotations]. [the point I make here is that every item in the list below* **was already in the story,** *yet I had failed to* see them as I wrote. I did not *experience what I had written. I believed I had no right to be disturbed.*

1.  The destructive force of myth. I know that much of my thinking then was magical; I understand now that each of us develops personal myths which we use to carry us along. I also suspect that our personal myths eventually damage us or kill us and need to be discarded, but if we do not understand where we came from we cannot understand the power our myths have over us. Myths are constructs and always separate us from reality. I do not disagree that myths are created by logical thought, however.

2.  Doubleness. If I looked at my life in P, I could not help but see that I attributed more than one meaning to every action, whether taken by me or others. I consider this way of thinking not so much paranoia (though it is) as a thread of thought that had followed me throughout my life which had its origin in the way my parents used me as a go-between in their own struggle with each other and my own intentions regarding that struggle. [Certainly, the events I have noted above were never discussed in my presence, so I was left to ignore, repress or misperceive their importance]. I was not always aware of this thread, but, having considered my own life to be one of neurosis, I consider the possibility that mental disturbance has both defensive and injurious functions. (I had only to think of those two palls to understand the force of doubleness in my life).

3.  Hiding in public view. Another myth which I adopted early in my life, whereby I believed that the only way I could live in the world in which I found myself was by hiding, but, contradictorily, the hiding had to be in a public space. One hides because one is ashamed and is ashamed because one hides.

4.  Thingness. Thingness is the adoption of the belief that every human being is also a thing, or an *It*, and a thing may be defined as an object which *may* draw attention to itself. The adoption of thingness is available to a solitary person who wishes to use philosophic concepts to justify his existence. It allows a man to consider himself equal to all others despite the individual idiosyncratic behaviors he despises in himself. [The mind is also a thing]. I adopted this view reluctantly and slowly. It is a preliminary step toward understanding that one is an object *and can be* a subject, as others can, also.

5.  Bars and brothels. These places provided the counterweight to anyone who believes he is thinking about his own life in moral terms; they teach a man that he has a body and bodily needs which he must consider whenever he begins his great philosophical quest. They are closely connected to the underlying stasis of one's mental life, moreso than the surface history one usually describes when writing one's history.

6.  [Triangular] repetition. The concept that neurosis is not just in the individual but in the members of his family. Under certain circumstances, the family becomes the neurosis, and the geometric shape of the family (in my case, father, mother, son) is repeated by the child in his adult life. As he grows he tries to recreate the triangle with other groups, friends, colleagues, not understanding what he is doing. It is a form of repetition, [and possibly a search for another family wherein one is recognized] that is, continuing an action that always

failed; it is a stupid act, similar to betting on a horse after it has lost the race, thinking it might have improved over time.

7.  Dreams. Dreams are ghosts that express wishes. It is less important to analyze them than to ponder them. Pondering leads to more pondering about how one ponders; dreams are a way of life.

8.  The myth-or-fantasy of saving parents. This myth takes precedence over the others in a family that should not have been a family in the first place. It may be only a cover for a more destructive myth, that is, the murder of the parents [Is it possible that one reason for the myth of murder to be covered over so diligently is because any child who considers it cannot yet even cross the street without assistance? I assume small children can reason]. It is clear that I do not want to discard the value of myths, but it is the way they separate us from reality that I must consider [and the way we use them in the process].

9.  The burden of consciousness. Many people must experience this burden but will not admit it.[13]

10. The City. A good place to be, where everything worth happening happens. The City is always reconstituting itself out of fire and destruction; it parallels my personal experience. It is where one goes to practice triangulation and repetition, which are difficult to do in the countryside.

11. Unraveling. The continual throwing off of one's identities, none of which seem to bring happiness or comprehension. It appears in Greek mythology in the Odyssey. It is, to me, the most important of the Greek myths.

12. The manipulability of mental disturbance. I had come to think of this concept in my own self-examination. It seemed to me that every mental

---

13 Mental growth can be painful when it outpaces the body's resources. Langer, An Essay On Human Feeling.

disturbance, even psychosis, including schizophrenia, has a component of intent, or at least usefulness. I believed for many years that I was mentally sick, [because I had always devalued the unchanging parts of my mind], though I functioned in society. I did not try to convince myself that the world is sick; that seemed no excuse. But I eventually saw that no matter how one defines oneself, each mind does its best to defend itself, sometimes by destroying itself, but always making the effort as a matter of logic and physiology. That is, illness has its own logic.

13. Platonic friendship. It has its genesis in envy, and possibly love, and is the adoption of someone to argue with mentally rather than in person. It may lead to growth or a feeling of defeat. It is part of the repetition one uses to overcome a parent who is no longer available to be overcome. It is father love/father hatred disguised as a philosophical concept.

The boundaries of my existence have been set forth. It is the terrain on which I played out my naivete that has always puzzled me.

I became interested in my past when I began to listen to the stream of thoughts that was running through my mind and discovered that most of the thoughts that occurred to me were nothing but lies, and the ones that seemed to come from the deeper places in my mind were often repulsive [and yet these were the most important ones]. The voice I had been using to live my life was lying to me every day, and I had always accepted it. It was me, after all; why would I lie to myself? I began to consider some examples, simple though they were. If I woke up in the morning and thought, "I feel miserable," I lived through the day with that as a beginning. But I never stopped to consider whether I really felt miserable; I had thought it, and it must have been correct. If a colleague asked me to lunch, I said "I'd like that"; but I didn't want to eat with him. I wondered if many words I spoke were out of politesse, and I was sure they were. Nevertheless, the words were still a lie. There were other examples which I will not repeat here. The point was that once I began to pay attention to that endless stream, I understood that more of it was untrue than true. I then considered the purpose of that stream. Was it defensive? If it were, it would have been justifiable in almost any context, whether at work or in social relationships. Could it have a moral, ethical basis? That was also possible, but only if we lie to ourselves for some higher purpose. This possibility did not seem right, neither logically nor emotionally right. Another possibility became clear (if vaguely): *I did not want to know what was true and what was false.* I knew that in the United States one can live an entire life not wanting to know the difference between true and false; I had lived for a long time that way. If I had not begun to listen to that stream with a sense of judgment, I'd have continued on my unknowing path. And I could not be certain why I had even begun to listen, but for some dissatisfaction with the way I was and lived. I was fortunate to have stumbled (in a sense of clumsiness) over my own mind. [When I say that the stream lies, that the stream itself is untruthful, it is possible that I am wrong despite my careful listening to it. But if I am wrong, it is also possible that the truth of the stream expresses itself in a code rising from the unconscious I do not yet comprehend. In fact, the stream may not even be speaking to me, but to another, an Other from whom it wants the expression of desire or, at least recognition. If that is so, I am merely *the interlocutor*, and my task is to redirect the stream so that it emanates from *"I,"* *and not "me"*]. I am mindful of a phrase I heard from Ericksen, another friend with whom I spent time when I entered P, who was speaking about someone we all knew—I am thankful it was not me, for it easily could have been: *"He locked himself out of his own mind and couldn't find the key."* When a child is locked out of his parents' minds, though they believe they are doing it for the child's wellbeing, they are, in fact, refusing to recognize him.

I am sure that this business of trying to remember is universal and I would not claim to be unique in any way (though it cannot be denied that it is an attempt to demonstrate one's own unique qualities). What happened was this: in listening to that stream, I isolated one word which put itself forward every day; the word was **WHY?** Why is a word we use in our daily lives all the time. Somehow it took on a new characteristic, as if, like an object with mass and volume, it tilted slightly to one side and made itself felt in a new way so I could view it from another perspective. Having turned on its axis, the word became not only new but familiar and frightening. [One can look at a word, too, as if it were a sculpture. Perhaps words are works of art].[14] It had always been there, and now I knew it had always been there, but it took on the aspect not of a word but a scream. It is a scream emanating from the body before the mind has words for it. By the time the mind has a vocabulary, the word has become embedded in the body where the mind cannot find it. I had always been screaming, but the millions of thoughts I had had in my life had muted the screams. Again, this knowledge does not make my life singular. It happens, though, to have become important to me to trace that word, that scream, back to its origin, whatever the cost, to put words before it and after it.

The question of "why" is useless if one only asks oneself "Why am I the way I am?" or "Why did this happen to me?" It is useless because "why" is *primal*. It arises before a child learns the word, but perhaps when he looks in a mirror for the first time. His physiological movements ask the question; his facial expressions, his stomach, perhaps his bladder and sphincter. Who asks such a question? The great monsters of history seem to have ignored it. From Atilla to Hitler, Churchill to Stalin, all have rushed past it. We might have expected more from Alexander, whose teacher, Aristotle, was so careful about definitions. It is a dangerous question, one learns, when one has speech. But the danger has not always been there, not when it first rose. Then, it was merely puzzling, or its context was misunderstood by the child and its parents. [I must consider also

---

14 I have referred to sculpture several times; it must be important; another example of not paying attention. Perhaps, without being aware, I am bringing shape, contour, color into these notes, *as if words themselves, and ghosts, exhibit these qualities.*

the possibility that in writing these notes I may be creating my own double, who I can love as I have never felt love for myself]. **WHY?** is a scream put into words by writers; every memoir is a scream, every novel is a scream.[15] I note that underneath the word "why?" lies the most basic question: *"How may I undo what has been done?"* In the end, one must work to recognize one's self. [I see that I have not asked an important question first: what was the timing of "why'; that is, what was I chewing on when it suddenly took on a clarity it had not had? But the answer to this question is lost; I will do the best I can.

And one repetition [which may actually be an answer]; no more beginnings. I repeat it to embed it in my consciousness.

Father was dead. Mother lived alone in the house. Fifty years of smoking two packs of cigarettes a day had killed him. Mother cried for a day, before she ordered new living room furniture, had the house repainted and new windows installed. They had been married for thirty-seven years. She no longer had to hide the chocolate bars smuggled in by her neighbor. She smoked her Lucky Strikes (she had smoked as long as had my father; aside from a stroke, she had suffered no permanent damage). No matter where we had lived, in an apartment or a house, our living space had always been permeated by two palls: smoke and anger.

I had thought for a long time that they hated each other, but I saw, I did not observe. After supper he went down to his basement workshop; he cursed her over the whirr of the power saw and the electric drill. She sulked in the living room. I went to my bedroom to read; I could hear his cursing through the heating flue. I could imagine her sulking. I often went outside to the front lawn, where I could lie on the grass and imagine breaking the windows; I thought, too, of making noise. It would not have changed anything. I could not have saved them. They did not want to be saved.

---

15 And some are, in fact, tantrums.

I will return to them, in time, in more detail, turning them about as if they (and I) were a piece of sculpture that must be examined on every side to comprehend its beauty and its flaws. It is only this page that I will attach to the wall of my flat with a push-pin.

It has certainly occurred to me that I have chosen the wrong word. the right word may not be "why?" It may, instead, be "how?" It may be that the two are inseparable, yet I have already taken the wrong path. I will take risk of discovering that I have been completely wrong; discovery is the goal, not rightness.

⟫⟫ ⟪⟪

## *The beginning of a middle.*

I kept a journal, haphazardly, after I moved to the City; I continued it later as it became what might have been a novel. Recently I began to reread it. I added comments to it, creating an annotated life. Everyone should have an annotated life, not only famous people or notorious ones. And the infamous ones always get one, but all are dead before the annotations are completed. Perhaps I will discover the reasons for concentrating on a brief time in my life as a defense against remembering the past. I must consider this possibility; it accompanies my belief that every act has more than one motive. It was only upon my annotating that I began to see the *other* history, without which the already written history would have been incomplete, a shell, not a lie, not necessarily inaccurate, but complementary.

In order to comprehend the stream that runs through one's mind one has to consider the myths under which one lives. Myths are dangerous, they cause murder and destruction; If we do not recognize them we live lives of fantasy. I only have to think of the Greeks with their *agape* and their *golden mean* which allowed them to own slaves and conquer cities, or the Japanese with their *kokoro* which means the "heart of things," which enabled the men to fight and kill and drink while the women went to moon viewing parties and wove silk and wrote the saddest poetry. I chose for myself the myth of the ape and the clown. Rather, I did not choose these myths, history had embedded them in me and they had to be apprehended prior to being removed, a process akin to a major essay in earth removal. Myths are earth after all with all of earth's qualities. Everything that has happened is buried there in the layer of myth which gives up its contents only under protest. The earth says "I will help you" but so much is buried one does not know where to begin digging. I do not like the ironic mode but it seems ironic that one has to disinter so much before being interred bodily. Then again I do not believe in cosmic jokes; the cosmos is terrifying but neutral so it is just another fact, this disinterment before interment. It is not funny, it is true, and not merely true; truth is not mere, is it?

‣‣‣— —•••

## *[The beginning of the original novel, in part]:*

*[I made two friends in P. It was with them I began my triangular repetition; one to combat, one to bear witness].*

A gorilla mask and a clown costume—these are the symbols in which a myth becomes embedded, an idea one carries in one's head that says it is possible to live in the world without self-consciousness[16]. I say it is a myth because, though it may be true for animals, it cannot be so for us (the connection between bumbling and clowns cannot be denied). This myth, which I carried so blithely

---

16 The gorillas were there from the time I was four; I was already afraid of them.

out of need and a certain elation which accompanied it, was the one I chose to live out that portion of my life in the city, where one may be a fool as long as one is able to earn a salary. Carrying as it does the symbolism of rage and hiding in view, it nonetheless gave a certain purity to my life; but, through a process of unveiling which was even more deeply the touchstone of that life, it had to be discarded. I will adopt another myth according to the rules I have set for myself, that is, out of experience and double meaning. Now I sketch my map [yet another way of describing a life's history] because, around me, people are talking of Korzybski, a Polish scientist who has written an eight-hundred-page treatise on the relation between science and sanity. I have not read it (nor has anyone else I know, except for Erickson, another friend, who reads and understands everything) but I am told it has one theme: *"The map is not the territory."* The meaning of this phrase did not have to be explained to me. The phrase struck me as if a heavy tree branch had fallen at my feet. That is, it told me *what could have been,* that is, that I had never understood the meaning of anything that had ever happened to me. In fact, I had refused to understand. The two symbols above, the mask and the costume, came to me slowly and only after much cartographic effort, though they and their counterparts are all around me (a tattoo, say, or a burn scar, perhaps a Borsalino hat). For reasons I did not understand, at one time the idea, the possibility of wearing these symbols in public thrilled me. I remembered the university student in Oregon who wore a burlap sack over his entire body to class for months. Permission to do so was granted by omission; that is, he was left alone. The reasons for his action do not matter to me; I am familiar with them. I can only hope he felt a certain exultation every day, in the anticipation of his classes and of his attendance, of his solitude in his canvas universe. Reading of him enchanted me, but not for years did I understand his importance for who I might be. He was hidden in view, just as is a myth which straddles two worlds, and yet did not have to be: anyone. Still, he was taken seriously.

Later I understood the meaning of clowns, too—they do as they please and we do not know them. Better, it is the arena of their performance that is most important. A space such as the circus ring, in which a clown is permitted to hide while yet remaining in public view, is as naturalistic as a glade and just as verdant. It stimulates myth to come forward, to take its rightful place in the history of one's personality. I have always wanted to dress up as a clown, but only if I could go about my regular business while I was garbed in clown *mufti*.

At home one evening, in the darkness of my room, while lying in my bed, it occurred to me to rent a gorilla mask from a costume shop, and to wear it to classes at the University where I was a student. I would put on my best (and only) suit, a white shirt, a tactful, understated tie, fully-shined shoes (in the years during which I attended the University, it was not unusual for students to wear business attire to class).[17] I would sit not in the front row but not in the last row, either. The idea was *to pay attention:* to listen to the lectures, to take notes. I was not joking with myself, though the elation this idea brought me was more than I could bear, and I began to laugh, thinking of it. [I did not know that the very idea was what psychoanalysts call a *fault,* an unconscious intention to erase the ego].[18] It was surprising that none of our neighbors called to inquire. That laughter—I will never forget it, and not merely because the idea thrilled me. A host of problems would certainly be created. One takes a step and has to deal with every consequence. No, it was the very *seriousness* of my intent that made the idea so important, to say to the world: *I cannot live with you unless I am hidden in plain view, and you, all of you, must go along with this idea. Then, I will be free—free to hide.* [I see now that the point of wearing the costume is to acquire control over the crowds who observe me]. All the time one lives one bends to the will of the world, until one finally takes

---

17  A certain vengeance against my father was implicit in the idea.

18  I cannot remember the events of the days preceeding the idea, which surely had created a desire to erase them from my mind.

that world at face value, that is, with all seriousness. After that, one either dies or sees everything from the center, rather than the fringe. [Sooner or later, perhaps never, one might give up trying to make the world fit one's needs; or one continues to demand it of the world by becoming an ape or a clown. I often fear for anyone who laughs]. Another truth I did not know: I wanted to live in paradox, without moving from one side to the other. This desire is not the same as immobility, it is riskier. One can see both sides and is tempted to resolve the paradox by moving one way or another. To *be*, in that situation, is to be alive.

I thought again of clowns, too, that night. How easy it must be to move through the world with no identity, or rather, with one's lack of identity hidden by greasepaint and baggy clothing covered with large red spots. I was a quiet, diffident youth, but as a clown my arms would move free of weight; I could jump two feet into the air and pirouette, landing on my shoes which were themselves two feet long. But keep in mind what I am talking about: the arena in which one dons the clown persona must be attuned to one's meaning. I sketch my map precisely to find the right territory. I am investigating the contours of an arena in which I could not suffer to have an identity. I wanted to be no one in the world and the world must play along. A clown suit is a lever that can move the world; it begs the laws of physics, I am certain. To have an identity means that one may die at any time [without ever having synthesized the original dilemma].


## [Annotation]

*[I had come upon the word 'arena' by accident, I believed, but it had a subsequent role to play in my father/son relationship].*

The costume shops were all too expensive. I visited them in the morning after laughing all night. I could not afford to pay two hundred dollars for a day's rental, and I had no interest in the body suit, only in the mask. To be able to live part of my public life wearing a gorilla mask—*without comment from others*—that was everything I sought. It was a way to make apparent what was hidden, without speaking of it. My disappointment was limitless, as was my fear. It was years before I understood that *looking* was my metier. *To look is to act. It was the only act available to me. Immobility does not impair one's vision!*

One might think it unnecessary to don the ape mask or the clown suit, to take on the persona. "Take on" is not really the appropriate term: the young man already is the ape, the clown. But he needs the costumes, or the imagined wearing of them, to place a layer, not between himself and the world, but between himself and what he thinks of himself, even if the layer is in front of the face. To be an ape or clown without the costume, or, again, the imagining of them, would be so painful, so full of torment, that it might be done only by one who has already disowned all shame, all self-loathing, and has accepted what is true—or what he believes is true—as absolute. Paradoxically, the idea of the costume is a necessary prerequisite for those who have not yet reached that level, who yet harbor in themselves a small voice that says self-effacement itself is a falsity which they may someday overcome. They have not come to believe yet that existence, qua existence, is the same for all, that is, a simple state of being which in itself is not shameful. Another reason for hiding behind a mask, or a canvas sack, is that the one hiding believes he has no right to be a madman. A curious contradiction exists; one wants to display his madness in hidden fashion *because he does not have the right to be mad! That right has not been given to him by anyone; he cannot insist on it, but nevertheless he will find a way to express it.*

The watcher does not want to change; he does not want his core to rise to the surface. Any change will be passive; that is, unavoidable. He is not hiding his face. Rather, he is hiding his shame and the shame of his shame. [Perhaps what he hides is also his desire, whether it is desire for the Other or he does not want to be the subject of the Other's desire. No matter; he is camouflaged]. [Shame is the refusal to be the object [or subject] of an *Other*; a knot that refuses to be untied]. the ape or clown wants and does not want recognition, and his costume displays his immobility.

## *[Annotation]:*

*The idea strikes me that I wanted to wear the ape mask because I was repulsive. Why else would I hide? Did the student in the canvas bag believe he was repulsive? Or did he think the world outside the bag was repulsive? I cannot speak for him, though I believed we were brothers under canvas and fake fur. But I wonder if the result of all that introspection I had done had led me to feel that I was repulsive, to myself and others. I was not then merely hiding in public view but hiding my apparent revulsion at myself from myself and others. It is a more natural, a heftier explanation for remaining hidden, not to avoid being seen, but to avoid being seen as a young man who despises what he (thinks) he is. If one has no talent for cynicism or sarcasm, and one is disgusted with what one has become, an ape mask, a clown costume, are certainly appropriate methods. It is one thing to hate what one is, it is quite another to permit people to see that hatred.*

If one can map an existence, then this myth of hiding in view has always remained on my map as a kind of capital city. One day, in fact, in a coffee shop, I stared at the face in the glass opposite my table. I saw a Jew, a youngish man with a high forehead and a serious face, serious to the point of naiveté. I might have been staring at that photograph of my three-year-old self, morphed into adulthood. I glanced away, but after a moment I looked again—one wants not to stare even if it is oneself at whom one is staring, but by then my expression had turned to whimsy. I began to interrogate myself: when did my life of hiding begin, not merely of hiding but of raising the act to mythic proportion? That is, when did I begin to feel ashamed? And who was I ashamed of?

If I thought about it, there were many possibilities to examine: when did the necessity of watching, as opposed to being, begin? Was it that first hurried masturbation at age ten, in a discarded refrigerator box laid out in ______'s back yard? Had I surrendered my self to its own contortions? Or was it when Lara, a woman whose actions I understood, left me? But these things were *actions* of a sort, even if not taken by me. I looked again at the face in the glass; this time I saw a gorilla, a great ape. I raised my fingers to my lips in a sort of tribute, then dropped my hand quietly to my thigh. [A sure sign of an early fixation which I had not begun to understand]. How many times have I looked at men and thought *"how ugly they are!"* only to observe them, those great apes, speak softly to someone, express desire, make a comment, or kiss a pretty girl? And it had always angered me to see it. What right did these apes have to live as everyone else did? [They may have been the robbers who beat my father!] None! Nor did I, who was also an ape. Only the handsome deserved anything, I believed, or possessed any grace. But now, after long consideration, suddenly I, too was an ape; I could see it in the glass. I had become what I had longed to be (and had feared, for I did not want to be defined, even by myself). And because I was an ape, ugly and coarse, I knew then that there was a chance for me. Though what I saw in the glass was a symbol of my own terror—my naked face—I was a human being, too, but even the handsomest of us were still apes. It was a miracle any of us were human. I could walk freely among apes, I thought. Later I found a book on symbols in the University library and looked up clowns. Here is the description I found:

*"Like the buffoon, the clown is a mythic figure, and the inversion of the king— the inversion, that is to say, of the possessor of supreme powers; hence the clown is the victim chosen as a substitute for the king, in accord with the familiar astrobiological and primitive ideas of the ritual assassination of the king. The clown is the last, whereas the king is the first, but in the essential order of things the last comes second.*

*This is confirmed by the folklore custom, mentioned by Frazer, in which village youths, during Spring festivals, would race on horseback up to the tallest mast (symbolizing the world-axis); he who came first was elected Easter king, and the last to arrive was made a clown and beaten."* Cirlot, <u>A Dictionary of Symbols</u> (1962).

I found nothing on apes, save for a cryptic entry:

*"With reference to mythic animals* (it continued) *treatment of this subject is to be found in the <u>Manual de Zoologica Fantastica</u> of Burgos y guerro (Mexico and Buenos Aires, 1957) in which such creatures are characterized as basically symbolic and, in most cases, expressive of cosmic terror."*

Even as a university student, I knew and didn't know myself.


## *[Annotation]:*

*[I had no ability to reflect. Wearing an ape mask was a donning of the very image of those gorillas of whom I had been afraid as a young boy]. A joining of myself to the robbers.*

The history of hiding in public view, certainly not specific to me, has as one of its problematic results a great difficulty in determining one's rights and obligations to others. Every social situation may become an agony of indecision, and every impulse to do for others must be questioned. The chewing on these questions thus takes the place of accurate observation insofar as it clashes with, or exists uncomfortably alongside, the conflict of appearance in society or disappearance from it. Another paradox: I had always hidden; now I wanted to draw attention.

I had missed an important idea: why create a map if it is not the territory? I answer my own question with a poor response, but it is all I have at the moment: First, the map, then, the territory. One must begin somewhere, even if intuitively (or by going in the wrong direction.]

Hart, who is a writer, sat on the couch in my flat, reading these words (as I read his, when they are posted weekly on the wall over his desk at his flat; perhaps he, too, believes that books ought to be hung, like paintings). His left hand held a bottle of Heaven Hill bourbon by its neck. The other hand held my manuscript, the pages of which he flipped. His Pall Mall lay burning in my clay ashtray at his feet. *"Yes,"* he said, *"you stare from a glade hoping to see a cunt staring back at you from another glade. You think a cunt has eyes but you are afraid to look at it except from cover."* He had got right to the heart of things, for he understood better than I that it was not enough to ask myself why I wished to hide in view; I needed to know what I wished to look at from behind my mask, and why. These words cut me, because a man who wants to see from cover believes that what he sees will come to him in a form he comprehends. He does not want clarity but release. Every clown, every ape hopes for release in what he perceives; otherwise, why does he look? my shame or seeing me seeing what I was ashamed to see?].[19] Ultimately, his cover will fall away under the assault of what stares back at him, and he will remain, naked, and, one hopes, unafraid. [If I thought a cunt had eyes, then I may have thought it was staring back at me, just as I may have thought penises were gazing at me, too. Were they seeing my shame or seeing me seeing what I was ashamed to see?] It would take a while to apprehend the meaning of what Hart said. Over time, as I came to listen to the endless stream of words that seem to rise up from my chest, I began to see that cunts, genitals, breasts had been a constant thread in those words. Then, though, I did not have the wherewithal to trace the thread back to its source; nevertheless, they were what I strove to see, as if I were trying to grasp, as an adult, what I ought to have grasped as a child but had barred myself from comprehending through immobility. I believe that I did

---

19 Apes in dreams have been said to represent polymorphous perversity.

not know then and am not sure now whether I am male or female. My desire to look at genitals of all sorts has never left me]. [I am reminded of Nietszche: "When you look into the abyss, the abyss looks back at you."] [I have only to recall those early memories to understand that they are all sexual in nature and that they all took place in bedrooms and a bathroom. I might consider who was getting pleasure therein].[20]

How can one trust a novel or a map (these notes are not so much a memoir or a story as an affidavit; affidavits have no arc, no boy meets girl [or boy], loses same, wins back same, in which the writer claims to remember events from childhood? [Though perhaps an affidavit is appropriate for a description of the unconscious]. The future grows like a cataract on the child's life that will hinder his vision as he ages, and any writer's description of his life before the age of ten has the feel not of memory but of re-creation; most people will admit, if asked, that they have no memory of any events before the age of four or five. Even a memoirist who adopts a cynical or satirical view of the beginning years of his life is not to be trusted merely because he demeans his past or the role he may have played in it. His life may have been perfectly unexceptional even in its emotional context.

All the same, one event is still clear in my memory; and if it turns out that my memory is false, that it did not happen the way I recall it, I may yet draw the correct conclusion from my imperfect, possibly unconsciously devious, memory. The fact that a memory creates an obsession is one of the worst grounds for attributing verisimilitude to that memory. Nevertheless, I became obsessed with the belief that there was a direct line between the myth of hiding in view and an event that happened long ago. They are two poles of a conflict I have never shaken off, between looking and participating, between wanting and fearing. It must have occurred in my ninth year, and it happened just this

---

20  I must have gotten pleasure from looking.

way. [Perhaps I continue to look at what I was not supposed to see as a child; can it be that simple?]

⇛ ⇚

On a Spring day in 195_, my father returned home from work with a pamphlet concerning the fate of the Rosenbergs, the convicted atomic spies, rolled up in his back pocket. He was deeply concerned about them and had often argued with my mother about their trial and capital sentences. He had officially joined the party in the 1940's (I learned this fact many years later) but his major contribution to it had been to make our tiny apartment available for use by his sister—who was also a Party member—for cell meetings. This generosity was wrongheaded, for my aunt had risen to a level in the Party that surely would have drawn the attention of the authorities,[21] but apparently my father had been adamant on the point, because sporadically throughout the year the members of my aunt's cell would appear at our apartment around midnight, trying, with varying degrees of success, to sneak up the steps to our second-floor flat without drawing the attention of our landlord, who lived on the first floor. By sunrise they were gone, leaving behind a pall of cigarette smoke that hugged the ceiling, and empty coffee cups. I learned about them only obliquely, but I sensed that they treated my mother abominably, as Communists were wont to do, since they were unable to be civil to a simple housewife even as they tried to save the world from itself. As my mother took their coats and laid them at the foot of my bed in the tiny bedroom where I slept, they blew cigarette smoke in her face and called her "Frau" or "Frau-Frau."

That evening the argument began at the dinner table and continued throughout the meal. I joined them from my sickbed (I was nearing my ninth

---

21 It is possible that he may have been concerned for her safety, too, though she had no friends who might have been engaged in espionage; their interest lay in union-building.

birthday and had stayed home from school with a stomach ache, possibly brought on by the constant haze of cigarette smoke which hung stagnant through the flat day and night). Finally, when I had taken my place at the table, their dispute reached its acme (or its nadir) and my mother began to cry as she cleared away the dishes. She was convinced, I suppose in hindsight, that my father, who had never in his life worked very hard, was showing the same incivility toward her as his Party member guests had shown. He looked up from his pamphlet, which he had spread out on the table next to his supper dish, and, angrily, he began to mimic her in the falsetto squeaky voice he always used when he wanted to be cruel to her. *"Mieu mieu mieu mieu,"* he said. And again, *"Mieu mieu mieu!"* She responded by turning her back to him and switching on the sinkwater at full blast.

I was as used to these arguments as a child can ever be, though I did not understand their political meaning, nor did I comprehend other meanings for which the political might have been a familiar screen. I knew only that they made me more afraid than their disputes over money or habits, [possibly because I believed I had to choose a side] and with my father's lips pursed at the flimsy and unworthy promises of "The General" (as he called Eisenhower) and my mother's shoulders squared to a sinkful of supper dishes, there was no longer any reason for me to remain in the kitchen. I pushed away from the table and went to my room, where I lay on my bed staring up at the ceiling thinking about my mother, whom I did not understand, and who offered me little protection, and my father, of whom I was afraid. He seems to have been a kind of crotchety Moses, unable to enter the land of Canaan though burdened with carrying the tablets of Socialist knowledge on his shoulders, unwilling to throw them to the ground in anger merely because so few people worshipped his god. But as a child I knew only that he seemed angry all the time. Even when he did a good deed it rankled him, and I had come upon him one snowy day the winter before as he put chains on the car tires of our neighbors, a charitable and completely gratuitous act. He lay under a Plymouth, hatless and gloveless in the bitter cold, blowing on his fingers, performing a task he had certainly volunteered to do, all the while cursing his life, cursing everyone's life, filled with the rancor that has always accompanied every good deed our line has ever done [which I have inherited].

Outside, the street lamps struggled into light (above all else, that is the part of this event I recall with the most emotion, almost as if they were stage lights preceding the rise of a curtain). The April dusk settled on our neighborhood. Through my window I could hear, from across the street, the shouts of the older boys who gathered every evening on the steps of a house across the street to harass the younger children who ventured out and to gather strength from one another's bravado. Their voices, sharpened on the cutting edge of puberty, rose on the soft, secret air and carried past the open window of my room, and I wished I could be out there with them, doing what they were doing, living unopposed. I desired unity…

I shifted my eyes toward the window, then to the kitchen, for I looked in the direction that I listened, having no guises. At that age, I already had to hide my entire body in order to keep my emotions hidden. I strained to hear the voices of my parents over the shouts from outside, but listening was difficult, for all adult talk seemed to flow away from me around corners and down stairwells where it left the apartment by the front door, spoken despite me rather than to me. That, too, I followed with my eyes, running after it to bring it back, to keep it within the house so that I might listen to it again and again until I understood it. Now I listened for its cadence, its unusual rise and fall, its abrupt ending that might make my pulse quicken and my mind shut. This time I heard nothing, and my heart opened a little.

I rolled out of bed and went quietly to the window which faced the house next door where the O___ sisters lived, unmarried women in their forties (I know now) who undressed before the unshaded window every night. [Even at that age I was curious about women's bodies, though I do not believe I had a clear idea of the mechanics of sex]. Their window was dark now and I sighed. I listened for my parents again and, hearing only murmuring—not the insistent kind which meant that my father was once again trying to explain his politics, but the softer kind that told me they had reconciled—I slipped out of my room and crept into the living room, whose windows faced the street and which was at the other end of the apartment from where my parents were. Quietly I climbed onto the sofa and raised my head to the level of the windows, with only my forehead and eyes above the sill. There, as silent as ever, I listened to the older boys who were gathered across the street as acutely as I had listened to the murmurings of my parents. It was through their words and gestures that I might learn what I needed to know: was it safe? Or was it dangerous? Their postures spoke to me, but in the end it was their words that would determine how it would go. One of the boys had not spoken since I had begun to observe them. I wondered if he was Mrs. C______'s boy, one of the few who had yet to bully me, knock my schoolbooks out of my hands, accuse or laugh at me as I ran up the street to the school bus every morning. In the deepening dusk it was too dark to make out anything but shapes. Two of the older boys seemed to be arguing and one of them, who had been sitting on the middle step, rose and faced the other, a tall, skinny boy. The skinny one pushed the other, who was stocky and who wore only a tee shirt while the rest wore long sleeved shirts. The lankier boy put his hands on the stocky boy's shoulders and pushed again, but the latter, his legs firmly planted, did not move backward. Without waiting for an attack, the other boy ran down the steps. When he reached the sidewalk, he turned and taunted the other, as if he had not already seen the danger he faced. *"You stink! You stink! You stink!,"* he shouted. (To be shouted at that one stinks was—and is, to me—one of the worst epithets one can hurl at another).

The stocky boy laughed, a laughter full of pleasure and cruelty and high spirits. It had overjoyed him to arouse such a response. He sat down again on the step, motionless, in the shadows of the other boys, oblivious to their existence. I watched him as one animal hidden in a glade might watch another in a jungle clearing. Sometime later in the night, my mother found me, asleep, and carried me back to bed…

On that day in my flat when Hart read the few pages I dared to show him, he had spoken other words that had a more lasting effect on my life. I can only paraphrase what he said, but in essence, it was as follows: *"One might say of you that you belong to that class of people who trust what you see out of the corner of your eye, or what you hear mumbled by a passer-by on the pavement, more than what you see or hear head on (for example, if you hear a gunshot)."* He finished by adding, *"I'll bet that as I say these words you are listening for their subtext, but there is none."*

Hart's words always had the power to harm (as did my father's), because I chose to acknowledge them (if not to hear them in their full sense). I am not speaking of mechanics, but of how the mind operates when primed. The word "Why?" seemed important. It is the plaint of one who has chewed on a question he cannot frame, seeking a response he will not comprehend. The word wants something taken back that cannot be, so long as the laws of time and space are obeyed. In this sense, "why" is similar to an argument in which one has been taken by surprise and tries desperately to travel backward to that surprise in order to speak the words which were caught in one's throat. It will seem contradictory that a myth of hiding in view might be accomplished by drawing attention to one's weirdness with an ape mask; but the myth itself—any myth—is an embodiment of a contradiction; it is the result of two uncompromising opposites which can only be reconciled by a leap into another dimension, i.e., the "other," where the world of subtext and paranoia rules.

Memory bends false, then, like Uri Geller's spoon. If I create a narrative—as today's sociologists and literary critics are fond of saying—will it be true? Or will it be merely the way I choose to interpret a series of events? I am aware of how faulty memory can be; nevertheless, if I do not make the attempt, I will never know whether it is possible to separate myth from reality, or whether the two are even so different.

*Much of my history has remained conscious and available to me. What I have never considered until now is the underlying cause of many events.*

When I was a child (I am forced to remember by the strength of Hart's comments) the appearance of cocoons in the trees of the neighborhood was an unwelcome omen of Spring. The winters were severe, and in the afternoons when the children on our block returned from school they usually stayed inside, secure in the warmth of their homes. But the onset of Spring brought all of them out to the street where I, as the youngest boy, was always a target for the teasing and mockery of the older ones. Even the few with whom I had played in their homes or our flat during the icy winters—as equals, relatively speaking—banded together in the warm spring air with the more aggressive bullies, who now appeared in their sleeveless tee shirts and carried loose cigarettes in their pockets.

The boys who lived on the street where I found myself were all older than I by at least three years. I may have been as intelligent as they were, but I was not as strong, and they found ways to torture me which, though not ingenious, nevertheless left long—standing marks on my mind. (I have been advised by Hart that I need to describe my physical appearance before I proceed, or it will be clear that I am not exposing myself. I was smaller than most children my age; I had facial tics; I wore corrective shoes; my right foot turned inward from two accidents; my eyes were hazel-colored. When I walked outside I often pushed my penis inward. I state facts as a favor to Hart). One of their favorite methods was the formation of a club. There were comic book clubs, card collecting clubs, and, quite simply, clubs composed only of boys who lived on our block. After they decided who the officers would be, no one was left but me. I was designated as the 'member'. Aside from the connotation of myself as a penis (which I do not believe they meant), I was thought to be weak, because I did not complain to them of my lowly status, and, when one of them held me in a headlock or threw my schoolbooks to the ground, I often ran home crying. But I had nowhere else to go; there were no other boys in the surrounding neighborhood with whom I could play, and I must honestly consider the possibility that after a time I took some satisfaction from being last in all things (which meant, in that small group, being third or fourth). [I did not know the meaning of clowns yet, i.e., that they are last but inversely first as substitutes for the King]. That is a hard fact to admit, because I believe I could still murder those boys if I were to meet them today, though I have learned that none of them have succeeded in their adult lives in the ways we measure success in our culture. Still, I carry with me all that was done to me by them. In that sense, they have beaten me, because in important ways I have become like them.

⟫⟫— ⟪⟪

Our street, our arena, sloped downward from the main highway to P., a large city on the eastern coast. An iron fence at the bottom created a dead end, beyond which were the tracks of the commuter trains to the city. On the other side of those tracks was a department store with a huge parking lot and beyond that was a wooded area thick with tall trees from which the cocoons hung in the weeks before Spring. None of us, even the bullies, were allowed to go into the woods, where mosquitos and tramps were thought by our parents to present almost equal dangers. The space in front of the fence became our playground. We shot marbles from slingshots across the train tracks onto the parking lot, trying to shatter the windshields of the automobiles. We wrote away for Army surplus weather balloons which we filled with air and sent off into the distance, hoping they would crash on the commuter train tracks. When the others were bored, I was tortured. Once I was tied to a tree in a neighbor's back yard, and for fifteen minutes at least I made no sound. I remember nothing of how I felt, whether I was frightened or embarrassed or ashamed or disappointed in my trust of these boys after they had put me to so much misery. [I believe now that trust was not a factor; I simply did not know to do anything else]. I remember only the trash cans which sat silently under the back porch of the neighbor's house. I think the sun was out, though I was locked in the shade of the tree. Victory for me then lay only in being able to wait until the boys returned to untie me, in other words, the only way I could survive was by waiting. That would have been true even if I had not been bound.

When the boys finally found the courage to explore that parking lot, which could only be reached by a circular walk out of our neighborhood, or on bicycles, they discovered a large, abandoned water pipe running across the farthest corner of the lot. At one time it must have been used to siphon high water from the creek that ran alongside the lot, but the creek had not overflowed in several years because part of its flow had been diverted to another creek nearby, so the pipe was now dry. The boys claimed they had crawled through the pipe from one end to the other. If I wanted to join their latest "club," I was told, I must do the same. The open end of the pipe was crawling with vermin; cigarette stubs lay all around the outside, where passing hoboes on their way to P—the wooded area around the lot led into the city—had most likely found an hour's respite or even, in colder weather with less mosquitos, a night's fitful sleep. I refused to crawl the pipe, not because I was able to stand up to them, but because it frightened me so much I was unable even to enter the first few feet. I ran home and left them there to laugh. It never occurred to me that they had never dared to enter the pipe, either.

⤜⤛

For reasons I did not understand I was in thrall to them, though they were not my friends in any sense. Perhaps it was the combination of the torturer who also protects and teaches. What I learned from them was to wait and to watch, but I did not learn cunning, nor did I learn how to take action. In these latter respects I was completely stymied.

Eventually I took on their bullying mentality. The few boys younger than I who happened to move to our block became the focus of my rage. How could I ever befriend those who appeared gentle? By the time they appeared, I had too strong an interest in paradox to walk away from the bigger boys. Emotionally, there was nothing for me in escape. Waiting; watching, without cunning or comprehension. These were my behaviors. All else was unintelligible to me.

If I needed to be reminded of these, I may only recall one incident that fixed them permanently for me. One of the new arrivals on our block, an Italian boy about my age (I was ten at the time) began to brag to us about his ability to shoplift. I say to 'us' because when he chose to brag, I was present. Thus, I was 'one of them' for the purpose of teaching him a lesson. The older boys challenged him to go to the department store on the other side of the train tracks to steal an item. They even told him what to steal—a fishing reel—and ordered me to accompany him so I could swear, if he returned with the reel, that he had not merely purchased it to increase his reputation in their eyes. I do not think I gave any consideration to the possibility of being arrested with him if he were caught; I had to carry out my orders. When we arrived at the store, I was told to stay in the same department, but not too close to him. I did not see him put the reel into his pocket, but when we left the store, I saw a bulge in his jeans pocket that could only have been the reel. When we returned to our sloping street, we could see the bigger boys gathered at the bottom in front of the iron fence, watching us as we neared them. When we were finally in front of them, the thief pulled the fishing reel from his pocket and held it in front of their eyes. *"Did he steal it?,"* one of them asked me. *"Uh-hunh,"* I grunted. *"You're sure?"* *"Yeah, he really did."* *"Well, that's pretty good,"* the older boy said. *"You should be proud." "I am; I said I'd do it and I done it,"* the thief said. He actually pulled a cigarette from his jeans pocket and lit it. None of us smoked, and he was going to add to his reputation by taking a drag on a cigarette without coughing.

*"Can I see the reel for a second?"* the older boy asked. *"Sure,"* said the thief. *"But you gotta give it back right away."*

*Oh, I will, I will,"* the older boy said. He took the reel from the thief's hand, lifted it up and down a few times as if measuring its heft. He then raised his hand to its full reach and threw the reel down onto the macadam paving with all his strength. The reel shattered into pieces, which the older boy then scooped up and threw across the train tracks. *"That's what happens to guys who steal!"* he said, laughing. The thief began to cry. The cigarette dropped from his lips as they quivered. He ran up the street, sobbing, and disappeared into his house.

I stood dumbfounded. I could not laugh; I was afraid to. It would have been an admission that I felt free enough to think of the older boys and I as an "us." I could not take that step, then, even if I describe it as such in hindsight. Nor could I take, in my heart, the thief's side; I would have bullied him, too, if not in front of the older boys. Though it was to the thief that they said *"Don't steal!"* I believed those words were also directed at me. My belief was directly in line with how they had treated me always: torture, protect, teach. [The evening prior to our leaving the street for the last time—my parents had bought a house in the suburbs—the thief found me out on the street. As dusk fell, he found the strength to tell me that he hoped God would strike me dead before morning. I was unkind to him, it is true, but I wonder now why he hoped I would die rather than the bigger boys who had treated him more harshly than I had. I imagine we were both afraid to lash out at those who were bigger than we were; we found each other instead].

***[Annotation]:***

*When I bullied the few boys who moved onto the street, I thought at first that I did so because I had taken on the mentality of the older boys who had tortured me. But I had not considered another reason—that any new boy would interfere with my relation to those older boys. In truth, I would rather have been bullied by boys with whom I was familiar than befriend a latecomer who might have become an ally if I had treated him with respect. I wanted to maintain my position as last in the race, because, in the theory of the clown I eventually discovered, last can be second or perhaps third, but on my street, no lower than that. It is difficult to describe an emotional experience; one reaches for the right words and usually exaggerates. I could say instead that after I threw a filthy bag into the face of one of the new boys, I ran toward the others, who had seen what I had done, to take my place with them, to demonstrate my loyalty. The activity after the experience demonstrates the emotion which accompanied it.*

One day we heard sirens in the distance coming closer to our street. My mother went out to the curb to see what was happening, only to see a fire engine pass by on the main highway, going toward the parking lot across the commuter tracks from the bottom of our street. I was home in my room with a plaster cast on my foot. A few weeks before I had jumped off a wall, following the boys with whom I still played through their bullying. We were going to put lit books of matches into the drainage holes along the wall because we believed rats hid in them, but I had landed on the alleyway on one foot and fractured my ankle. My mother was fascinated by fires and, with another woman who had come out to see what was going on, decided to follow the fire truck. I could only walk with crutches, but she did not want to leave me alone in our flat; she found my old baby carriage in a closet and told me to come along with her. I hopped to the stairs, descended on my behind, and hopped again down to the pavement, where I climbed into the carriage, and we were off. We could not cross the train tracks; we had to go up to the main highway, turn left, and go two more blocks before we could enter the parking lot. When we got close enough to see the fire engine, we discovered that there was no fire. Instead, firemen were dragging the creek which ran alongside the lot. As we watched, more neighbors came to the scene. A few minutes later, two firemen stepped down into the creek, wearing thigh-high boots, and climbed back up the bank carrying a young boy. At the top of the bank, another fireman passed them a blanket with which they wrapped the boy's body. It was clear now that he had drowned. We caught a glimpse of his legs protruding from the blanket; they were dead white, as if he had been in the water for some time.[22] He may have been swimming with some companions, but if that were the case, they were nowhere to be found. My mother and her neighbor began to look around but there were no young boys watching. I doubt now that if they had been there they would have admitted to it. There were no signs along the creek warning of danger; it was not very deep; but even the bigger boys from my street knew better than to enter it. We left after seeing the firemen place the boy's body in their truck. I have never forgotten the whiteness of that boy's legs; that image will remain with me forever. Nor have I forgotten that I, an eight-year old boy, was wheeled to the scene in a baby carriage. It must have embarrassed me greatly, yet I remember none of my emotions from that day. Possibly, none of the boys from my street were there; I may have escaped their teasing by chance. Still, I knew I had watched the aftermath of a drowning while I sat in a baby carriage, and that was embarrassment enough. I may have also seen the aftermath of a death that occurred because his friends, who in my mind ought to have protected him, ran away. I do not think we spoke a word on the way back to our flat.

---

22 An image that would return to me later as one of the 'word pictures' that rose from the depths of my mind years later. It must have arisen at a time when I was experiencing fear without knowing its origin, but the timing of its appearance is lost to me.

## *[Annotation]:*

*I have not fully considered the meaning of that sudden desire to wear the ape mask at the University. Only now do I wonder if I had made an unconscious decision to define myself as a hider, with no clear idea of that from which I was hiding. I wonder now if it had something to do with an incident that had occurred earlier, when I was still being bullied with those boys I played with. (I say 'with' instead of 'by' as if I somehow enjoyed taking part in the bullying as a victim). One day when I was about thirteen they invited me to play with them on the lawn of the gentler—if I can make such a distinction—bully, and I went with them thinking we all might play mumble-peg or touch football. After a few moments of such play, however, they tackled me and threw me under a small tree toward the front of the lawn. Then, they pulled up my shirt, kneeled next to me while pinning my arms to the grass, and began to pound my chest and stomach with open palms until my torso was red and sore. The act was called 'giving a cherry-belly'. I cannot recall the emotion I felt at that moment; it would be false if I claimed to. But one thing I remember clearly is that I made a conscious decision to surrender! I did not try to escape. I would like to think that my decision was made rationally, in the hope that they would, from then on, leave me alone, realizing that the usual response from me, crying and writhing to get away, would not be forthcoming. However, I cannot think that. I simply gave in. From that point on, I was free of them, but not free of victimhood. It was a choice I did not understand I had made, not even when the idea came to me some years later to wear a mask. [To hide, and to be seen hiding; this is the acting out!]. [I also believe that if I had fought back, it would have been by lashing out at the 'gentler' bully for not protecting me. My mother's failure to protect me from my father may have been the unconscious motive here for my anger at her].*

One evening after supper we were playing ball in the street when a storm blew up suddenly, bringing lightning and thunder. Rain pelted us as we ran for the cover of a nearby porch covered by a fiberglas awning. The leaves on the Sycamore trees sagged groundward from the beating they were taking. It was the kind of rain where each drop is so heavy and falls so fast that most of it flies back into the air an inch or so when it hits the sidewalk, and we could see this effect clearly from the porch where we stood protected, leaning over the railing. The sound of raindrops falling onto the awning was deafening. Even as a boy I must have felt the mysticism of this natural event because I still remember it. None of us spoke; bullies and victim alike were silent in the face of what we were watching. The tableau had a sense of realness to it that was different in kind from our daily lives. There was an animal-like quality to our waiting, because, in a sense, we were not waiting at all; we were experiencing, though we could not have described it that way. The memory of that event convinces me of one thing-that children can exist for moments of great seriousness and existential reality; they are more than creatures of immediate need. Perhaps if a child has enough of these experiences he reaches a tipping point, after which he may begin to ask himself about their nature. Perhaps this is because every child who watches silently such a rain is for that passing moment a man as well as a boy, for he is locked into a kind of mature quietude that does not ordinarily appear in males until they are much older, if at all. Something about the intensity of concentration focused on the storm transcends boyhood and hints at what is to come—the inner silence of the grown man. What was most amazing about this experience was that, after the storm had passed and the sun again beat down upon the street, no one spoke. We climbed down from the porch and went to our homes, each to continue to be molded in our idiosyncratic ways by what we had experienced. Later, much later, I took a simple lesson from that day: a brutal silence has a calming, leavening effect on all who take part in it. For a few moments, we were all monks in the monastery of a thunderstorm. Nature produced a unity I had not expected, and which I did not ponder, until now.

There must have been something pleasant about that experience, or *grounded*. These kinds of moments are stripped of self-consciousness and steeped in *experience*. Pure thought must be like that, I suppose. Is it not true that a woman is never more attractive than when she is concentrating fully on something to the exclusion of her surroundings? It is also possible that in every life a few events are experienced which carry a simpler message: there were other histories one might have lived. the event was likely the first time I had ever experienced myself experiencing; it came by chance; there was no way to seek out another one. For a period of five minutes we were *being, that is, we had stepped out of time.* There was no love, no hatred, not even awe, no opposites, no thought, no thinking. We were animals.

## *[Annotation]:*

*This event was an awakening, not a grounding. A child is too young to understand an awakening. It lies somewhere in the mind, waiting for the child to mature. The older man who was the child may recall it at a particular moment, and then it will grow into its own meaning; then he will understand that at the time of the event he did not have that which was necessary to understand it. There is little difference between the experience of being beaten and that of being grounded; both result in one's experiencing one's experience. Perhaps it is the sense of complete weakness that accompanies the former which enforces the sense of shame, which later becomes a defense, an avoidance of pain before it occurs.*

One more event, which occurred much later, reinforced my growing belief that there was an *Other*, [a term difficult to define; let me suggest it is only another unlived history, in which one has been recognized] but I was wrong in thinking that it was mystical. And it also came by chance. That time, I was on a bus traveling into P to take my army physical. As I sat with many other young men from my neighborhood, I looked at the stores and homes we passed and recognized them because I had often shopped there. But I was in a different world on that bus. I could not have gotten off; the thought of doing so never occurred to me, though I am sure I was apprehensive. The war was on; stories of young men my age trying to cheat the draft were circulating. One had shot a gun off next to his ear to make himself deaf. Others were supposedly starving themselves. All were drafted despite their attempts at evasion. I knew nobody on the bus, though we were all from the same area. In a sense I was inhuman, able to see my life passing by but unable to experience it. The bus ride had the same kind of naturalness to it as had our watching the storm, but it took considerable effort to understand why it should be so. As the bus left my neighborhood, I felt more and more that I was leaving my life without having experienced it. But I did not feel grief, only a sense of displacement akin to that feeling of awe and *otherness* I felt while watching the rain.

These events remain with me for reasons that may seem unrelated to their theme. That is, I understood from them much later that despite what I felt about myself, my apeness, my personal myths that arose from my experiences, there was, is, an overarching sense of naturalness to be experienced, a naturalness which makes every human being equal before it. It was that knowledge of equality in nature that I sought for the rest of my life without ever being able to put my search into words, possibly because when I stepped away from that naturalness, I was no longer the equal of anyone, at least in my own mind. But

I must caution myself: If I had not gone to live in the City, I do not believe I would have considered or recalled this part of my past. It was the ferment of the City and what I observed there that nudged me backward. The City was a wider arena.

What are all these events by themselves—an idea that caused great excitement but never came to pass, an argument that led me to stare at boys being free and, in truth, brutal—other than disconnected happenings? A life has a million occurrences, and hardly any two of them may be placed one with another in a meaningful way. But as I did not do then but can do now, I can say that they convinced me-without knowing that I had been convinced-that I was and always would be isolated and a watcher. I could not move toward either end of the spectrum they provided, nor could I accept my immobility. The solution I chose (or which was offered to me rather as if it were a card from a deck fanned before me by a conjurer) was immobility and denial of immobility at the same time. This choice invariably leads to tension; in fact, it is the definition of tension, and when puberty eventually arrives, it is tension with a sexual meaning. My inclination became, and remains today, to observe, to stand back, yet to desire frightfully for contact with what I am seeing. And because I cannot take part fully in what I see, I misperceive it. The importance of my map-sketching explains itself in this misperception, for it is an attempt accurately to place myself in a context so proper that I cannot deny what I describe. Simply, I will draw myself into a corner from which I cannot escape. It was my isolation that led me to raise to the level of grandeur the title of *accomplice,* because, when one has become a watcher, one begins to believe that what one is observing is separated from oneself and therefore not as pure; but one is, in a way, taking part. Watchers believe they are purer than all others and that is why the act contains elation, or at least denotes thrill. Knowing this to be true, I guarded against it. How could I be an ape if I were not ape-like? So, I also wanted to hide in view, but the method that occurred to me had not come to me by chance. It was predetermined by a prior idea and my relation to it, that is, the idea of the ape-ness of all men and, I think, of their essential shyness. [And the fear of apes I had as a child]. An idea becomes a talisman in just this way, and in time, I entered the city of P. with the force of my myths pushing me as from behind, and the certainty of my belief was reinforced when I went to a sculpture exhibit at the Academy soon after I entered the City. The life-size sculptures of human forms by Segal were on display. I walked among these figures, almost brushing against them at times, entering a revelatory world, for I would never otherwise have had the opportunity to stand next to construction workers having lunch or a family at table and to stare relentlessly as I did that day. To look, to stare or ogle—even to leer—I would reach out and touch people's bodies if I could, but it is not permitted, except at sculpture exhibits.

*The stocky boy-I'll call him F-who crowed on the step taught me how to masturbate. After the teasing abated and I took my place in an unsteady triumvirate, I was protected as a protégé, a step below that of friend. That is, only they could torture me; but I was also protected; no one else could bully or threaten me. So it was that when F and I crawled into a discarded refrigerator box in F's backyard, and the teenager next door began to pelt the box with rocks, it was F who charged out and chased him back into his house, while I huddled in the box, afraid to look out. When F returned, full of that bravado I had already seen, he crawled into the box, unzipped his denim jeans, and, lying down in the narrow space, began to stroke himself. I had never seen anyone do that; at ten, I still believed a penis was for urinating. "Do it like this," he ordered, and showed me how to move my hand over the shaft of my penis (it is a conceit to call it a shaft at that age; he did not touch me) until a feeling I had never known before arose in me. Oh education! Oh friends! What did I not own after that? It still made a difference that he tormented me daily; yet he had clarified for me something I would never lose, the image of one who educates, protects and also tortures. If I elevate this image to the stature of a myth, it is because he moved that image in time from my father, who was, after all, not around most of the day, to the present. From that moment, he transferred to himself (and to his friend) some of the power my father held, and made it, in a sense, contemporary. They bestowed on me a secret which I might keep from him. In this way I was elected clown by the neighborhood boys, because I was last, last to know, last to understand the link between aggression and sexual excitement, and the smallest. What was I doing in that box? I imagine F could have strangled me. Perhaps only that older teenager who threw the rocks at the carton saved my life. And why did I go into the box? A secret wish to die or to be molested? The event has the quality of molestation! I cannot know what F had planned; I can only vaguely comprehend the repetition of ego-weakness I had already begun to suffer when challenged by a man or boy older than I. What was my wish but to be swallowed up in that weakness by another male, as I had already been swallowed up by my father, to whom I always gave in?*

Choices always present themselves to a watcher. Though I never wore the gorilla mask, other ideas which did not become a myth and which I ultimately rejected occurred to me: to follow someone, anyone, who I saw in the street, to make such an act my work for an hour, a day, or a month. Upon thinking about it, I understood immediately that I had no goal in mind; yet there must have been one, one I could neither reach nor acknowledge: the adoption of the life of another or joining another family, undertaken merely by tracking. Tracking is another form of disguise—merging one's life with that of another allows one to slip below the surface of another's life. But this idea did not thrill me as much as the mask or clown suit, perhaps because such an act leads naturally to a *story*, a series of events in the life of another in which I would have to immerse myself. But I am not a natural storyteller, nor do I see anyone's life as a *story*. I see no arc in anyone's life, not even the greatest of men. And I am too silent; rarely am I able even to listen to the facts of another man's life, unless I am seeking pleasure. It was only by looking that I made sense of the world, and tracking increases the risk of being seen. It creates a relationship, even if the person being followed does not know he is being observed.

What did occur to me, in the end, was more painful, as it came to light a few years later while I lay on the couch at the office of Dr. Gold [later to be described] and was my attempt to describe for him the paradigm of my life in a way other than discussing my own ape-ness, which, though I had almost accepted it (in a metaphorical sense), was not a subject about which I could yet speak freely. One afternoon in early Spring, rather like the one on which I had observed from my window the boys across the street, with bees riding the warm air currents up to the open windows of Dr. Gold's study, shortly after we had begun our session, I described for him the structure of my family unit, weighted by years of watching, listening and anger. It was not a tainted description, for I had entered that zone of talk in which one speaks to oneself with wonder, as if no one else were in the room and one was discovering something for the first time, that is, as if what one were describing had never been true until the exact moment one spoke of it.

*"I am straddled across my mother's thighs as she sits on a chair, facing her with my penis inside her, while, behind me, my father has inserted his penis into my anus."*

This image came to me unbidden, which was cause enough for me to fear it yet also to trust its validity as an apt description of my position in the family (and on the earth). *I was doing and being done to:* that was the dominant image of my life. It was the first sign that the history which, in my mind, belonged to me, had another side for which I had no referents. One may spend a long time becoming accustomed to such an image if one is fortunate enough to have it made conscious. Much thought has gone toward becoming comfortable with the image as something metaphorical rather than obscene. [It was not only metaphorical; it was accurate in a way that goes beyond metaphor, for it showed both halves of those opposites I mentioned earlier, brokenness and unity, with sex as the unifying force of synthesis, as well as punishment, humiliation and desire]. I surely am not alone, however, either in my metaphor or in my creation of it. What is miraculous is the idea of a middle-aged automobile mechanic and a housewife becoming the subject matter of the metaphor. One knows afterward that possibility is endless in this world. I imagine Dr. Gold asking a relevant question: *"Which part did you enjoy the most?"* That question, whether Gold asked it or I asked it of myself, was meaningful. It led me to ask, a long time later, whether we have two sets of memories which exist alongside one another [and whether I was as polymorphous-perverse then as I was as an infant]. One set is that of events, working, playing, being; the other is the set of quick images, almost lithe in their movement in and out of consciousness, which compose the sinew which holds together the first set. I hope to speak later of a raincoat on a window sill, an old soldier mumbling to himself as he walks along the pavement, (I have already spoken of a high back porch under which trash cans sat). All these images are of *things* (a human being is also a thing). I ask myself whether it is possible that *things* are what binds memory. [If I want to be immortal I must consider myself as a thing as well as a human being].

## *[Annotation]:*

*Now I had two images to work with, that of my mother in the bath, and that of me penetrating and being penetrated. Taken as one singular symbol of a particular family history as joined in my mind, the symbol takes its place alongside all the other events, the street life, the years of schooling, illnesses. Thus, two separate histories exist whose interlocking connections are not obvious to me, nor do I understand that it is so for everyone. Becoming a watcher does not embed this lesson; one is not watching oneself while observing others, or, at least, one does not understand that one is watching others because of the psychic history rather than the event history.*

*I will mention this paradigm again, but I am certain that I began my time with Dr. Gold with a strong desire not to have him take it away from me. I valued it as a possession which I believed expressed in compressed form my goodness, my generosity, my sacrifice, as if I were only fucking my mother to reconnect her with my father, as if I were a volunteer savior of a marriage, that is, a* **catalyst.** *An image such as my paradigm is so rich in meaning that several ways of looking at it appear to me. But the most frightening view, which never entered my mind at the time, was the view which included the definition of a catalyst, which disappears after it has connected two substances. Plainly, the paradigm itself was an offer to mother and father of my own suicide. It represents, in fact, two meanings; a desire to connect them, and a desire to die after the connection, clothed in a generous and lustful act. It also indicates, in the clearest possible way, that I had taken in their struggle and could find no way to consider it with the intellect of a child; my only choice was death, [or, at least, punishment] which is less fearful than annihilation. It is unpleasant to discover that one has wanted to die after only four or five years of life; my fear of death has remained incomprehensible to me until now. The unity I had wanted I already had; a triangular death struggle. [There is another possible explanation which I have considered: that having my mother was so important that I was willing to be punished by my father to expiate my guilt].*

*If I have not completely made clear the issues over which my parents struggled, it may be because it was the aura of conflict in our household that entered my mind and remained there, rather than any particular political or personal issues. I would have adopted their conflicts without understanding them, simply because that aura frightened me and I sought the comfort that any child would have looked for. It seems certain, however, that neither got what they expected from marriage. I now know that a catalyst does not disappear but moves on. This knowledge does not change my thinking about the paradigm.*

⟫⟫⟫ ⟪⟪⟪

Hart has been reading my notes again. This is unusual, for just as he papers his walls with the pages of his novel-to-be, I hide my work. But I have a hunger for praise which grows as I make progress in sketching my map, only to be brought down to earth by his comment: *"A demeaning portrayal of oneself as a naif aligns the cynical self with the world's view and assumes the world's view is correct; but it is not. The description itself is merely arrogant."*

The very fact of his being here in my flat, as we wait for Ericksen, another friend, to arrive before going out, recalls for me another corner of the blank square on which I began my cartographic effort, the idea of *triangulation*. By this term I mean the creation in my mental life of groups of three; a mother, father and child; a young boy watching two other boys fight and creating an emotional triangle from what he sees; Ericksen, Hart and I having an acquaintanceship. I can see that this mental operation is ongoing and meaningful, but I cannot say truthfully that I understand why this should be so. As I went here and there in the Central District of P with my friends, both of whom had to be with me for me to attain the fullness of an evening spent in bars, the idea that I was *recreating* a group of three flitted in and out of my mind; but at other times, when I was on my way to a brothel or sitting at a bar alone, it was more difficult to concentrate on this idea because I was too busy watching, or asking questions (the latter of which I used to control my world and to make it safer. If one is talking in a bar [or, later, in a brothel] with a young Negro girl, or a Korean, and one asks *"And do you have children?"* or *"And who takes care of them while you are here?,"* is not the goal one of safety, of creating a more familiar world around one in the tiny cubicle or bedroom one might find oneself in?).

My list of myths, all of them false, or, if not false, contingent and based on false premises, might go on and on. I state only a few of them here because these are the ones that return to me often, carrying with them for that reason the power of meaning and the sense that, in their totality, they were the boundaries of my existence. When [incomplete] ideas repeat themselves, they become myths.

It is true, of course, that one can misunderstand oneself completely. Yet I have already said it is also possible to misunderstand and still come to the correct conclusions, even if they are only contingent. For a long time after I came to P, specially after I had begun to converse with Hart about films-his favorite topic, other than Balzac-I believed that it was the director Hitchcock who had stated in an interview that his method was to subordinate his subject to his object. From that statement I understood him to mean that he used his subject matter, which was film, to work out the central question of his life, which was his object. I later reread the interview and found that he had never made such a statement. Someone else had actually said the reverse, i.e., that the question was the subject and each film an object to be manipulated in a way that aimed to resolve the subject. But had I not formulated the statement in just that way, that is, had I not misunderstood it, I would never have been able to begin my map sketching. It would never have occurred to me to begin thinking seriously about the images and the ideas that always seemed to recur to me at unpredictable times, or which seemed merely to thread themselves throughout my consciousness over the years. One's myths recede into the background, as Kita describes, but that background creates a kind of microcosmic static that results in background noise, to which one pays no attention until a Korzybski comes along and a single sentence out of eight hundred pages causes everything else in one's mind to recede into silence, a silence just long enough for the realization that one is being driven through a lifetime by memories that have receded into the background, where they became myth, where their force, for good or evil, remains limitless. One's myths have *been* one's life. It is the discovery of a single sentence such as Korzybski's that produces a *gap*; if one peers into the gap one may see all that yearning which has been missing or overlooked in one's life, all the possibility and impossibility the argument between which one has never been comfortable.

One cannot explain a myth on its own terms. It stands on the border between two worlds which rotate upon the axis of a sun. I can say only that I saw these recurring ideas as objects on a map, but the map itself had no boundaries. If I determined those boundaries, might I not step over them? I will describe only a few events that occurred when I moved to the city of P, and I provide this description for myself to determine whether they can be understood in such a way that fills in some of the gaps in my comprehension of my past that might explain what I have become. I do not expect complete, even partial success, but it is the work I have chosen to do. I am learning as I go along in this experimental examination. Experiments often fail or prove something entirely different from what the experimenter expected, or they prove nothing at all. Yet, they must be done; physiology alone drives them forward. [Hart once asked me why I had ever come to the city if all I did was go to see women dancing nude and look for call girls. As I later discovered, it was precisely for that reason, though he had convinced me to enter P as if it were a walled city].

⤜ ⤛

*It is only in a city, The City, that one can come to comprehend that one lives with two histories; it is only in the city that one is forced to come to terms with the fact, because one cannot live in a city without being forced to observe the two histories of everyone with whom one comes in contact. Even so, the mist of events covers the mist of that other history, resulting in a furious struggle which can only be understood as the meaning of one's existence. And the under-history, if I may call it that, is composed of 'things' as well as psychic events. I have only to look at what I intend to consider: genitals, ashtrays, Kleenex, sculpture; these 'things' will take their place in my mental apparatus, have already acquired meaning. I had found a broader arena and exchanged the idea of a mask for a set expression on my face, which could relax itself under certain conditions [such as being in a booth at an adult bookstore or being with Hart and Ericksen].*

Spring comes late to the city of P, because of its latitude, which is similar to that of Paris. Winter storms which begin in the south sweep upward to the coast near where P lies, and warmer temperatures do not appear until late April. As Spring approaches, the azaleas in the garden behind the Museum of Art are the first flowers to bloom, almost without any of P's citizens noticing them. Soon afterward, more azaleas open around R Park, near the southwestern corner of the Central District. Blue, pink, white blossoms suddenly appear, all fighting for their individual destinies, where the day before there seemed to be nothing but dark shoots uncared for by human hands. Many of P's streets have names taken from the vocabulary of the local indian tribes who flourished there three hundred years ago along the two rivers that limn the Central District: Shackamaxon, Lenape, Delaware, [there are also Spring Street and Summer Street] ; and spring seems to approach P along the banks of the Western River as if by canoe, floating gently but inexorably toward the Central District and through it to the Eastern River. There, the grass fattens along its banks; the deck hands on the freighters moving downriver discard their sweaters and, in their tee shirts, wind heavy ropes around bollards. Flowers, then grass, then the musculature of working men are back in the world. Gulls from the bay, sixty miles to the South, begin to appear on the Eastern River; and above the marshland on the far bank, ravening hawks circle and glide over the copses that have not yet been torn down for development.

On a long quay by the Eastern River was an outdoor cafe where Hart and I could watch the barges slip southward with barrel loads of waste on their decks. Water lapped onto the quay and sprayed a fine mist on which sunlight reflected, and the bargemen ignored us as they clambered over knotted ropes topside, checking the barrels for play. Once we had seen a man fall from one of these barges, a ship so loaded with cargo that it could not have turned back to pick him up. We sat watching while a police boat came alongside the man, who treaded water for thirty minutes until he was pulled from the river. The entire time he held in his hand the leather boots he had been wearing, loathe to give them up to the current.

It was at this cafe that Hart described for me the reasons why I ought to live in P.

*"Think of Greece three thousand years ago"*, he said. *"Athens, say, and what must have been going on there a thousand years before the birth of Christ. At the very least there were armorers, candle makers, hide tanners, farmers, winemakers, grape growers, potters, road builders, stone masons, sculptors, usurers, teachers, students, oracular seers, thinkers, drunkards, rebels, builders of temples, driers of brick and clay, cart makers and smiths, stable boys and breakers of horses, soldiers and shipbuilders, religious leaders, statesmen, ne'er-do-wells, prodigal sons, whores, courtesans, crutch makers and woodcarvers, prisoners and gaolers (English words which we believed carried a certain cachet often appeared in our conversations), ruffians and homosexuals, gods and perverse thrill seekers."*

Even then, before I came permanently to P, I thought I understood what he meant. Now, when I stroll down the pavement and see drunken ex-soldiers mumbling ("Yes, Sergeant! No, Sergeant. Sorry, Sergeant!") and women who beat their heads against trees in R Park, when I see the lawyers with their ties tucked in and the vendors of scarves, fruit and handbags, when I pass the characters who define P, as in a sense the Duck Lady and the Stock Exchange Screamer do, [Later to be described] I feel the straight line between Athens and P. We have steel and migraines and cigarette lighters but we also have those who were in Athens and businessmen and lawyers to boot. If I dwell on what Hart told me that afternoon I realize that we wanted time to stop, but there is no doubt in my mind that some essence, some golden nugget of reality has been passed on from Athens, or Mohenjodaro or Peking or Timbuktu to us here, now, and we in our fashion will pass it on too, even if we fail miserably at whatever we attempt, because we came here. Every human being contributes mass to P, if nothing else, and mass, compacted tightly enough, discharges energy. When I lived at home and went outside to lie in the grass, wanting to howl at the moon in despair, I did not know any of these things. My body knew it, that ungainly mass of fat and bile. My father must have known it as he cursed and mimicked and hammered in his basement and swore again. I did not know that he knew, but that kind of behavior bespeaks knowledge, knowledge bent and misshapen by time. It is possible my mother also knew but took something gentler from her knowledge because she had been born in P and would die there and accepted what happened there with equanimity as my father could not, for where she saw individuals he saw masses and well-fed bourgeoisie. He had failed and believed a price should be paid though he hated to pay it. And that was one more reason why I saw that straight line between Athens and P which Hart described, because I, like the Athenians, strove to propitiate my gods—my father and mother—and my myths-as Hart did in his fashion and as I think Ericksen did, also. Here, in P, those mystic shapes still exist and force themselves upon us from within.

To live in P, with its music, bars, brothels and motion, I would have to live the life of an accomplice (I had experience as such) and an accomplice cannot hide. A watcher is always in complicity with what he sees anyway because he does nothing to interfere with it. He is as responsible for the suffering or joy he observes as those persons who are undergoing life within his view. Whatever was at my core would have to be played out in the arena given to me. I had no desire to watch grass grow. I wanted to see men and women living, apes, if you will. Almost against my will, (but not quite completely, I know) I joined that motion.

⟫⟫—⟪⟪

I did not go to P to make my fortune, as any young man in a Balzac novel would surely have done. It seemed predetermined that I would never have money or position. And even when one moves to a city one does not enter it right away. As men did a thousand years ago when they came to the gates of walled cities, one must symbolically stand and wait today until someone opens the gates. Entry is a procession which occurs over time and requires method and ritual. One falters in the beginning because this knowledge can only be gained by experience. For example, merely to find a bar or cafe to call one's own is a task that requires tact and patience. The first step, I learned from Hart, is to buy a quart of beer at a local taproom and to leave quickly. [Was he a torturer, a teacher, a protector?] It would be a mistake actually to sit down and order a drink the first time one entered a bar. This act, repeated several times, allows the bartender to learn one's face, perhaps even to assign one a nickname after a period of weeks. One might end up being called "Mr. Bud" or "Quart o' Piel's." After a few weeks of these actions, one may enter and sit quietly at one end of the bar, where suddenly one is changed from "Mr. Bud" to "Draft o' Rock." After that, one is free and may sit at that bar for the rest of one's life if one chooses. One might even be asked to run errands for the bartender, such as turning off the lights after last call, or taking the nightly six-pack out to the police squad car that pulls up to the front of the bar and sits, its engine idling, every night at two a.m. I performed these rites in a bar called M's, across the street from the building where I rented my flat, and I was accepted. Once I became known, there was no need even for me to speak to anyone. I was part of the *mise-en- scene* and thus contained the same qualities as a booth, a door or a stool. [Another thing to which attention might be paid]. Entry into the City is entry into one's self; both are rituals.

⇛ ⇚

The flat I took was in the Academy of Music District, on the third floor of an older building that had a travel agency and a restaurant on the ground floor. The day I moved in, Hart came over to watch the process. I brought only a few pieces of furniture from my home, a small bed, a couch, and a chair which

I had not wanted but which my father had insisted I take. It was pillowy and one sank down in it as one sat. I placed it in a corner, and whenever I became frustrated over the next several months I would hit it with a baseball bat or a golf club. [I had brought a set of clubs with me, a symbol of the suburban life I could not wholly part with]. After a year or so most of its stuffing on the back end had leaked out onto the floor, and I swept it under the bed, not bothering even to sweep it into a dustpan. I came to think of it as *that chair.*

*"There are cats in this building,"* Hart said when he walked in. A small window in the bathroom was open, and he leaned out to take a look. *"Just look at the filth on this ledge,"* and through it we saw what appeared to be several pounds of cat droppings on the ledge just beyond the window. I leaned out, too, craned my neck and saw a cat lying on the windowsill of the flat above mine. *"There's the explanation."* *"Find a whisk broom,"* Hart said. I had only a long broom, which I slid out the window. I put on a pair of woolen gloves and, with Hart holding the window sash up, I slithered out onto the ledge and swept the cat feces off the roof onto the parking lot below. When I climbed back inside, I threw away the gloves, washed my hands and lit incense sticks, which I placed in a glass in the middle of the bathtub. Hart had brought two leaded glasses and a bottle of Heaven Hill bourbon and he poured the tawny liquid generously. We touched glasses and drank.

*"Aside from my father, you are my first visitor,"* I said.

*"After the stench leaves, you can even have a woman over,"*

*"Maybe it will even be Lara."* Lara was a woman we knew whom everyone was after. She was a patient of the same therapist whom Hart and Ericksen saw. I had met her only once. It had become common knowledge [morelikely only a rumor begun by another patient who saw an opportunity] that she had never made love to her husband. Why would Hart suggest her, when he wanted her for himself? It is clear that I had already taken a subservient role with him, yet I would remember this night later as his intent became

clearer]. And anyone my age or older, even younger, would have had more sexual experience than I had.

*"I'd hardly expect that. After all, I'm not very slick, am I? Just look at where I live."*

I waved my arm toward the middle of the room, almost bare but for the chair my father had insisted I bring.

*"You don't need to be slick; you only need to know what a woman is looking for. Even the ladies' men hanging around her may not know that." ["And they're all patients of Dr. Gold, not very adept at dealing with women."]*

That was true. Lara was a beauty and a man who could pay attention to her might have a chance with her, if only because she in her turn was a woman who could pay attention to a man.

We were sitting by then, Hart on the couch and I on the floor [already in the subservient position, as the women were in the loops I watched in 'adult' book stores]. Hart had lit a cigarette and given me one, also. I thought then of my situation. All of my life until that day I had lived at home. My parents had wanted me to remain there, but upon my telling them that I had rented a flat, they had given up their opposition. Now I possessed one room, a closet, a Pullman kitchen and a stench-filled bathroom. All I had brought with me from home, excluding my clothes and toiletries, were the bed, a couch, a table and *that chair.*

My thoughts had drifted and I realized that Hart was speaking to me. *"................ Ajax, a mop, sponges, paper towels and plenty of them............... Oh! and Brillo, too.,"* he was saying. *"I'll get everything right away,"* I told Hart. *"Let's go out later to celebrate." "Yes,"* Hart said, *"We'll celebrate the cleaning of the cat shit."*

Though this conversation was of a type that I might learn from, despite its banality, it seemed to me that it was making Hart uncomfortable. Perhaps in his role of advice-giver he was thinking aloud of his own desires. In fact, he had an interest in Lara, the topic of which had been momentarily side-tracked by the need for cleanliness, but he would enjoy taking her away from me more than approaching her first. Lara had the quality—and it was not one she might control—of being more attractive to men when she was already with one. When Hart said he was leaving I did not object. I watched him descend the steps and then, locking myself in, began life in P.

The Academy of Music District was close by an elegant square around which rose stately apartment buildings. Across the street from the building where I lived was a bar called M's, and on late afternoons in the Spring I sat near its open door with my newspaper, watching the people of wealth alight from their cars onto the parking lot across the way (the same lot onto which I had deposited the pile of cat droppings), dressed in smart, cummerbunded tuxedos and taffeta gowns, taking an early supper before the nightly concerts. At night, back in my flat, I lay on the cool linoleum tile floor with the lights off, listening, and watching the tip of my cigarette glow and darken in the shadows. From the parking lot below came the sounds of doors being slammed shut, engines being gunned, the crunch of tires on gravel. Around the corner, on the walls of the Academy-which was a hundred years old-the reconstructed gas lamps (as I imagined them) fluttered in the sweet breeze. Outside, the night was an amoral soup into which I might fall eventually with a noiseless splash. I did not know how much I wanted to be amoral, and I often left my flat about that time to walk through the Central District from River to River, feeling miserable and marvellous at the same time. In the brownstones and row houses yellow rectangles of light shone everywhere, and I knew people were *doing* things. I had only to glimpse a shadow pass across a lighted window to believe that, in the City, anything was possible. High above the brownstones, I saw the lit windows of hotels. In the rooms, I imagined men in rumpled suits who threw down their baggage on the clean beds. Tired from their cramped flights and long cab rides, they looked down at P with their Adam's Apples bobbing as if they were looking at the veldt, wondering *"What's down there?"* I thought the same way I imagined they thought. Nothing has happened to change that and I have now been in P for quite a long time. Dr. Gold had once remarked to me, as I described my walks through P, *"When you are not thinking about fucking you are pretty shallow."* It hurt me to hear that; part of my sorrow lay in knowing that he had only to utter a word for me to believe it implicitly. But I had merely to remember one event that occurred shortly after I arrived in P to know that his words were accurate. I had been on a bus traveling toward the Western River. The bus passed a pleasant string of shops which gowned itself in more furtive fashion when dusk fell. In the rear of a used-book shop a bare bulb burned solemnly. Nearby, a lone woman hugged a parking meter. As the bus went by, a man turned the corner and approached the woman. He reached into his pocket and our eyes met through the glass, as we both had the same thought: *"How much money would he need?"* On that bus, and from then forward, I understood that the onset of dusk is a votive song… It never occurred to me that I may have been looking toward every window for the purpose of recreating a primal scene (which I may never have actually seen)—in which case I was, without thinking about it, desirous of seeing it for the first time, in order to move on to the genital phase of a man's life… [Had I been a watcher for so long in hopes of seeing that alleged primal scene?].

⇛ ⇚

Whenever I entered the City from my flat there appeared a world of older and wiser men who stood behind me and slightly to my right, just beyond my peripheral vision, as if they were looking over my shoulder while I lived, benevolent private detectives, in a sense, whom I did not know I had hired. They seemed to follow me but not to interfere as I corkscrewed into the future. I was too wrapped up in my own concerns to notice them, then. Now, as I

84

make this effort to recall, I see that they were always there, but I knew not how to take advantage of their presence. (I am reminded by Hart that the phrase *I knew not* appeared in DeQuincey's <u>Confessions of an English Opium Addict</u> as another example of having to borrow because I have no originality). I speak not only of Dr. Gold, whom I saw every week, but of Tony, who tended bar at M's, also of Rubin, the great poet, who said *"Men have a sexual thought every five seconds"*... One lies on the floor of one's hovel dreaming of glory and reading novel after novel of young men in the city (and Hart and I had read most of them) yet comes away with nothing but confusion, or a bravado which is pure stupidity, while, not ten feet away, a man is observing one who has seen one's forebears, but one thinks of that man as no more than another piece of the *mise-en-scene*, placed there for one's own gratification. [One does not know yet that he, too, is a thing to which attention may be paid]. One speaks to him in passing, but his presence has no meaning. Later, he and others like him become the signposts to which one's memory returns. I spent much of my life in P in the presence of such men, sitting at a table in M's or lounging in Dr. Gold's offices, talking to whoever came by. The presence of older men comforted me....

⇒⇒⇒ ⇐⇐⇐

I think now specially of Tony, the bartender at M's, whose word, as with many people who go to work after four o'clock in the afternoon, was less than his bond, but in his case, the difference was negligible. When I had followed Hart's instructions over a period of weeks and become known at M's, Tony promised me that I would never need worry about how much I drank there-he would always see to it that I got safely home. The first time I fell asleep there at a table, drunk, I awakened in the middle of the night lying in the foyer of the building where I lived, propped up on the landing between the inner and outer doors. I had learned that Tony would cross the street for me but he would not climb stairs. I may exaggerate when I say that one cannot make a discovery more exciting than that one, but I say it anyway. So Tony and I got along fine, mostly because I never spoke more than a few words to him at any time, and those mostly on the order of *"glass o' Rock, 'kay?."* When I first found M's I was at a point many young men reach when they live alone in a city (though few will tell you of it without prodding) where, but for work, I would not speak for days at a time, particularly on weekends, preferring instead to lie abed in my flat, daydreaming or merely dozing. Speech, to anyone, was a minor victory over the forces of solitude. My reticence was not so much deliberate as it was a part of my personality, and over a period of days I would become jumpy of people. When I finally spoke, my first words were always high-pitched and full of phlegm and often had to be repeated. To enter a place such as M's and to order what I wanted in a clear voice was an act I never performed without it being preceded by a violent pounding of my heart and an almost blinding narrowing of my vision, excluding all but me and Tony, whom I saw as at the end of a tunnel or as through the wrong end of a pair of binoculars from where I stood on the other side of the bar. The few occasions when he and I spoke were revelatory, for to be able to speak one sentence in public had become a measure of my worth. Everything depended on it. I sometimes wonder if people can understand how it is that to be able to order a drink can become an act that means literally everything. There were times when, if Tony had said to me *"Speak up, damn it! I can't hear you!,"* as I had seen him do to others when he was in a surly mood, I would have turned away and left the bar, never to return. There is a way some people have of screwing up their faces and asking one *"What did you say?!"* several times in a manner that makes one think one has not asked a question but has committed a crime. Tony had that good bartender sense that told him I was to be left alone (I hadn't the power to say it myself). Some period of change or reconstruction had already begun in me, and if I knew not what it was or even that it was happening, he appreciated my solitude and the tremendous effort it took me to break through it. He never embarrassed me. He was a man. He did not interfere with my *becoming*, of which I was not aware.

To say he was a man, given how I have begun, is not enough. Rather, I should say I was unconcerned with his bravado or his ability to earn a living for his family. I mean that I could well envision him crouching behind fronds in a jungle, picking nits from a fellow ape without the slightest hint of self-consciousness. Tony was what he was and was unconcerned with hiding. He did not judge himself. He had no interior dialogue with another soul.

I may think also of McManus, who had ruined his back during forty years as a stevedore, and who hobbled down the street with his overcoat full of papers, applications for disability, letters to the editors of tabloids which he wrote but which were never published. Worse, his wallet had been stolen in an adult bookstore, along with all of his identification cards, and he had every day to walk to the public library, where typewriters were available for public use, to make reapplications for his driver's license, social security card and Medicare card. I have seen him spy a fifty-cent piece on the pavement in front of M's and cover it with his limping foot as if it were the hope Diamond, glancing quickly and furtively around to see if anyone else had seen his treasure (only I had).

I cannot pretend that I was conscious of having taken sustenance from these men; but their presence in the narrow area in which I existed (I was *existing* at that time but not *living*) created an atmosphere of comfort, if only because they were not harsh and made no judgments of others. Or, I should say that if they behaved harshly, they did not dwell on their actions. I was permitted to be 'not myself' in their presence. To be in their presence was to lose some of my imagined uniqueness and brought a certain fear with that loss. If these men were sick, and I was in their presence in P, I must have some of their qualities, too. A certain denial began to weaken, imperceptible, perhaps, but for the anxious state I often felt.

There were other patrons whom I saw frequently in M's who were-and I describe them in the gentlest sense-disturbed. I think specifically of Richard, who had urinated in his trousers and thus saved his own life. When mobsters entered his small jewellery store demanding protection money, his first thought had been to run into the vault, lock it behind him, and blow out his brains; his fear was incalculable. Before he could carry out that plan, he wet himself. He felt such a fool, and it was so strong an emotion, that he collapsed, and the extortionists ran from his store. He often sat in complicated discussion with Bradley, a schizophrenic attorney, who had never practiced law. Bradley's parents had stopped giving him money after he finished a year of spending a hundred thousand dollars on whores. In a sense, it became more important for me to know these facts (or to believe their stories were factual) than it was to have Tony and McManus in my sphere, because with the former, I understood that the collective force of P had routinized our various idiosyncratic ways of living. I was sure that if Richard's jewellery store had been in a suburban strip mall he'd have killed himself immediately, and that if Bradley had lived in the country he'd eventually have joined Richard or fallen under a pile of rotten autumn leaves on a country lane, leaving his aged parents to consider the dual experience of relief and despair. Instead of these deaths, these men were known. For a few hours each night they were forced to become socialized and acclimated to the noisy clanking weather that hovered in M's a few feet above our heads.

Others stood out for their bizarreness, but also because they provided a watcher with impressions that were long-lasting. I think now of the man who screamed in front of the Stock Exchange Building every weekday. I do not know his name. He appeared to have suffered a brain injury, for one side of his head was deeply dented. But every day he was driven to that corner by his brother (as I learned from passers-by over a period of months). Immediately upon climbing out of his brother's car, he lit a cigarette and began to growl, producing a sound that could be heard a street away and several floors upward. Whatever the agony of his life had been in its original form, one could assume he had made an *adjustment* and no longer expressed it internally. Now each growl was a sort of pronouncement which he made every day; from nine o'clock in the morning to four o'clock in the afternoon he often spoke quietly to the young workers; he smoked their cigarettes; they bought him sandwiches from luncheonettes. He *hung out.* One could not say that he was not sick, but he managed to live a routinized life by expressing his despair in a routinized way. I would speak of his courage but that had been lost; he was impelled to act as he did. Nevertheless, his actions were, over time, meaningful for me, for they were additional varieties of city behavior which were naturalistic. It was a pure stroke of fortune that I did not consider his behavior in the usual context: *Thank heaven I am not like that.* Rather, I marvelled at the ability of P to accept him and to adapt to his actions. And he was not unique. Several streets away an empty store front had been besieged by a middleaged woman who quacked like a duck for several hours at anyone who passed by. I do not know her name. She lived in the Western District and rode a bus to the Central District several times a week. She trembled as she quacked, yet I once happened to observe her boarding a bus on which I was traveling to the Western District. She sat quietly, without tics or tremors. When she rose to leave, she walked calmly to the front of the bus. She had not made a sound during the ride.

These two people were, for me, examples of the power of the City. In essence, even severely disturbed persons had, for want of a better word, *work.* They seemed able to make choices without thinking about them; that is, they had instincts. I, believing I had none–or that I was terrified that I might act on them—envied that part of them which was able to keep living. Compulsive acts are work, or at least a substitute for it, for they are measures of accomplishment in the same way as are the number of widgets per hour produced on an assembly line.

One spends years writing one's story and in the end sees it only as another morality play—good against evil. Perhaps someday I will have wisdom; certainly I had not got it then. It was blind luck that prevented me from being murdered in the street, the way I ambled along staring up at cornices and gargoyles or gazing into the eyes of passers-by. I wanted to write a song of P, as <u>Ulysses</u> is a song, for the innermost voice is a continuous song, one never-ending upheaval of the unconscious, a rearranging that ceases only with death. But then, a song affirms because it is music, because it has form and because the intellect that molds the form to its content creates a style; and I could not affirm anything. I waited only for the word, the one word that would set me vibrating as if I were a string on a base viol, the great Shudder, a shudder I wanted and did not want at the same time. I saw greatness in everything, even collapse.

And I did not know what that word might be, so all Winter that year I walked from River to River, sometimes with Hart, often alone, measuring the distance which our District took up between those flowing borders. There was no heat in my flat and my landlord, who was a lawyer, refused to make any repairs. Many evenings I went at six o'clock to Hart's, where he, too, slept fitfully on the bare floors of his trinity in a sleeping bag, warming himself with occasional gulps of whiskey. Islands of dirty snow shrank from the curb as I made my way, and the doors of abandoned cars swung to and fro in the biting wind. At my knock, more often than not, Hart bolted forth holding a quart of beer wrapped in a paper bag, a flask in his coat pocket, his earflaps down, and we were off, briskly. *"East or West, my man?"*................ *"Pick it, sir!"*.......

➤— ⫷

## *[Annotation]:*

*It is easy to see that the word "why" disappears in the city milieu. There is simply too much to see. It is only after a certain amount of experience has built up that one might—and it is a tenuous might—consider how one has come to be where one is.*

The fifty dollars I had lent Hart two months before had finally been repaid, but after only an hour and a half in my pocket it had already begun to burn.

We drank whiskey at M's which we paid for with wrinkled dollars. Three vodkas straight up, a snifter of cognac, a Yuengling draft—I was reaching a mood and trying to hold onto it, full of ideas for the next chapter of a novel that I probably hoped, unconsciously, never to finish; but then the two girls came in and sat in the booth behind ours, and I could see it was going to be a difficult time keeping what remained of the fifty dollars as Hart's face turned serious and he crushed his Pall Mall in the ashtray. His voice, which had been well-modulated as we spoke of films and books, rose sharply and John Ford and Hitchcock were forgotten as he began to discuss that year in Paris when he studied at the Sore-bone. He fished a crushed pack of Gaulloises from his shirt pocket and lit one elaborately, then cocked his head toward the ceiling, the better to allow the pungent smoke to drift over the girls' heads. Soon they were sitting with us and Hart was ordering drinks all around.

As soon as we learned that their boyfriends had just been arrested, I understood that my fifty dollars was not going to remain in my pocket. The girls were trying to collect bail money; the arraignments were set for later that evening. They were moving from bar to bar, flirting just enough to pry money loose from the likes of us before their men were brought into night court. I understood right away that Hart wanted the money I had, because he intended to put some effort into convincing them to accompany him back to his house. He was not going to give them the money for nothing; there was a certain amount of fucking to be done first. [He may have had only a bit more experience with women as I, but he was a better actor]. It appeared to me that I would be useless in that endeavor. Each of the girls had small roses tattooed on their shoulders and their conversation was interlaced with the word *fuck*. They made me uncomfortable. There was nothing for me to do but leave. I was faced with a dilemma: either I had to admit my limited sexual experience (which I was not yet willing to do, and certainly not to these girls) or I had to go. I chose to go. But I had to give him the fifty dollars before I could leave.

On this evening Hart's dog had come with us and his leash was wrapped around a post in front of M's. It was now my task to get him back to Hart's house. I took Hart's house key, which I would have to leave under the mat. Soon I was out on the sidewalk, where I unwrapped its leash from the pole and let myself be pulled along by the furry shark he appeared to be to anyone who crossed our path. The dog sniffed at every mound of slush as I stumbled along with him. I was thinking of the fifty dollars and how much it would have gotten me at the Nude Dancers, a strip club in the Central District. I would never see it and looking felt like a burden rather than a way of life.

When I got to Hart's house I let myself in and removed the dog's leash from his collar. I was not going to leave without finding out a few things. In his library, where he wrote, I began to open the drawers of his desk, looking for something-I did not know what. I suppose I wanted something back for having given up my fifty dollars so quickly. In one drawer I found a pair of panties; they lay on top of a sheaf of poems. Pens and erasers were scattered over the desktop. In another drawer I found an envelope that looked familiar. Inside was a story I had written and left with Hart for him to read. I flipped through the pages, now full of red pencil marks and hand-written critical comment. At the bottom of the last page was his conclusion: *"The writer who cynically aligns the world against himself is in fact a naif, and does not believe he is wrong!!"* He had signed it *"Dr. Doom, Professor of Leer-ature."* He had graded it as well: an 'F' covered over with an 'A' in differently colored ink. I stood there wondering if Hart had ever intended to return it to me. After a moment I began to take notice of the dog, who was noisily gnawing a bone. When I locked the door behind me I left the key under the mat. I walked back to my flat thinking of a book I had skimmed recently, called *The Three Christs of Ypsilanti*. It was about three men in a psychiatric hospital in Michigan, all of whom claimed to be Christ, who had been brought together by the hospital staff to see what might happen. I imagined Hart and I being introduced in the same hospital: *"Mr. Hemingway?............... Meet Mr. Hemingway."*

*"Stupidity is a disease," I say, though in my internal dialog I give Hart the words. Hart, with whom I shared a certain time in my life (it was he who met me in the University cafeteria when I first came rushing in with gorillas on my mind) "And for many years you were seriously ill" . It 's true I have always been a bumbler; clumsiness is an emblem of one ' s imprisonment; one wears it at one's peril, like a convict's uniform. Still, I believe he is correct, though in this country, one who confesses great sins or heroic errors of judgment-and in America these are indeed sins- does so not for release but for approval. That is so the public may truly comprehend the magnitude of his mistakes . If one agrees with such a confessor, he is likely to become enraged. For in confession of this type there is no magnanimity, only rancor. And the last thing a young man wants to know is his own rage. I think of Hart, for example, and how much he drank not to feel, not to be clear… How noble we make it in our culture to avoid clarity. Yet a man without knowledge of his own anger is a dangerous man. He steps between two people, then away, and suddenly the two are fighting. He compliments one and one feels raped or denuded . If one touches him one touches foam. Push through the foam and one will be burned. He is disjointed, with a body like a roadmap that has been unfolded and refolded incorrectly. His arm knows nothing of his foot. His head is ignorant of the stomach. His extremities all work against one another. He is a moving force field of pain, and his presence, if one is not careful, will surely seem like a dryness in the air that comes before a thunderstorm. Rage, not heredity, is the etiology of this disease. Bumbling is only the major symptom, and one has only to look at those bumblers who stumble about jabbing one with an elbow, a knee, a forearm to understand that stupidity and clumsiness are cloaks for a rage that cannot be spoken openly. Not because the clumsy have no eloquence, but because they do not understand what underlies their actions. They are more expressive with a jab to the fleshy part of one's arm than they could ever be in speech. And bumbling is a topographical act. It is because I have always thought of it as such that the idea of*

*making a map with ideas was so appealing. It seemed appropriate to my position in the territory I wanted to examine.*

*Whenever I listened to Hart, that is, as I put my own thoughts into his head, I began to feel a kind of anxiety. I thought—without parsing it out—that I may have chosen the wrong man to overcome, and that is what I intended. He sounded sometimes like a Henry Miller in training, long monologues such as the one I have described above. But he also spoke often of Balzac and the great scientists. It seemed that he had many models to choose from, all great men. That, I was familiar with, believing as I did that I had no identity but that of watcher. But I wanted someone with whom to argue, not to emulate. I wanted to prove that I was right, that everything I thought was right. If I succeeded, I would overcome my father, for whom Hart was acting as a proxy. [Hart, clever as he was, may have understood this and would have enjoyed acting his part]. I saw, though, that it might be difficult with Hart, because, no matter how many models he had, he was as bright as I thought myself to be. How could I ever win an argument with him? Unless, that is, I made it my own by incorporating it into my mind. I could argue with him without his presence, slowly, with method, as I could not have done with my father. Hart's attitude toward me was also one of bullying; by my mental conflict with him, I was also working out my position toward the bullies of my youth. It is difficult to consider that I may have felt love for them; but the repetition in which I found myself could not have been only for the purpose of overcoming my father; I wanted to re-create the affection I must have had for him and the boys who tortured me.*

I speak so much of Hart because he became important as a signpost. As I walk through P, even when I am not with Hart, I have a silent dialogue of love with him, in the Platonic sense. It is to him I speak when, whether out on the street or alone in my flat, I want to justify my puritanism (I place a small "p" at the front, because it does not seem to me to be a religious instinct so much as a punitive one), into which I always plunge after an evening at the Nude Dancers or at the loop stores. He does not suffer me gladly; his is the voice of desire and impulse; mine, the voice of restraint and sterile observation. [At least, I have projected my own desires into him]. And I cannot forget that he has told me how stupid I am. [He knows that I am bright; I understand, at least, that his comments have a purpose]. Yet it is I who speak for him, more eloquently than he would speak for himself, because I want him to love me more than he does. It is I who put the words of abandon on his lips, I who absolve myself of my imagined sins. I honor Hart by incorporating him into myself, albeit as an *Other* from whom I want recognition, and I honor myself by creating his love for me. In that way I maintain some of the *Other's* magical protection. When one chooses someone with whom to argue one asks that person to *heal*, not to cure, but to *heal*, and in the most primitive way imaginable: *"Let me no longer be rent!"* I do not know yet that he is someone whom I *must* overcome, now that I am away from home and no longer around my father, of whom I am still afraid. Nor do I know that my love for him is as my love for my father. I believed that I could only be loved by someone I had conquered.

## *[Annotation]:*

*The genesis of platonic friendship is envy and repetition. The envy is displaced toward a relationship of internal dialogue (or argument). It is an attempt at growth; it turns a perceived enemy into one with whom one grapples. It is a kind of defense. One cannot say openly that one envies a supposed friend because the friend has qualities one lacks (and may always lack). The perceived superiority of the friend is internalized and is then used to debate all sorts of issues. The debate acts as a struggle to free one's self by overcoming the perceived superior. Platonic friendship also repeats a relation from the past that has not been resolved. The overcoming of the platonic friend is an attempt to overcome the father (if the relation is between two males). It is debatable whether one can develop a platonic friendship without having been the lesser person in a previous relation. I assume that the seeker of such a friendship chooses his platonic friend for psychic reasons of which he is unaware, though his unconscious knows quite well what it is doing. The tragic part of the dialogue is that one finds one's self loving the other, as one loved the original other. Love is then seen as brutal, an approach-avoidance dance which must contain brutality in order to satisfy. [I did not intend to write a love story, but it seems that every story begins with love, before the trouble begins]. "I saw Socrates (in Hades) and he seemed to be in love with Hyacinthus—at least he was refuting him most." –Lucian,* True History. *[the Oedipal conflict was never resolved]. I have learned that my repetition was also a search for an Other, for in my family there was no Other. I believed I wanted unity, but what I sought was recognition.*

The difference between Hart and I appeared immense at first. I walked along the sidewalk at midday in this city of ours, shadowed everywhere by concrete, and on the pavement before me I saw two well-dressed gentlemen approaching. I asked myself: *Should I pass them on the left or on the right? Oh, never on the left!* That would force me to pass close to the doors of an office building, where I might be smacked by someone running out through the glass double doors, and I'd have thought: *But I had to get out of someone's way!*" In the muscles of my chest, the rancor that was always present, waiting only for the thought to express itself, would turn fitfully and awaken, opening one scrunchy eye sticky with sand. *"Well, I'll pass on the right, then*............... *No!! Why should I give in to these thugs in pinstriped wool?*............... *Then, I'll walk between them*............... *Impossible!!"* They are too close to one another, and the sidewalk is too narrow to part them. This analysis occurred in the time it took to walk ten feet, and in the end I made the decision to pass them on the left. The tall building with the double glass doors loomed over me as if it were alive, my heart pounded, I was defeated.

What could it have meant? Was the building a symbol, some monster out of my past, the Scylla or Charybdis of an inability to turn this way or that which repeated itself upon the occasion of every choice? [It did not occur to me that I was, simply, disturbed]. Whatever it was, it had taken on *significance*, and my argument, the one I had chewed on since time began, had almost driven me mad. A decision to go left or right had become the living embodiment of my conflict, to live or die, to look or participate, to unite or dissolve. How should I ever pass between two posts, or climb a stair beginning with my right foot?

For me, then, every object and action had meaning aside from its appearance, and that meaning ordered my chaos and made it bearable. The relation between objects, buildings, men was never *neutral*, but was always enhanced or undermined by my actions. For me there was an *Other*, and all acts and things were connected by its existence because it was within me and because I was afraid of it and wanted it at the same time. Being in me, all things became its representation. What amazes me now is that I lived my life then despite the restrictions that abided with this *Other*. It was the living embodiment of the sacrifice I had made upon one half of myself splitting apart from the other half. The act of cutting off becomes, itself, an object. [And what is the Other, except what is not, or cannot be, or never was, a recognition, perhaps it is a 'what might have been'? An absence made present by its very absence, all the states we wish to approach but are afraid to acknowledge].

That was not at all the way Hart lived. Hart was not watchful of the universe, but at ease in it. Of course, no one who drank as much as he did is well, but whatever his fears were, they did not transform the very nature of things. he was not bound to anything or anyone by destiny. For Hart, a bus was just a bus and a drink a drink. [He was Aristotelian in his bones]. In short, I was religious, almost an animist, and Hart was not. Yet I did not believe in a god, and he may have. Hart acted without regard to the consequences of nature; nature was not after him. He had no *Other* comprehensible to me.

Our many discussions were literary but imprecise. I was unable to read anything at that time but Sherlock Holmes mysteries. Yet, if Hart said that they were only good "bad" literature, I became enraged. One day he said, *"I prefer to read Celine and Stendhal.............. There is a tension in them, of synthesis attempted, even obtained.............. You can feel history moving alongside them as they work out the politics of their era........."*

*"That is a judgment so pompously devoid of meaning it makes me want to throw up,"* I replied. *"What is any other era to me?.............. I am a Twentieth Century man, a fouled up Twentieth Century son of a bitch, as Salinger says!"* (I had read a few novels at the University and could quote as well as Hart).

*"It's the age of Romanticism that lives on, pal........."* said Hart, with the emphasis on the "pal"-has anyone ever called anyone else "pal" without its carrying with it the connotation of derision or bullying? *"That is our age, our true age, anyway, a time when young men on the prowl could make their mark."* [Now that I recall this conversation, I am struck with the unpleasant thought that the man who I have chosen as my platonic friend, to whom I will assign all the counterarguments to my own dithering, can be as bullying as those boys who tortured me when I was a boy, or as judgmental as my father].

*"But you could not call Stendhal a Romantic.............. he produced the first existential protagonist, Julien Sorel..............If anyone was an extraordinary nitwit it was he.............. He took a shot at the woman he loved, did not even manage to kill her, and lost his head for it.............. What is Romantic about that?"*

*"There was a time when you could be a fool and still succeed, my man, but that time is gone.............. If you are going to be a fool today, you have got to live in the past, but with a certain.............. Elan!.............. That's it.............. That is the word I want.............. Elan!"*

*"Yes, elan, that's it all right..............Men live in the past all the time now, and then, when they do go off, they plead insanity.............. And when they do shoot, they don't miss either, as Julien Sorel did........."*

Hart believed that one should enter the city with the goal of fame and fortune. Otherwise, why be there at all? That was what his heroes had done, Julien Sorel, e.g., even the two fools in *Sentimental Education*. But I had come only to see and did not meet Hart's criteria of heroism. Consequently he treated me as a *naif*, and perhaps rightly so, but for the wrong reasons.


## *[Annotation]:*


*[This is not true. I had escaped, with no other conscious goal but to leave; I did not know what to do with freedom, though I had thrust it upon myself.]*

On the shelves which covered every inch of wall space in the tiny room in Hart's house in the River District (it was a trinity and we were on the second floor, above the kitchen, below the bedroom) were almost a thousand books. Whenever Hart was forced by lack of money to find another flat or house to rent, the books were the only items he put in storage. They had to be kept at all costs. Here, they covered the walls and spilled out everywhere onto the floor. There was hardly room for two folding chairs among the stacks leaning everywhichway. I believed Hart without reservation when he said that Celine and Stendhal (and Balzac—how could the creator of Rastignac not be included in Hart's pantheon?) were the writers he most loved. If I scanned the shelves-and I was intimately familiar with them, for I was at Hart's house whenever I could not be alone, where I sat quietly, drinking or daydreaming while he went about his business doing housework or even going to the store for groceries-I would see every novel they had ever written, most in hard-cover. These were men who did indeed create a "shelf," as we had often spoken of doing ourselves with more than a note of futility and the failure of which we would forever bemoan. The attraction of these writers for us (and I came to think as Hart did about them) was complicated enough. Maybe they did not beat their wives or refuse to bail their offspring out from gaol, but clearly their human failings were major: Celine, anti-Semite, raving lunatic; Dostoievski, gambler, almost-executed revolutionary (or was it reactionary?); Balzac, money, money, money, everything was money, etc. None of it mattered, though. We'd spend our days comparing ourselves to them at each stage of our respective careers, and as we aged we would find other writers whom no one had ever heard of until forty (Hammett and Beckett were already lined up). I note, however (and that phrase *"I note"*-how many times have I read it in Genet?) that the two Frenchmen of whom I spoke earlier were not the most prominent on Hart's shelves. No, the centerpiece of that room, the locus to which one's eyes eventually turned when one had fully entered the space, was not fiction at all. It was, instead, the two-volume unabridged set of Bertrand Russell's *Principia Mathematica*, whose robin's-egg blue spines, which were always kept free of dust, immediately and strikingly set them apart from the mass of gray leather and sunlight-faded paper binders which bracketed them, most of which had been purchased at used-book stores or flea-market tables.

*"Aren't they great!?,"* Hart would say, flinging his arm toward the shelves. *"The bastards who run these used-bookstores wouldn't know a first-run edition if it fell on them............... These books will be worth a fortune someday if I can keep paying the storage fees........."*

I did not reply; nor did I want to talk. I coveted not the valuable books but the esoteric ones, the early Foucault, for example *("I, Pierre Riviere, Having Murdered My mother, My Sister and My Brother")*, purchased at a used-bookstore, or *Contemporary Novelists,* a *five-inch-thick* compendium of every major and minor novelist writing in the English language still living, with critical commentary and a complete bibliography.

But the scientific texts were the bulkiest, and, aside from the *Principia*, the most prominent. Physics texts, mathematics, nuclear science, computer principles, systems analysis—if I had not known better, I would have believed that Hart revered science, and it was true he had spent a small fortune (relatively speaking) on these books. Whenever Hart had been employed, his income had been minimal (which was true of Ericksen and I as well, no matter that we had degrees and intelligence). Yet Hart had always spent lavishly on books and the materials of art.

In fact, it was the materials of art that were a matter of great concern to us. The art-supply store clerks knew us by name. Though Hart had his singular fascination with old books, it was the tools of art which enchanted him: slant-top desks made of close-grained wood; bonded paper and fine German or Swiss fountain pens; stencils for the title pages and chapter headings of his novels-in-progress. Utrecht's, Taws, Ginn's, Pomerantz'-the finest stationery and art supply stores in P: we spent money there we could not really afford. A man such as Hart might bustle into M's at five-thirty in the afternoon, barely a half hour after leaving work, with the pre-dusk sun still burnishing the stained glass windows, climb up onto a stool, and pull from his knapsack a complete set of coloring pencils, a compass, twelve blank notebooks of architectural paper, bottles of India ink, and a hundred-year-old copy of the poems of James Greenleaf Whittier, all of which would be dumped unceremoniously onto the bar (with the exception of the Whittier, which was set down gently away from the beer dregs), the better to display each item, one by one, for the thrills and edification of the rest of us.

*"Jesus, that's a Mont Blanc,"* someone might say. *"They're worth twenty-five dollars apiece!"* But Hart would merely extract a ream of bonded paper from a shopping bag, which he had set down at his feet and which seemed ready to burst. *"Wait until you see this Eagle paper,"* Hart would brag, and our examination of the paper would be accompanied by comments on the quality of Hart's writing and the need for another, softer kind of paper as opposed to the bonded type. But Hart would only laugh his conspiratorial laugh and crane his neck to look for Tony, who always approached Hart torpidly, his face full of anger at Hart's ecstasy. Hart might already have dropped fifty dollars worth of supplies on the bar, but then he would say *"I'll have a double of Imperial and a round for all my friends!."* [There was only me, perhaps one other]. His

arm would sweep across the bar the same way it swept across his bookshelves, and when the drinks arrived he would grab his shot glass and raise it to us, laughing. *"Drink up.............. I've just cashed my pay check and I've still got forty dollars left...............!"*

A silent envy hung over us as we gathered closer to look at what Hart had purchased. No doubt the compass, precision-tooled, with a finely lathed handle, was a marvellous instrument. But Hart was a writer, not an architect; what would he ever use it for? And the India ink? Or the architectural paper? *"So you say,"* Hart would reply. *There is always a use for this stuff............... It's the same theory as applies to highway construction: build the road first, and the cars will come to it............... Well, buy the best and you will find a use for it...............God, I love having this stuff............... I love it.............. "*

I always thought Hart's logic was farfetched, but I had nothing to say against it. Had I not behaved as bizarrely, purchasing stiff manila folders by the dozen, the better to hold the finished chapters of the novel I hoped to write, and box upon box of tab dividers, the better to organize my work? And then there was my four-drawer file cabinet, which had nothing in it as yet but socks and shirts. I took what Hart offered, the Imperial, and drank quietly out of my shot glass.

I had had several jobs before I left my home, cab driver, gas station attendant, factory work, office clerk, and the scene reminded me fully of the few men I had known in my working life who were fanatical about the *schtick* of office work but whom I had never observed actually *doing* anything. The sharpening of pencils and the organizing of their materials was what fascinated them, rather than writing or creating. At the bottom of their sickness was the equivalence of every movement with the investigative method of Sherlock Holmes, the very detective for whom I had been mocked by Hart for appreciating. They went about their preparations with the same methodical deliberation Holmes exhibited but which today denotes, in a business setting, only congenital idiocy, and they conducted these arrangements with the tenderness of a gorilla caressing its captured maiden (was I so unlike them?). To watch them prepare was to witness balletic movement on the business floor. They sharpened their pencils until the points could excise a mosquito's prostate. The swept their desktops with Pledge and soft rags. They put every item in its proper place, pens, erasers, ink-everything was ninety-degree angles; curves were not permitted. And when they were all through, when the preparation was complete and there was nothing left to do but begin the work, they sat up straight in their rolling chairs, gripped their writing instruments in the preferred hand, and tried to keep from shitting themselves. [They appeared as pilots who could not gun the engines and head on down the runway]. As they sat, seemingly relaxed but actually vibrating inside as if their lungs were tuning forks, they slipped into a dream state where all was peaceful and there was no such thing as argument.

In like manner, Hart and I, too, prepared to become artists as opposed to *artistes*. [I believe we had defined artist as 'artist' and artiste as 'failure']. We purchased the tools, prepared our desks, cleared our minds of all that was extraneous to creation (other than the endless analysis of our positions in space, about which we intended to write with greatness), but, in the end, what we did in the evenings, when supper was done and the dishes lay unwashed upon the table, was another story, and as yet we had nothing to show for it but notebooks full of half-finished poems, drafts of novels sent to agents but put aside for a year after being returned with pleasant letters that anyone else would have found encouraging, brilliant paragraphs that went nowhere. We were as enmeshed in form as those office workers I had seen, as if form alone would carry us through. That is why Hart bought hand-tooled compasses and I spent my time in P staring at mens' pants cuffs to see which ones wore floods and which ones knew how to dress well.

It was because of this insistence on *form* that I finally understood the real reason why Hart had so many scientific texts on his shelves, and why I, too, had begun to buy them. *It was because we wanted to stop time.* Hart believed that if he were to apprehend the theory of relativity, were he to grasp the absolute simplicity and undeniability of that famous equation , [and after that, quantum mechanics] everything in life would fall into place with a satisfying *click*, the kind of sound one hears when one has fit together perfectly the pieces of an expensive mechanical toy. [In other words, we hoped for a catharsis]. The courses we could not afford to take would no longer have mattered. The winters spent without heat, the women we were afraid to speak to because we had neither money nor style, the novels we did not write, or that we wrote in our heads but not on the bonded paper-none of these things would have mattered. All the wrong choices we had made would not have mattered, either, because, paradoxically, *knowledge is denial!* We wanted to stop time the way one might stop a photon experimentally, by tricking it into slowing down, so that for one instant, and one instant only, time would be *confused*. If we were to understand relativity, and if we stopped time by tricking it, we would have triumphed. Then, would we be able clearly to estimate our positions latitudinally and longitudinally [I am attempting the same end by describing my life in the form of a map] and, also paradoxically, thereby escape what we already knew-that all the rest of our knowledge was useless and limited, and in fact (though we referred to it merely as a way of life and of thinking that one chose freely) there were real reasons why we were in psychiatric treatment.

Yet, sometimes, when I looked at Hart, when we were sitting on his two wooden folding chairs, leaning back against his bookshelves, and he had just lit one of his unfiltered cigarettes and was blowing the smoke up to the ceiling with his head tilted back, arrogant without knowing he was arrogant (perhaps, after all, he did, if it pleased him), I saw all that was necessary to produce that novel to which the expensive paper and the fine instruments ought someday to contribute. Intelligence, arrogance, stamina—are these not the qualities one needs? [Much reading has informed me that these qualities lead to therapeutic disaster]. And I did not think for one minute that Hart (or myself, for that matter) were incapable of getting by merely because we had had so much psychiatric treatment. It was the age for therapy (we called it shrinking), and there were plenty whom we passed every day on the sidewalks of P who met all the criteria. One did not stop living or working just because one thought one was crazy. Our opinion of ourselves was as subjective as anyone else's might be. Besides, there was no sense diagnosing ourselves or anyone else under or near the age of thirty: have you ever heard the nonsense the young speak? And we were just on the cusp of thirty ourselves. Why, Hart might end up a corporate executive, and I'd be in the National Academy.........

Meanwhile, Hart remained himself. If I describe him now in the past tense it is only because the image from which I write is taken from a memory I retain from one such night. At five feet eleven inches, he stood naturally at ease, without awkwardness or tension. An inward tension, however, gave his face, in repose, a curious, puzzled expression. His cheeks were pale and slightly puffy, as if they had been made by an excellent baker, but the puffiness was usually unnoticeable unless he had been drinking heavily. Then, his complexion shone and highlighted the swelling under his eyes. He was reed-thin and had no stomach, particularly in the Spring after he had eaten nothing but vegetables all Winter. His hair was thick and straight, cut short on the sides and back, high on top, and parted, if at all, down the middle. [Had he seen photpgraphs of F. Scott Fitzgerald?] Or Red Grange?] His eyes were light brown or green. He had all his teeth and did not need glasses.

Generally, he wore corduroy pants, a shirt, and old but stolid work boots. He owned little clothing, but what he had was of good quality, and he went regularly to the laundromat, where, while his shirts and underclothes tumbled dry, he sat and thought. His clothes sometimes gave one the impression that he had, at one time, been wealthy (for example, the Harris Tweed sport coat), but which had been left on a dirt floor for his dog to curl up on. [I learned, though, from living in P, that good tailoring on ragged clothing is noticeable and has certain benefits, i.e., people come to believe that one is either wealthy but eccentric or that one was once wealthy but has fallen].

He smoked every day, but moderately; but he drank in gargantuan quantities—sometimes two fifths of whiskey a day. Though he might drink nothing for weeks, he always began again. Once, at a party, I watched him drink six bottles of beer, some wine, several shots of whiskey and an entire fifth of mescal, after which he stated his desire to depart because he was hungry...

His true profession was writing fiction (one may have a vocation even if one never completes anything), though he was an excellent cook (he had talented hands; he was also wood carver) and could have made his living as a high-priced chef were it not for his drinking. He wrote naturalist fiction and poetry; yet no one he portrayed was ever completely lost to the elemental forces of nature because his subjects were always redeemed through his (Hart's) own sacrifice, as if he could not bear to let the very world he saw and described, which was the lower-class, working-poor world, destroy them without also giving back something of himself to that world. He gave up a portion of his talent to allow his characters to survive with more clarity. He did not write to resolve his pity but to clarify it. he made fun of writers whom he called *"those university types who annotate everything [as I am now doing]....... . If they shit once, the number of little balls has to find its way onto the page, like the Holy Trinity or the Four horsemen."* How odd, then, to be watching, years later, a showing of *Breathless* on television, only to see Belmondo, taking leave of Jean Seberg, shadow-box his way down a Parisian sidewalk. I would later see Hart dancing his way to the last seat on the West-bound bus on a cold night in February. I saw *"Bullitt"* around that time, too. For days afterward, I wore a raincoat with a turtleneck sweater underneath. All that time, I suppose we were annotating ourselves......... [I was so busy trying to compete with Hart that I did not understand that I loved him as I loved my father, an angry, demanding love. It did not occur to me that Hart [and my father] had loved me, too.].

[I should note here that Ericksen, another friend who accompanied us in our wonderings, (I have given him this name because in Scandinavian it translates to 'always power') did not respond to Hart as I did. Whereas I argued with Hart, silently, to overcome him as I saw the similarities between Hart and my father, Ericksen had a very acute mind of his own which did not require him to compare himself with anyone. [Now that I write these words, I am reminded of two items I mentioned earlier, i.e., platonic friendship and the repetition of triangulation (as a way of comprehending, in spatial terms, the past). I am beginning to understand that any *map* I may create in order to consider the question, that is, the word *"why"* is going to be nothing more than the names of the people I've encountered]. [I also note that my love for Hart, which was not obvious to me then, was a genuine love that, if I saw similarities between Hart and my father, would certainly have come with any repetition of the original triangle]. Hart had other qualities, though, which were akin to those of my father, which I denied at first; a sense of superiority of mind, an entitlement to interfere in the lives of others because he knew what was best for them]. I had yet to comprehend a fact which Dr. Gold would demonstrate later, that all of us were living on a curved surface rather than a flat plane.

## *[Annotation]:*

*Hart's bookshelves now remind me of the shelves in my house during my youth. On one shelf,* And Quiet Flows the Don, *on another,* Peyton Place.

⫸— ⫷

Hart, Ericksen and I often spent our evenings together. We'd show up at M's separately, drink, and go on our way. Afterward, we went back to our flats, also separately. I do not recall any decisions about where to go; I recall only where we ended up. I recorded only a few evenings. Imagining myself as Celine at the time, my notes contained ellipses, as if I were writing, speaking to my notepad, in short bursts of action reflecting the action I had observed. Rereading these notes now, I am surprised; they seem somewhat accurate. I may have been an accurate watcher, so that my recollections of watching became accurate as well. I read these pages now, with the history I have described in mind, to ascertain whether my actions in P might be said to be the result of that history. [Certainly, my history of watching–if not voyeurism–runs throughout my notes, which are more than the mere observations of a lonely, virginal young man].

⫸– ⫷

......... There is no whiskey sold in this place, the Bar of Nude Dancers.............. If you want to drink, you must buy your liquor elsewhere and bring it here in a flask or a six-pack.............. The barmaids serve only set-ups, that is, glasses with ice and tonic water or soda.............. It is illegal in this Commonwealth to sell alcohol in bars where women dance nude.............. Of course, the dancers could wear pasties two millimeters thick and the liquor would flow like water from a tap, but the intricacies of the law are not what we are about..............

The bar is a large circle around which almost fifty stools are aligned.............. The stage is a rectangle within the circle.............. Both are the same height.............. While the women dance, the barmaids run back and forth in the space between, providing fresh ice, water chasers, perhaps even mixers..............

Tonight is Camera night.............. The place is crowded with men, young, middle-aged.............. Old men, men over sixty, do not come here.............. I know, because I have been here often and have noticed their absence.............. I do not know why they do not come here . . . . . . . . . . . . . . Perhaps they no longer care or never cared, or it is too much aggravation . . . . . . . . . . . . . . Maybe they cannot afford it . . . . . . . . . . . . . . Or they are married and come from a generation that will not step out, as the younger men do . . . . . . . . . . . . . . One thing is for certain—several men have cameras with flash attachments, little Kodaks, the mass production type, or Polaroids . . . . . . . . . . . . . . Perhaps they are afraid to use regular cameras, the kind for which you must take the film to a drug store for development, because the film might be confiscated . . . . . . . .

Tonight I am out with the writer, Hart, and the painter, Ericksen. . . . . . . . . . . . . . . We are all about the same age—early thirties . . . . . . . . . . . . . . Years of psychotherapy have undone any dreams we might have had of a long professional life, let alone of grandeur . . . . . . . . . . . . . . This is our entertainment . . . . . . . . . . . . . . We've spent our adult lives thinking about ourselves, examining every little cranny of every neurosis . . . . . . . . . . . . . . All our energy has gone to that . . . . . . . . . . . . . . There is not one car between us . . . . . . . . . . . . . . I own the only suit . . . . . . . . . . . . . . Ericksen has one pair of Johnson & Murphy shoes he bought five years ago . . . . . . . . . . . . . . I still remember how proud he was . . . . . . . . . . . . . . No one complains . . . . . . . .

It is eleven o'clock . . . . . . . . . . . . . . One does not come here first on a night out, but toward the end, after a night of drinking or merely wandering and talking . . . . . . . . . . . . . . To see these nude women, when one has no money and no way to convince them of one's unique sincerity, causes only sadness and frustration, so what would be the sense of coming here at, say, eight o'clock? No, later is best, when one can leave and go home, perhaps with one last good drink brought in from the bar across the street, to dull whatever it is one thinks about when one has gotten into bed . . . . . . . . . . . . . . Still, we have to do this . . . . . . . .

*"Oh, it's not that bad!,"* Ericksen says, looking at my face . . . . . . . . . . . . . . I am never able to hide my emotions . . . . . . . . . . . . . . Whatever I am thinking is immediately apparent . . . . . . . . . . . . . . he reads my face like a ticker tape . . . . . . . . .

The women . . . . . . . . . . . . . . . Or, the girls . . . . . . . . . . . . . . . Do not expect a fanfare; It is not that way at all . . . . . . . . . . . . . . Every girl has three dances in her set . . . . . . . . . . . . . . It is a quota set by the house . . . . . . . . . . . . . . . We watch one put her quarters into the jukebox, a ritualized behavior which gives the girls a sense of control . . . . . . . . . . . . . . Her index finger slides up and down the glass . . . . . . . . . . . . . . A railinged stairway descends from a loft over the front of the bar directly to the stage . . . . . . . . . . . . . . The girls dress(!?) in the loft, come down to select their tunes, return up the stairs, then begin their act by descending again as the first song begins, slowly, making love to the railing . . . . . . . . . . . . . . No, not making love . . . . . . . . . . . . . . . . . . . . . . . . . . . . . . . . . . . . . . . . . . . . . . *attaching* themselves to it as they descend . . . . . . . . . . . . . .

When she first appears, the girl wears a diaphanous gown or wrap . . . . . . . . . . . . . . From Baum's, probably . . . . . . . . . . . . . . All the dancers buy their costumes there . . . . . . . . . . . . . . It is always discarded after the first dance, but, until that is over, she plays with it as she dances, twisting it about her body like a wreath of transparent gauze . . . . . . . . . . . . . . The stage lights in the ceiling, red, blue, white, illuminate her as if we were in a real theater . . . . . . . . . . . . . . No, this *is* real . . . . . . . . . . . . . . As in a play, for example . . . . . . . . . . . . . . Red is the dominant motif, yet all the other colors in the spectrum are easily distinguishable . . . . . . . . .

These moments are so important to me . . . . . . . . . . . . . . Why? Years later, I remember them eidetically, as if I were watching again . . . . . . . . . . . . . . Perhaps eidetic memory is not completely lost over time . . . . . . . . . . . . . . This is how I lived, and what fascinated me then has never lost its power . . . . . . . . . . . . . . Each memory is like a tangent touching the circle of my life [or, morelikely, the triangle], which I cannot see . . . . . . . . . . . . . . It is as if I could figure that life out mathematically, if I had enough memories tangent to the circle, describing it fully . . . . . . . . . . . . . . It means nothing to me that so-and-so's vagina caressed the railing as she descended awkwardly to the stage . . . . . . . . . . . . . . Well, at any rate, I do not want my picture taken, even though I'll never see it . . . . . . . . . . . . . . I want the only record of this evening to be my recollection of it . . . . . . . . . . . . . . *"You're already worrying about running for office,"* Ericksen says, his mouth curled into that little moue around the lip of a glass of ice water . . . . . . . . . . . . . . I recognize the ridiculousness of my feeling; still, I put my hand to my cheek as the flashbulbs go off . . . . . . . . . . . . . . Or *do* I? Now I cannot remember . . . . . . . . . . . . . . But it is the girl's entrance that remains in my mind: her movement, the curve of her calves under the gown, not how I responded, or my shame, or my lack of shame . . . . . . . .

A few brief moments have passed; that is all it takes, yet the first dance is over and we've seen nothing . . . . . . . . . . . . . . A forearm, a knee, a quick glance at a calf . . . . . . . . . . . . . . We're patient, though, and soon the second dance has begun . . . . . . . . . . . . . . The wrap is draped carefully over the railing . . . . . . . . . . . . . . The girl begins to edge closer to the rim of the stage near the footlights . . . . . . . . . . . . . . Finally, she is nude, except for a g-string . . . . . . . . . . . . . . Then, she slips that off, too, moving to the rhythm of the jukebox music,, and we all stare . . . . . . . . . . . . . . See the vagina! That's what is important, isn't it? See it as long as you can . . . . . . . . . . . . . . See as much of it as you can, but *see* it! Her choreography-if one can call it that- carries her in a wider circle as she nears us . . . . . . . . . . . . . . But now she stops, near center stage, and kneels . . . . . . . . . . . . . . She displays her vagina to the men on the other side of the bar . . . . . . . . . . . . . . They look, silently, their gazes going right through her and us . . . . . . . . . . . . . . A few young men are laughing; one rolls his eyes, but other men, men in their forties, look almost grave . . . . . . . . . . . . . . Now she swivels and shows it to us, while the others see her rump . . . . . . . . . . . . . . The music plays, we drink and stare . . . . . . . . . . . . . . The vagina has been displayed, and we all know it's in our midst . . . . . . . .

Around the bar, I see no particularly responsive behavior, except for the gigglers . . . . . . . . . . . . . . No one is talking, except for the younger men, because no matter what pose we take, this is serious business . . . . . . . . . . . . . . There's money on the bar that wasn't there a minute ago, ones, perhaps, maybe a few fives.............. No, I doubt it.............. Ones- they're more sensible.............. I sweep the bar with my eyes but I can't tell the denominations from far away.........

Some of the young men, the few whose faces register nothing, are boyfriends of the dancers, or friends of the boyfriends.............. The boyfriends are here to protect their girls, or to protect their economic interest in them; the friends, to protect the boyfriends in turn.............. No matter how they posture, though, it must be difficult for them, too.............. I disdain them; they don't trust their girlfriends; they let their women dance here, but they themselves are imprisoned by their acquiescence.............. We, the unattached, would walk on our toes for a week if one of the dancers took the time to have a drink with us at the bar, or merely stopped to exchange a few words with us.............. But these boyfriends won't have it.............. *"Here!,"* they say.............. *"You can see it! You can even touch it with a dollar bill! But you can't have it! It's mine!"* Why do they show it to us, then, as if it were a wild stallion they had tamed? When they can't even enjoy it themselves?.............. Well, who can answer that?

I try to avoid thinking about that, and I feel pity, instead.............. Not for myself, or the boyfriends, but for the other men, particularly the black ones.............. They seem at ease here, and I feel something for them.............. It's not pity, actually, but a kind of distanced well-wishing.............. Whatever I may think about black men, here I like them.............. They're relaxed, watching the dancers.............. The black men don't look at the other men the way I do.............. They look only at the dancers.............. *"That's my meat and potatoes!,"* their eyes say.............. I like them also because they don't care if a girl's got a pocked face or if her buttocks are flabby.............. I can see in their faces that their appreciation's the same.............. They're not thinking *"What a pig!"* That's a white man's invention for sure, that phrase.........

The third, final dance has begun . . . . . . . . . . . . . . The girl stands up, moves, circles really, to the edge of the stage in front of two men, three men . . . . . . . . . . . . . . One leans forward with a dollar bill between the knuckles of his index and middle fingers . . . . . . . . . . . . . . She smiles? I can't see her face . . . . . . . . . . . . . . Closer, closer . . . . . . . . . . . . . . She's on her knees, now . . . . . . . . . . . . . . The man with the bill leans forward and thrusts his face into her crotch with a wavering motion, as if he's saying No! No! even as he moves toward it . . . . . . . . . . . . . . His hands squeeze her buttocks . . . . . . . . . . . . . . A second man leans over him and kisses her breast . . . . . . . . . . . . . . Then it's over, and with their money between her fingers like so many fans she rises and sways toward us . . . . . . . . I'm afraid to kiss her, even if I get the chance . . . . . . . . . . . . . . Not that she might have a disease . . . . . . . . . . . . . . It's these men! They might . . . . . . . . . . . . . . Oh, I *would* kiss her! Her face could be any face . . . . . . . . . . . . . . All faces of all dancers are kissable! Beauty is certainly not a factor here . . . . . . . . . . . . . . One thinks nothing of beauty . . . . . . . . . . . . . . Who cares for it, anyway? *Coming!* That what this is all about, I think . . . . . . . . . . . . . . Or, at least, it's about not worrying about beauty because beauty here is *stupid!* Stupid and senseless . . . . . . . . . . . . . . Look at what's staring us in our faces! Don't tell me about beauty! . . . . . . . .

We're entranced, the three of us . . . . . . . . . . . . . . Ericksen smiles shyly . . . . . . . . . . . . . . I love that smile . . . . . . . . . . . . . . It's so uncorrupted . . . . . . . . . . . . . . *"She's a woman!,"* it says . . . . . . . . . . . . . . Hart is so drunk his face is maroon . . . . . . . . . . . . . . But he's shy, too . . . . . . . . . . . . . . I feel so dirty because of my hunger and my belief that I must *see* everything . . . . . . . . . . . . . . it's overwhelming . . . . . . . . . . . . . . I haven't a clue what anyone else feels, except what I can see, or think I can see, on their faces, in the sweat cooling on their foreheads . . . . . . . . . . . . . . Here, I'm separated, even here . . . . . . . . . . . . . . Hunger of any kind feels dirty, doesn't it? Whether it's for sex, or food, or riches? Why shouldn't we all have what we want without being at odds with our desires? But, there it is . . . . . . . . . . . . . . In the end, we each give her a dollar, but none of us kisses her . . . . . . . . . . . . . . The music ends and she disappears up into the loft . . . . . . . . . . . . . . Not even a goodnight kiss . . . . . . . . . . . . . . I remember the map of my emotions and the route I took, and how *seeing* was everything . . . . . . . . . . . . . . But I couldn't tell you what color her hair was, or her eyes, or whether she wore earrings . . . . . . . . I wonder if my father ever saw anything like I've seen tonight?

Immediately we pour into the cold night air, checking our pockets to see what's left . . . . . . . . . . . . . . Almost eight dollars apiece spent tonight . . . . . . . . . . . . . . This can't go on . . . . . . . . . . . . . . As we leave I see Arielle, a whore, playing the pinball machine in the lobby . . . . . . . . . . . . . . She doesn't notice me, and why should she? I've seen her going into the Sirens Cafe, next door to M's and across the road from my flat . . . . . . . . . . . . . . She's six feet tall and her hair, when it's not braided and stuffed into a turban, hangs to her waist . . . . . . . . . . . . . . I don't bother to point her out to Ericksen and Hart . . . . . . . . . . . . . . We've never even spoken, Arielle and I, but as long as Ericksen and Hart don't know about her, she's more mine than theirs . . . . . . . .
Good—byes all around, slurred but meant, nevertheless . . . . . . . . . . . . . . *"Got a cigarette?" "Here, take one . . . . . . . . . "* *"No, no . . . . . . . . . . . . . . . . . . . . . . . . . . . . . . . . . . . . . . " "It's okay . . . . . . . . . . . . . . Here . . . . . . . . . "* Our hands in our pockets, chapped, our chins down to our shirt collars, we drift away . . . . . . . . . . . . . . *Should I go back inside?*, I wonder . . . . . . . . . . . . . . Hell, I haven't any money, and someone's got to put Hart on the bus; Ericksen did it the last time . . . . . . . . . . . . . . Then, I'll go home to bed . . . . . . . . . . . . . . There's nothing like smoking a cigarette when it's twenty degrees outside and there's no wind . . . . . . . . . . . . . . Every toke is like a mixture of high-octane gasoline and cool air . . . . . . . . . . . . . . I'll feel like a dynamo by the time I get home . . . . . . . .

>>>—<<<

Next morning I wake early.............. There's an argument in the flat upstairs—it's the two lesbians who own the cat, and I listen intently............. The terrible names they're calling each other and it's only six thirty! But I'm all ears for the terrible quiet that always precedes the soft *plash* of a fist ramming into flesh.............. It's what I do best: *attending*.............. And I hold my breath not to miss a word.............. But I've heard this before, haven't I? And soon I begin to drift.............. On the corner last night, waiting for the bus with Hart, he shadowboxed down the pavement.............. Passers—by crowded against the stone buildings to avoid him, and when the bus came he skipped aboard, dropping all his change on the floor next to the fare box, laughing all the way to the back where he flopped onto a seat.............. I leaned in to pick up the coins and deposit them in the slot and waved good—bye mentally to Hart's dancing back, bobbing and weaving toward the last seats............... He's never failed to get home........

It's time to go to work, but I don't want to get up.............. Instead, I parade mentally through the morning rituals.............. What does the color of the sky say, as it slips through my curtains? Stay? Or go? How will it be today? Will I stumble on my words or avoid humiliation? I can understand as I see through these questions why the nights are so important to me.............. I make a decision and throw off the sheets, but, swinging out of bed, I spy the box of Kleenex on the night table.............. There's time for delay, and I reach for it to pull out a few white sheets, and begin to stroke myself, smooth tactile strokes, thinking of the dancer, how I'd like to have her here with me.............. I finish, remembering how I felt last night, just *looking!*, knowing it had nothing to do with the unspoken bleakness of it all, because it wasn't bleak at all, knowing what I'd have said to her if I'd had the nerve: *"Wonderful!.............. how wonderful you were! It was marvellous!"*........

*[I was moving relentlessly forward toward* overt *looking. That night I imagined the ape mask was unusual in that I was not peeking through the blinds at my bedroom window at the window of the young woman who lived next door. I had learned that with Hart and Ericksen at my side I could go about without my imagined mask. But I see now a backward movement, a desire to return to my bedroom in our apartment, where I could look into the windows of the house next door. There had been so much discomfort in my early life, yet I brought it with me when I moved to P.]*

What I do in the daytime does not concern Ericksen or Hart.............. I might be a bank robber and they'd never know it if I didn't let on.............. And when I admitted it—as I surely would—it would be in the evening, standing up against a crowded bar, shouting my secret into an indifferent ear, as one of them stared straight ahead into the mirrored wall opposite, glancing left or right at breasts, hips, cracking nuts between his fingers and popping them into his mouth, expressionless............... *"You're kidding, right!.............. Well, I noticed you're drinking better whiskey"*.............. But, after that, what is there to say?.............. An admission like that should draw a response, even it's untrue.............. So, one mutes one's news, good or bad, knowing it's irrelevant.........

Sometimes I go places with Ericksen and Hart—to see the Nude Dancers, say.............. But other activities I take in alone.............. What I want is sex, or at least the idea of sex, but what I do not want is recognition, either of myself or by others.............. The Talmfud says that private sins are the worst because they deny the presence of God.......... I understand this in theory, because once one has committed even one act that one considers a sin, though it is never done again, it takes on a life of its own and pushes God aside.............. Whether this theory is true, I know not. . . . . . . . . . . . . . Nevertheless, I save for myself some acts I do not want them to know about. . . . . . . . . . . . . . I am sure that if I admitted these acts they would understand in a flash. . . . . . . . . . . . . . But the telling of it would undo me. . . . . . . . . . . . . . Too, I have my own questions to chew on, which are not their questions. . . . . . . . . . . . . . *Seeing* is what I am about. . . . . . . . . . . . . . *Seeing* again and again and again, never tiring of what I view, only turning the vision about at every conceivable angle, as if what I were seeing were a puzzle to be solved by applying the correct geometry. . . . . . . . . . . . . .

Today I am out again, alone. . . . . . . . . . . . . . It is colder than it was the night of the Nude Dancers and I do not want to walk too far. . . . . . . . . . . . . . Around every corner lies the sharp slap of a gust of wind. . . . . . . . . . . . . . Piles of trash with nowhere to go are swirling on the sidewalks and I am the only one on the pavement who is looking at the faces of passers-by. . . . . . . . . . . . . . I could walk over to Hart's flat, but he'll only want to go out himself and walk from River to River before finding a bar. . . . . . . . . . . . . . He's got no heat in his trinity and a brisk walk is the only way he can keep warm. . . . . . . . . . . . . . I could also walk to one of the loop stores. . . . . . . . . . . . . . For two dollars I can have a late afternoon's entertainment. . . . . . . . . . . . . . It's an easy choice. . . . . . . . .

Behind the racks of magazines and paperbacks, men pace the corridor lined by the film booths. . . . . . . . . . . . . . If one were to enter a bookstore to browse the shelves—that is, a regular bookstore—and if one returned a year later to browse again, one would find the same books, but for the latest best-sellers. . . . . . . . . There is a continuity created by economics and cultural preferences that leads people to buy books they've read about or heard of from their friends and classmates. . . . . . . . . . . . . . The writers of the Pantheon are always selling, even from their graves. . . . . . . . . . . . . . But if one were to do the same thing here, nothing would be the same. . . . . . . . . . . . . . There is no such thing as a popular sex novel. . . . . . . . . . . . . . Everything here is disposable, because it will be replaced by photographs of newer, younger more concupiscent men and nubile girls. . . . . . . . . . . . . . What does not sell is thrown out or returned for credit to the wholesalers . . . . . . . . . . . . . . . This is the epitome of the brown—wrapper industry . . . . . . . .

The cashier shouts at us from his raised counter in the front of the store . . . . . . . . . . . . . . . *"No loitering !* . . . . . . . . . . . . . . . *Pick a booth!* . . . . . . . . . . . . . . . *NOW!"* . . . . . . . . . . . . . . When he shouts we scrabble about for a time, the way ants will when a child places the barrel of a cap pistol over them on the sidewalk and pulls the trigger . . . . . . . . . . . . . . . But we always slow down and straighten out, because we do not want to be interrupted . . . . . . . . . . . . . . . Iron bars on three sides of the cashier's platform protect him from those of us who might disagree with his technique . . . . . . . . . . . . . . . The cashier is aware of our tensions, and so we force him to remain alert even as he forces us to keep moving . . . . . . . . . the store is another place in which I am learning that I am not unique . . . . . . . . . . I belong to a group . . . . . . . . . .

In the middle of the corridor a huge black man is standing perfectly still . . . . . . . . . . . . . . . All his clothing is drab, dark . . . . . . . . . . . . . . . He's got a mean look, full of hate, pale dead skin reflecting nothing even as the corridor lights flash in roseate bloom . . . . . . . . . . . . . . . He's looked at all of us as if he'd like to stab us in the back, but the cashier is not shouting at him . . . . . . . . . . . . . . . As it is everywhere else, the big fish are left alone, while the rest of us swim about as best we can . . . . . . . . . . . . . . . The cashier will not do anything about the man—he would have to leave the protection of his grill-sided platform . . . . . . . . . . . . . . . Some of us are wearing bulky coats because of the cold, and we have to squeeze close to the doors of the booths so as not to touch him . . . . . . . . . He's like the spider in my dreams that crawls across the edge of the carpet in whatever room I am dreaming about . . . . . . . . . . . . . . . I have managed to confine my fear to this one danger, this mental tic, as if I looked at a rhinoceros through the wrong end of a telescope to make it manageable . . . . . . . . . . . . . . . I am able to slide by his back to go deeper into the corridor . . . . . . . . . . . . . . . As I browse, the sheer busyness of all of us begins to drive him toward the front without anyone actually touching him . . . . . . . . . . . . . Perhaps he'll drift away to the next place to frighten another knot of business-suited voyeurs . . . . . . . .

I cannot see clearly the expressions on the other men's' faces . . . . . . . . . . . . . I do not look at them unless they are far enough away and I can sweep them with a glance that takes in everything around them, too . . . . . . . . . . . . . That is how I saw Mr. Drab Clothing . . . . . . . . . . . . . I know some of them by their mode of dress, though . . . . . . . . . . . . . Mr. Black Cordovans . . . . . . . . . . . . . Mr. Wool Gabardine Slacks With Cuffs . . . . . . . . . . . . . Mr. Corduroy Overcoat, the cloth of kings . . . . . . . . . . . . . It is not proper etiquette here to look directly into another man's eyes . . . . . . . . . . . . . This business is such a personal one, and no one wants trouble . . . . . . . . . . . . . A single glance may send things tumbling out of control . . . . . . . .

Everyone studies the posters on the front doors of the booths . . . . . . . . . . . . . These are still shots from the films, and one looks always for a special woman: the woman with the *form of forms, the one who means everything* . . . . . . . . . . . . . Then, after one finds her, he trashes her image by masturbating in front of it . . . . . . . . . . . . . But each man must have his vision of what his particular form is, and the personal meaning that accompanies it, because we, all of us, study the posters carefully and reject most of them . . . . . . . .

What I look for here is love . . . . . . . . . . . . . Not to get it but to see it . . . . . . . . . . . . . If I can see it I can ape it, and I will believe I appear more normal to the world . . . . . . . . . . . . . I have not learned yet that it is the normal world that is nudging past me in this corridor . . . . . . . . . . . . . That epiphany is, as yet, far away . . . . . . . . . . . . . But I think love must be in one of these films, and I am determined to find it . . . . . . . . . . . . . I am sure it is here: the evidence that people *do* it and *feel* it . . . . . . . . . . . . . I think it is in their expressions and the way they touch one another on the screen . . . . . . . . . . . . . It is of no consequence that I have not found it outside this corridor . . . . . . . . . . . . . I believe it is here . . . . . . . . . . . . . Certainly I do not want to watch expressionless automatons going at it . . . . . . . . . . . . . I want to see emotion, or, at least, the theatrical expression of emotion . . . . . . . . . . . . . . Perhaps, looking at these loops, I believe I have a better chance of seeing a true expression of suffering, or ecstasy than I might if I were watching a film in a general—audience theater, or on the street . . . . . . . . . . . . . . In a loop, a man or woman might fall out of character only for a few seconds, but the very amateurism of the cast and the camera operator increases the possibility that such a mistake will go unnoticed or will be left in, whereas, if it were a serious film, such a failure would surely be cut . . . . . . . . .

I pick a booth and step inside . . . . . . . . . . . . . . The film I want has a voluptuous brunette who reminds me of Lara, a woman I know whom I still see in R Park sometimes . . . . . . . . . . . . . . The things I see in this short loop are those I would never have thought to do with her . . . . . . . . . . . . . . I was so shy! . . . . . . . . . . . . . . Now, when I watch the loop, I can imagine myself as I might have been, then, had I not been so at odds with my own desires, so unwilling to see them as merely human . . . . . . . . . . . . . . After slipping the bolt on the booth door, I put a quarter in the slot and turn the arrow to the selection I've chosen . . . . . . . . . . . . . . I lean against the far wall so that the projector, which is behind and above me, can project the loop over my left shoulder onto the door . . . . . . . .

On the screen a man is speaking with two young women,—(it has not occurred to me that I am watching a triangle) one of whom is the brunette . . . . . . . . . . . . . . I see them only from the waist up, but as the camera pulls away to take in more of the room, I see that the women are playing with the man's body, running their fingers under his jeans and shirt . . . . . . . . . . . . . . He is sitting on a sofa with his hands resting on his thighs . . . . . . . . . . . . . . As the women begin to undress him on the screen, I, too, pull down my zipper, stuff some Kleenex through the opening, and grasp myself . . . . . . . .

All of these loops have the same story structure (one cannot call it a plot) . . . . . . . . . . . . . . A man and a woman, or two women, are in an apartment in an unnamed city (one thinks of a city as opposed to a town only because of the

availability of actors, film equipment, and self-related fantasies) . . . . . . . . . . . . . . .
One of them is having a birthday, perhaps, and there is a quick shot of a cake
with candles on a table . . . . . . . . . . . . . . But soon everyone is groping everyone
else, touching, feeling, rubbing . . . . . . . . . . . . . . It is not Tolstoi, but the natural
evolution of Tolstoi in a culture that claims to love God . . . . . . . . . . . . . . There is
no sound, and the poor acting magnifies the loop's tragic aspect . . . . . . . . . . . . . .

What strikes me most about these loops, though, is the veneration
and honor in the women's' eyes as they potate, guzzle, nuzzle and suck the
ponderous cocks one always sees on the screen . . . . . . . . . . . . . . I have never seen
such idolization and regard in actual experience . . . . . . . . . . . . . . I would distrust
it if I were its recipient . . . . . . . . . . . . . . All the while they smile up at him, often
with their mouths full of him, while he reclines dissolutely . . . . . . . . . . . . . . Thus,
he is passive in the scene but presents the image of strength and dominance
because the cameras are placed primarily below or at the same level as the
players . . . . . . . . . . . . . . This rule applies to the loop no matter how plain, ugly
or even repulsive is the man's appearance . . . . . . . .

When the loop is over I put another quarter in the box and the loop begins
where it left off . . . . . . . . . . . . . . My attention begins to wander—that is, I have
not sufficiently identified myself with the male because, in the actual film, as
opposed to the come-on picture from which I chose this loop, the women
do not resemble anyone I know, not Lara nor even Arielle, the whore—and I
begin to notice things I hadn't noticed before . . . . . . . . . . . . . . On the door of
the booth, for example, someone has written his name (I say this with absolute
certainty), but for a few seconds the trio's legs are in the way and I cannot
make it out . . . . . . . . . . . . . . When, suddenly, everyone changes positions,
it becomes clear: **"MIGUEL"** . . . . . . . . . . . . . . A telephone number follows,
ending in two zeroes . . . . . . . . . . . . . . It must be a municipal government
number, I realize . . . . . . . . . . . . . . No private residence would ever have such
a number . . . . . . . . . . . . . . *"Who would answer?,"* I wonder . . . . . . . . . . . . . .
Does working for the government permit leisurely assignations in cheap

hotel rooms such as exist in this neighborhood?............... Or Holiday Inns?.............. Before I can even begin to follow these questions to their logical conclusion, I notice that the blonde's got a nose like Hart's sister's nose, strong and almost perpendicular to the plane of the floor, while the man's cock has a large, blue vein running up the side............... Now the apartment seems more European that American, perhaps as much because of the way the players' hair is cut or the few pieces of furniture we are permitted to see............... It is odd how one's analytic skills do not cease merely because of the milieu in which one asks them to operate............... It may be that I become more focused when I am viewing a loop because there is something I want to know or prove............... Probably, the elements of secrecy, danger and shame combine to sharpen these abilities.............. After a time, one begins to use one's head, no matter what the subject......... Every booth is a glade...........

........ . I am not alone here............... Everywhere close by are men............... Men who were in a meeting where someone was using a pointer to explain bar graphs on a chart, or who were dictating a memo when they looked without thinking at the stenographer who was sitting across from them, men who just stood up and pushed their chairs away from their desks, made their excuses and left hurriedly to get over here............... Why are they not in a men's' room stall somewhere, I wonder, thinking of their secretaries or of the waitress who poured their takeout coffee this morning?............... What is the necessity of having the image on the screen before us?............... It must be that we must know for certain that other men *do it* , that the impulses we have do not occur in a void [It is always difficult for any man to believe that any other man has sex]............ . . It validates our desire to come here, without making it necessary to speak of it............... But one comes *close* to something here, too, something with sharp edges............... To stand in another man's place while watching him is both homoerotic and ego-strengthening and so creates its own conflict.............. But to view is to investigate, and to investigate is to capture........

........ Then, too, there is the danger.............. Once, not a month before, a scream arose from one of the booths.............. I was in the middle of a loop and did not react right away, but many questions filled my mind............... *Was it the police?*............... *Or a killing? Had someone decided, finally, to act?*.............. How horrible it was to hear it.............. There was fright in the scream as well as pain, as if a man's very being were trying to escape through his throat.............. Cautiously, I pulled open the booth door, thinking now of escape.............. The cashier ran by me toward the larger booths in the rear, a blackjack in his raised hand.............. Then, shouting.............. *"Wait!?"*............... *"Out!!"*.............. *"Get out, you bitch!!!"*.............. Men leaned backward against the thin panels between the booths, trying to avoid being touched.............. Soon the cashier reappeared, dragging a young man toward the front, a frail-looking white man wearing a suit, his legs flailing as the cashier pulled and shouted at him.............. Then the blackjack flashed.............. A brief aura of blood mist arose as if it were a tiara.............. Just as quickly, they were gone.............. I never learned what had happened.............. Surely I would not ask anyone, nor would they ask me........

........ When the young man's feet had disappeared through the beaded curtains separating the booths from the book racks, I felt safer.............. I closed the booth door and put my foot against it.............. Out came my Kleenex.............. Many images flickered before my eyes: everything but what was on the screen; a dancer who had smiled at me at the Nude Dancers; a girl on the subway to whom I had given my seat; a woman I remembered from another loop.............. All of them coming to me, loving me........

The shuffling sounds of the men pacing the corridor and the clicking of the film being taken up by the projector pierce my memories and return me to the present, but their regularity produces a pleasant sensation in me, too . . . . . . . . . . . . . . The strong pull of the *Other* floats along atop this rhythm, reminding me that in another loop store someone wrote **XAVIER ThE MAD** on the wall of a booth in smeary red marker . . . . . . . . . . . . . . What did he mean to say, aside from the obvious? . . . . . . . . . . . . . . Perhaps I could write **CLICKY** on the wall of this booth, because i often click my teeth while I am watching the loops, I have so much tension . . . . . . . .

What I am learning here is that any woman will do, despite the care we all take in choosing the right loop [None of us have learned an important lesson from this view—Love has nothing to do with beauty; we'd love the woman who loves us if we weren't afraid of appearing less manly] . . . . . . . . . . . . . . One can see the flickering image of a woman on the screen, a woman whom one does not know, will never know—she is across the country or fucking in a loft in Manhattan under stage lights—but one still entertains the most intimate and lurid fantasies about her . . . . . . . . . One places oneself up there on the screen and it almost takes one's breath away . . . . . . . . . . . . . . I have already forgotten about Lara . . . . . . . . . . . . . . It takes only an instant of thinking of her to realize she had left my mind completely for several minutes . . . . . . . .

On the floor, pushed by mens' shoes to the sides of the booth, are rumpled paper towels and some tissue that appears still moist . . . . . . . . . . . . . . Even the inside of the booth door is covered with dried stains from men coming on it . . . . . . . . . . . . . . I think sometimes it might be well if all of us identified ourselves on these walls, not for the sake of advertisement but as a monument, a list of those who have never given up searching for that veneration that we see only on celluloid . . . . . . . . . . . . . . If I ever sleep with a woman, and I am underneath her and she is moving at her own rhythm, her eyes staring at something over my left shoulder, I will look down the lengths of our bodies to watch what we are doing, to see if it is really love, to see if it matches what I am sure is love, because I have seen it in the loops . . . . . . . .

### *[Annotation]:*

*[Only now do I understand that the door to a booth is also a mask provided to me and the other men by one who knew how many of us were walking about with masks. I had thought I was unique but I was not. How striking that there were enough of us to encourage a commercial enterprise suited to our needs].*

*[I have not considered an important question: why was I able to stare at a real cunt only in the presence of a triangular relation, when I had to be alone to watch the loops? In the triangle, the shame is controlled; alone, it appears and I bathe in it, not knowing that shame and the cunt are as one]. Also, I am yet a virgin].*

*[I will watch films of two women and a man, but not films of two men and a woman. The latter make me uncomfortable; there is a not so subtle undercurrent of homosexuality in the latter. There is a limit to how many penises I can see in one film, and I am too uncertain of my own desires to face them on the screen, even behind the closed door of a booth]. [If I explained that to Hart, he might say Oh, of course, I saw that in you right away." And I wouldn't want Ericksen to know, either]. The essence of doubleness makes its appearance here, a hiding of desire, (a desire not at all understood as a child, but frightening nevertheless) behind a mask, in a family unit, repeated again and again].*

*[Something about these adventures reminds me of the bullies from my youth, though my experience with them is several years behind me. I had never seen my mother's vagina, though I had seen her naked in her bath. I know now that I had always wanted to see people's genitals, men, women, my friends. In that refrigerator box I saw for the first time a young boy's penis]. Sometime afterward I saw the penis of his close friend , who had usually taken part in the bullying but never seemed to have gotten much enjoyment from it [perhaps taking my mother's place in another triangle] when I visited him while he was lying in bed with poison ivy all over*

*his body. As he turned naked under the sheet I quickly glanced. I had once tried to look up my mother's skirt and she told me never to do it again. I had to go to P on the commuter train many times, though, and, whenever I could, I looked surreptitiously at the crotches of women sitting across the aisle from us; it made no difference whether the women were young or old. I had to look. A final question arises: did I want to see people fucking? Or did I only want to see penises and vaginas? It is perhaps true that in my desire for unity I considered that a knowledge of genitals, from which I was barred as a child (but for seeing my mother's breast and my father's penis as we peed together in the toilet once) might be an answer. [I did not know whether I was male or female]. It is no accident that as I become enmeshed in the relation to Hart and Ericksen my sexual desire began to appear [in secret, though, bringing with it an argument, under a conscious level but powerful, between homesexuality and heterosexuality. This conflict, which I could not speak of to Hart [Ericksen might have understood it] may have pushed me toward sex with a woman]. [Hart's comment about coming to the City to look at cunts was accurate; it was another way I had brought my childhood history and fantasies to P.] Freedom for me was narrowly defined: the freedom to look at naked bodies. [I suppose I wanted love from anyone, male or female].*

⫸ ⫷

One corner of my flat was devoted to my typewriter, which sat on a small table with just enough room for an ash tray beside it. On nights when I had nowhere to go or did not feel like walking about the city, always looking at women disappearing around corners or entering cafes with handsome men or having to jump out of the way of Mercedes sedans speeding through intersections in the Central District, I looked at the page in the roller, where I had noted some of the events of the past several months. The lure, I should say the pull, of the street was strong [as strong as the lure of past misery] and I had made few entries.........

March __: *One of the dancers on break looks at me and smiles . . . . . . . . . . . . . . I look to my right and my left, but then I stop myself, decide to accept the attention. My throat tightens and my forehead tingles with anticipation at the possibility she will speak to me. "Will you buy me a drink?," she will ask. But when she reaches my stool she breezes right by. There is a man sitting behind me and it was he at whom she was looking . . . . . . . . . . . . . . Now I have a problem: what to do with the emotion she has engendered in me. I look down at my glass and then, slyly, at the man. I hate him. His ears are too big; his teeth are crooked. I look at her again. Now she is fat and her face is pockmarked. A second ago she had excited me merely by walking in my direction . . . . . . . .*

May __: *A dancer leaned her chin onto the proprietor's shoulder. "Are you in love?," she teased him. "My lips are sealed," he said, "but your pussy isn't." "I'll bet you'd like to know." She went over to the jukebox and put some quarters in, then returned to his side. "Don't you ever want to do it?" "I'm retired." "You're tired?" "No, Retired! Every time I jerk off I put a hundred dollars in the bank." "how much do you have in your account?" "Seventy-five dollars . . . . . . . . ."*

July ___: *A dancer stares at a young Italian boy as she dances. At the end of the song he nods at her. "Yes," he says. "Yes, what?" "Why they don't applaud." She nods in agreement. As she danced men prodded dollar bills at her, leaning over the men in front of them. The proprietor points to the men who have contributed. A black man next to me speaks without taking his eyes from the girl. "Why does a pretty girl like that have to dance here?" "Because a lot of men want to see it . . . . . . . . ."*

August __: *The idea of exploding my present self and reconstituting a new one is central to my story, whether or not it ever gets put into written form. A self that is always malleable always looks for high ground on which to make a stand, and always dissolves again when the high ground does not seem like the right territory, because the self is unwilling to experience itself negatively. Even when it chooses to remain unified, it feels the tug of chaos, because dissolution is always one element of its being. . . . . . . . .*

*Sept.__: Hart with a dancer, saying things to her: "God, you're a whore" and "You have such whore-like qualities." He meant these remarks to be complimentary, because to him whores are soft and their sweetly pungent odors are so adaptable to one's pleasures. All the time he was saying these things he was trying to lift up her blouse, which she had put on after her set and she was not sure about him so she kept pulling it back down. It reminded me of one of those signal devices on ships: Blink: blink: blink. "I love the way you walk," Hart said. He was not trying to placate her. It was his way of recalling a visual memory of some actual whore whose flesh shifted subtly from side to side as she walked across a room and connecting it to the dancer as if she were the woman who was the subject of his memory. It was his way of becoming ready to accept her as someone who had beauty in her own right and who would carry forward for him the visually memorable tradition which was in his head all the time, his confirmation that she was woman, as if woman were land and all land a part of a unity of the essence of land. A woman carries a lot of responsibility for Hart. She is the repository of every experience he has ever had with all women. There is only one woman but she is all women and the last one in the sequence is the principal. It was all very mathematical, but it led to this conclusion: he had to make the last woman the carrier of all who had come before her. She symbolized infinity. She was woman to the nth degree. "All philosophy becomes mathematics," Hart says. But he is paraphrasing Sonntag. . . . . . . . . . . . . . . by way of Bertrand Russell. . . . . . . . . [I wonder if I was as jealous of my father as I see that I am of Hart, yet I do not believe that Hart had much sexual experience; perhaps it was the way he described women that impressed me].*

*Oct.__:A young artiste in M's. He is short and thin, and the women tease him but none will share his bed, so he sits at a table building a house with swizzle sticks, getting drunker, the dexterity in his musician's fingers shining brighter than the neon sign outside. There are people to whom you wish all the luck in the world, but you don't want to be there when they get it. . . . . . . . . . . . . . .*

*Nov.__: I have spent the week making notes on the five books I will write: the present one, children, call girls, blackmail, and thirty-six hours in P, which will be a neomodern retelling of Ulysses. Something has happened to me! I have no belief that these books will come to pass. Rather, a sense I can only define as a great yearning has come forward. But since Hart has told me not to pretend naivete, I will not mock myself for this yearning. Doctor Gold might say it is only the oceanic feeling which prefigures a religious desire. I may find someday that it is only a leap backward to my year as a four-year old, when I likely felt omnipotent. I had, after all, by then found that discovery, creativity were available to me; once I knew that shitting made my parents happy, I could then shit words. [As I read these notes I see how strong was my desire to be recognized, which had never merged with the stronger desire to see].*

### *[Annotation]:*

*I am stunned by these notes in one respect: the economy I have shown by merging all of the facets of my life in P as they were at home; watching, hiding, endless sexual curiosity, changing identities, repetitive mechanisms. [Looking and hunger were my life in P.] I feel a repulsion for the person I was then, a feeling that I could not put into words; even now I judge that young man harshly. How immature he is!*

⟫⟫⟩— ⟨⟪⟪

*It was inevitable that I would come to psychiatric treatment; not because I was flailing about, but because Hart and Ericksen were already seeing a psychiatrist, and I often accompanied them to their sessions, where I would sit in the waiting* room, keeping silent, watching the people, mostly young, who occupied the chairs or sat on the floor smoking, arguing, staring or, sometimes, crying. When Dr. Gold came out of his consulting room with a patient one day, he looked at me and asked "Did you want to see me?" I rose from my chair without hesitation and followed him down the corridor. That is how simply one's life veers in a new direction, though the force of the vector of change is but a soft wind at one's back. [I assumed that my two friends were healthier than I. I did not assume that any of the other patients were. I did not know them yet. At first, they joined in my mind those persons I have described earlier, bartenders, screamers, longshoremen, the oddballs of PJ.

If I have given the impression that I had some understanding of the repetition with which I was acting then, I have been inaccurate. I saw only afterward how I was playing out a geometric structure, how I was substituting Hart (and Ericksen) for the ghostly figures of my past. I was, in my essence, not an "I," and could not have used an "I" to consider a "me"; that is, I had no ability to consciously create a construct with which to examine my actions. There was no spatial relation between "I" and "me" yet which would have allowed me to listen to the thoughts running through my head. Self-loathing and shame are frightening when one has not created a logic to explain them, especially when they have, as all disorders do, a form and function of which one is unaware. Watching became an escape, both a way of avoiding insight and learning how others lived. If one is fortunate, one might begin to examine the envy which results. Envy has the potential to create that spatial construct which separates "I" from "me," but first, one must talk. And one must talk to a listener, aloud. With time, the number of persons in the room increases, from two to three, or even four. Another fact that one does not know: the repetition, the triangle, are not about overcoming a parent, but about overcoming the constant argument writhing in one's belly.

⫸ ⫷

*[Annotation]:*

*[One begins psychiatric treatment as a 'result'; the antecedents are unknown or vaguely suspected.]*

A man undergoing psychoanalysis a hundred years ago had not long to wait for a diagnosis. Three or four meetings with the alienist and then a session at the latter's desk, sometimes with the entire family present, to hear from the alienist's mouth the concise statement of the problem and the likely prognosis. "You have a schizophrenia of the hebephrenic type with an accompanying hysterical reaction." (Today one remembers James Stewart informing John Wayne of his fatal disease in "The Shootist": "You have a cancer!") The patient then says, "Thank you very much, Doctor," and shakes the alienist's hand. The patient might then be invited to stay at the alienist's hospital for an indeterminate length of time, even to share dinner at his table. Even the sickest people were treated as mature adults with an illness. Dr. Gold had no such method. He knew the jargon—as well he should—and his letters to draft boards were known to have caused receptionists to step away from the counter to confer with sleepy security guards. But he would never tell you what was wrong with you. That was for you to figure out, over a period of some years.

I accepted this method with no hesitancy, because, as I said, I had been accompanying Ericksen and Hart to their appointments with Dr. Gold and his colleague, at their offices in the Central District. My impression of psychiatry was at first no different than it had been after seeing The Shootist, that is, formal, an agreement between grown men who were peers in all respects. I learned otherwise.

One may be given any label up to the age of thirty, and yet, what does it mean? You may take a Rorschach, but you will not be told the result. Besides, how many fusilages must you see in the blots before an idea comes becomes clear to you. [It may never become clear]. Of course one has spent months in one's flat watching soap operas or the news, or is bored, or is unable to get women. These are measures of our inability to find what we need in the civilized world. But let us speak to someone for a few years, once, twice or several times a week (with summers off) and we shall see. We shall see.

Many psychiatrists do not have waiting rooms in the ordinary sense. One enters through door A, then through another door to the consulting room, then leaves through door B. Appointments are scheduled an hour apart, with five minutes for escape and for the psychiatrist to undergo his handwashing ritual, which he disguises by taking his empty coffee cup into the bathroom (which he enters through door A). Who knows you are disturbed? The maintenance man, maybe, or the coworker in the cubicle next to yours who hears you mumbling or confirming your next appointment. If one lives deep in the City one's family sees one rarely. One might appear on Thanksgiving, but in the melee around the table and with the uncles playing pinochle, the children destroying the basement, one's madness does not stand out. If anything, the relatives appreciate one 's quietude.

Dr. Gold had turned the method on its head. He wanted to learn. Hundreds of us walking the streets, lonely acid freaks with drooping faces, heroin users, thorazine shufflers, alcohol-besotted executives, Darvon freaks and schizoid social workers, quiet voyeurs. What did he know of us? He wanted to find out a few things, and soon he was in it up to his neck. With an adventurous mind and a total disregard for his home life, he saw patients at eight o ' clock in the morning and finished up at midnight. If one could not come to his office, he saw one at his home.

On any given day might be found in his office patients who brought transistor radios with earplugs to listen to music and avoid talking; patients who sat in the corners behind the Italian neo-Deco chairs, hugging their knees to keep from flying off the face of the earth; patients with guns in their briefcases; patients trying to goad other patients into fights without themselves becoming involved; patients who were fucking one another; patients who hated each other; patients who were fucking patients they hated; patients who had driven to California and back six times in one summer and who no longer spoke to one another; patients who couldn't fuck; patients who just the week before had tried to uproot Sycamore trees with their bare hands; patients who sat in rockers fourteen hours a day; patients who hallucinated but who held executive positions; patients who shot smack; patients who walked along the sidewalk as if every step were a step down; patients who held hands and patients who had to be forcibly separated; patients who couldn't utter a syllable (what did they do when they went back to his consulting room?); and raconteurs who couldn't be shut up, speaking their ghost tales to the walls...

### *[Annotation]:*

*[I sense my own bitterness as I write these words; it was the bitterness of a youngish man who believed he did not belong with these people; he had yet to understand that he was one of them].*

Out of this *schmeck,* Dr. Gold created order, of a sort. While we were crazy we could be his world, swirling around him as one's thoughts swirl around one's head. We had no responsibility for our sicknesses because, in a sense, we had all been thought up by him. We did, would do, what he thought we would. He knew what we were going to be when we recovered (a relative term, but meaningful to us nevertheless), so he let us be whatever we were then. He had plenty of disappointments—car wrecks took some of us, cancer, others; one caught cold and died of convulsions within the week. Dr. Gold had said it himself often enough: one might know exactly what one was doing, one could watch the upheaval as from a distance, and still the world would hurl one into space. Some think the crazy are dead, but things happen to the dead, also, as a kind of extra burden. So it was with us. Dr. Gold had thought us into the world we inhabited, but sometimes the unexpected occurred, and there was nothing he could do but wait…

A patient of Dr. Gold's with whom I had spoken sometimes while I waited for Hart or Ericksen to finish their sessions told me, in a low voice, that he had always begun his own free association in Dr. G's consulting room by mentioning the same image: he was fellating a horse. I began mine by imagining Hart fellating a horse. [I believed I had no imagination; note, though how quickly I changed the identity of another patient to Hart]. In many respects psychiatric sessions are a means of learning to *play*—with words there is always the possibility—but Dr. Gold was not playful in one respect: He never inquired whether the two horses were identical. The question remained: why did these images come to mind—to two minds respectively? I speculated that Hart sought the essence of a powerful steed, that his horse was muscular and swift. It would be unthinkable for me to imagine him fellating a swaybacked nag. I, in turn, sought the power I believed Hart had; in my mind, he *was* strength. I distinguished the two processes. His image (as I imagined it) came from inward need; what would have followed for him in the consulting room was an explanation not soaked in envy and paranoia. My image arose from emptiness and imitative desire [and homosexual panic]. But Dr. Gold rejected my analysis: the image was the image, in his way of thinking, and comparison itself was a mechanism to be analyzed. Well then, I thought, comparison itself derives from despair comprised of envy and paranoia; I did not know my territory. Now you are entering the sphere of metaphysics, Dr. Gold said. You are talking about talking about language. But you introduced the concept, I answered. I imagined Frank, one of his other patients, suddenly sitting bolt upright and putting his fist through the wall next to the couch on which I lay (he had done so). I described it and Dr. Gold said that image would not have occurred to Hart if one were to disagree with him. He suggested that I wanted someone else to express my rage on my behalf. Why do I not think of myself fellating a horse?, I asked. It was a rhetorical question but Dr. Gold answered it anyway. Why do you not think of yourself punching the wall? he said. I do not act, I said, I only see. But you only see others, he said. [Was I Hart's horse?]. [It was frightening to hear, from another patient, the kind of thoughts that were often in my own mind; no wonder I borrowed them so quickly].

The issue one faces in the consulting room is one of freedom. Freedom is given to us and we do not want it. We have always had it and it has been too frightening to contemplate. *"Make me better!"* is what we seek, at first. *And don't ask me why I came to P!* Of course, in a short time I was to mention the paradigm; it seemed to float upward so quickly, though softly that I could not have stopped it without biting off my tongue. I had dived into the sexual pool of my unconscious by allowing myself to be pushed off a diving board.

*A penis, when working properly, is the antithesis of irony. It knows what it wants and directs the body to obtain it.* That may be what this process is about: the shedding of the ironic mode without growing a new one, as a snake does. One day I said to Dr. G *"Hottentots! And Bottenfots! and poppenshots!"* A sentence that seemed to come out of nowhere. *"Are you making fun of Hottentots?" "Yes, and I could not abide it, so I added nonsense words." "Hottentots frighten you?" "I don't like a vacuum. It permits images I do not want. Violence; there is violence in Hottentots, and a lack of pretense." "Who do you want to kill?"* I cannot say you, I thought. *"They Have bones in their noses,"* I said to put him off. *"Have you been dreaming?,"* Dr. G asked. *"Yes. I was on an escalator, grown as I am now, in a department store. I went down on it to a desert, growing smaller as I descended." "Escalators are in department stores. Were you shopping?" "Yes. For an identity." The basement of the store was a desert. Protruding through the sand were pieces of an automobile. "Cars are ego,"* Dr. G said. *"My father worked on cars." "Are you a smashed car?"* One millisecond of a familiar image: my father's penis in my rectum, my penis in my mother's vagina. *"We are not analyzing my father,"* I said. *"Why not. One ball of wax per family. Oh, and send in Hart, will you. I want to hear about a horse."*

These samples of therapy did not occur all at once. It is only possible to describe the process by condensing it into small examples. I have made myself seem more aware than I was, more willing to appear reasonable. Of course Dr. Gold saw my pose early on; he did not challenge it. How is this process connected to the shedding of identities? I believed I wanted to be only me, not anyone else. But then, after more time with Dr. Gold, I considered the dream again, which I spoke of to him, filling in parts I had not considered before:

*I stood at the top of an escalator at night. I was in a deserted department store. Behind me were appliances, washers, dryers. I stepped onto the escalator as a young man; at the bottom, I was a child. The floor on which I found myself was composed of sand and dirt. Buried in the dirt were parts of an automobile.*

What was the auto parts dream about? A gift, I think, from an Indian-giver. A desire to have Dr. Gold take me back, a pictorial description of a broken family and my own broken self. Or, a wish for the destruction of the family, which I saw as soon as I could see anything. The wish: that destruction! The sex: ownership of my mother? It was not the family's destruction; it was father's! [I.e.: I wish I'd killed him a long time ago]. Or perhaps it was a wish to destroy Dr. Gold. As soon as I began to think of myself as a thing, that is, as a piece of a destroyed automobile, was I not back under my father's control? Freeing psychologically? How can it be both? Because it gives me an identity which I believe I chose myself, even if it was predestined by the very theory my father espoused. What a contradiction. [It is a truth that we are always free; there is nothing in the cosmos that prevents us from freedom, only human beings. It is one of the most frightening experiences to begin speaking words one does not even know were in one's mind; only when one begins to avoid censoring them does the freedom one has always had become terrifying and therefore real. With practice, one might grasp that terror; one might even become its wary friend. Its absence, which has been enforced, has still been felt as a presence, for an absence which is finally known becomes a presence]. [I was still thinking of myself in the Psychoanalytic paradigm of Oedipal struggle. There were other frames of reference I had not considered which might have been equally or even more accurate]. [Reciprocal gift-giving and a challenge]. [I presented the paradigm and the dream to Dr. Gold as gifts, without knowing that they were intended as such. Perhaps they were challenges, as well. [I am a man! They said]. He presented me with a room in which to speak freely; that was a gift I could take only with trembling hands.

*In fact I came to think of my time with Dr. Gold as a period of reciprocal gift-giving. Over time, I gave him four or five gifts without any conscious knowledge that I was doing so. He did not open them; it was for me to unwrap them while he held onto them. The first gift was the paradigm, which I mentioned blithely with no thought of what it might mean; the second was the dream, which has seemed to contain several meanings [these were expressions of infantility]; the third was my telling him of my proposed novel; the fourth was my theft of another patient's free association; the last was my explanation of the Euclidean way I explained my actions. In return, he held my gifts, often frustrated, perhaps thinking I would never comprehend their meaning. It was only the final gift that he returned to me unopened. Only long after his death did I open it, to find that I had used the wrong geometry to describe my life, my repetition, my overcoming.*

⟫⟫ ⟪⟪

In the waiting room, sharing a joint with Hart and Lara, the ceiling pink like sunset. *"Do nothing 'til you hear from me,"* a song line running through my Head. I am talking to myself now, not Dr. Gold. All is friendship and friendship is technique and love is technique. We all pay weekly for a new ball of wax. *E pluribus unum!* [Lara leaves first; a moment later, Hart disappears. the only reason these facts do not increase my paranoia is that I have not been seduced yet by Lara. Whatever Hart sees, he's already preparing for conquest, a reversal of our roles which is unfamiliar to me]. [Only after I had described this scene did I realize that it has all of the elements of the family constellation: a woman I wanted but was afraid to attempt to get; a man who also wanted her, a man whose ability to have her frightened me. At that time, I experienced immediate weakness whenever anyone disagreed with me, followed by rage. It may have been only that I had never believed Lara would have anything to do with me that I did not, in that waiting room, collapse.]

Dr. Gold wanted me to accept my complicity. That is, I should admit that watching is pleasurable, and that it carries with it its own guilt, that it is a means of controlling my world. If I am a complicit watcher, why not a complicit actor? [Because a watcher accepts what he sees and does not try to change it; it is his entertainment; an actor acts]. Ideally, I should end up screaming on his couch: "Frauds! Hypocrites! Bastards, cheaters, liars, human monsters! I hate them all and I hate being alive!" But instead something else happens: the Other becomes real, something to look at, to turn around in my hands as if it were a block of wood, a thing with substance, mass, width. It is *recognition*. It is my interpretation of events which is faulty, not my memory of the events. [I am doing the same thing with myself, but I am unaware of it].

And in the middle of it all are the pictures which seem to come from the depths of my mind, lithe, small squares, Kodaks from the past slipping upward and down again, teasing me: me as a child of three, being teased by a neighborhood boy and feeling a warmth of love I've never recaptured; the boys I watched from my window pulling down my pants the following year and giving me a cherry belly; my father tearing the entire house and garage to pieces looking for his glasses; the spittle on my jacket at the school playground. Everything true- all the emotion that these pictures engender that is too dangerous to acknowledge—has been split off and orbits the core in pieces, meteors of lust and murder and love. To call these emotions desire would be euphemistic . I've thought of killing everyone I've ever known, even the ones who've been good to me. The homosexual panic I felt as transference began to gel, the impulses to bite off my tongue or cut off my penis. Ice at the center, pictures in black and white ...

**What to do? I've rowed my little boat into the middle of a vast sea and all the words I used on land have not been useful. Talk of the weather? ask Dr. Gold about his health? Describe the pictures? Let my mind wander. But that's not possible, is it? Put the evidence side by side. Oh, I did punch one of those boys in the head for no reason? He beat me up, then. Remember the new boy on the block who grew flowers? I tore them out by the roots and scattered them over the pavement. And don't forget Frank who shoplifted the fishing reel that the bigger boys smashed on the ground to teach him not to steal. It all spirals down to an image: riding my tricycle while my father watches. He's angry about something, but I don' t want to acknowledge it. I might die or be swallowed up. I've always remembered the event, but not the emotion. That is, I have not been there! With Dr. Gold looking at me, quiet, no more farting or cracking his knuckles or answering the telephone while I try to hold on to a thought, the anger I, too, felt comes roaring back. I scream to push it away but it comes on like a bus. BANG!, and it's there and I don't step aside. A little piece of my self returns and I lay there stunned. Three days later I'm still lying on the floor of my flat. I can' t smoke, I can't eat, not out of fear but out of ease. I exist and nothing else. I exist.**

*[Annotation]:*

*After I made this note I remembered something; I had broken a neighbor's window with a bat when I was about three. I wondered then if the catharsis I had, involving me riding my tricycle on the same pavement where that window was, was not at all about the tricycle but about the anger my father [and I] had when I broke the window. I had transposed the events and the anger he expressed about the broken window, as well as my own three-year old's anger. The catharsis was about another event. It was a distortion of time from one instance to another. Yet, the emotion that was released, the energy it had taken to bind it up, was significant, no matter the transposition of one event for another; in fact, it was a lesson in inaccuracy. Moreover, it was a frightening demonstration of the fury which had grown in me from the first years of my life, which must have begun to grow well before the event I have described. It did not occur to me that I was furious at Dr. Gold; to acknowledge that would have destroyed me; I'd have drowned in my own guilt. [I saw him as physically weak (which he was not, though he had suffered several heart attacks). When that catharsis occurred, it seems now that my rage at Dr. Gold was too terrifying to express directly; I diverted it toward my father, saving Dr. Gold from my wrath. It was another gift I gave to him, as if holding on to my rage was a gift!].*

What is missing? The questions that should have arisen afterward. What was being repressed was not only the emotion, the anger, but the fear of that anger. The anger was dangerous, as it should have been, considering my father as the angry man he was at that time. I consider now the later years, when I still lived at home, when I feared his death when he went out every morning to work, and I waited in front of the house on late afternoons for his return. But I was not talking to Dr. Gold then, and I did not know that my waiting on those afternoons was, in a way, a death watch which I could not admit and would have denied if someone had pointed it out to me. A question Doctor Gold never asked: How could a four-year old boy have developed so much rage? [I was not allowed to be angry [nor could I allow myself to be openly afraid] because it would always have engendered anger or worse toward me. Thus I was afraid of my own emotions and the emotions of everyone else].

I have recalled more of the day of the catharsis. Two of Dr. Gold's patients, young women who were part of that waiting-room group that I had dismissed as *not like me*, had walked me home, gotten me up three flights of steps—which was farther than Tony, the bartender at M's, had ever carried me—and laid me out on my couch. After they left, I believe I slept. Any further description would be a reimagining, surely inaccurate. I will dare, though, to imagine anyway what would be consistent with the event itself. That is, I imagine myself, having brought forth an event from the past into the present, having the mind of a child of four, *also in the present.* In that mind, there has already been a *disruption.* There was an expectation of warmth, there was no 'yes'; there was no 'no'; there was no philosophy; there were no inconsistencies; there were no themes; there was hardly any language; there were no questions. I was not yet split. But in the morning I will wake up and yet not know how to live without being split. *But I might know that I am split!* Disruption will appear as a comfort, and I will not, for years, see it happening. A lesson has been missed: emotional expression is useless if it is not explained with words. Words!

## *[Annotation]:*

*The ease with which the paradigm and the dream arose from the lower tiers of my mind was misleading; only when the cathartic experience occurred was the force of repression made clear. And the image it finally brought forth was misplaced in time. The emotion itself was of an earlier event; the deepest part of my mind would not give it up without distorting its position in the timeline of my life.*

*I became afraid of being hospitalized for several months; I kept an overnight bag on a pedestal near the door to my flat. Dr. Gold could have told me to go, but he never did. Instead, he gave me a prescription for stellazine, which I put away behind some books on a shelf. I pretended I had lost the pills, though I always knew where they were. I wonder now if I was entering a transference psychosis; I wanted him to be a protective father and I was (unintentionally) willing to become psychotic to force him to take the fatherly role. He'd have known I was too frightened to go crazy, and he rode out that fright until it abated. It would have been the antithesis of going off balance, as it would not have happened voluntarily, a leap of faith into disequilibrium. That is, it would have been no risk, but rather, an avoidance.*

*Our histories are "why". Freud says (I paraphrase) "why" is the result of constitution and events. Paz says I am not in history, I am history. I am flattered by Paz' statement (though he was speaking to Mexicans), frightened by Freud's. But that is no more than a repetition of what I have become used to, the double meaning of words, extended to the double meaning of my and everyone else's individual history. To become psychotic is to take one's self **out** of history.*

It is clear that in my sessions with Dr. Gold, despite the freedom he offered, there was much I did not speak of. Masturbation, virginity, yearning, my nightly search for women. I do not think I ever explained my triangular theory or my repetition compulsion. He, however, saw and heard what was missing, the absence that was a presence, and he allowed me to continue in my ignorance. That was his gift to me, though it may have given him fits waiting for me to show any sign of reflection, that is, an *I* listening to a *me* with the possibility of discovery. In passing, I recall now two events that demonstrated a small but significant change. I began my free association one day by shouting *"Avast, ye landlubbers!!,"* which made Dr. Gold laugh. And another time I began my session by speaking baby talk for five minutes *"bagagooboobagagaga…"* Both of these events exhausted me; freedom is exhausting.

One day, on the couch, I had been thinking of something classical, having purchased a copy of Bulfinch's Mythology. I thought I needed a background in Greek classic literature and myth if I were going to write one of my novels [One day in P, a neomodern tale of a late 20th century Ulysses/Odysseus]. What came to mind was the story of the Golden Fleece. Without saying the words, I thought, *I'm a lamb and he's fleecing me of my money with commentary…*

This thought, in a way, was a sign of change, in that it was sarcastic rather than purely angry. It was also a way of distancing myself from any affection I may have been experiencing for him.] [Without being conscious of it then, the importance of the word 'commentary' would later make itself felt after an observation by Ericksen].

I avoided the mention of "fleecing" by talking about the Odyssey, which I had read several times. I had outlined every chapter as well. It was going to be the template for my great novel. Dr. Gold asked me if I had gotten to the part of the story in which Penelope weaves a shroud on her loom for her father-in-law, Laertes. I had, but he leapt from his chair and went to his bookshelves where he pulled down a Bulfinch's. *"Look up Laertes."* It seemed that while Odysseus was away at the Trojan War, his wife Penelope, despairing of his ever returning, was weaving a shroud every day for her father-in-law, Laertes. She had promised all her suitors that when it was finished, she would marry one of them, giving up any thought of Odysseus ever returning. But every night, after she had finished her day's weaving, she would secretly unravel what she had done that day, postponing the decision she did not want to make. Dr. Gold then made a comment which glanced off my mind as soon as spoke the words [He was directly hinting at repetition, but he couched it in "unraveling"].

*"Perhaps you unravel every time you might be forced to choose an identity other than that of watcher, or whenever you have to make an actual decision about who you are...* ["i.e., you are the angry son of an angry man. Is that the total of you?"].

When Dr. Gold said I reminded him of the Shroud of Laertes, I took the wrong meaning from it. I thought he did not mean that I became someone different after a time and then dismantled that personality for another. I think now he meant that I perceived myself as a certain kind of person for a time, then discarded that perception when I realized I could not contrive to act in conformity with it [and when it did not achieve my fantastic desires]. My complicity theory was an unwieldy way of carrying out this discarding, as I understood each time that my impulses were not conforming to the false perception I carried of honesty, gentleness and generosity of spirit and weakling victim. I always returned to the stream of misery underneath. *I was putting off the ownership of my mind, which was owned, in the fullest sense, by my father.*

Dr. Gold explained: *"Perhaps the shroud is for your father, and you don't want to finish it. If you do, he'll die, but so will a part of you that you don't want to give up. Which, by the way, is also him."* He might have said *"this man at whom you are so angry—he was a ditherer, and you are, too."* But he didn't.

The simile, almost a conceit, actually, was not such a good fit, but it appealed to my hatred of myth and the way I thought of myself. I wanted a new paradigm; the old one with me in the middle of a couple of middleaged parents was not working all that well. I thought, I'll adopt it as the new paradigm of my life. [It fit in another way, as well: the shroud was for my father as was my unraveling, i.e., a continual delaying of his death until I could recapture him as a man other than he had been for most of the time I had known him].


### *[Annotation]:*


*[I wonder now about Penelope's motives as I expand my research into my own. Perhaps she was unraveling the shroud each night hoping that Odysseus would never return; perhaps she wanted to sleep with Laertes before he died; or perhaps she imagined sleeping with all the suitors in a giant orgy and unraveled the shroud to keep that desire from coming to awareness. What I understand now but did not then was that the process of unraveling was (and is) a repetitive fetish, a driving away of an awareness that is unbearable [That I am what I am and I have defined myself accurately, a frightened, beaten-down, disgusting coward (which, according to my certainty about everything I think, will never change)]. That may have been one reason for Penelope's repetition, mixed with the conscious reason (which was also a fantasy) that it would bring Odysseus home if she kept up the repetition]. I chose the Title of these notes, then, because it has the kind of double meaning I saw*

*in all action and all speech]. [Unraveling is one kind of repetition, overcoming by proxy, another]. I had not seen another reason for the title, either: burying a father. Perhaps the unraveling was a kind of dithering; I had not yet gotten the strength to kill him off. As long as I could remain tethered to one persona after another, I could avoid killing him. There was an inverse ratio between my own freedom and his life span, as if he'd give up the ghost if I settled on a comfortable way of being. I was afraid to kill him off mentally. I needed him in my mind; I had no way to work through the double need of wanting him to die without wanting the part of him inside me to die. That is, I did not know I could live without the parts of him of which I felt myself composed. I did not want to be the King; I would always settle for being second. I punished myself in order that he might continue to live. [I claim to hate myth but myths are what I have lived by!]. [Have I unwittingly resolved the paradigm?].*

*Let me try to put a few things together. A scene on a bed, a memory of pleasing my parents (and myself) by defecating), learning how to masturbate, my father in bed all day, fucking my mother while being fucked by my father (and imagining Dr. Gold asking which I liked more), paranoia, the deliberate frustration of desire, all these form a history which can be examined or ignored. I look for reasons given me by writers and philosophers to examine this psychic history, and I find Descartes, who tells us in his Meditations that he will spend his life studying himself. This support is invaluable; a great philosopher and mathematician has told me I have the right to root around in my histories as if I were pulling dingleberries out of my rectum (which is an activity surely related to one of the histories). I might add a few things here: shit has been a constant theme in my mental life, beginning with that first memory. (I had once said to Hart that I wished to sit on my birthday cake). Shit and penises, and vaginas. I had seen my father's penis, and the penises of the boy in the refrigerator box and his friend and fellow bully, when I visited the latter in his home as he lay in bed naked but for a sheet, covered with poison ivy. Oh, I was curious! My mother would not let me look up her dress [I was four or five] but whenever we were on the subway, I always tried to look up the skirts of the women sitting across from us; it did not matter whether they were young or older. I had to look].*

*Other memories adding to one stream: my raincoat on Zola's window sill [later]; watching television with my parents; watching Zola wipe her vagina; on the bus going to my Army physical; watching Lara cry; these are the real history. And dreams are the attempt to merge the two histories.*

*The framework in which I think about behavior is opposed to the way my father thought. A Communist never has to think about the "why" of any act. he has already defined "why" as the result of opposing classes. I've been reading Trotzky's <u>The Russian Revolution.</u> He's a good historian and is factual; he goes far enough to analyze the personalities of Nicholas, Alexandra and the people who surrounded them at court. But he stops at a certain point when his analysis of their psychological makeup clashes with his certainty that things could not have turned out differently because historical forces had already been set in motion which were not to be denied fruition. This kind of thinking, which my father accepted (though he never explicitly said so to me) has never found comfort in my mind. What it has done is create a conflict between acting on behalf of others and acting on my own behalf; it has also created a sense which has never left me that I must not succeed. How I ever did reasonably well in my work life and romantic life remains a mystery to me. Perhaps the adoption of the words 'must' and 'should', which are the wellsprings of a fascist mindset, were of use to me in ways I did not understand. It is almost as if, with those words, I created a set of rules by which to live, which sometimes worked to my advantage. Strange, though, that anger was often the motivating force behind many actions I took; or, if not anger, vengeance. Anger is a unifying force against chaos. [In a way, these notes are my counterhistory to the rules by which I lived].*

*What is the result when the words 'must' and 'should' are combined with the unspoken message 'don't get angry' which comes from parents who sulk? It can lead to suicide as a 'must'. Other memories constituting a history: the trash cans under the back porch; the bear![23] Dreams merge the two histories of event and perceptions in the midst of events. Words are ghosts.*

*To put it another way: an argument has been going on in your mind since you were a child, but it has always been carried out in a childish way, because it has been interrupted by a din shouting 'why did you do this to me?'. The din has always interfered with a logical way of approaching the argument. A man comes along who, by virtue of his history and his very existence, comes to represent one side of the argument. As you interact with this man, the argument becomes clearer, more focused. the argument may have been a dialogue with your father, or an internalized struggle between mother and father, but fear, among other factors, made it difficult for the argument to clarify itself. Now, though, the man, your friend, by how he acts toward you and what he says to you, begins to replace your father in the argument. Now you begin the attempt to overcome your friend, mentally speaking. In doing so, you begin the attempt to overcome your father. You believe that growth will follow, that as the argument becomes clearer, you will become more you. It may be uncomfortable to become more you, but without knowing it, you are taking a risk you have not taken before. There is a logic to repetition. You may give up the desire to overcome him when the past catches up to the present. [In a sense the argument is an evasion. You have introjected a parent [or a mother-father unit] whose presence in your mind is painful. You believe you can exorcise them by repetitive argument, even with a substitute. It is going to be an unsuccessful enterprise, but one that may be necessary to repeat. An understanding of the repetition is more important than the repetition itself. You are, in a way, memorizing an equation until you apprehend that the process by which you are*

---

23  A dream in which a bear climbed a firescape and entered my room through a window.

*memorizing it is faulty]. The tragic facet of this repetition is that you are also trying to learn how to love!*

## *[Annotation]:*

*I consider the Golden Fleece with another event which was evidence of a kind of transference to Dr. Gold, but which frightened me. I went into his consulting room ahead of him one day and sat down in his chair. He immediately lay on the couch and began to talk as if he were a patient and I were the psychologist. I listened for a minute or two; it was upsetting. I felt responsible for his wellbeing; the burden was overwhelming. I stood up, stupefied, and we switched places. I note this event not because of its character, but because I had thought "I want to be like him," but I had no idea of the burden which would have gone with the imitation. At the same time, I thought, I knew, actually, that I had failed him. He needed to talk to someone, and I had been afraid to listen. My father would never have spoken to me about himself. All I knew about him came from direct experience of his moods or from other relatives describing him. I was coming to care for Dr. Gold, and I did know it. The combination of desire and fear prevented me from trying to overcome Dr. Gold; that is, I hesitated to replace my father with him. I needed my father, or the view I had of him; I could not give him up yet for another father.*

*Beginning treatment in desperation, finally deciding that one needs to talk, does not release, but only covers with a thin sheet, the resentment one feels at needing to talk. The demand for help carries with it a sense of abasement; it is this sense that one tries to pretend does not exist that motivates the dare in the dream.*

*I have never considered until now the possibility that my intention to write a modern version of the Odyssey was unintentionally a plan to make the antagonist of the novel a selfish young man who has not gone off to war but has run away from his father after blinding his younger brother! Even in my nascent writing career—I use the word "career" with sarcasm—I could not avoid recreating my own history without being aware of what I wanted to do.*

⫸ ⫷

*The expression on my father's face when he entered my flat for the first time was priceless—the sudden drop of his jaw in dismay at its tiny-ness and its drab colors, followed immediately by his attempt to smile, which did not fully succeed. But it was I who had to remain. His only form of insistence was that I keep that chair, the one I battered with a golf club when I was in a surly mood. He had refused to take it back and I was stuck with it. It became the focal point of my anger as I aped his cellar behavior. When I finally got rid of it, dragging it down three flights of narrow steps, its stuffing trailed behind, rather like the ashes of Pompeii, I thought cutely. I was still his son, in all respects.*

*Thinking about him too much always drew me to thoughts of Hart and whether Hart was a fascist. The idea came out of the air but I chose not to suppress it, for there must have been a reason why I chose Hart as the person with whom to have my internal dialogue. It seemed that I had created a form of triangulation by entering P. That is, the two friends with whom I shared my time had in many respects those qualities I had found so frustrating in my father and mother. Hart was always right, in my mind; Ericksen was incomprehensible to me. I demanded more from Hart and assumed he had something to give; I left Ericksen alone. I had brought a template with me when I entered P, and I had begun to fit within it those few persons with whom I associated . . . . . . . .*

⫸ ⫷

*My father wore sleeveless undershirts and boxer shorts. He had to have socks without elastic at the tops, which my mother was able to find in department stores. He shaved with Treet blades which came in little green plastic boxes. Every morning he covered his face with shaving cream using a white-handled brush with soft, brown bristles. After he had shaved, he shook Dr. Lyon's Tooth Powder into his cupped palm, rolled his wetted toothbrush in it, and brushed his teeth. He wore suspenders and always, even when he was out of work, put on a clean shirt and tie, which he tucked into the shirt between the second and third buttons from the top, as he had done in the Army. The trousers he wore could not have been expensive but they were neither "floods" nor baggy. He was, within the means available to him, fastidious in his appearance. His shoulders were sloped, accounted for by Ricketts when he was a child, but he stood straight and did not slouch when he walked.*

*On the bureau in my parents' bedroom lay the Daily Worker, rolled up and rubberbanded. The rectangular green container of Treet blades gave perspective to the white and black cylinder of the newspaper. A box, a cylinder, the shaving brush an obelisk on its handle, the bristles light brown toward the end, darker at the base where the whisker-dust collected. At the kitchen table he read the Worker from first page to last (as he read every newspaper), carefully folding the pages back and running his index finger down the middle to avoid creases. My mother, an afterthought in the house, sat with her chocolate bars hidden under the cushion of the soft chair, her detective magazines on the table under the muted light of the lamp. Later, when he descended to the cellar to work with his power tools, his curses rose through the heating flues into the upstairs bedrooms, muffled by distance but still vehement and articulate in their cadence.*

*These facts, but most clearly the image of the geometric forms on my father's bureau, I compared with Hart, of whom I thought, "he looked about himself and saw stolidity in every form." He saw that the shapes and forms about him were unyielding; they were solid and did not shimmer in bright light. Nowhere did he see the treason of a mirage. What he saw was real; it was firm; it was geometry. It was that word: geometry; somehow it applied to both of them. Perhaps if I were to send them hurtling toward each other in a cyclotron, the collision would occur not in a tunnel but in my own mind. I could not take the analysis any further; I knew only that they both had adapted themselves to the geometric forms of life whereas I was a stumbler who saw danger in buildings and chairs. They were as unyielding as any geometric form. I had been born gentle as they were but they had grasped something I never had: serve they master and it will all work out in the end. I wished to incorporate their strength, but even had I the means, that strength would have entered a void. Not long after I made this comparison, I learned that my father was dying, and I returned home to take responsibility for his care.*

In the last stages of my father's illness he slept for hours, days… He didn't want to eat… He dreamed… He claimed never to have dreamed before… Now he confided to me that he dreamed of California. *"What do you think it means?"* he asked… I was surprised at his question… It might have meant he credited me with some knowledge he did not have… It was not easy for me to respond with an *"I don't know,"* though I believed I did know; the dream was about death, being carried away to a far place… *Do you think I can beat this?" h*e wondered, and again I had no answer that would have been other than a lie…

…He sat in a soft chair in the bedroom which had been mine when I lived at home… A black nursing aide stood out in the hallway… Every day she tried to force-feed him his medicine, after which she sat in the kitchen eating lunch with my mother… *"You're very sick."* I managed to say…

We all wanted to tell him the truth, yet we wanted him to get better, too, and not to suffer. But he became depressed and sank, until his doctor said to me, "It's not the cancer that is killing him, it's negative thinking." So I gave him a pep talk—*"You can make it"*—I told him, yet he sank even further, but the next day he ate breakfast, had my mother call a taxi, put on his clothes, and walked out of the house. He and my mother, along with a neighbor who helped lift him in to a taxi, *"Let's shop and get something to eat,"* he suggested.

At a diner, he ate a cheeseburger, French-fried potatoes, and a milkshake. He told a joke. After lunch he insisted that they stop at a hardware store, where he bought light bulbs and fuses. When they got back to the house he went down to the basement and changed all the fuses and climbed the stairs again without help.

*"I'm a little tired,"* he told my mother, *"I think I'll take a nap."* The next day he was back in the hospital, and when the hospital decided it could no longer help him, we put him in a nursing home.

The manager of the home had no legs; she travelled the corridors in a motorized wheelchair. She told me that she, too, had been a patient there. It was supposed to be a convalescent home, not a place to die, but she was the only person I had ever known to have recovered, and even she had never actually left.

*"He'll get excellent care,"* she told me.

I was trying to be careful, in a role I had never had to take on, so I checked out the rooms and tried to ask the right questions, while I fought against the words that kept running through my mind: *"Do it! Just do it! "*

He was put in a room with a madman, an octogenarian with senile psychosis who punched anyone who came near him. The old man ' s family had money to pay for around-the- clock nurses, but still he had to be tied to his wheelchair and he kept tipping it over. I begged the manager to move my father, but it took another week before he was shifted to a different room, and he himself had insisted that the psychotic was no problem.

Every night after supper, when he had been healthy, my father disappeared into the basement of his house, where he kept his woodworking tools, a router, a table saw, an electric drill with a set of bits. At irregular intervals he would bring forth his creations to display them to us before taking them to art galleries where he left them on the cheapest consignment—portraits, modern-designed picture frames, framed prints, clocks, cabinets, even a set of dishware he molded by hand and took to the local art school for baking in the school's kiln . *"Why don't you make a business of it?,"* he was asked, mostly by friends who wanted "just a small piece for the dining room." But that would have killed him. It was bad enough that he cursed aloud all the time he was in the basement, curses which made their way up the steps to the kitchen or through the heating flues to our bedrooms upstairs. And he mimicked people while he worked, too—mostly my mother—while he worked the power saw and he thought he couldn't be heard . When I found myself, after visiting them, running back to my flat to hurl books at the walls, emptying shelf upon shelf in my fury at one imagined slight or another, I remembered that mimicking. *"YIP, YIP!,"* he said, (being my mother asking him why he wasn't earning more money) *"Yip, yip yip!."* The sawdust flew and he (as my mother) tried to bury himself in it. And the curses still rose through the sawdust .

He also spoke to the mirror while he shaved. He simply could not do anything that was called work, even if in fact it was not work. The very idea of calling it work aroused too much conflict.

When he became ill, my mother helped as best she could, but it was just at the end of their life together that she could do the least for him. She had always been a bad cook, and what she made well he would not or should not eat. And she spoke loudly, a trait superattenuated by her fear of his death, yet which permitted him to exacerbate his own fears, for, when he was awake in his room, he listened intently to every word that was spoken in the living room downstairs for news of his own fate, or, at least, the peculiar twists of the road leading to it. *"Am I going back to the hospital? All right, I'll go,"* he told me. *"But will you get me a decent room? ."*

*"Yes. I'll get you the best room I can,"* I said.

*"And don't send her (meaning my mother) up here with any more of that mush!"*

*"She's doing what she can,"* I said, helplessly, unwilling even then to permit him any of his uncut bitterness. I was still in the middle.

So all of our old roles reestablished themselves in his dying, my father bitter, my mother unable, and me, helpful but doubting my own strength.

My father had known he was ill for a long time, months perhaps, but he did nothing about it. My mother had just suffered a broken hip and had spent two weeks in the hospital herself. My father's sister, who was in her eighties, had had a stroke and was also hospitalized. He ignored the way he felt and stayed in bed for a few days. A certain fastidiousness kept him from investigating the source of his discomfort. He told himself it would go away.

I, who seldom visited, noticed something, but not anything specific. When I visited my mother in the hospital where her hip was mending, I lit a cigar in the corridor outside her room and offered him one, too. He scowled and looked doubtful. *"They're not so good for you,"* he said, turning down the cigar. I agreed, seeking every chance to agree in our long history of opposition (our similarities of behavior having gone unrecognized by both of us). I saw a tiredness in him, but not enough to think of rationalizing it to myself. Later, waiting in the train station for a ride back to town, I began, without realizing the extent of my own fury at what must have been happening, to smash my umbrella against a bench until it was ruined.

I arrived at the house one day to find my father slumped over at the kitchen table. He was not even smoking, though he had smoked three packs of cigarettes a day for forty years, mostly unfiltered Lucky Strikes (until the Surgeon General's Report came out in 1964, when he switched to filtered Winstons). I knew he was trying to quit, but I did not see the fear behind his attempt. *"How is Aunt L.?,"* I asked. She was home, answered my father. He had visited her twenty times over a five-week period that Winter. At first she had not even known who he was. *"My Brother?! Awww! Really?."* But now she recognized him yet had no idea how great a part he had played in her—albeit limited—recovery. Now he was at home , too, my mother having sent him back from the hospital to get some rest .

A month later my mother was home but something was not right. My father had a cold that would not go away. I did not visit but I called often.

*"Has he gone to the doctor?," I asked her. "No, the doctor comes here,"* she said . *"Is he any good?." "Your father likes him."*

It was a source of continual rage to me that they told me so little, that it had to be dragged out of them in just the right way or they would not tell me even the simplest details. A week later I asked again, and was told that x-rays were to be taken...

I went to the hospital and found him waiting for an elevator, having already been x-rayed. He seemed tired but glad to see me. Whenever he was in a new situation, he appeared to become younger and more curious, as if his antennae had opened and expanded. I could imagine him pushing his bony chest against the x-ray glass while some bastard in a lead apron hid behind a stone wall. His acceptance was not what I had anticipated, because he had been such a household tyrant. I did not doubt my historical view, but I wondered at the contrast I saw that day. He asked me if I wanted to get some lunch, but I told him I had to go back to town. Immediately I felt I had said the wrong thing, but then my father's throat rattled, actually rattled, and I told him to get home to bed, trying to bury my feeling of having disappointed him in concern for his wellbeing. I felt I should have gone with him, perhaps was afraid to do so, but he seemed unbothered by my refusal which made it worse, in my mind. I did not say to myself, 'He agrees he ought to be in bed', but instead I thought 'I hurt him so much he doesn't even want to show me how he feels'. I always took responsibility for the way anyone felt in our house no matter how farfetched the logic of it was.

So home he went, but when he got there he could not sit still. He went down to the basement and fiddled around with his tools but he could not concentrate. As soon as the doctor had told him about the need for x-rays a buzz, like a constant internal din, had begun in my father's body, as if a motor had been turned on, the motor of eating, of keeping alive at all costs. He couldn't turn it off. He was somewhat successful in putting it out of his consciousness, but the trouble was, it wasn't in his consciousness; it was in his body and that made forgetting it impossible. He considered drinking, but he had never been much of a drinker, perhaps a shot of whiskey at a funeral or a family gathering, a beer once every six months, and, besides, beer wouldn't do the trick. He had never deliberately befogged his mind—he liked thinking too much.

Of course, no one knew what he thought. He was a mystery, he knew, to my mother and I. His convictions were no secret: he was a socialist, an antifascist, a Marxist-Leninist—but what he thought about all day, when he was driving around or eating or resting—that was unknown. He smiled once thinking of his secrets and felt the machine's power dim for the first time…

It was part of his essential cruelty to be secretive, for he knew well that my mother and I wanted to know what he thought about things, and he enjoyed our not knowing.

The doctor called and told my mother that my father's room was ready at the hospital. Tests had to be done, methods of treatment explained. When I learned this, I knew the worst had come. I was already there when my father arrived, with a new robe I had bought him…

One day after a visit to the hospital I came home and began to throw furniture around the room. In my bedroom I ripped all the linen and blankets from the bed and jumped onto the mattress where I flailed my arms violently, until the bed began to move away from the wall across the floor. I threw the pillows off and ran to the kitchen where I threw some pots to the floor, then ran to the front door, which I opened and shut with such force that the building next door shook.

I sat down and thought about the rage. I was angry he was dying but I also wanted him to die soon. I had realized he might hang on for some months and I did not believe I could stand to visit him much more. For years I had seen him (and my mother) only sporadically; now I had to see them three times a week. And how could I overcome a dying man? Perhaps, now that I might overcome Hart, I believed my father was unnecessary to me.

I returned to the hospital a few days later. He was asleep in his room, and I sat in the soft chair and watched his slow breathing. I did not want to disturb him but he always woke up soon after I arrived. He'd look at me, say my name, and I would tell him to sleep, but he rarely did. I thought there should be a presence in the room. He had always come to the hospital when I was ill and had spent weeks at my mother's side when she was hospitalized. I had known a young man, a patient of Dr. Gold, whose wife had slipped into a coma after a series of convulsions. She spent the last week of her life on life-support systems, and her husband had said: *"Call me if she changes"* and went home. I could not do that, though I felt the man was probably right. I felt everyone else was always right and hated doing "the right thing"...

My father would not eat, and when the orderly brought his supper I always encouraged him to eat just a little, but he could not do it. It was as if he were saving all his strength for something else, dying, perhaps, and he would not rouse himself for such a minor task.

In August, after he entered the convalescent home, I decided to go away for a week. I asked the nurses if I ought to go, and they told me to get away, so I left, for the beach. I gave my mother the telephone number of the hotel and told her not to call unless he died. She didn't call, but I was besieged anyway, by Annabelle, Hart' s girlfriend, who happened to be staying nearby. She was lonely and wanted company, would I accompany her to supper? Would I like to go swimming? She was bossy and demanding. She liked no restaurant, no wine, insisted on waiting two hours in a drafty bar where she had been told the food was excellent. Each morning I left my hotel room earlier in order to avoid her calls. I lay on the beach in cloudy weather, listening to music, swimming once in the morning and once in the afternoon. I did not think about my father too much...

After a week I returned to face another problem. My mother said he wanted to come home. When I walked into his room he said *"Will you give me a minute?"* and I turned around and went out. A moment later I went back in. He was propped up on two pillows, thinner than ever. His face was calm.

We talked about the beach, the news; I read the newspaper to him and he asked me about the Israeli peace accords. My mother came in with a friend who had driven her over, and we all left the room . *"All week he asked where you were,"* she said. *"But I told him where I was going,"* I answered. *"He forgot, and he's been asking about coming home."*

*"It's not a good idea"*. . .

*"We could get nurses."*

I realized it was she who wanted him to come home. He had not been asking about it at all; he knew he would die there in the Home. *"I'll talk to him about it,"* I said, and returned to his room to say goodbye. I bent over and kissed him on the forehead. *"I'll be back Tuesday,"* I said. *"And we'll talk about when you can come home."* "Okay," he said. He was in tremendous pain.

*"Do you want a shot?"* I asked. *"No. All right, just one,"* he said. I asked the nurse if he could have some morphine. *"I'll bring it right in,"* she said, and in a few minutes he had been given a shot. I watched. It was the only time I had ever seen him take any pain medication. He died the next day.

My mother and I and her best friend went to his funeral in a black Cadillac. In the back seat she cried, I cried, her friend cried. Back at the house my mother cried some more, but she managed to eat two sandwiches. And she smoked a Pall Mall.

As I wrote of his death, without too much embellishment—as if death can be embellished—I experienced a sadness which was not oppressive but which still made itself felt. What did his death have to do with *why?* I expected Dr. Gold to make a joke*: "He'll be fucking you up the ass for the rest of your life!"* (He remembered everything). Yet, why was I sad? Missed opportunities, i.e., the offer of lunch? Or a more acute reason: I would never overcome him in his life. In that sense, the comment I imagined from Dr. Gold was astute; my father's death did not mean he had gone from my mind. Hart made a poor substitute when I considered the matter. There was another reason that I did not consider: he had cheated me out of the opportunity to excise him from my mind before he died.


The day before my father died, when I visited him in the hospital, when I read the news to him, what would have happened if I had asked him if he knew how close he had come to destroying us, my mother and I? That would have been a confrontation I could never had made; I had already confronted him once, when he was shouting at my mother in the cellar while I was there, and I had picked up that ashtray and thrown it to the floor, and again, after I had left the house, when I returned to tell him and her how they had failed me, he with his betrayal and her with her passivity [as had Dora those many years ago]. These actions had not worked, and I had known they had not. If such a question had any meaning, it would have been clear that I wanted to speed him along to death; he had become a burden I could no longer deal with. I had acted the part of the good son; it seemed the proper course, but there was a history behind us that could not be fixed nor could it be brought into the present for examination. We had never been together in the present; we were only together in the past which was still with us in the present, but that past had not been brought forward; it was too late. And I had seen my father treated with cruelty and carelessness; I had seen him surrender.

After his death I found his wallet in the room—my bedroom—where he had spent the months leading up to his final hospitalization. In it I discovered a newspaper clipping. It was a quote from Pascal's *Pensees*: *"The eternal silence of these infinite spaces frightens me."*

There is no overcoming; at most, an accommodation. And no mourning of consequence. How could I mourn when his essence was embedded in me? My father already took up space in my mind; I'd have to find a comfortable chair for him in which to recline, while I went about the rest of my business. Moods come without effort; what is to be grasped, if at all, is their rhythm. Once one feels the rhythm, it may be possible to climb upon them and ride them to an uncertain future. [I was so fixated on the nature of the relation between me, my father and my mother at the time I wrote of his death that I ignored the deeper, unconscious connections that bound us together, the paradigm, the oedipal struggle, the tortured version of love and shame that accompanied our lives and sat at the table with us during every meal. I remembered eventually the nights we sat in our living room watching comedies of family life, I Love Lucy, The Honeymooners, Make Room For Daddy. I sat on the floor, my parents were on the sofa, each at separate ends. When they laughed, I turned to see that they were really laughing. If they weren't laughing, I turned to see why. *Why* was always there, but hadn't turned itself the right way, yet]. [I must have loved him fiercely, almost incestuously].

*I cannot tell what impression these memories make when they are recalled on the page and replayed through the reader's mind. It seemed important when I began, to describe accurately, that is, within the limits of my recall, allowing for but trying to avoid embellishment, for I am susceptible to copying the form and style of whomever I happen to be reading. If I should pick up, say, a Japanese novel in translation, by Soseki, for example, or Saito, who wrote The Kobe hotel, I am immediately struck by the humility with which events and emotions are written on the page. Only a Japanese writer can express self-loathing or witlessness without interfering with his telling of the story or creating in the reader a feeling of disbelief. For weeks afterward my notes—this journal, if you will—ape that kind of description. Let me switch to Lost Illusions by Balzac, and my journal becomes florid and full of rhetorical flourishes and loses all direction. I should cross out the word 'susceptible' above and insert the word 'prone'... There, I have done it.*

The position of a son encouraging a parent to continue living is so foreign to most people that one has no experience in it. One can only try to remember what was thought and felt during the conversation, but the awkwardness which is natural to any exchange between child and parent is made even worse by the shadow of death which sits at the table with us. When one believes that his father has never thought much of one—no matter that one cannot really know what any parent thinks—and yet asks that father to go on, one stumbles and judges himself harshly.

Some time after his death, I dreamed once again about my father. I was in a synagogue, about to go up to the Bima to say a Kaddish for him. Two burly men in suits were standing beside me. As I began to move toward the Bima, they held me back. It was not possible for me to have the conscious thought: "He's finally dead!" Nevertheless, the thought must have been close at hand. I was not rid of him, but I wasn't going to honor him either. It was that division which I had never closed that held me back. The argument lived.

⟫ ⟪

I am reminded now of two observations I made earlier. First, Dr. Gold's comment that when I wasn't thinking of fucking I was pretty shallow. I feel a fury now at his having said it, perhaps because he defined me, identified me when I did not want to be identified. But as I read my notes over and over it seems impossible for me not to have agreed with him immediately. Second, remembering how Hart wove his way to the back of a bus—though he was drunk- recalled Belmondo dancing down the street in *Breathless*—which Hart had surely seen—was a sign I did not understand at first. It is as if he, too, was looking for an identity, or rather, he had adopted one from the films he loved. When I entered P, I was still a watcher, [Dr. Gold did me the honor, or dishonor, of giving my behavior a name: scoptophilia], but the life around me had by then begun to change me into something else, a temporary consumer of new identities, as if I were trying on suits in a department store. I, too, had tried on Steve McQueen (I wore a turtleneck sweater and a raincoat after seeing *Bullitt*), Penelope, weaver and unraveller of a shroud, psychiatric patient, writer. Yet it seems now as if I were trying to overcome a man who was traveling the same path, the only difference being in his choice of characters to put on, legendary writer, legendary movie star, legendary anything. He was acting out a Balzacian character come to the City to make his name and fortune. I have little choice but to conclude that I wanted to be like a man, to overcome a man who was as false as I thought myself to be, who had as little depth as I myself had been told I possessed by Dr. Gold. [I wanted to love a man, a father, but the fury I had brought with me prevented me from doing so]. [I cannot deny that the fury was intended to blind me to the desire to love a man sexually].

⫸—⫷

The narrator had reached a point at which he had become sick of himself and of his constant use of the first person (as he knows Stendhal worried about the same problem). If he were bored, what might a reader—if there were a reader other than Ericksen—think? All the writer's perceptions appeared to be nothing but clichés: "Save the parents"; "the Other as a reaching out to what has been forgotten," etc. He didn't want to think about it anymore. He still believed he was an ape, a clown at heart; he could not rid himself of the memories of being bullied and teased by his so-called friends. He could not rid himself of his 'inside father' without destroying himself; nor could he murder the "outside father." He understood his own history only fitfully. He had reached an impasse, without understanding that the dead end which loomed was the beginning that all humans who think must face. He had not comprehended the most basic truth: that life occurs while chopping onions on a cutting board or standing in line at the supermarket (or the unemployment office). He had begun to feel that his map-making was a fraud, a way to avoid being human, and that he had learned, if at all, nothing that other people didn't already know. He had wanted to make a new discovery that would show the world his brilliance as a thinker, yet his efforts had come to nothing. The emptiness of this unwanted discovery—that he had failed—brought on a headache, but there were neither aspirin nor whiskey in his flat. M's was closed; there was nowhere to go. He lay down on his bed with an ashtray on his chest and smoked desultorily, glancing at each wall of his flat (as his father had done). It crossed his mind that the ashtray he was using had been made by his father, but as yet this fact had no clear meaning for him.

As he smoked, he began to look closely at the wall next to his bed. It was stuccoed, but the builder had neglected to place wire mesh between the gypsum and the stucco. Consequently, the vibrations caused by the heavy traffic outside had led to cracking and bubbling in several places. The writer observed that the wall looked like the wall next to the couch in Dr. Gold's office, the one in which Frank had punched a jagged hole which Dr. Gold had never bothered to have repaired. How like Frank, thought the writer, to reach out and destroy a thing, a wall, out of frustration with ideas. A thing, a wall, is solid. If you strike it, dust and silica fly out from it, but it maintains its essential character. Even the dust drifting down onto the couch or, in the writer's case, the bed, was composed of things, as were the cracks which radiated from the hole. Hart, the writer's friend, his platonic debater, believed Wittgenstein was right: the world was composed of facts, not things. But the writer said to himself (and, in a sense, to Hart) it is things to which he always seemed to pay attention. Things bring forth emotions and caused him to remember. People do not affect him in that way; only things do, he pondered. But, he considered, people are things, too, objects with weight and mass; I attend to them too, don't I? If so, I must be a thing, also, a human thing. He found some comfort in this thought, for it cut against the grain of a lifetime of considering himself as an outsider, a watcher, a disturbed person.

As he followed this train of thought, the sounds of the street which came through the open window seemed to bear out his reasoning. A horn blew and he thought of the parking lot below, where he had thrown the glass against the far wall which Frank had held in his trembling hand some months before [a foretaste of that to be described herein]. The memory of the glass led him to consider Lara and what he had felt for her, that, for the only time in his life he had known someone, had probed in and about the mind of another human being (as she had done to him without apparent effort). He understood that he'd have to describe that episode, too, when he could fix it securely in his mind. The cigarette he held in his hand reminded him of his father, for cigarettes, in his analytic way, stood for truth, the intake of truth, a bond he and his father had shared in lieu of speech. Cigarettes said to him "I am with you; I am standing next to you." [They also said "Kill the father whom you have brought into your soul and can only slay by slaying yourself]. And then he thought of Hart and the way they had stood on street corners smoking, facing the street without looking at one another as they took in the passing scene. Perhaps, he reasoned—for his thoughts had excited him, had pushed away some of his boredom and self-sickness—perhaps I am a thing! I am human. I am human and I am a thing. [He also remembered a quote from John Ford: *"A man rolling a cigarette is more interesting that a man saving the world."*]. The memory pleased him.

The further he went in this vein, which, he realized, was not a debate with Hart or a session with Dr. Gold, the more excited he became. He crushed his cigarette in the ashtray and lit another (perhaps to take in more truth, symbolically, or to continue his own dying before an actual truth might make itself felt) and he realized that the ashtray itself, which was made of clay, had been made by his father, who had shaped it by hand in his basement workshop. His father had taken the piece to the local art school, where he asked some students to bake it in the studio kiln. He had taken the piece home, glazed it, and asked the same students to bake it again. The angry communist had created a thing, and it was a useful thing, too. Now the writer, frightened of the sudden surge of anger he had just felt, jumped out of bed and walked to the refrigerator, found a few slices of processed cheese, ate them hungrily, leaned over the sink to gulp down some water, and lay back in bed, still hungry, thinking to himself, If I'm a thing, all people are things, the corollary being, if

I am a thing, I am not only an ape. He wanted to giggle, but he followed his line of thought. He might honor human things (still feeling the pang of his recent silliness). If an ape or a clown can be a silly thing, why cannot he? He ought to try on the persona [without a mask] (he did not use that word, but he knew what he meant).

With yet another cigarette, he considered how a thing exists in itself; it draws—possibly- the attention of all other things to it, just as they, in turn, draw it to themselves. He pondered. I can't call things "themselves," can I? Then, "Why not? Can I not be human and a thing as well?" He began to grow terribly tired then, managed barely to crush out his cigarette in that ashtray before he was asleep. He had not even switched off the lamp on the night table behind the bed.

When he awoke it was morning and rain pelted the windows. His first thought was one of embarrassment at the line of thought he had followed before falling asleep. He allowed the embarrassment to remain while he rubbed the sleep from his eyes. When he felt he could see clearly, he looked around the flat. The walls were still there. The linoleum tile on the floor remained, scuffed as ever. The refrigerator continued to make its usual noises. His hands grasped the quilt, which had slipped down over his knees during the night, and he pulled it up to his neck, as his mother had done for him when he was a child. He fell back to sleep thinking of nothing, or, for an instant, pebbles in a stream, ice cold spring water flowing over the pebbles as he stepped gingerly from flat rock to flat rock. Afraid still of anger, afraid of elation, afraid of fear, he slept. He wondered, before sleep overtook him, whether he might just be working toward another *persona*, but he was truly exhausted and that thought sank below consciousness before he could parse it further. He suspected that the idea of *thingness* was another evasion, another way to explain away his essential immobility. Before he could consider the idea, he was asleep.

*[Annotation]:*

*As I moved like a caterpillar toward apprehension of that inner argument which was always taking place, my anger began to make itself apparent as I viewed it from outside, from Dr. Gold's view, which I was taking on as my own. I could not, however, scream at him, for I believed it would destroy him. He waited, with frustration, to see how I would resolve this business. One day when I was angrily complaining about some slight my father had directed at me years before, Dr. Gold suggested that I go out to the street and punch the first person I saw. Of course I could not do that, as he knew; he also knew I could not redirect my rage toward him. It was one of several attempts to nudge me toward standing outside myself, which took months, if not years to accomplish. I could not trust myself or him to adopt that outside view. Nevertheless, the primary struggle was becoming clear; what remained was my inability to describe it in words.*

⸭⸭⸭ ⸭⸭⸭

It seemed as if my dreams and my reality had a symbiotic relationship. Just as a bird might spend its life on an elephant's back, nourishing itself on the parasites and insects which might otherwise sicken the elephant, while the elephant, in turn, provides a feeding ground for the bird, which no longer has to compete for its sustenance with the other birds in its environment, I saw that my dreams were feeding off my reality by becoming clearer as I continued to consider my past... At the same time, my reality was taking comfort from my dreams, as the dreams sucked the past from my mind and placed it in front of me where I could examine it with more clarity. In a sense, my dreams were intruding into my reality, not as enemies but as companions. Of course, it could easily be perceived in exactly the opposite way. My reality was sucking comprehension from my dreams by making the present clearer and, surprisingly, somewhat more enjoyable.

The idea of this symbiosis continued to puzzle me, however. I was uncertain what to make of it. The very idea that I had to make something of it may have been the most puzzling aspect. I was groping toward a way of being that cut completely across the concept of identity, but I was also on the middle way, rather only part way through a trek of which I could see neither the beginning nor the end. [As long as my father lived, the idea of *thingness* would not have occurred to me].

It was already late afternoon when I walked one day through the Central District all the way to the bridge over the Western River near the University. The sun was still fairly high in the Western sky, and as I crossed from one street to another, it left me first in brilliance, then in shadow [as did that photograph]. Eventually, I came to the flat grassy swath near the bridge, under whose shadow sat a concrete block which must have been a platform when passenger trains rode over the tracks. The block had, at one time, a roof, which was now gone, probably because it had been fashioned of tin and had been stolen by metal thieves, but from each corner still rose rusted steel beams, now bent and twisted as if they had been wrenched out of shape by a giant hand twirling nothing weightier than a soda straw. Around the concrete block lay almost an acre of weeds and patches of sand, with small sections of grass that had not been cut for many years. The entire space was still owned by the railroad which maintained the track, which ran parallel to the River, for its freight hauling. I knew the railroad was in bankruptcy and was not going to spend any time or money on the land abutting the tracks. As I climbed the concrete steps which had been hewn out of one side of the block, I could see the River gently lapping against the large stones which formed the abutment on the Western side. The River was calm and was almost never roiled by ship or boat traffic.

Dr. Gold had said *"Take your ideas from your environment,"* yet I would not have paid much attention to those words if they had not been spoken in the weeks before his death, but we tend to remember deaths by recalling first the weeks which led up to them, perhaps as a way of that death somehow fitting more clearly in the ongoing stream of events, thereby lessening its impact as well. Now, I sat on the block and looked up at the twisted beams and the sandy patches surrounding it, and I recalled another dream I had had when I first began to talk to Dr. Gold but had, I thought, never related to him.

In a way with which I had become familiar, the dream slipped away from me immediately, probably because of its importance. tried to recall it for a moment but I soon gave up. I continued to sit, however, and thoughts about P itself began to arise. P had been a center of commerce once; now its manufacturing plants were almost all abandoned. Hats, locomotives, menswear, steel, freighters and warships, all of these things, real objects with weight and meaning and usefulness, had been made here and sent all over the world. The Central District had been encircled by manufacturing plants, which now sat empty, with smashed windows and crumbling brick, their walls covered with graffiti, surrounded by the same swaths of sand and weeds in which I now sat.

Hart and I had spoken of this deterioration often as we walked through the Central District. We knew that most of the area through which we often strolled had burned to the ground at one time or another. In the Nineteenth Century riots had occurred, with loss of life and near-anarchy. Religious riots, workingmen's riots, strikes, all had contributed to the swirl, the tearing down and rebuilding of P. Explosions, ships sinking in the Eastern River, all shaped the history of P. We believed it been no different in Athens, a city thousands of years old...

Yet P remained. Thinking of it, I wondered if, as so many cities had done, whether there was another way I might consider my constant throwing off one identity after another, not as a way of hiding, but as a way of regenerating. Perhaps the dream which had come and gone so quickly (it came back later, it was the auto parts dream again, which I had presented to Dr. Gold) was a wish to be regenerated, to be put back together, even with rusted parts, to have energy to rise out of the desert in which the parts were half-buried. [It was as if the desert in the dream and the parts buried in sand were the ruins of an ancient city which might, with effort, be uncovered by archeologists who would then unearth its history, too]. It seemed that P remained alive not by any conscious effort, but because something emanating from its citizens in their struggle to live and work was determined to keep going. If I were a citizen of P, might I not be doing, unconsciously, the same thing, not so much because I was dissatisfied with how I saw myself, but because I simply wished to stay alive. It was my corporeal body that was pushing me along, despite my fear, my self-loathing, my misperceptions. I turned around to look once again at those twisted steel beams. They were certainly a sign of decay, with their oxidized surfaces rusting in the setting sun; but they were also strong and unyielding to the elements at their core. Only their surfaces were ugly; but the sun shone on them just as it did on the grass, the skyscrapers I could see to the East, and the University students going about their business across the River. I felt a desire to connect with all of these things, because I, too, was a thing. I sat on the surface of the world as securely as a building or a mountain. From where I sat, the entire universe stretched out; the space I occupied was equal to any other space, from the point of view of that universe...

I had walked to one of the few areas in the City in which the difference between concrete and nature, between what the City looked like now and what it might have appeared to be long ago, had narrowed over the years, as parts of it reverted to their earlier form. Dirt, weeds, scattered clumps of grass, a building disassembling itself through snow and storm and summer's interminable heat.

The evening had become dusky; a few stars glimmered, the early moonlight cast the twisted beams in shadows that lay horizontally across the weeds. I happened to cast my eyes on a rock near the base of the block which seemed somehow out of place, bigger than the stones which lay scattered here and there among the weeds. I bent down and peered at it; it seemed to have been ground into the sandy gravel so that only its top third was visible. It was less than a foot from one corner of the block. I wondered how it had come to be in that particular spot. Without thinking, I reached down and grasped it with one hand. It was firmly embedded, and I had to use both hands to get a grip on its irregular surface. Finally it gave way and I knelt looking at the base of the hole I had unearthed. An object glittered in the moonlight. With one hand I reached in, pulled it out and held it aloft to capture that moonlight. It was a toy sheriff's badge, made of plastic but painted in a shiny silver. I understood then why the rock had been tamped down so strongly: it was a marker. Some child, probably a young boy, and his father-or so I imagined-had placed the rock over it so they could find it again. I imagined the boy returning to this spot only to find the badge gone, and a feeling of sadness enveloped me. I had thought to take the badge, more or less as a souvenir, a reminder of the day, when the sun, the moon and my inchoate mind had all met at this place, but now I felt like a thief stealing a memory from someone whom I could only imagine. After a moment's reflection I pulled my shirttail out from under my belt and wiped the badge clean as best I could, as if I were cleaning my eyeglasses. I found some unused Kleenex in my pockets and wrapped the badge. I placed it back in the hole and put the rock over it. When I had pushed the rock down as much as I could with my hands, I stood up and put my left foot on it, grinding it deeper, twisting my ankle back and forth (That is, I hid it and crushed it downward at the same time). When it seemed to be set the way I had found it, I stepped back and looked around. I saw no one; no one had seen me. I walked away quickly, my mind whirling…

Instead of walking back through the Central District I decided to cross the bridge to the University campus. There, life thrived, and I wanted to be a part of it, even if I were only a mote of dust flitting down the sidewalk, passing through a beam of light from a streetlamp. When I reached the other side of the bridge I stopped to glance at the window of a bookstore. The theme of the week happened to be philosophy, and there were several books on display by famous thinkers. Two of them caught my attention. One was titled "What is Meaning?" I paid no attention to the title of the second, but it was the author's surname that I recognized: it was the same as my own. I had heard of him but had never seen one of his books. He was, as far as I could tell, the only person in the history of time with my surname who had ever attained recognition. I had never met him and did not want to, for there was certainly nothing I could say to him that I thought he would not already know.

## *[Annotation]:*

*It has just occurred to me that the description of the badge found in the dirt is somehow parallel to the description of the auto parts dream. In the former, **I put the badge back in the dirt and cover it up again! It is as if I am letting the dream go back to wherever it came from, because I have the strength to do that.** And the phrase I used when I had this thought was that "I was putting the dream back to bed"! Back to the childhood of my past. Also, I was allowing the child who had put the badge in the dirt—with his father, I presumed—to return to his childhood as he pleased, if ever he pleased, perhaps with his father, I wondered, in a father-son relation that I had not had, discovering their past together. I had acted generously. It seemed that there were other paradigms I might have considered, had I been able. It was an act of self-creation at the same time, paradoxically bringing my own past up to the present, thereby changing that past and changing my future. Perhaps that is why, when I looked in the window of the bookstore and saw a book on display by an author with my last name, I felt no envy. Again, I would not have understood this idea if my father were still alive.*

At some point during my walk, as I recrossed the bridge, I think it was, I experienced that anxiety which, though I cannot say it was vague, was nevertheless somehow unable to break through and make itself fully felt. It was as if my mind had decided to tell me that the world was still a dreadful place and I would never be comfortable in it. A bit farther on, though, for an equally unknown reason, what came to my mind were two events I have mentioned before. One was the thunderstorm I had watched under an awning with the older boys who had made my young life miserable with their teasing and bullying. I recalled the silence all of us maintained during the fierce lightning and roar of thunder. Another was the feeling of separation from the world I had felt while on the bus going to my army physical after I had received my draft notice. It occurred to me that finding that sheriff's badge in the dirt near the railroad tracks might have something to do with why I was recalling these two events, but I could not work out in my mind the exact connection. But the surprising recall of these events led me to consider them in greater detail, hindsight, perhaps. I asked myself about the sensations which had accompanied those events and discovered that they had been, in a sense, grounding forces, not as unpleasant as I had thought or wanted to think because of the situations I was in then. Instead, it seemed to me that I had on those two occasions been a grownup, an adult considering the world and his place in it. Also, those events did not stop time, as Hart and I wanted; rather, I had stepped out of time. I was being! Reconsidering those sensations as somehow completely human and mindful—mindful is the closest word I can use—almost seemed to let stagnant air out of my body. It was as if I was experiencing the same sensations as I had then, but with a sharper memory and a measure of distance which allowed me to appraise them differently. I had been *alive* then, and I was alive now. When I put that badge back under the rock, I was a grownup! [I had even ground the rock into the dirt as I had imagined the boy's father having done]. [the boy's father and I both wanted the boy to remember!]. The discovery of this continuity gave me comfort. Moreover, I saw that I was able to comfort myself. *As I walked back to my room I began to hum a tune, which took me a while to recognize: it was only a few bars of Tchaikovski's violin concerto, which I had been listening to on my phonograph recently. I understood that I had been humming it for several blocks before it made itself fully conscious. I seemed to be comforting myself with those few bars, too, and that led me to another discovery— for as long as I could remember I had had melodies in my head which came and went seemingly without reason. I had never bothered to ask myself why a particular melody appeared at a specific time, until this instance.* **The melodies comforted me! When I needed to be rocked, cradled, swaddled, they appeared.** *Had my mother sung to me?* [Melodies became the internal comfort object]. I had not recognized them as such until, probably out of a certain necessity (which they recognized before I did) they began to make themselves available to my consciousness insistently). **I had rediscovered my mother.** Shortly before Dr. Gold died, another dream may have foreshadowed this discovery. *I dreamed of a tall stele in a cemetery.* When I awoke I thought: *Mother!*[24] *I wonder if I had to get rid of father, at least to come to terms with him, in order to find mother again. [An internal struggle begins as a unity; only when its parts begin to separate is it possible to examine each separately].*

What is *groundedness* but an apprehension of one's history? It is not a matter of knowing one is alive, but of grasping the wholeness of that life from birth to the present. And wholeness is a misnomer; what must be apprehended is broken and spiraling forward constantly; what is sought is a way to grasp what is always moving and reconstituting itself. There were themes which ran through my mind, sometimes for a week, other times for a day, intermittently at best, so I was not aware of them for long periods. I had to return to the journal I had kept while I lived in P to see if I could determine what they might have been. One might think that one always knows what one is thinking, but the reverse

---

24  A poem by Charles Reznikoff about his mother is titled "Stele."

is more accurate. A thought might occur in passing, only to recur a few days, a week later. At each time, one pays little attention; it is only one thought among many, and one is working or loving or falling asleep. Only when one begins to look for the theme does it appear, and then in fragmented form. Of course, the idea of platonic friendship was one theme; the myth of triangulation, of recreating a constellation of an ill family with groups of others with whom one associates, was another. But these themes which I identify now did not make themselves apparent until I made the effort to find them. I have put the cart before the horse by identifying them at the beginning, perhaps because I do not want to lose sight of them after struggling with difficulty to find them. There was never any certainty that I would listen to my own stream of thought and sift them from the thousands of thoughts that occur every hour of every day. Once found, they may yet offer no answer to that "why" I spoke of.

What was that sense experienced during the thunderstorm that seems to important, so valuable now, but which spoke only mystery as it occurred? Was it only a sense that life, true life, though undefinable to a ten-year old child, actually existed with a fullness that might be experienced? Or to be fair, a sense that a fullness had already been lost, which could only be recaptured by chance, without foreknowledge, as if to remind me of what had already gone, a kind of comfort on earth, a belonging without fear, as if the sky opened and spoke to me the words "you're on your own, don't be afraid." [As soon as we emerge from the womb life changes from 'perhaps' to 'impossibility', and all we have for 'perhaps' is our imagination. The will to succeed eventually fails to bring us back to 'perhaps'. We are offered a glimpse, occasionally, when we are making supper or taking a walk, but the glimpse comes from nowhere we know. There is a 'nowhere'; that's all we know, and it cannot be searched for.] It teases us [Ah, Lara!]. Later we die, thankful for the teasing]. [*The idea of thingness can also be considered with the idea of chance, that is, the possibility of recognition by another human being. If possibility exists, my yearning, though vague, justifies its own strength and is not meaningless. It accepts reality*].

I am not so much angry at my father now as I am ashamed of him and of myself for having, in my case, an education which I feel is inferior and for which I blame him. I have written down this observation after reading part of The Interpretation of Dreams. While I was reading I was thinking that I do not have enough knowledge to interpret my own dreams or anyone else's, and that led me to thinking about my lack of a classical education and the impact of that lack on my writing. I cannot use but a few classical allusions nor can I create parallels between modern people and ancient gods, etc. My success in law has not dissipated that shame; it has always been on my mind, sometimes clearly, other times vaguely. With Dr. Gold I talked about the anger I felt but not about the shame I felt for both of us; that was my father's unwitting legacy, made more forceful by my observation that my male cousins on my father's side had all attended private schools and, later, Ivy League universities or small colleges with excellent reputations. [My desire to have my son attend good schools and universities was driven by more than love, more than wanting him to have an excellent education; it was a means for avenging myself on my father, working off my own shame by ensuring that he would not have to undergo the same experience].

**[Annotation]:**

*Yet another example of a kind of repetition, i.e., placing myself in a position between two families, neither of which I believed I belonged to.*

My father was five feet four inches tall; he was completely bald at thirty; he blamed his baldness on his barber's use of Kreml. He dressed every day in a shirt and tie, tucking the tie in between the third and fourth buttons of his shirt, as he had done during his brief time in the Army. I shave and see his face in the mirror, as I also see the earlobes of one of those cousins who had an excellent education, and the broken nose of an uncle who was a longshoreman. I think often with affection of those cousins with their excellent educations but hardly at all of the longshoreman who was one of my mother's brothers; yet if I am ashamed of my father and of myself why not think more of my mother's family? I have always defined them as schleppers, eastern Europeans with their crassness and unknowingness. I wanted little to do with them; it would sanction my shame to spend time with them. [But I belonged with them, too, and shared the qualities they possessed]. I cannot throw off the cloak of my arrogance; sooner or later I suppose I will, later rather than sooner would be better. He could have made more of himself, my father could; he was determined not to. He shouldn't have taken me down with him [Another issue encompassed by the dream]. I'll have to reason out the connection between penises and shame before I'm through; that's for certain. It's what happens when I read Freud. One thing is clear: it is useless to be angry at a father whose qualities I have; nor is it useful to be self-loathing for the same reason. Let me stand still for a while; let me be *inbetween without shame!*

## *[Annotation]:*

*What is it like to be comfortable on earth? [I see by the above notes that I am beginning to consider my life as part of a larger community, of not only mother and father but the aunts, uncles, cousins on both sides of my family.*

It is the filling in of the gaps that is important. We remember events but not the emotions or the circumstances which surround them. It is these latter things that are the missing pieces. If they are not recovered, our memories remain as fragmented as pieces of a water glass dropped from a table onto a tile floor. The shards spread out and end up under cabinets or out the door. Recreating the glass becomes difficult; the largest piece may never be found.

And as soon as you begin to examine the past you simultaneously object to the process. Aren't you satisfied with your life as it is? Have you accomplished enough? Have you formed attachments with others? Each of these questions has more than one answer and you must choose among those answers given the risk that you may give up the whole business. What urges you on is the sense that you have never been comfortable on earth and you have never made an accurate statement about yourself to anyone. You have always lied, not out of concern for propriety but out of fear of self-discovery. You cannot help but go ahead. ***Love lies in the accuracy of self—description.***

These missing pieces are the actions I take now, smoking, nervous tics (father drumming his fingers on the arm of the chair in which he sat when he made a decision), sadness in brief bursts, the ways I relate to friends (spatial shapes, triangles), fear of obligation–father always acted on behalf of others with rancor, though he did the acts anyway. Are these repetitive acts signs pointing to what is missing? Taking their place in the present as a way of finding that past in the present? And do we not attend to this action because the mind itself is always changing its configuration? I look for what is missing and what was missed, and it may be a giant hole, an abyss, with nothing at the bottom but more nothing. Perhaps discovering that lack is also a discovery of what surrounded the lack, the conundrum of any life in which a body resides. [the absence that is also a presence].

*When I had almost finished these notes I took* Ghosts *from my bookshelf. On the frontispage I had penciled a note to myself: "Are these repetitive acts pointing toward what is missing, or are* they *what is missing, taking their place in the present as a way of bringing the past forward, as if one's mind says to one "I challenge you to pay attention to me, I can teach you to put some of the shards back together." I had considered triangulation as* discovery! *Repetition, of course, did not work; it was a failure; but in an almost perverse way it reversed a position I had long held, i.e. 'success is failure', for its failure was, in its own way, a success, for it washed away a fog I had cherished, but left me as a person who did not fit.*

*I have said that I stole the idea of 'thingness', but I see that it was not by chance that I did. Considering myself as a thing or an it was a way of considering myself as a unitary being. Every thing, every human, is in a sense a unit, a single object which may capture someone's -another thing's—attention. Of all the ways one might try to describe identity, thingness is one that cannot be discarded for another if one does not feel comfortable with it as a definition.*

The catharsis in Dr. Gold's office was insufficient because I was unable to put the recalled experience into words. [Because I had no words at the time of the original event!]. There was no risk, no learning involved, only a set of circumstances. It is **the risk and the after-reflection** that matters!

## *[Annotation]:*

*It is becoming clear that the novel I thought I had written was the beginning of a stuttering, stumbling attempt to apprehend an internal conflict. I read these notes and see how fright and determination fought one another, each becoming stronger as I staggered quite unwillingly toward a grasp of how my mind worked.*

*My life in P continued while I spoke to Dr. Gold: [I learned that Hart had been right about why I had come to the City; I doubt, though, that he ever dove into the infantile sea that was driving me. Meanwhile, I became, with that mixture of fear and determination, a person who (sometimes) took action . . . [Of course, becoming through action = reification, a Marxist conception, a rallying cry!] . . . And the action I took was sexual contact, not 'looking'.]*

⫸— ⫷

I climbed the steps of a brownstone in the Central District not far from R Park... In the pocket of my raincoat was a rolled up Daily *News*, which I intended to present to my hostess as a kind of gift... I was about to experience my first purchased encounter with a woman (I may also characterize it as a lesson in the conflict between ethics and desire, though I had ethics only on the surface and my desire was frozen)... That is, I was going to become a participant rather than an observer... Hart and Ericksen had become concerned at how isolated I had become... Except for work, I hardly left my flat... Even then, I went only as far as M's, directly across the street... I had begun to buy whiskey by the bottle in order to avoid going out... There were dust balls under my bed as big as tumbleweeds... When I came home from work I immediately fell into bed and remained there until late in the evening, exhausted... My assignation had been arranged by my friends, and I did not know how to avoid it... Thus, the brownstone...

On the second-floor landing I came face to face with a full-length mirror... For a moment I was given back to myself... I looked even younger than my youngish years... I did not know it would be months more before I met a woman who was not a call girl... I did not see an ape in the glass, but a frightened young man... I had never admitted to Hart or Ericksen that I had little sexual experience (the word 'little' is an exaggeration)... Yet I intended to give Zola (she had a *nom de travaille* which I will not repeat) the *News* in the same fashion as guests who bring a bottle of wine, as a gift of entree... I knew nothing, absolutely nothing... But as I walked to Zola's, into my head sprang the vision of a calling card delivered by a butler into the parlor of a British manor on a silver plate (called a salver, I believe) which I must have seen in a movie... Putting my own strangled twist on that image, I bought a newspaper at a corner stand to present to her... Figuratively speaking, its function was similar to that of the broomsticks that soldiers in the War were shoving into tunnels to see if they were booby-trapped... I carried with me the form, the image of a penis in that rolled-up newspaper, almost as if I needed the symbol if the reality of the assignation turned out to be unpleasant or unnerving...

Zola's flat was at the rear of the third floor... Each floor had a long corridor running from front to back, with a solid wooden table along the wall where the mail for the floor's residents was placed... On each table sat a forlorn lamp atop an age-dimmed doily... At the second-floor landing I met another full—length mirror, and again I paused to stare at my reflection... I was excited, breathless... My raincoat, corduroy pants, wool sweater, seemed to me to be a costume for a role in a play for which I had not rehearsed... I did not see the potential murderer that Lara would see... My mind was racing down the corridor, expectant, numb... Just then, a door somewhere above me clicked shut and a man brushed by me and descended the stairs... He was my nightmare, all right... I got a good look at him, too... I, who usually forgot a man's appearance within seconds... My heightened awareness left him as an eidetic image upon my senses... A fine suit girding but not quite disguising a fat belly... Teeth like little mesas gleaming as if in sunlight... A red—stoned ring on his little finger... He was just the kind of man I had imagined would enter the elevator as I stepped out onto my call girl's floor... I immediately turned around to watch him descend the stair, and, as soon as he was out the door, I, too, fled the brownstone, found a diner, ordered coffee, lit a cigarette, sat there with my chest pounding...

People came and went, dishes clattered... Smoke rose... Through it all the man's fat face remained a foot above the seat rest opposite me... Until what I wanted began to change him, ever so slightly at first... The ovals of his cheeks sharpened... Cloth transformed itself from cotton-blend to pinstriped wool... The clear greed I thought I had seen on his face was now sorrow... I thought then (how easily we comfort ourselves when we have true need of it) of Frederick March and Kim Novak in Paddy Chayefsky's *Middle of the Night*, the middle-aged widowed dress manufacturer and his abused young secretary... The image was like a soothing voice saying *"Go back... Go back..."*

This time I bolted past the mirror, and Zola opened the door to my timid knock… She wore the first peignoir I had ever seen, sheer black, with only panties underneath… Her breasts appeared small, but her nipples were taut… Except for my mother's breasts, and places such as the Nude Dancers ,I had never seen a woman's bosom in the flesh…

*"… You must be…?"*

*"And you're…?"*

*"Come in, come in… I knew you were coming… Let me look at you… My, you're handsome…"*

I pulled the *News* from my pocket, but the words of greeting I had planned caught in my throat… She was taller than I was, blonde but with black roots… She appeared to be in her late thirties… All I could think was *How will I do?*…

*"… Tongue-tied, eh?… Well, take off your coat… Is that today's News?… Here, I'll take a look while you get acclimated…"*

That last word-*acclimated*-was so unsettling I could hardly move… To me it meant there was weather in that apartment, a warm wave I might thaw in, letting the salt in which I had been preserved dissolve in sliding rivulets… Slowly I removed my coat and laid it on the bay window sill… Zola sat in a chair, with the paper on her lap… Outside, passers-by must have been striding briskly along the pavement, streetcars were gliding by… The day was gray with the pallor of late afternoon, the street lamps not yet lit…

*"Should I sit down?,"* I asked…

Zola suddenly jumped out of her chair and threw the paper to the floor… *"Be with you in a 'sec,"* she said… *"Take off your shoes… get comfortable"*… I looked around, searching for evidence that this was a room where sin occurred, but I saw nothing out of the ordinary… A few chairs, a half-made bed, an open closet where several dresses covered with dry cleaner's cellophane hung…

*"Do you live here?,"* I asked…

*"No… I have another place near R Park… This is just for work…"*

I was staring at the open closet... *"Oh, you mean those!... A friend gives them to me... Are you ready, by the way?... Get in bed, I'll be right there..."*

I began to undress, slowly, while Zola went into the bathroom... She hung the peignoir on a hook and removed her panties... I wanted time to move almost with reluctance, though, as I recall the scene, I am not sure why... Perhaps it was nothing more than a middle-class desire to preserve capital... As I pulled off my socks I saw her bend over the toilet and swab herself with Listerine... At that moment I was a voyeur as well as an actor, come to see as well as do .

Oh! What a person she was!... Gentle, matter—of—fact, a psychiatrist of touch... On the bed we fumbled... It was awkward and it made her awkward, too, for a moment... Her hands gently rubbed my back above my shoulder blades... Never before had I been a lover!... I thought of the man with the teeth like mesas... He probably had not even been here... I needed to think that as I changed from desirer to coveter... Well, it was over like *that!*... I had gotten inside her, but barely... A silent howl of self-derision rose in me and subsided just as quickly...

That was my only crescendo of feeling...

I did not know what to do, then... I lay next to Zola, wishing only that I had more money... *This takes money*, I thought... *I'll have to get it*... I felt its lack more acutely than I judged my performance...

Dressed again, I watched her go to the toilet... This time, she sat, juices seeping downward, and swabbed herself again with a washcloth...

*"Where shall I leave this?"* I asked, holding some bills up... I wished I had hundreds of them...

*"On the table there, under the ashtray,"* Zola said... She wore the peignoir again... She sat down in the chair and picked up the *News*... I picked up my coat, wishing she would thank me for the paper... It seemed important to have given her something... But she was lighting a cigarette and noticed nothing... There was no reason why she should... Her telephone had not rung during

my stay; I noticed then she had turned it off with a switch... She realized it, too, because she noticed me staring at it and turned it back on... Immediately, it rang and she picked up the receiver... *"Oh, hi!"*... And I took my place in line, neither first nor last... I waved good-bye, and let myself out... She was laughing with her caller...

On the landing I looked in the mirror and saw the same youngish man who had climbed the stairs a half hour before... *I'll be back*, I swore... I immediately walked over to a branch of the City library and spent a half hour mindlessly browsing the shelves... A tingling in my groin remained with me even as I put distance between the act and the present... I wondered if I smelt different or if anyone might notice something about me that was different than it had been an hour ago... *Books!*, I thought... *Books will save me."*... In the Architecture section I found a book on the architecture of the homes in P, Colonial, Georgian, Art Deco... One of the photographs in the book was of a four-story brownstone similar to the one I had just left... The house in the book—I should call it a mansion rather than a house—had belonged to the _____'s, a Nineteenth Century baron and his family; it was now a preserved historic landmark near R. Park. I wondered whether a rich man had owned the building in which I had made my assignation. Somehow I began to convince myself as I read that I had undergone a kind of historical experience, not in the sense of my own history but in that of the City. If a rich man's home could become a whorehouse a hundred years after he had lived in it, was I not now a small token in the historical fare box of P. This thought was as exciting to me as that of the sexual experience I had just had. But when, after another half hour, I wandered out and through R Park, I remembered only two things with lucidity: how I had lain my coat on the window sill—my only natural and unawkward act; and Zola swabbing her crotch... Two actions so perfectly human that they were the distillation of familiarity with other humans... These two images seemed to be an accurate measure of the gulf between Zola and I; yet I would remember them and would use them... They formed the corners of a template I was creating in my mind, even if I believed that, as to the latter image, I should not have seen it…

Later I described the entire experience for Dr. Gold… I waited for him to comment on it, knowing that no matter what he might say, I would hate it… He was prescient… *"Some learn to fuck… And some fuck to learn"*…

*And another: [Finally, Lara!] .*

*R Park lies on the Southwestern edge of the Central District. Set on two square blocks surrounded by tall apartment buildings, it is one of four parks laid out by the founding father of P. The other three parks have deteriorated because the neighborhoods in which they lie have become slums and the City spends little on their upkeep beyond a few plantings of seedlings, but R Park has remained well-kept. Every year its grass is resodded and its statuary rebronzed. For many years the horticultural society tagged its several varieties of trees, from ash to willow. In the Spring the sun rises directly over its Eastern rim and arcs across the Park all day until, around six thirty, it disappears behind the apartment buildings on the Western side. Blue and pink azaleas bloom along all four sides. The park's design, consisting of a wide, oval path inside its rectangular borders and intersecting paths from each corner which meet at the fountain in the center, was meant to take full advantage of the shade offered by the trees and neighboring buildings. I came there often when I first entered P, to sit and smoke and watch human beings being what they were; when I began to go to Lara's flat, I would stop there on my way over to prepare myself. It was one of the few places that one could still hear the mournful blare of freight engines as they pulled long trains across the City through the cuts built by the railroad. Sometimes I thought, as I watched, that if I could describe R park accurately, I might think of myself as a writer.*

I lay prone on my linoleum floor, smoking, again listening to the sounds of the street through my open windows, trying to decide the exact moment when I would sit up, pack my gear and move on to M's. Someone rang my bell, and when I opened the door and peered down the spiraling steps, I saw it was Frank, come to pay me a call, Frank, whose girlfriend, the (in my mind) fabulous Lara, I had once usurped (though the force used was negligible) and for whose loss Frank still deemed me blameworthy. Frank was muscular and bright, spoke cautiously as if he were checking every word against an internal Thesaurus. The many acid trips which had brought him to Dr. Gold had left his face unlined and youthful, but had also caused his skin to sag, to look as if he had hurriedly put on his face as he left his flat and had not got it to fit quite right. I let him in, offered him my one good chair (*that chair!*) and offered him something to drink. I hoped he would not throw the glass, as I could not afford another television set. That I gave him a glass instead of a paper cup may be a sign of trust the origin of which I cannot understand.

Except for a few words of greeting, he said nothing. he seemed to be staring at the wall behind me. I tried to read his expression, but, as always, that led me only to fear. We lit cigarettes and imagined entire conversations, rewriting our brief, shared history. Silent myself, I waited for him to speak, meanwhile trying to remember that history and asking myself why I might yet have to pay for it.

To be in Frank's presence was to be close to menace, for he did not know how strong he could be in frenzy. He was known for having tried to uproot a Sycamore tree with his bare hands, on the University campus. His gentleness— when it came upon him, told one nothing because it did not seem to come from within. It was a behavior separated from its generating source, one more chunk he had split off from his center. It, too, like his rage, orbited in some arc whose precise calculus was unknowable, as was the time of its appearance. He and his qualities were like so many unruly comets. How amazing that a person rings one's doorbell after six months and one merely lets him come in without a word, though he may have returned for the sole purpose of destroying one's flat.

That word: *usurped.* It was the wrong word. *Luck* was more appropriate. Or, perhaps, *unluck,* if there is such a word. I had believed I was simply the only man in P. who could look into Lara's heart and divine that it was clear and good. That belief is the kind that occurs to one when one has lain alone in one's flat for days or months until, suddenly, a woman pays attention, even fleeting attention. Before one knows it, one thinks he is the answer to that woman's prayers; one has already assumed that she has prayers. Other men— and they hung about her like gnats, a cloud so thick it obscured her vision (and mine)—understood not a thing. They wanted only to sleep with her, or to rest their heads for a time on her bosom. She could have killed people, slit their throats, actually, and yet I would have marvelled at what potential she had for being *herself.* That was the curse I carried: to be able to divine something of value in only one other person, who cared nothing for my opinion. That was the only time it had ever happened to me.

I had just moved into my flat, but every evening, as dusk fell, the sharp blaring sounds of the street drew me out, even if I had just returned from M's. I did not want to remain inside staring at the furniture, all of which I had brought with me from my parents' house. A glance at the bed in which I had lain many evenings listening to my father's curses curl upward from the basement through the heating ducts finally drove me outside. I packed up my money, cigarettes and keys and left the flat, thinking I would visit Lara and Frank at Lara's apartment. (I differentiate between a *flat* and an *apartment.* She had two rooms and a kitchen on a well—to—do street). She and Frank had invited me often since I had come to the City; her apartment was already a place of pleasant memories for me. Often we sat on the floor and listened to records; more often we talked and analyzed our neuroses and those of the crowd at Dr. Gold's. Not five minutes later, in R Park, I passed Frank, sitting on a bench. I had known him first from Dr. Gold's, where his reputation was already made; when he had moved in with Lara, taking his place as her man of the month, I had been puzzled at the combination, but I had not understood then the choices Lara made or the reasons behind them. Now, he smoked, one leg folded over the other, his cigarette between the second and third fingers of his left hand. Perhaps I had seen Eric von Stroheim hold a cigarette that way in a film, but I cannot be sure. I might have thought: how seriously we take ourselves when we are psychotic. Instead, I approached him, sat gingerly on the bench, and asked for a light.

We smoked while the sun set over the apartment buildings on the West side of the Park. A few brilliant bursts of light shot through the leaves which were just blossoming on the trees, their thick trunks dappled where children had torn off strips of bark. As dusk fell, Frank leaned over and pinned me to the bench with those serious, contracted eyes behind which I saw frenzy.

*"I'm going to the movies to see 'I Am Curious Yellow',"* Frank said. *"I hear it's pretty sexy; come with me, won't you?"* He rolled his eyes and screwed up his face in an approximation of a leer, but he was such a serious fellow generally that it did not work. I was too shy to comment on the movie, but I was not going anyway. I would not admit to Frank that I could not see a movie like that with others; I would have to go alone, if at all. If I were going to see it, I needed to be unfettered by the need to wonder about what my companion was thinking and what I might think about that...

*"I'd rather go over to Lara's and talk,"* I said. *"You'll be back later, won't you?"* But he had already leapt up and disappeared into the darkness. I did not see him again for six months. [I had never had a woman *offered* to me before, though it is possible that there was a homoerotic element to the gift; if I'd have gone to the film with Frank, we'd have watched people fucking together, as two brothers might be watching a primal scene. I did not want a brother, which may have made all the difference].

That evening at Lara's all we did was talk and sing childhood songs we both seemed to know though we had gone to schools miles apart. I remember not a word of what we spoke—though I am sure I told her of my father's murmurings and the loneliness of every room in my parents' home—it is the *feeling* I recall, that I have never felt since. I had never been seduced before, nor did I understand that Lara seduced me merely by being herself. The seduction brought with it a terrible fear that she would leave me (she did) and another quality I did not expect, the realization that I *knew* her in a way I was unable to know myself. That was a realization she *permitted* me to experience.

A moment came, around midnight, when we realized Frank was not coming back. I did not understand it, then, but I believe he meant for me to go to the movie with him so we could watch it together as he transferred to me his magical power to fuck Lara. [I had not thought through what I have annotated before]. Instead, I sat next to Lara on her sofa, and, when we had run out of songs to sing and peace hovered over our heads, she leaned forward and unbuttoned her blouse, starting at the top. It billowed slightly in the breeze from the open window, and when all her buttons were undone her breasts lay before me like lazy cannon guarding her flanks. They were open to my caresses, but the way she looked down at them, each cone pointing slightly to the outside, I understood that she had feelings about them—they were too big or too little, I did not know which—but I could see she thought about them and I wanted to be careful not to bruise her.

(After I came to know her better, I understood that she would have considered the night a success even if Frank had returned; the excitement of him walking in on us would have given her great satisfaction, and I had no idea of the danger I was in). But all I said was *"You are so very pretty."* I had spoken while looking at her breasts, not her eyes, and a moment of uncertainty came between us. I was sure I had made a mistake. Then, I looked properly into her eyes and at her nose and at the drop of sweat glistening above the delicate oval curve of her upper lip, shifting my eyes as I had seen women do in movies, and, thankfully, she looked down again at her breasts, smiling faintly as if to say *"I know… I know what is happening here."* My heart sank, though my face, I believed, revealed nothing, but then she did not smile anymore and instead she leaned forward again from her waist, her face tilted upward, waiting for the kiss. *"I'm like them, I'm like everyone else,"* I remember thinking, and I kissed her so sweetly that the drop of sweat rolled from her lip onto mine and the salt taste glazed my tongue.

Later, I wanted to tell her that there would always be one truth she could never deny—though she might not feel its emotion or accept its logic—that there was in her a wealth of clarity. Clarity was a given in the equation that described her position on the earth's surface. I was too afraid to say this to her, though, and when I saw her again we spoke only of regular things, people we knew, our childhoods. I had seen her in Dr. Gold's office many times, always crying after her sessions. Nothing thrilled me so much as that crying. It led me to believe that a process existed by which one could recover (though only women seemed to experience it). The excitement of watching someone change had begun to change me in return. One could let go of things, I saw. I was demure and icy, yet it excited me to see someone apparently moving from one mental place to another. I believed then in *progress*.

I was a dangerous man because I did not know myself. But I knew her, and a few days later I brazenly told her what I thought she was going to do. *"You'll be fucking motorcycle bandits for the next few years, trying to get one of them to kill you or come close to it…"*

*"D'you think I'll succeed?"*

When I spoke to Lara of clarity I meant to say that in her consciousness every thing existed for itself. She saw through every object's symbolic function and every human being's self—delusions. She went straight to the first cause. If she had walked the earth five thousand years ago her own tribe would have killed her as soon as she spoke her first words; her first grunt would have been one of derision. She saw back to the beginning of time and forward to infinity's middle and she saw it all clearly. I exaggerate, out of love and respect (I make my friends larger than life in order to honor myself). She was afraid, too, because she was human; but her essence, her spirit, had no fear, no more than a tree might. She avoided the people she might devastate—women who were not as tough as she was—I was wary of her only woman friend, who was similar to her in many respects—and men who loved her illy. It was a negative compassion she had, but an understandable one. There was no rancor in it.

She accepted what was true as true, not as defeat.

Some people stink of the present, but she was a rose of all being. When she decided to go off balance, to upset the equilibrium of her own lunacy, she did it immediately and without regret. When the stroke was complete, she began to heal herself…

So, she was becoming herself; she had finished with judging. Yet there was a tension in her because she was groping toward something. I say *becoming* because she was not yet fully *Lara*, but neither was she impeding the process.

Just to look at her I had to bring forth new resources I had not yet touched. her large breasts tapered and sagged angularly outward. A touch of baby fat on her legs gave a wondrous depth to the curves of her thighs and calves. Every woman to whom one responds emotionally carries about her like an invisible aura the silhouette of the *form of forms,* that perfect form for which one has been waiting all of one's life—one recognizes the form before one recognizes the person. I spent hours trying to discover just who it was who had had that silhouette, who had been the primitive template from which Lara's figure sprang to my mind at once as one to be desired. It was not my mother—at least, not as I remembered her as a younger woman. I searched through hundreds of family photographs looking for a neighbor, an aunt, a girlhood friend of my mother's; I was unsuccessful. No matter. I believed Lara had been painted by an artist whose forte had been depth perception. She had more *three—dimensionality* than any woman I had known, and I did not feel comfortable with the way she looked guilelessly into my eyes, because I knew she saw not only the lust, for which I would have been embarrassed in any case, but my rancor, my righteousness under which lay a bedrock of rage, and confusion, the blurry everywhichway I saw myself even as I believed I saw her clearly. It was as if, were I to gaze into a mirror, I might see, rather than my own reflection, hers. I wanted more than anything to *look* at Lara, to search her face for all that might be there, for good or bad, to see if her expression might tell me whether my destiny hung in the balance. [I have since learned that, in a sense, she was the *Other*, an object I desired and desired to *be*]. She knew me.

That first evening, without Frank around to glower, we talked for hours and I do not remember a word she said. how could I ever recount an entire evening? It is the *tenor* of it that remains with me, not the words but the grammar of the scene itself, in the way one might remember not a single raindrop but the clean, purified smell of the grass when one has stepped outside again after the rain has stopped, with the sense that something has perhaps burned off above the tree line. One can depend on it to be that way because nature has its own grammar...

She wanted me to kill her—that was the problem. I was dangerous precisely because I had learned nothing from my brief history. That is, I was angry and did not know it; I experienced everything as from a remove; my life was measured in its iciness. But, paradoxically, that was why I was in line with the rest of the motorcycle bandits and men like Frank who might go off at any moment over the most minute issue. I, with my corduroy pants and my white shirts, my almost—virginity and the communist politics which gripped my heart like a diastolic claw, was as murderous as the rest. Men like us—all men, I suppose—as soon as we open our mouths women know we are ignorant of all that is within us. It is their genius that, though they must act out of competing motives of desire and pity and self—interest, we assign all to desire. And she saw right to the heart of me, to the overflow of helpless hunger and the rancorous well of enmity, and yet, and yet, she sought me out. All the while I thought I was chasing her and thinking pretty love dreams (tempered with a dose of reality regarding Frank's psychotic strength). But Lara was not perverse. *"Oh, I want you... Oh, I love you...!"*—these words never escaped her lips.

I had no comprehension of Lara's personal mythology. I know not today why she needed to court killers. There was some desire, perhaps, to prove to herself that her father had been the killer she'd thought him to be (in a psychological, not a real, sense). I knew only my own personal eschatology; it was not semen nor pussy nor bitch that concerned me, but spiders and tics, twitches and tremors, the pulsating blood vessel under the eye or in the forearm muscle near the elbow crease, the obscene cracking open of the universe. My universe; my shallow, shallow egg.

Whatever it was for Lara, it had something to do with that equilibrium she had deliberately surrendered. She had no control over what she did. Her shattered self was calling the shots because it was on the move and no longer sick in the same way it had been, and she had to trust it. She had leaped into an abyss and was going to trust her *self* to let her hit bottom gently. That self—trust was incomprehensible to me yet I saw it clearly, as if I were an émigré looking at the Statue of Liberty through a steerage porthole. Whatever had caused her to shatter in the first place—an unsure, angry father, perhaps—was present in me, too (I did not know it). Her soul, her essence, groped to feel its own rightness in the presence of yet one more careening male mind. Its pieces were turning from side to side, now, trying to find the right way to interlock, because all that instability created tension; it craved an answer (sometimes a final one): the proof that it had been right to shatter in the first place. And when it saw a leather jacket and two days' beard growth on the same man (or confusion sitting astride anger) it said *"go there!"* and she went, because her instinct told her to go.

So I had been chosen for my inner qualities. I might yet kill her myself. Any woman who looked at me would have seen my confusion, but who, other than Lara, would have seen that confusion's potential? How lucky I was! To be loved for what I most feared in myself, by someone who almost, *but not quite*, needed to bring it forth. I say "not quite" because, when I think back on it, everything she did for me was like a cauterizing needle applied to what burned and festered in me. Instead of pushing me beyond control, she deadened my rancor and turned it into authentic human feeling, something palpable I could grip. It was more charitable of her than I could comprehend. I might have expected her to have pulled me apart, afraid to admit how fearful I was becoming of myself (it was the tidal pull of her desire) yet wanting to give her what she seemed to desire—aggression, if not outright violence. But it never happened...

It never happened because I *liked* her. That may have given her pause. She could not, or would not, ignore that; it had a temporary but telling effect, because I longed to be with her. Love is not love but twenty things at once, and she whom one loves may pick and choose among all the things one offers. Lara chose the chance of murder, but with it she got... affection; and since I did not know I wanted to kill her—only she knew that—I knew only that I was afraid of myself but that my love for her was genuine. I was given an ally I had not expected: the real secondary warmth one takes from loving another human being without knowing why. That warmth stood before me and pushed away my rage, which came and went independently of everything else; or so I thought.

I was about fifth from the front of the line, as I remember. My turn had come in the Spring, after Frank disappeared, and by June I, too, was gone. I even met the man who would take my place one evening when we were relaxing at Lara's. He came by to sell her some grass, a young artist already on parole. We got along well and I liked him, but though not a word was spoken of it, I knew he was the one. He would not have been there if he were not. I could imagine him in my mind's eye, waking up some morning in the next month or two, well after the work hour had begun, asking for breakfast, and swinging determinedly at her jaw when she did not get up fast enough.

She did not *want* to be hurt, not really, but she was investigating something—those few seconds that began to tick the instant she knew she might be hit. She was examining those seconds for all their attendant possibilities, for their didactic, heuristic functions. I say this with some anger, for I did not hit her, did not think to hit her, yet failed to hold her. That was her task, that investigation, to examine those seconds. Their existence was a *must* which necessity itself required her to examine. There were questions to be answered: what was the configuration of forces that existed at that precise moment? Who had demanded her death? Her need for unity had gotten her to the point where she understood what questions had to be asked. Now she had work to do. What was the meaning of that moment that had to be replayed again and again? *The creation of her universe of sickness.* And what had happened at the instant of its creation? *She was weak and she was her father who saw her weakness, and she could not bear to be either, so she strove at the same time to be weak and not weak, but she saw it from both sides and judged the moment harshly...* Each time a man almost hit her the moment of her original death was re-created. When might she freeze the frame?

She doubted her own leap into the abyss; she was trying to hedge it. I say these things from hindsight. I have thought of it for months, and the appearance of Frank at my door convinced me that my instinct was correct...

Every night for a week I went to her flat after work. Each of us looked for an opening (though it is almost ridiculous to say that I did because such maneuvering was not within my ability). I was being caught up in her liberation before my own was ready to begin, before I knew I might even have a chance for that sort of thing. She stroked my hair and said, softly, *"By the way, you've been here for a week now and you've only fucked me the one time. Even Frank did me more than that."* *"Let's go to bed, then,"* I said, but she was ready for me, wrapped as she was in a large bathroom towel, smelling of shampoo. *"Ah, but I've just washed my hair and it's still wet."* She examined my face as if it were a slide on a microscope. I could almost see one of her eyes shut as my bafflement turned to anger...

But I could only remain angry for a short time. Often, she was sad and I wanted to cry as I looked at her sagging face. Dr. Gold had said, as he had also described Frank, that it was acid that caused the sagging, but it made me want to cry anyway because I thought my tears mirrored what was in her heart (and if they had, as I ask now, what good would that have done for either of us?).

One day I was speaking to Hart on the telephone. Lara was fellating me as we spoke. It was an act with complicated meaning. She became connected to Hart on the other end of the line. He wanted her, too, and she knew it. This act was her way of fellating him, too; I was the connecting link (the scene reminds me now of my paradigm—being between my mother and father: were they using me, or had I placed myself between them in unconscious generosity mixed with desire?). Then Lara teased me and drew me away from the sense of the conversation; that was her second intention: to make me angry. That I might become enraged at a gratuitous sexual act which brought me pleasure—this was complication beyond measure. My ignorance saved me; I comprehended nothing. All this is hindsight. She might have said only *"Why don't you get angry enough to kill me?"* Around a circle we moved; in the center, the unacknowledged true love I believe we had for one another, the residue of all the manipulation that had brought us together in the first place, the umbra of our intentions, the knowledge we did not know we had that said *In the end you'll be changed but you will not die,* which most people who call themselves daring or passionate or merely foolish would never admit was really there. Our separate knowledges of this truth, which perhaps only our bodies knew, did battle in that center. Perhaps I should not call it battle; I do not know, but there was something in that middle space, where our separate ignorances met, beyond rage and manipulation, that became a human tithe we made in the highest form of charity, as Maimonides describes when he speaks of the recipient who does not know who it is who has built him into a whole man.

It ended abruptly, as it ought to have. One evening, I noticed that her face was was sagging again. I looked at her and began to sob. I stifled my tears and went into the bathroom, where I cried for several minutes. I was crying for ten years into the future, when we would no longer speak to one another as we passed on the street. When I returned to her living room, Lara told me to sit down. I sat on the rocker next to the sofa, and she knelt on the floor in front of me, as adults might when about to speak seriously to a child.

*"It's time you left. I can't have people crying over me."*

I had thought my crying was a sign of my love, but compassion was precisely the wrong response.

*What do you mean?*, I said.

*"It's like this. I like you well enough, but we're going nowhere. In two years we won't even say hello to each other on the street."*

I saw she had waited until I could not cry any longer before she told me we were through.

*"What am I to do?,"* I asked.

*"What are you to do...?... You're to get out!"*

Constant in her character, she slammed the door behind me as I went down the steps. Loud as it sounded, it was an elegant, nuanced action—I might yet run back up the stairs and kick down the door with my booted foot. How fine we would feel, then, in our mutual terror, examining our equally charged moments at the same time but in different universes. I took the slammed door as a sign of love, and continued down the stairs, carrying my anguish before me as if it were in a wheelbarrow...

≫— ≪

Later, in my drought (when I learned what it meant to walk for miles every night), I thought it was only proper that I should suffer more, from a mathematical point of view. I had had my moment of clarity, but I had failed, also. I did not have what it took to tear another apart looking for the human core, tossing away flesh and sinew as I fought my way to the center. Nor did I know it was a good thing I had not. Instead, I thought it was one thing to have seen clearly into the mind of another for a second; I was yet an idiot savant as to the rest of the world. I had discovered one talent: the power to look into the soul of a woman who not only gave me that power but who might have killed me sooner or later or forced me to kill her. When once you have had a glimpse of something in yourself that seems more real than any other thing you have experienced, and when you do not have the wisdom to recognize that it was only the natural presence of another human being that brought forth from you what you were powerless to bring forth on your own, you are lost. You are not only lost; you are falling…

Six months later, Frank leaned forward in my chair, his gaunt fingers wrapped around the glass. My memories had consumed about thirty seconds of our time. He hefted the glass in his hand, as if measuring its weight, and glared at the blank television screen as I contemplated his hand, alert for tremors of enmity. Without either of us looking directly at the other, we yet stared each other down. We were like two gunmen in an existential farce, neither having guns, only the idea of a gun, each wanting the other to draw first (to prove that the guns did not exist).

Finally I said, *"Throw it if you want."*

The silence continued as he thought it all through. Neither of us really wanted to do harm. The part of the catalytic equation that was needed, the plutonium that sets off the uranium, was missing, was that very moment probably working through her instant of *reconnaissance* with one more villain.

*"Well, you did take her from me,"* Frank said finally.

*"I do not see how you can say that. It was you who left. What did you want to see that idiotic movie for anyway"?*

*"I wanted to see what you would do, and you did just what I expected—you fucked my girlfriend!"*

That was said quietly, with more power for that. And he was still gripping the glass.

*"None of us lasted very long, did we? I was out in less than a month, myself, and guess who moved in?"* (I gave him the name of the doper who had brought over the grass one evening).

Frank's rage was diverted for a moment, and a puzzled look came onto his face. He repeated the doper's name several times, as if he needed to memorize it in order to find it in the telephone book. His hand slowly lowered to the armrest of the chair; his grip on the glass seemed to lessen perceptibly.

"*Jesus!*" he said. *"I'd have to break into jail to settle up with him, wouldn't I?"*

A few minutes later he was gone. I stood in my doorway and watched him go down the steps. I was thinking *"You poor, hapless cueball"* I laughed upon thinking of that phrase, perhaps in nervous relief, perhaps because I was not sure to which of us it applied. I was still laughing about it later, but before I stopped laughing, I opened the back window of my flat, the window that faced the parking lot, and I hurled that glass as hard as I could against the far wall. If Frank ever came back, I would have to have paper cups.

## *[Annotation]:*

*[I understand now why I believed Lara was (and is) a genius, but it is a self-serving understanding. She was trying to repeat something that had happened long ago, to get back to it in its original form, to be in it. It was not any different, except in her individual circumstances, than my repetition of groups of three, but for her own knowledge and her purpose. I had met a woman who was trying to overcome, who had more courage than I, but her acts of overcoming resonated in me at a deep level; it reached me. And I ought not to omit another fact: the quality of rage in my character of which I was not fully aware had been attractive to Lara]. [But I was not going to hurt her; the act had never occurred to me. In that regard, I was no longer useful to her; I was not a threat]. Yet, If I learned anything from Lara, and I did so only later, it was the enormous strength we carry within us to close off parts of our lives, and the equally strong effort it takes to strip off the thick layers of that repression.*

*Looking and fucking and raging and stumbling and drinking and yearning—for all I know I was hardly unique.*

*I have read in a novella a description of another city located between two rivers. The author described the rivers as if one had male qualities, the other female qualities. This description recalled for me my walks in P, almost always at night, after Lara ended our brief affair. It occurred to me that I have earlier described the Eastern River as one of commerce, ships with freight moving toward the Bay downriver, whereas the Western River had no ship traffic to speak of and had always seemed gentler, undisturbed by its connection to P. I wonder now if, during those walks, I was unconsciously going back and forth between male and female, Mother and Father, as I trudged along in my despair. Certainly I'd have been doubting my manhood during those walks. I cannot recall any of the thoughts I must have had; I assume I spent months asking myself what I could have done to remain with Lara and berating myself for failing to hold on to her. [This assumption is not correct; it is more likely that I always feared it would end but would not admit it. It was doomed from the beginning].*

⫸ ⫷

*Winter passed… It had been severe and I was tired of walking the streets with Hart to keep warm…My heat had been off for weeks at a time, and when I complained to my landlord he called me a Shithead and I hadn't the nerve to hit him… Hart called me a fool and I believed him… "You live in a building full of degreed transients… landlords can do anything to that crowd."…. He was right but I was hurt by his words… The landlords and tenants were all of a piece—suburban bastards with mouths full of late 1960's gabble and souls hard as scarabs… The had all been born of the same mother and she had left them under the back steps to drink rainwater… They had not forgotten that desertion… They understood one another…*

*And another:*

A mugging occurred late one night on the Western Bridge leading to the University District. A man lay bleeding on the walkway while footsteps receded in the distance. Below the bridge the dirty water lapped against mossy stones. To the Northeast, lights twinkled in the tall buildings of the Commercial District while charwomen mopped their floors. The police found an incoherent young man bleeding from the nose, his wallet gone. An officer leaned over the parapet but saw nothing but blackness. The young man was so confused that the police did not believe his story. Twelve hours later he was admitted to the state hospital for observation while facts were sorted out from fantasy. Later that day Ericksen telephoned me to let me know Hart had been committed and had been trying to reach me.

*"He wants you to take care of the cats while he's away."*

*"Away? That's a fine way to put it. What seems to be the problem? And whose cats?"*

*"I don't have a clue, but I'll meet you tomorrow at the station and we'll go see him. It's out in the country somewhere, and he still owes me fifty bucks."*

The next day I left work early and met Ericksen. The City train took us to the terminus where all suburban transport was re-routed, and we boarded a bus. The route took us over winding roads lined with willow trees whose branches dragged across the top of the bus as we went. Fine needles of light like laser beams threaded their way through the leaves onto the road. On the low hills in the distance the flowers seemed to glisten. Ericksen stared out the window while I focused my attention on the neck of the man sitting in front of me. I wondered why Hart was really in the bin. It was sure to be his drinking, but maybe it was something else. Perhaps, I thought, it might be the slowness of producing 'literature', or perhaps Annabelle had kicked him out once and for all, or, worse, had admitted all her affairs. Then again, the failure of his restaurant might have been the final blow, though how he could have expected the landlord of his dilapidated building, who was also a restaurateur, to permit Hart to compete with him was a question Hart had never truly faced. I thought then that the cats Ericksen spoke of must have been Annabelle's.

I felt a certain amount of guilt over this train of thought, because I had often wished such a fate on Hart. I considered that I might at that moment even be envious of him now that he was putting the finishing touches on his legend. I had no wish to become his Boswell, though that is what I have become in order to describe my territory with as much accuracy as I can, but I was tired of people coming up to me at parties and asking *"How's Hart?… Is he writing by the way?… Say hello to him for me, won't you?… That's a good fellow."*

Ericksen interrupted these musings. *"You see the way the sun's shadow seems so much more intense as it strikes different materials? Some materials reflect different shades of gray or black even in the same intensity of sunlight."* He pointed to a white stucco house in the distance, shaded by azaleas in its front yard. *"I've never noticed that before, but I'll take your word for it."* I wondered if he was thinking of his career, such as it was or might be. *"It's important for the painter, even the sculptor for that matter, to understand this phenomenon, so that he knows he may have to paint one part of a surface 'deeper' than another contiguous to it to make it appear in the finished work that both areas reflect the same shade… It's a matter of laying on thicker color, you see"…*

I would not have replied to this analysis anyway (in fact, it was extremely observant, but I could not admit that in the circumstances), but luckily, the bus came over a long rise and the hospital appeared in the distance. It appeared to be composed of several brick buildings in the sprawling modern style, none more than three floors high. Hart greeted us in the lobby of the Administration building, a large, airy space full of vinyl, where patients lounged about smoking cigarettes or waiting for medication. Hart wore street clothes and aviator sunglasses. He came forward and shook our hands warmly, seeming in perfect health.

*"So you're here, too,* he said to me… *What a nice surprise"* . .

*…I don't understand?… I thought you'd been trying to reach me"* . . . .

*"Let's go to my room. We can talk there."* …

We followed him down a tiled corridor (it reminded me of the corridors in the building where I worked) to a stairwell and up to the second floor, where he led us to a small room with walls of yellow-painted concrete block. (This space, too, reminded me of my office cubicle). He had a bed, a closet, a few armchairs which were bolted to the floor. The windows were made of plexiglass and, though unbarred, could only be raised a few inches. Through them I could see the white stucco house Ericksen had pointed out. On the night table were two books Hart had in his backpack when he was collected on the bridge: Wittgenstein's-*Logico-Philosophico*-Tractatus, and, of all things, *I, The Jury*, by Mickey Spillane. Hart saw me staring at them. *"They both believe the world is made of facts, not things, my man... Compare and contrast!... That's the way to think about the world..."* Hart sat on the bed, removed his aviator glasses, and lit a cigarette... *"Gentlemen, the smoking lamp is lit"*...

*[I did not agree with Hart's statement. As little as I knew about philosophy, I knew enough about Spillane to be certain that he did believe the word is composed of things, namely, bullets, fedoras, dames. I asked myself silently whether my dialogue, my Platonic conversation with Hart, was nothing more than a streaming hatred covered over by a pretentious, sophisticated idea which was full of holes. Yet, I sat and observed. I also compared and contrasted; I did not argue with Ericksen, I had not argued with my mother, I did not argue with Dr. Gold—I had tried, but he rightly ignored my efforts. At that moment, Hart was my father and I hated him; I was not going to give him the other side of any argument, at least, not aloud.*

Hart was in an excellent mood, and this was my first look at him in months. His ruddy face, his cowlick, the goodnatured expansiveness of his arms waving in all directions as he did when he entertained in his book-lined room at his house-none of these qualities had changed an iota.

Ericksen was the first to speak... *"Excuse me for saying this, but you don't look as if you belong here... You look better than we do, if I might say so"*...

*"To tell the truth, I don't belong here, thank God... I'm only here because of Annabelle... And thank God again, for the insurance"*...

*"Annabelle!,"* I said... *"What's she got to do with it?"* Annabelle was Hart's lover, a sculptor who made only torsos, many of which could be found leaning against the walls of her kitchen.

Hart blew a curl of smoke out of his pursed lips. *"She wanted to take a vacation and I haven't got a dime... You remember I lost my job last year and my unemployment compensation's gone, too... We always split our expenses down the middle and I just didn't have any dough"...*

*"You couldn't have lain in bed for a week?"...*

*"Well, you know how I drink... She thought I might leave the gas on or drown in the tub... Say, what's the difference, anyway?... I'm sure as hell comfortable here"...* Hart scratched his back with a comb and yawned contentedly...

*"Where is she, then?"...*

*"She went to Atlantic City... She loves to gamble, you know... Anyway, she'll be there for a week, then she'll come and collect me here... I'll want you to check on her cats, by the way, she left them at my house... That's my main concern."...* He reached over and switched on the radio, began snapping his fingers to the music... *Oh, and I may have left a candle burning somewhere in the house... I know you'll see it, if the house is still there"...*

*How the hell did you get in here, then?,"* Ericksen said... *"We heard you'd been mugged"...*

*"I made that up... When I got here I told them I'd been drinking two fifths a day... That's an automatic entry under my plan"...*

*"So that's why you've been calling me... To make sure Anna's cats haven't died?"...*

*"I haven't been... Who told you that?"...*

I looked at Ericksen, who was staring out the window. True to form, when people fight, he slips away. Had he hoped to get his money if I were here with him?

*I'm disgusted with both of you!,"* I said, and then the argument began in earnest. Names were called, blame was assigned. Hart called me a 'sucker'; I said he was a 'thief'. I hated him, then and I hated Ericksen, too, who had got up and left the room. I hated Annabelle most of all, for I blamed her for everything. I felt that I had no family and Hart had, even if his was careless and thoughtless.

After a few minutes of shouting, Hart became overcome with fatigue. He crawled into bed and drew the blanket up to his neck, but he had one more shout in him. *"Annabelle !,"* he rasped... *"Annabelle is not responsible... I am my own man!"*...

*"I refuse to go to your house... And Annabelle's goddamned cats can go to hell!"*...

*"Oh, well,"* Hart said, with an air of resignation. *"They'll be alright for another few days or so, I suppose."*...

I stood up. *"And that's goodbye!"*...

*"If it makes you feel any better,"* Hart said, *"I'm getting loonier the longer I stay here"*...

I turned from the door. *"Fuck!... Give me your house key."*...

Hart fished through the drawer of his night table and retrieved it. *"I'll stop by to get it when I'm out of here."*

⫸ ⫷

Hart said once that one had to choose a beggar carefully, and he chose the word beggar rather than panhandler because it was more literary; as I walked in the freezing cold with the wind lashing my face at the turn of a corner, I saw beggars still on the pavement, trying to put together a few coins before finding a step to sleep on. I tried to ignore them; I felt during my walk that I was a beggar, too, an emotional one, an unsuccessful one on that score. It occurred to me that I might remove the wool cap from my head and stand still, holding it out for affection and respect rather than coins. The thought passed quickly, however, and anger took its place. When I reached Hart's house and stood on the front step I was outraged. At last, I opened the door.

Right away the cats were at my feet rubbing their cheeks against my pantscuffs and I knew Annabelle hadn't left them any food. She'd had it all figured out-I was right on schedule. In a cabinet I found some dry cat food and fed them out of dirty plates from the sink. I was happy they were alive. The furry shark had died some months before. While they ate I went upstairs to Hart's bedroom/library/den. I was in no mood to observe the etiquette that solitude in another's home demands. Immediately I began to rifle through Hart's desk drawers. I found old manuscripts which I had already read and tossed them on the floor. Beneath the old Underwood portable lay another pile of papers turned face down. The top one was a note from Hart to Annabelle, which he had probably never let her see. *"You are the only one who means anything to me. If you left me I would have to go and live underwater. But I have no gills and could not breathe."* I went back to the desk and put the note on top of the pile. On the table next to Hart's soft chair was the burned-out candle he had left; I found a match and lit it, then placed it carefully on the desk. I looked more thoroughly through the papers. One sheet had Hart's writing credo on it, or, rather, it was an example of that for which he had always strived, compression, the entire world in every sentence. I read it for the first time:

*"My first destination was Tishewitz. I put up with an acquaintance of mine, Reb Bruch. He sent for the sexton and a few householders. While waiting for them, I stood by the window and studied the market-place."*

Now, I recognized this paragraph. It was taken from a short story by I. L. Perutz, whose slim book of stories I owned. I had no idea that Hart had ever read it, but as I was now going through his private papers, why should he never have done the same in my flat? A minor writer, Perutz, dead by 1915, but—just look at that paragraph! Four sentences tell us everything—the journey, its first leg, the players, their importance, the situation of the Reb's house in the heart of the God-forsaken village, the window through which Perutz views the life of the town. Four sentences. If only I had written them, I would be satisfied. A strange place to experience an epiphany, since I did not believe in epiphanies.

I slipped all the papers back under the typewriter and sat down in the soft chair. The room was a mess. On one wall a crack in the plaster radiated tiny fault lines in every direction. I was reminded of the hole in Dr. Gold's wall. Pieces of a broken dish lay on the floor with cat feces hanging over their rims. Cause and effect was apparent everywhere. The candle began to flicker and I reached over to steady it. After a while I blew out the flame and sat there in the dark. Hot phlegm rose in my throat. My cheeks burned. I felt then that all life was a vicious argument, which all the asylums in the world had not room to contain…

*And one for good measure:*

*On the street outside my office an unmarked police car rammed another car to stop it. A burly policeman waving a pistol ran up to the window of the rammed car and shouted at the driver to open the door. The driver, sullen, Negro, hapless, refused. The officer ran to the other side of the car where he tried to pull open the door, but the driver had locked it. My allegiance kept shifting as I watched. He must be a crook, I thought. But then I said to myself, I don't like that cop, either… What kind of man jumps into danger that way? I remembered an event that had happened when I was a child. The police stopped my father's car one night because he had boxes of spark plugs on the back seat, which he sold in his business. The police made us get out of the car and they asked him about the boxes. After they heard his explanation, they pulled me aside-an eight year old boy-and asked me the same questions, trying to trip us up. At that age, I did not know how to be a fool yet, and I gave them the same answers my father had given. They finally let us go on our way. I wanted to help, but I did not know who I was supposed to be helping. I did not know where my loyalty lay. I had become a philosopher without knowing that I had.*

My supervisor's voice drew me away from the work I was doing at my desk for a meeting in her cubicle. She had the only enclosed space in our office; as I went in behind her I caught R, whose desk abutted one of the prefabricated walls that enclosed the supervisor's space, sliding his hand into his desk for his stethoscope, which he sometimes placed against the wall to listen to our conversations…

In an office like ours, where everyone was afraid, the employees always told everyone exactly what they were doing. *"Well, that's THAT!,"* they would exclaim, slamming a file shut, *"The Wellington matter, closed! Now I can begin the Slavin investigation."* An office is a place of horror, no matter what anyone's intentions are.

I had found work at the Institute for Dispute Resolution, a non-profit organization which tried to resolve neighborhood disputes before they became lawsuits, fistfights or worse. Someone had figured out that every case we might resolve saved the court system money, so the City put a small part of its budget away every year for the Institute, and private donations made up any difference between our budget and the City's contribution.

We were a forlorn crew, and no one was pure in that place, except Eleonor. She was the only pure one.

Our offices were housed in a large, two—story building that had been a clothing factory, later a welfare office. The building sat in a run—down area on the demographic edge of the Central District. We worked on the second floor, which consisted of two large rooms. The back room, almost windowless, was where the negotiators' desks were placed. We did our administrative work there and took telephone calls, which were difficult to hear because we were packed so closely together. Our desks were jammed together and telephones were allotted one to every two or three desks. The telephones rang constantly and were answered by whoever was closest.

The front room was separated from our quarters by a large set of red double doors and, for some inexplicable reason, contained several church pews where visitors could wait for one of us to bring them to the back. The only employee who worked in the front room was the receptionist, who sat at the deepest part of the room opposite the red doors. Visitors approached her from the stairwell—there was no elevator—and her desk was, for reasons never explained to us, on a raised platform about six inches off the floor, so visitors felt as if they were approaching a judge. The receptionist's sour demeanor did nothing to discourage that impression, and when someone approached her she announced that person's name in a brutal voice. Only then did one of us rise to maneuver through the maze of desks and furniture to push through the doors and greet the visitor. The waiting room was five times too large for its purpose, for we had hardly any visitors, but it gave the receptionist a sense of power which, all things considered, she was fortunate to have. When she paged us, none of us looked up because the sound of her voice meant we had a visitor and we did not want to see anyone. But when Eleonor was paged, we all looked up to watch her go through the doors, because it was often her husband who was out there and he was probably drunk.

Eleonor was disheveled, sad, lumpy, timid, thirty-five. She could not be liked because her timidity was too imposing. It had the same quality as her fleeting self—confidence: a refusal to consider itself. It turned only outward without wisdom and angered those who faced it, and she employed it deliberately rather than fighting for herself, as if there were a principle, an erroneous one, behind it. If I compared myself to her, though, she had more courage than I. If I'd carried through with my gorilla mask, if I'd taken the risk of letting the world see my shame, the shame of my shame, I'd have shown bravery that she demonstrated every day by not hiding herself. She was lost and did not bother to hide it from us. Her lost self was transparent. She was not *performing.* She was not acting out. Yet.

Her face was thrust forward, unlined, like a young gnome one morning when she heard her name paged. She looked for a moment like a deer that has heard a twig break in the forest. Impatiently the receptionist repeated Eleonor's name, and Eleonor rose from her chair and squeezed through the narrow corridor between the desks, barely keeping her balance. She hurried past the supervisor's cubicle and pushed open the red doors. Everyone watched her go out except the supervisor, who encouraged timidity. She had been a politically active bookkeeper and had obtained her position by patronage. Often she called us in the late afternoons and gave instructions by telephone while the clinking of glasses and jukebox music could be heard in the background...

When Eleonor entered the waiting room her husband was there, sitting in a pew, drunk. He had lost several jobs in the last few years, forcing Eleonor to find work. (The supervisor enjoyed having control over people who absolutely needed a job). Eleonor's husband was always rude to the receptionist (whose description of these events I have borrowed from) but when Eleonor appeared he began to pay her a kind of court, dancing like a boxer and hurling questions at her that he had surely asked her many times. *"What?"* he asked, pointing to the double doors, his face reddening with the effort. *"Zatcher workplace?...  Zatcher office?"* Then he howled. *"Yuk, Yuk!,"* rocking back and forth on the balls of his feet, his face florid from the high—calorie diet of the authentic drinker. Eleonor listened, her face appearing to twitch as she raised her eyebrows at everything he said. She seemed to be waiting for a reprimand to slip out from behind the red doors like angry smoke. In a barely audible voice she whispered to her husband, *"Please... Please go home!"* That was how it was for her.

⟫⟩ ⟨⟪

A friend of Eleonor's told her about screaming as a therapeutic technique. One could scream in the privacy of one's bedroom or basement, and all the demons of the past, all the reprimands and punishments of a lifetime would go flying out of one's throat into the stratosphere. The method appealed to her because it was parallel to her timidity; that is, she did not have to speak to anyone. After a week of screaming at home, she appeared one day in the office. She was calm and felt like a pioneer. For the first time, she explained, she felt as if she were making progress. Life was endless progress, she said, and one stood still at one's peril.

She screamed in her basement, she informed us. She sat in a chair or lay on a cot while her husband drank upstairs. First she cleared her throat by drinking Coca—Cola. Then she began to scream as loud and as long as she could stand it. That was all there was to it. At first she could only scream for a few minutes, but after the first night—after her husband had fallen down the cellar steps running to save her life—she had explained to him that in fact she was saving her own life, and she began gradually to increase the time she spent hollering until, by the end of the first week, she had a daily schedule: come home, change clothes, eat supper, set her husband in front of the television, retire to the basement, scream for twenty minutes, take a shower.

*"You feel marvelous, afterward,"* she said. *"Your past becomes remarkably clear... All the obstacles to your success—which, by the way, you have placed in your own way—are overcome... Your childhood lays itself bare and you come to love yourself..."*

Before Eleonor had begun to scream, she had come to my desk one day after her husband had made another of his appearances. her head hung so low it almost lay on my desk, her fine face was red with the blood of despair. *"The supervisor permits his behavior,"* I told her. *"No weakness of ours is too base for her to expose."* I felt my stomach tighten as I said these words, as if a choice should be made or I would be destroyed, but for me it was not time yet to stop suffering. After a week of screaming, though, Eleonor told her husband not to come to our offices anymore, and she began to take on more assignments. She was feeling powerful and surer of herself. She had talked to me only once since she began to scream: *"If you screamed instead of paying all that money to a psychiatrist, you could have a new car by now, a Corvette, maybe, or even a Porsche."*

I began to observe Eleonor during the day, as if the Institute were a laboratory and she were an experiment. I expected that the supervisor would not let her sense of well—being continue. A polarity grew between her and the supervisor. Some employees thought this polarity was a good thing and that Eleonor would loosen the bonds that held us all. I was not one of those. Others thought it was folly. One employee, a practitioner of yoga, said *"I've been in the Army… You have no idea what supervision is until you've served your country."* Another, who always argued with his head down as if he were disagreeing with one's shoes, pointed his finger angrily at the yoga practitioner's wing tips. *"I am of the opinion,"* he said, *"that her screaming represents total contradiction from praxis, or action. It is entirely internal, therefore totally opposed to any communal activity. It is individualistic and should be eliminated."* The yoga practitioner, who could be counted on to throw off his cloak of sensitivity in the face of any statements on morality by others, reversed himself and declared that screaming was an entirely harmless activity. *"What's good for her is good for the community,"* he said, meaning us. *"She has every right to seek self—fulfillment. That is, after all, the ultimate goal of revolution." "You won't even know when the revolution has begun,"* the other countered, but the yoga practitioner merely gave his co—worker his broadest smile, the one he reserved for those *who do not know. "And what do revolutions solve? Do they change human nature? Of course not. Only meditation does that."*

Eleonor had now begun to scream in the basement of the Institute. The building guard let her into the boiler room every day at lunchtime, where she screamed for a half hour, the agony being drowned out by the noise from the huge heating system. After screaming, she wiped her face with a towel and ate a sandwich. The guard spoke of her as if she were the goddess Athena. The polarity I spoke of took on a life of its own as employees chose sides for their own reasons. Finally, one day Eleonor went into the supervisor's cubicle for a meeting, harsh words were spoken, and Eleonor hurled a telephone book to the floor to emphasize a point. That was that; she was suspended indefinitely.

The employees held meetings in nearby luncheonettes, but no one knew what to do or whether anything should be done. After these meetings, the supervisor's snitch rose to go to the bathroom, went downstairs and called the supervisor from a telephone booth. In that way the supervisor found out what was said without having to open her cubicle door. At the same time she humiliated the snitch, because we all knew where she was going when she left the table. Even the snitch had to be kept at a disequilibrium. In the end, I was chosen to approach the supervisor, because it was known that I had seen a psychiatrist; my fellow workers believed I might be slightly less likely to crumble before her.

On my way to the supervisor's cubicle I watched the non-negotiating employees line their desks up with all materials perpendicular. I saw the man who sat directly behind the supervisor's cubicle remove his stethoscope from his desk; I saw the snitch pretending to work. I looked down at the tiles on the floor but they revealed nothing to me. My behavior of choice—noticing—was working well, but I felt distinctly uncomfortable as a representative of another human being. I knocked on the cubicle door and was told to enter.

I have waited until now to describe the supervisor. I believe my hesitancy is a function of my own fear of her, which was magnified by the way her cubicle was designed to create dissonance in her visitors. The chair directly in front of her desk had a solid bottom; one could not put one's legs under it as one can in almost every type of business chair. There was an ashtray on her desk but it was kept at the furthest corner from the visitor's chair. If one wished to smoke one had to lean forward awkwardly, taking the chance that one might spill cigarette ash on the supervisor's papers. The chair in which visitors sat faced the sun, which lit the supervisor from behind in the late afternoons, which was the only time she would meet with any of us. I wanted to get our meeting over with quickly, so I spoke before I even sat down.

*"We'd like you to rescind Eleonor's suspension,"* I managed to say. Those were the only words I was able to speak.

I expected nothing. The supervisor was a liar. Under every lie, of course, there is a set of truths yearning to push off the burden of falsity, but I saw no chance of that happening here. She sometimes said yes but she always meant no; if she said maybe she meant never. One had only to read her hands, because even as she spoke she gripped the armrests of her swivel chair in a powerful, sinewy motion. When she spoke her lies her body told the truth, yet she took no notice of the contradiction. One knew as one spoke to her that she was no longer interested in what one was saying by the way she seemed to go to another place in the middle of a sentence. She never looked at the speaker; she looked over the speaker's shoulder or off into the distance, and one could see she was out there somewhere hurting someone or firing them, perhaps even beating them. Whatever it was she was doing, one could see she was *winning*. Her manner reminded me somewhat of Hart, who had been a wrestler in high school and who sometimes remembered his successful matches in the middle of a conversation. She reminded me of him so clearly because when they returned from wherever they had been they both had the same expression. From that place they had brought back some of its marginal protection, for suddenly her face, as had Hart's, took on a cunning look as if she had had an idea in that place, a real brainstorm that would resolve everything and there was not going to be any trouble because now she was back to put it into operation. When she turned back from the wall or the distance it was as if one were speaking to an angel—her face was unlined, her eyes half—closed—a tricky, playful angel, one of those who had lain back when Beelzebub fell out of heaven to see if he'd land face up. I wanted to slap her with a galosh, then, but all she said was, *"Of course I will rescind it. She can come back tomorrow."*

When Eleonor returned to work she was more powerful—in her own mind—than she had ever been. During her suspension she had found a teacher who undertook to show her how to focus her energy to make her screaming more productive. *"I think it is wrong '*, I said to her one day. *"There is no clarity involved… Things find their own unity… You cannot impose unity on them… It's the old goo—goo principle; when in doubt, be as childish as you can."* She rose from her chair and left, unmoved. She no longer spoke to us, in fact. With every scream another crime against nature flew from her throat. If one believed in spirits, here was the explanation: shards of the pasts of all the screamers in the world floating by like coal dust. Her screams filled me with dread, though I only heard of them and never experienced them directly.

⟫⟫– ⟪⟪

In the Fall, as the air became cooler and the smell of burning leaves rose in the streets, a group of Negro[25] men and women who had moved into a home with their children near the University District began to point rifles out of their upstairs windows, frightening their neighbors, (also, for the most part, Negroes) who, until then, had been willing to put up with the group's stray dogs who barked all day and defecated on the sidewalks, and the garbage they threw into the street, and their children whom they kept home from any schooling. Along with the rifles came bullhorns, with which they excoriated their neighbors for not living a pure life, and loud music which they played from giant amplifiers late into the night. The neighbors asked the police to intervene, but, given the racial polarity in P, they moved slowly. The police seemed unable to comprehend the struggle between two groups of the same race. No matter how they dealt with the problem, they would be seen as brutal. The police suggested that the Institute might defuse the situation with less danger. The supervisor, sensing a chance to obtain victory no matter what the result, assigned Eleonor to meet with the group.

---

25  At the time these notes were written, the term "African American" had not been coined yet.

The members of the group in that house might be called 'the people who say No!' No! to the Water department whose water they were stealing. No! to the Electric Company, whose kilowatts they were stealing. No! to their neighbors who had never faced a threat such as they presented and who were struggling to pay their own mortgages. No! even to No! There was no Yes! for them. They had not developed any philosophy of Yes!; they were not there yet. They knew only that organized society had to be rejected. One might even sustain a certain sympathy for the idea (how could I not?). My allegiance had always been with No! though, as I wanted to be a part of the world as well, my allegiance was also with their neighbors, who were, for the most part, working class people. While the people who said No! were in that house debating whether to eat packaged meat and what to do with the cellophane wrappers if they decided meat was acceptable, and whether to send their children to school, their dogs were attacking passers-by and their trash was bringing in all of the neighborhood rats. Everyone wants to say No!; what stops most people is their inability to carry No! to its ultimate conclusion, which is death. The group had never read Bartleby, or learned that death is the price of a life lived without irony. One would have expected them to find a place in the country where they could say No! to cows and trees, but I understood one thing clearly: they needed to say No! to the City. I might want to say No! to the past and the people who raised me, but the group needed to say No! to P because it had raised them.

The group's house was detached from the homes on each side. The police had surrounded it at a distance; for several days they did nothing but observe. At night, when their shift changed and the night officers arrived, they saw on the rickety open porch a cinder barrel burning, while two young black men cradling rifles sat on rocking chairs, smoking cigarettes and laughing at the spectacle. On the night Eleonor was supposed to try to meet with them, I stood behind a fence a half block away. I was afraid for Eleonor and her imagined power, and I wondered what the supervisor would obtain from this meeting.

As Eleonor walked toward the house, the knitted frieze of the wire fence through which I watched her made her appear to be walking faster than she actually was. Even from where I stood I could see that her face was composed. Gone was her dishevelment, her timidity, the limpness of her posture. I had a scattered thought of Susan Hayward as Barbara Graham in *I Want to Live*, walking bravely to the gas chamber.

Eleonor, who had also said No! to living a life of complication and despair, had now reached the sidewalk in front of the house where the group which had said No! watched. A woman who said No! was being watched by five television cameras and hundreds of police as she stood in front of the two riflemen. Her pug nose and the gold tooth of one of the riflemen were later visible on the late television news and visible again on the following morning's television news. Everything was clearly delineated except for the path of the bullet which exploded from the rifle of the gold—toothed man as Eleonor turned away from him after failing to reason with him successfully and her body fell to the sidewalk saying NoNoNoNoNo!

⟫— —⟪

I went to see Eleonor in the hospital. A fierce gun battle had erupted after she had been shot, but she was pulled out of the way by a few brave police. Several group members died. The following day, the City razed the house. In her hospital room, Eleonor's husband sat, sober, with his hand holding hers…

How much emotion could I put into this tale to make a crime palatable? There were many times during my life in P when I found myself lacking method, if that is the right word for how to live. But when I find myself thinking I have no method, I will remember that Eleonor had one and I did not. I went to see the supervisor after I left Eleonor's hospital room. I wanted to ask her how she could have sent Eleonor on such an assignment. She would not answer my question; she said only that I had no business even being near that house. I must have had quite a painful expression on my face, because she added a few words as I left her cubicle. *"This is MY kingdom, and none of you have the strength to take it from me!"*

➤➤➤ ⫷⫷⫷

Her comment made me wonder about purity and what it means to strive for it. Is it the constant attempt to go back to the past and somehow clean it up? To make it more acceptable? To rearrange what happened in one's life? *Or, to destroy it?* And what of the parallel life one leads while making such an attempt? Aside from my belief that, while clarity is important, the past itself cannot be re-conceived, only brought forward in pieces for examination, I could not even answer my own questions. After the incident, I worked and kept quiet. I, too, used to believe in the dissipation of emotion through screaming, but I no longer have any faith in that. Whenever I had to speak to the supervisor afterward, I imagined our words rising and spinning through space in a helix of rage, bound up, clinging, green, unable to let go from their violent, defensive embrace. But they were words, not screams. She was one I would never overcome. I wonder what battle, what topography Eleonor and the Supervisor were repeating? It occurs to me now that when I was sitting in the supervisor's office I had thought of Hart and the similarity of qualities I saw in him and the supervisor. That similarity may have stopped me from asking myself: 'what would Hart or Ericksen or Dr. Gold have done?' I had no business being in the middle of the struggle between Eleonor and the supervisor, yet I had placed myself there though I had no affection for either. I do not remember whether I ever told them what had happened. I hope I did not.

➤➤➤ ⫷⫷⫷

*A late night telephone call from Ericksen... "I was mopping the floor at the hospital when two men in overcoats burst into the room where Mc____ the criminal lawyer was dying."... Tubes ran into and from his body, some bringing life, some taking it away... His daughter was sitting in a chair by his bed reading a magazine when the men leaned over his dying bulk and growled... "The money, you bastard... Where is the money?"... By the time security arrived they were gone, and he died the following night... I knew that Mc____ was the man I had seen giving out money at the Sirens [a bar next to M's that was also a brothel] to the working girls]...*

⫸— ⫷

To listen, to ponder, to agree or disagree, to *speak*, endlessly—this is why we are alive. And this is the secret I have learned about Ericksen, for he has become a hermit of sorts, but if one gets him to talk, he talks—about mythology, and Husserl and phenomenology and art and music and politics. No subject is foreign to him-he who said once that he felt the cold North wind blowing through him-he is storing it all up in his hermitage but he knows there is something in him of value, not to himself alone but to us. He, too, believes there is a pot of gold at the end of the rainbow and he spends his time soaking up all the knowledge there is so that he can TELL US! What an achievement this is! I have always leaned toward Hart because it was with him I had my dialogue, but it has always been Ericksen who had more to tell me, and I never recognized this truth. We are all so taciturn, except for rare machine-gun outbursts of knowledge. He alone, silent as he is, has yet been able to close the gap between what he has learned and the ability to speak it. And I once called it gabble. I am ashamed of what I have not understood.

In a way this fact fits in with what I have attempted to do in my poor way. I have read enough of those precious little novels... Their authors have not got a clue what has happened to them... There is no plot, but not because life has no plot, or because they decided not to create one… Instead, every paragraph is shaped, sculpted almost to the point of corruption, the beauty chisled away and left on the floor so that nothing is left but deadness… Luckily I read Petronius, and saw that one could find the fragments of a two-thousand year old story and discover a world of gossip. I wanted this story, this affidavit, to be gossip, too, never mind that you do not know a soul in these pages… *"I write for a hundred years from now,"* Stendhal is supposed to have said… I know by now I will make up whatever I want about Stendhal…

Ericksen is fastidious in his personal habits… He is always neatly dressed, though he can afford only chino pants and inexpensive shirts which he buys at Woolworth's… I have bought clothing there as well… One needs a certain anonymity when buying clothes… The worse one feels about one's self, the more secretive one wants the purchase to be… At Woolworth's one cannot even try things on… One merely pulls the item from the rack, holds it up against one's torso, and, if it appears to fit, one pays for it at the register and leaves the store… As careful as Ericksen is about his person, though, none of us have seen his flat… I know from his description of it that he has two rooms near the University, across the Western River… It is a rough neighborhood, full of transient students, low—and middle—class homeowners and a steady population of venomous, disaffected teenagers who are fond of stepping from the shade of Sycamore trees in the early evening and clubbing the clueless… Ericksen has been beaten twice, once in the foyer of his apartment building as he tried to hold his two bags of groceries in front of his upper body to ward off the blows from a dozen fists… But danger is not the reason we have not been to see him… He has never invited us… Instead, he meets us in the Academy District…

More than Hart or I, Ericksen sees his flat as a home… On the road for twenty years, flopping in the flats or houses of others, lying on the floor in a borrowed sleeping bag more often than not, he has created a nest filled with books and records… *"Next week I'll have you guys up,"* he says in all sincerity, but it never happens... He's always busy, or exhausted from painting and working, from sweeping floors and emptying bed pans at the hospital. Besides, what is to be gained from sitting in his flat drinking beer?... There will be no one there but us, and we'd be together only because we have little money and no women, but even those reasons are not the crux of the matter... It is that there is no *possibility* there for Hart or I... Nothing could happen there that would enhance our egos... It is almost better to sit drinking in the backyard of Hart's trinity, looking at the pile of trash behind the adjoining shell, throwing our empty beer bottles through the glassless windows or smashing them against the shell's crumbling brick walls... It is so desolate that one thinks *it can't get any worse than this... This place could be a restaurant in six months with a lot of work... Hart will be upstairs screwing a waitress and I'll be sitting at the bar entertaining someone... it's just a matter of a small loan from the S.B.A....* At Ericksen's I would be thinking *This is the kind of place I'll be living in when I'm seventy and unmarried...* None of us believes we will end up in squalor, but I think we all worry (to ourselves) that we could end up with a night table, a broken radio with its antenna pointing out the window, and a noisy refrigerator jammed into a room or two... We're old enough to think about it... We're on the cusp, anyway...

My relation to Ericksen was one of freedom, of which I was unaware at the time. Freedom because he was not an object for me—I had not understood yet that I could think of persons as things, objects. Because I had no object relationship to him, I was freed from making him a part of my internal argument. He was part of that argument as a witness, that is true; but he was not the person I sought to overcome. By being himself, he permitted me to be myself. There was no intention in that permission he granted. I did not have that permission from Hart because I could not give it to him; thus, he could not give it to me. I would not have wanted it; it would have had to be taken, an act I could not undertake so long as I needed him to remain part of my fantasy of overcoming. Whether he was a substitute did not matter.

At M's one night, I told Ericksen how I had climbed a narrow stairway the week before in an old building near S Street... I could not have admitted it to Hart. It is possible that Ericksen was familiar with what I described, but I do not know. I wanted him to know that I had become, in a hesitant way, an actor.

*"At the top of the stairs I entered a small foyer at one end of which stood a table with a register book on it... A woman opened a side door and pointed to the book... 'Sign it', she said... her instruction stunned me, as I had not expected to have to identify myself... I signed the name of my colleague at the Institute... 'A.S.' He was the man who mentioned 'praxis' earlier... .Donating his signature was the only thing he had ever done for me... He was a man so afraid of other people that when he had to speak to them he looked down at his shoes and gestured toward the ground... Now I had taken his name in vain to sleep with a stranger... Desire brings much silliness to sex when one is estranged from one's essence... I* continued... *"The tittering of women's laughter rose over a faux wall, and the masseuses who had no clients watched me through a mirror I knew was false... I did not choose one of them; rather, one had come out to get me... Quickly we made our way to a small cubicle containing a raised bed similar to a hospital stretcher, a chair and a coatrack...*

*... Of course I wanted to concentrate on what was before me... The girl was attractive and did not rush me... But in the cubicle next to mine a drama was playing out... I had seen him as I walked by, an old man—I judged him to be at least eighty... A glance to my side and there he was, sitting on his stretcher draped in a towel... All your ideas* (he looked at me, then) *about why we see only young men at the Nude Dancers—and you've pointed that out, haven't you?... But I never paid the slightest attention, did I?—They went out the window... And this old man was complaining, no less... He wanted someone to fondle... But there are no eighty-year old women who can be fondled, I suppose... Some verbs are barred by the passage of time... I heard everything over the transom... My ears*

*were straining while my hostess tried to ignore the scene unfolding next door…
Someone padded into his cubicle and his whining lowered to a murmur as I waited,
breathless, more for what was happening to him than anything my hostess was doing
to me… I'll tell you, every nerve in my body was tingling… I never felt so alive…"*

This story, which I told with some hesitation, was informative for two
reasons, because I understood first that Ericksen, whom I had always thought
to be reserved and cool, had no criticism to present, nor mockery… *He could
have any woman he sought,* I thought, *yet something about the drift we were
all in permitted him to understand what I had done…* Second, I saw that I
understood nothing of the need or reasoning that had led me on, but, rather
than making me afraid, my tale was frightening to tell, and liberating to me…
[Was I telling Ericksen that I loved him? Or that I no longer needed Hart?].
Or, was I admitting to him that, though watching (or listening) was my métier,
I had taken a hesitant but firm step toward action, an admission I had never
made to Hart?

Ericksen said once that paintings by Kandinsky are remarkable for their
generous swaths of color which dominate the space within the frame. Primary
colors, red, green, yellow, are pleasant to look at for long moments; they do not
tire the eyes. His early paintings, made before he began to paint geometrical
shapes in space devoid of identifiable images, demonstrate this quality. In
the later paintings the primary colors do not dominate the space. Ericksen's
paintings also use green and yellow, but they do not have readily recognizable
forms. In Kandinsky's early work there are human beings present, though they
may be placed in corners; nevertheless, though primary colors predominate, the
human forms balance the picture and assure the viewer that he is looking at a
village and is meant to look at it. Ericksen's forms are alive but hardly human;
they are grotesque shadows which are not reflective of substance elsewhere. It
is as if the shadows are substance but not counterbalanced by any other masses
in the frame. Yet the pictures are powerful because the forms are in a repose

that suggests that movement will occur very soon. Ericksen's forms *think*; they are *pondering*.

Ericksen sought refuge in formal thought, which comforted him. He attacked the problem of art in this way, by analysis, posing a question to himself, then answering it. His discussion about art was a sort of practice for meeting Hart who, after all, owed him money that he sorely needed. I did not understand this process at the time, for I was very angry at Hart. We both were, but Ericksen chose to think in analytical terms, while I chose to fret. Yet I envied Ericksen's ability to fill his mind with topics on which to expound. Every time he spoke I learned something, though I often wanted to reject it. From him I learned something I would never learn from Hart, who was building his literary legend, that is, to choose the subject one wants to investigate, and then to choose the characters who one will manipulate during the investigative process, just as a painter chooses his subject and the colors he will use to depict it.

⟫⟫⟩ ⟨⟪⟪

*Christmas Night and Erickson and I were sitting in my flat waiting out the last moments of the holiday. In my rocker Erickson moved forward and backward silently. Outside, the streets were empty and we were maudlin. Erickson had not spoken to his family in five years. He was very cool about that break—at least, he appeared so—but his pain, as I imagine it, would have been reflective of my own and I decided to make a move. I grabbed the telephone and dialed my parents' number. My father was still alive at the time.*

My mother answered, surprised to hear from me. I called them about once a month, but I tried never to go to their house. Perhaps they'd developed a decent relationship in my absence—as if I thought I had been the glue that held us together, but I kidded myself that they did not speak to one another without me there to carry messages of disappointment and rancor back and forth.

I wanted to speak to Dad, I said, but he's apparently angry at me for not calling enough, and he will not come to the telephone. I want to ask him a question, I say, just a simple question. Don't get him riled up, my mother says. I do not consider the possibility that if I upset him it is she who will suffer.

I insist, I say, while Ericksen rocks gently, not saying a word. He's an expert at ending up in the middle of disputes without taking part—he's always in someone else's flat or home. God only knows what he's writing in his journal. I may appear in someone else's work if I don't hurry with my own. *Just put him on!,*" I shout. Finally he picks up the telephone and I ask my question. *"I just want to know"*—my heart is pounding—*"which is more important, me, or Communism? Just tell me that one thing, will you?"*

He slams the telephone down and I dial again. After several rings my mother answers. What did you say to him? he's madder than ever. *"Put him on,"* I say. *"Put him back on!"*

*"No,"* she says, *"it's useless. Please hang up."* *"I won't!"* I say. *"He's got to get back on!"* In a few seconds, he does, and I repeat my question. I'm growing calmer as he becomes angrier. Again, he puts the telephone down but doesn't hang up. Ericksen has not spoken; he seems to be paying no attention, but in a way I believe I am doing this for both of us. I feel foolish in his eyes but I might be brave, too. One cannot think through these paradoxes while one is being a fool. Foolishness is action, whatever one might think.

*"For God's sake,"* my mother says, *"why are you doing this? I have to live here. You don't."* *"Put him back on,"* I say.

Now, he's determined to speak. *"There are three things that are important to me,"* he says. *"Your mother, you, and Communism."* *"What is first?"* I ask. *"Communism,"* he says. *"Always has been. Always will be."*

Thanks, I say. *"How are you and Mom doing? Everything okay?"* Erickson is looking at me. I have neglected to tell him what my father has said. I have never asked him whether he heard my father's reply. *"Why don't we go out for beer?,"* I suggest, and he's putting on his coat before I even rise from my chair. At M's we drink without talking but I'm feeling pleasant. When he leaves I shake his hand and wish him a good holiday. I offer to walk him to the subway but he refuses.

At my flat I am contemplative but I think a great weight has been removed from my shoulders. I know my place in the scheme of things. I am number two, or three; but the top spot, that is reserved. I won't have to worry about that anymore. [I have forgotten my research on clowns, that the last is second]. The following week Dr. Gold is stunned and cannot believe I've done what I did. *"Are you crazy?!"* he asks. It is a statement, not a question. *"What did you need to do that for? Are you some kind of pain freak?"* He's sitting close to me and and leaning forward, paying absolute attention. *"I am not Jupiter or Saturn any more,"* I say. *"Now, I am Venus; no, not Venus, Mercury, or whatever's two planets away from Earth. And yet, I retain my orbit."*

*"And what is he"?* Dr. Gold asks. *"Is he still the Sun?"*

A few weeks later, my father came to my flat. He climbed three flights, carrying bags of groceries. I opened the door as he reached the landing outside my flat and told him to fuck off; I refused to take the groceries. He began to descend the stairs, and before he turned the corner at the next landing, he turned to me and said *"I'm a survivor."* That was his only explanation. I did not see him again for several weeks, until one night he again rang my doorbell. Again he climbed three flights, this time carrying a table he had made in his basement shop. I let him in. He carried the table through the door and set it on the linoleum floor. It was made of birchwood, he said. It looked incredibly strong; I could see how many layers of varnish had been laid on its flat surface, for it shone under the dim light of the tall lamp I had purchased at a thrift store not long before. He moved the table over to a wall near my bed, stood on the bed, then on the table. He had not removed his shoes. He jumped up and down several times to show me how sturdy the table was. There was no doubt about that. We could have jumped on it together and it would have taken our weight easily. He stepped back onto my bed, then to the floor. We had exchanged only a few words before his demonstration, none during it. He walked to my door, we said our goodbyes, and I kept the table. There had been no overcoming, no triumph; harsh words had been spoken, but it seemed that for once we were thinking alike: *a rapprochement!*

*I had unwittingly loosened the triangle. In fact, I had tried to smash it to pieces. I consider now that I had chosen to expose myself to Ericksen, and that somehow, the act had led to a kind of equality with my father. It led to another conclusion, too, which took much time to settle in, that I did not need Hart. In fact, he began to avoid me, and I saw him rarely afterward. Of course, I had forgotten Dora!*

⫸ ⫷

## *A Sort of Ending*

Dr. Gold dead... Impossible! I cannot believe it. I went to his house last evening, where he had been seeing patients in his den... The house he loved that he had paid for with cash because no one would give him a mortgage with his history of four heart attacks. His wife answered my ring. *"He's in the hospital and I'm about to go see him. Want to come along?"* But I could not bear to. Instead, I went back into P and drank whiskeys at M's. The next morning she called, to say he was gone. I went right back to the house. Patients were everywhere, sitting on the floor, leaning against trees out on the front lawn, making coffee while his wife made arrangements. Lara was there, Ericksen, too. There was no talk of guns or valium or dope; even the schizophrenics seemed better, more subdued. Later, at the funeral, a girl who had not paid him in seven years sobbed. *"I'll never get over this!,"* she screamed at his coffin. The funeral made me think of us, his patients, as having been released when we had not wanted to be, as if we were born in the wild and had been domesticated, only to be set free without having learned how to survive. I had a dream about Lara around that time. It is instructive that Dr. Gold did not appear in it. She was wearing a raincoat, walking up to an airline ticket counter, mumbling to herself. I thought about it for days until I reached a tentative analysis. The raincoat protected her against the tears to come; she would be traveling by herself now; and she was mumbling because she would have to talk to herself, now Dr. Gold was no longer around to listen. It all left me with a bitter taste. I was in the same position, but I had dreamed of her. It did not occur to me that I might have created another triangulation with her and Dr. Gold, which I had never considered.

But if the dream meant that Lara would now have to protect herself against tears, and would now travel alone, what meaning could I attribute to myself for the dream? I asked this question of myself not out of egotism (though every question one asks about another contains the seed of self-absorption). I merely speculated that dreams must be personal to the dreamer, and this one must hold a personal meaning for me as well. Perhaps it was an attempt to keep the triangle together, the one that, in my imagination, if not in reality, existed between the three of us, but I could see nothing in the dream that would lead me to that conclusion. On the other hand, I did not exclude the possibility (rare for me) that, whatever love is, I had experienced it with her, and with Dr. Gold, along with genuine empathy for her loss. Had I ever felt such love or empathy for my mother or father? He was gone, but she lived still. Perhaps I had experienced, somewhere along the way, some similar concern for them if only because of the way I saw them living their lives, each longing for something, personal or political, they would never find. I had not. Somewhere on earth there may have been a child who had such empathy for his parents, but I was not that child and I had known no one who was capable. As I thought more about the dream, I began to wonder if a sense of pity, or compassion may be a more accurate word, might be a more worldly way of creating my map than dwelling on the angers, disappointments, and whining to which I had committed myself on the couch at Dr. Gold's. it might be a better path to consider the past as a sort of semi-blind historian rather than a watcher. Were I to go in that direction, I would not revise *facts*, at least to the extent I could discern them clearly. They would continue to be as clear as my memory could make them. My response to those facts might yet be inaccurate, or deliberately wrong. But if that were the result, I might have the opportunity to consider the deliberate errors. They, too, may lead to clarity. For a time after Dr. Gold's death, I went often to one of the parks in P, where I sat on a bench and talked to him as I had done in his consulting room [a term I have borrowed from Arthur Conan Doyle, I see]. The park was near the bridge over the Eastern River and was the least used of the four which the founding father had laid out. I could cry, laugh, mumble or scream; the traffic across the bridge drowned out any sounds I made. After a month or so, I stopped going there. I understood then that it was myself to whom I was speaking.

⋙ ⋘

After Dr. Gold's death I found myself taking closer notice of what was happening around me; I had no goal, except possibly to take some sustenance from my surroundings. [He had said once that the City has an effect on its inhabitants that cannot be separated from our individual lives]. I went to R Park and sat on the bench Frank had occupied that evening when I had been on my way to Lara's. It was toward the end of Winter. I watched the people going by pushing their bodies through a brisk wind, scarves wound securely around their necks, heavy overcoats still necessary.

A truck carrying a crew from the Parks Department drove up on the sidewalk next to R Park. The men jumped out and began to stretch yellow tape from tree to tree until they had roped off almost one eighth of the Park area. They took a break and smoked; then, while they chatted under a large elm, another truck came; this one being a flatbed. From the rear of the flatbed the second crew unloaded shovels and pickaxes, rakes and trowels. I walked over to where I could see the back of the flatbed; there were many squares of sod lying stacked. A few men stepped under the yellow tape; one pulled a thick packet of papers from his jacket and unfolded them. Both men studied the papers, until they appeared to agree on where to begin. One pointed to the others who were outside the yellow tape, gesturing them to climb under the tape. These men came forward wielding the pickaxes and shovels. Soon they had dug up a considerable amount of the dead, yellowish grass that winter, dogs and frisbee players had destroyed. The first truck left, but the flatbed had been unloaded in the meantime and driven into the Park on one of the macadam paths close to where the digging was ongoing, and the men who had not been digging up the dead grass now took over. They carried wider shovels, almost like snow shovels, with which they picked up the dead grass and began to throw it onto the flatbed. All the while this activity was taking place, people had stopped to watch the men work. Passersby would watch for a minute, then move on, wrapping their scarves more closely around their necks. The cold did not seem to bother the crew; they were wearing sweatshirts but no coats; a man who seemed to be a crew chief had brought coffee from a coffee shop near the Park. It all seemed like satisfying work, useful now to the crew and useful to us when Spring came. [Watson's Annals, a month—by—month history of 19th Century P, came to mind then. Something about what I was seeing got me thinking again about the City in which lived. I later went to the Central Branch of the Free Library where I found a copy, and I began to visit it, wandering with no intent among the shelves. I may have had a goal,] [I am reminded only now of the longshoreman I knew at M's, who went there often to use the typewriters on the mezzanine. Yet another older man whose ways I would begin to adapt as my own].

*If I had not put these words to paper I would not have seen the regeneration I experienced, perhaps because there was no one to overcome any more, no platonic friendship.*

I must return to the dream once more.

*I stood, as an adult, at the top of an escalator in an empty department store. Behind me, in darkness, a floor filled with appliances, washing machines, dryers, stoves, all white. I stepped onto the escalator. As I rode to the bottom, I became smaller, until I was a child as I stepped off. The floor to which I had descended was barren, a desert. But buried in that desert were parts of an automobile, sticking half out of the sand.*

I never gave much thought to this dream until I began thinking about what I was doing with Hart and Erickson, and the idea of triangulation. How had I chosen them as companions in P? I assumed that my being with them was not random-there were others I could have befriended. I noticed now that I had added a part of the dream–the white of the appliances. It must have been important, because I had omitted it previously. I could only wonder at what 'white' meant to me as an adult on a couch; perhaps it was the idea of purity which I was giving up as I descended on that escalator.

Why are dreams important? Because we yearn for a comfortable narrative— not for explanation so much as for ease. When we interpret a dream we think we are finding a psychological truth. But we also want to comfort ourselves—to think and feel that we are placing ourselves accurately in the endless stream. To examine a dream is more than a search for truth; it is a desire for a confirmation with which we might live comfortably—that is, we want to be equals with our histories, as we see those histories. We want to walk side by side with our lives, as if they were friends with whom we could have a pleasant conversation, punctuated by those silences that indicate unspoken agreement.

*This is not an analysis I might hide in a dialogue, pretending it came out of a conversation with Hart or Erickson. It is too personal. As Hart did say once, though, it is what occurs to you while you are chopping onions or preparing a roux to which you ought to be paying attention. I see now that every person with whom one comes in contact, every mother and father, every friend, has a symbolic significance for the endless stream of language which never ceases until death.* **Every person is also a word!!!** *Is this point the one where the confluence of persons and things—or Its—coincide? That is, symbolically in the stream?*

*In language the equation is as follows:person = word; thing = word; ergo, person = thing. [if a = b and b = c, then a = c]. [Of course I had not considered that all persons may not be words; I am not a logician]. In the mind, whether conscious or unconscious, every word is also a symbol. We forget this doubleness when we think and when we listen to ourselves thinking; this forgetting is the crux of a problem in thought and language and apprehension of reality. A thing does not lose its symbolic significance in the stream of consciousness merely because it is identifiable as a thing. One can see, e.g., a tiger or a picture of a tiger and one knows that it is what it purports to be, a tiger, that is, a word and a thing. The observation does not interfere with the symbolic value 'tiger' may have in consciousness.*

Which raises a question: is careful movement important? Cooking a stew, planting impatiens, lighting a cigarette—these are our most valuable behaviors, and the least mundane.

What is written on the page is false. This is the corollary to Korzybski's theorem. I note that 'false' here does not mean 'lying'; it means only a failure to render accurately, because the word **cannot be** the thing! It is a representation, but not the thing itself. This conclusion certainly contradicts my logic, but I continue in the belief that a mistaken idea may yet take me somewhere worth considering.

The auto parts in the sand were things. Each piece was a universe in itself, but it was also a thing, with two or more meanings, as is a myth. (As I am, in a sense, a myth, a story that is not true, a story that is not the thing itself, not I). To put the pieces together was to put myself together, but it was also to put my father back together-and my family [that is, to make a myth true!]. The idea I had been looking for, and 'looking' is the apt word-was to save my family. My failure to do so-not literally mine but for my mythic purposes mine—is what I have buried. But one never can inter these intentions entirely; our myths are created to disguise them so they can walk among our conscious thoughts without being recognized, just as I desired to walk among men without being recognized. And how I and my intention had succeeded! All my looking, my sexual longings, the knowledge of my parents' lies, the primal vision—we think these are what we are concealing, when all along it is only a simple, and yet exalted yearning for *ground* and connection to mother and father, and to be recognized that we conceal because otherwise life would be unbearable. I cannot deny that there is another way of looking at the dream: it was a challenge to Dr. Gold. *"You can't fix me!"* The first lie is thus told by the patient: *" I want to get better."* What he means is*:" please hurt me"!*, or *"Let's see what you can do, Mr. Doctor"!* There is a sequence he wants to follow. Hurt leads to pain; pain leads to rage; rage leads to unity. The unity he seeks is of the many impressions, lies, clichés hurtling around in his brain, all of which serve a common desire, the desire to avoid annihilation; for what would happen if all of those impressions, etc. were to fly outward, to hover over the patient in the consulting room, free of that unity? No patient wants to answer that question; hence, the first lie. Freedom has been defined as the freedom to remain sick, as far as the patient is concerned, without defining himself as sick.

*Mental disorders, whether predisposed genetically or caused in part by chemical imbalances, are both controlling and controlled. To experience them is to develop a relation to them; once that relationship is made, they take on the role of any object-relation in one's behavior; that is, they affect it in deliberate and unintentional ways.*

*Once one develops a relationship with one's illness, the parts of that relationship that are difficult to look at with clarity will become unconscious; at least, if one does not like that term, it can be said that they become more difficult to locate with accuracy. They will affect one's behavior, though, as if they were unconscious. It is this effect that makes talking a proper adjunct of medication. If one understands one's illness but not one's relation to it, one remains in the muck. And in that muck, one causes suffering to others. As Doctor Gold put it, one "bumbles toward paradise." I considered the dream in another way, too: as I stepped on that escalator, with all those appliances behind me, washers, dryers, I was moving from cleanliness and order to the filth of that sandy bottom—perhaps the same sandy bottom on which I had sat on the potty. I wanted Dr. Gold to help me to see, to use my hands, to dig up the parts, to have courage.*

*The autoparts dream was a gift. It was an emptying of my bowels, and a rebirth, recreating the scene with me on the potty and my parents looking on, smiling. The dream message, and wish, was this: I give you my gift, I make you happy, look at my prowess, be my father and mother.*

>>> — <<<

*Erickson made a fantastic observation after he looked at my notes. "You are writing your own Anti—Talmud!" I was surprised because even with his breadth of knowledge he saw its structure immediately—a revelatory story, with Commentary, and Commentary on that as well. My very own upside-down Common Law!*

I had my platonic dialogue with Hart because I could not have it with my father. Hart was a stand-in. And Erickson had to be present because I needed three people in the little universe I had created. In this universe I might acquire the means to save my parents and to put myself back together. [It is likely that I wanted to kill my parents as well, him for his brutality (as I saw it) her for allowing it]. I understood a question Hart had posed once (or had I, taking Hart's role, posed it to myself?): Why would a man who claimed to enter P with his myths of hiding in view spend his nights looking at cunts and breasts, never growing or progressing? Because, I reasoned, it did not matter what I did in P, or what I saw or experienced. What mattered was the creation (the re-creation) of three. [And, perhaps above all, looking [one who looks also controls!]. If one cannot act, he can look, and remember, and spend a good part of life asking himself that essential question: why?]. The question I had always chewed on-where was my place in the three? If I were a clown or an ape, what matter? That was a role I took in a set of three. At least, I had accomplished one thing: the giving of equal weight to every idea, no matter how silly it seemed. If any one thing had cracked me open, that was it, and I am not sure I realized it at the time. [It occurs to me that in my repetition with Hart I wanted not only to overcome but to be recognized, that is, loved by another as I wanted father-love]. It seems that as a parent becomes part of us, we want to love and kill that parent within. The identity we deny in our repetition is that of being a walking, talking conflict between love and hatred. I repeat the question Hart had posed (or had I, taking his role, posed it to myself?): why would a young man who claimed to enter P with his myths of hiding in view spend his nights looking at cunts? *Because I was practicing!* [I was going to remain a curious child until I got it right and had an answer for that three-year old]. It did not matter what I did in P; what mattered was the recreation of three. [And I did not know whether I was male or female]. It is an honor to create a platonic friend; it gives him the respect due to one who might be more brilliant; because he is given the opposing position in all arguments, it places him on a higher level, and doing so shows a fear of his intellect. Whether he knows that he occupies a position from which one will seek to overthrow him cannot be determined; but that is the risk imposed on him whether or not he is conscious of it. It is, for me, a repetition of the position of the clown who is always last and thus second. If the platonic friend is not overcome, at least I will place, as the second-place finisher does in a horse race (what does this have to do with sucking off a horse?) Or a way of killing father after the fact! To lose is to win by coming in second, as I knew as soon as I read the book in the library about clowns!

I have manipulated the idiosyncratic meaning of my characters to work out the meaning of the triangular relations of my past. Isolation, observation, anxiety, these are my methods, and, instead of thinking, I looked at breasts and cunts. But one is pulled by life's circumstances into life itself. What one has always thought of as the *Other* is now seen not as illness or as alien but is only the nameless pull (I wrote "pall" at first) of human beings toward one another, which sickness distorts into symbols and not discourse (it is a discourse, but a symbolic one). It was Hart's talk about the importance of P, when I had first arrived, that reinforced the way I considered my task. That is, I act as if I am writing a description of reality, but in fact I am manipulating characters and words to tell a story. The reality about which I write has been reduced to a manipulable reality, and thus loses some of its accuracy.

***Groundedness occurs when we experience how we experience. The death of a father is not the end of his relationship*** with his son, but the beginning. Whether the son grieves or rejoices is unimportant and has little to do with what he will feel later. At first, the son runs his tongue across his lips to see what he can taste of that death, whether it be bitter or sweet, salty or acidic. He may taste nothing; in time, though, there will be a taste; he does not yet know to expect it. For good or bad, the dead always return. More accurately, they never leave; learning that truth is growth. A final thought in connection with that groundedness: to a child, silence is external; to a grown man, silence is internal. [A year after Dr. Gold's death, I had another dream: *my parents were shooting at each other, while I watched.* It seems that I now knew a bit about "why"; that gunfight was occurring in my mind and heart and gut. I had a long way to go*]. **But it was the first time I put the conflict outside of myself to observe it.**[26]

**A winding down, a revving up.**

Now I've spent so much time talking about looking to the past I ought to consider why I have concentrated on such a relatively short period in my life, particularly what Hart and Erickson have to do with the past. I saw this question, one more 'why?' as a difficult one. I wondered if I really did not want to consider the early events. After all, how could I bring them into the present in a form which would include the emotions I felt then, and my memory– anyone's memory, for that matter–is always suspect. The memories I was able to bring forth might not even be mine; someone might have told me about an event at which they were present, which I could not recollect; perhaps I had taken it as my own as a result of having remembered the event as it was told to me rather than as I recalled it. I wondered if I could have discussed *any* time in my life just as meaningfully. These thoughts brought only fatigue, not clarity. I considered what I'd written, looking for some kind of answer in the words instead of the past. It began to come to my consciousness that the time I was describing and the people I knew during that time seemed to be a kind of repetition of an earlier time. I had never understood my earlier years in a Euclidean way; that is, the triangular form my family had taken and the effect that a change in one side of the triangle affected the other two parts. It seemed to be a reasonable way to consider those earlier years, given the paradigm I had described earlier. Was it possible that my relations with Hart and Erickson were an attempt to *practice* a clearer examination of those earliest times. Surely, I had need to overcome Hart, if not physically, then intellectually.[27] And perhaps Erickson was a required participant, a

---

26 *And my mother, too, had a gun!*

27 As I write I realize that I may have chosen Hart because in the depths of my mind I had already decided that he was not as astute as Ericksen.

neutral observer for the most part, but an observer necessary to complete the triangular form. This way of describing the period of which I speak felt like the correct fit and brought me to consider another element; that it was not enough to overcome Hart. Someone had to see my victory! I could go far enough to consider that I needed to overcome Hart because I could not overcome my father. They were similar in personality, and I sensed a hardness of belief in Hart, likely because he was arrogant in the areas we discussed. I did not go so far as to equate Erickson with my mother, but I saw that it was necessary to have someone from whom I could silently seek a kind of affirmation of what I strove for. In that sense, it was understandable to have someone with Erickson's characteristics as a friend who would be present often enough when Hart and I were together. I would not possibly get affirmation from Erickson, but he would bear witness; and I did not expect criticism from him. If I did not manage to defeat Hart—at least, defeat him psychologically in my own mind—Erickson would never comment on it (though I was sure that he would understand the dynamics of my relations with Hart but they would have no intrinsic meaning for his own life). Or, perhaps they would, but it was not my concern then. It was not only the geometric form that I was repeating; it was an attempt to dive into the universe of the first years of my life as if that universe were an ocean from which I might bob up to the surface having grown gills. [I believe that, having finished these notes, a change occurred during my life in P, and I may have chosen that period without understanding that if I examined it, I might see growth]. The psychic turmoil I experienced in P mirrored that which I experienced during the earliest years of my life. If my time in P may have had no zenith, it produced the words to describe my life, that is, the words that made the scream part of a complete sentence, perhaps even a paragraph. I may have been repeating a time of sexual curiosity in which that curiosity was never satisfied or deliberately repressed by mother and father. Of course, it was also a systematic regression to that childhood curiosity which has remained until now.

Extreme self-awareness must begin as a protective mode. When I ask 'why?', what I am really asking is this: why did I develop that mode? There are some obvious answers: emotional danger in the household; threats perceived (and real) in the neighborhood; inner thoughts too frightening to accept in the context and the age at which they came, that is, without knowledge that those thoughts were not unusual even to a frightened boy. The self-awareness develops in that topographical way I spoke of earlier, that is, in the spatial relationship between the listening and watching and the stream of consciousness, so that one grows to be watching both the outer world and the inner stream, both of which have historically presented danger, either physical or in unwanted emotions (which were appropriate when first experienced but continue to be felt without context). The tragic result of this dual attention is that one uses vision to protect oneself but does not attend to the effect on the stream. The situation is one which leads to a habit I never really broke, of having to spend time at the end of each day putting the day back together. Did I make any mistakes? How did I feel at every moment? Was I laughed at? What began as a reasonable protective mode now becomes a barrier to growth, intellectual as well as social. And there is nothing in one's experience that supports giving up that mode. One accepts a muted life, or becomes cynical and sarcastic, though the sarcasm is moderated because it can lead to being attacked. The beginning of paranoia lies in watchfulness.

It bothers me that I have chosen to answer "why" with nothing but incidental events, descriptions of things, people, the City. It may be in my defense that I ought to go back once more to consider the idea of geometric thought with which I began. The triangle I considered still seems important, but in an infantile way, as if my earliest impressions were of geometric shapes, which in turn shaped the process of observation with which I looked at the world. A nude dancer is geometrically a triangle made of two breasts and a cunt. The cunt itself is a triangle. Another triangle is composed of two bullies and a frightened young boy. A family is composed of three sexual beings fighting for control, arguing and sulking, ignoring the bedrock of desire that the Greeks knew of three thousand years ago but which the family played out as both myth and reality; and Hart, Ericksen and I, the subject for endless repetition of the same triangle. I could choose to conclude that I, all of us, are stuck with that spatial way of perception from the beginning; the only way out of it might be to try what I chose, to become a thing, or rather an It, at least, to consider myself as one. It gives off a kind of equality, thingness does, particularly when one asks why and finds that his history can be described as nothing but a series of the perception of things, a thunderstorm, a bus ride, a raincoat on a windowsill, a rocking chair and a well-beaten chair, teeth like mesas, a badge buried in the dirt of a disused park. It's true we are not only in history but are, in fact, history, but the perception of things seems like as good a way to be in history as any other, and it does have something to do with "why", even if I do not know why. I ought to include one more thing here: an azalea bush. When I still lived at home and wanted to get away from the triangular mood that slipped into the house under the front door, when I watched television sitting on the floor of our living room, constantly looking backward to see if my parents were laughing or sulking, I sometimes left to step outside to our front lawn, where I could lie under the large tree and talk to the azaleas my father had planted along the edge of the driveway. I spoke to them articulately in a way I couldn't have spoken to my parents. The azaleas, though, only bloomed for three or four weeks, and eventually I was out there in all seasons, until I finally left, with my silences intact. I never liked azaleas after that, until I went to P and saw them announcing the coming of Spring in R Park and outside the Art Museum. It was a return to things for me, which I did not how to take advantage of until now. Speaking to flowers is certainly an animistic way of being, primitive, regressive, but in some cases, soothing.

⟫— —⟪

Isaiah Berlin describes Marx as believing that man is a thing in the natural world subject to the same natural laws as other things. This statement makes me wonder if my choice in 'Shroud' to become a thing is first, an unconscious desire to be ruled by the natural laws which govern things, and second, another failed attempt to strip away what is in me that is father and/or mother, which in the end only shows me to be more like them than ever, an amalgam of them. Looking for what is him in me fails once again [perhaps because I am ideas rather than spirit]. I thought becoming a thing was a way to an equality of all things which would destroy my self-conscious hiding, but in fact it is merely a step toward the materialism of my father. But it is more than that, too; whether I am human or thing or both, I have put myself in fate's hand.

Berlin's essay has made Marxism clearer to me than it ever was before, specifically in its explanation of the theory being based on the natural law of man. In its genesis, the theory does not seem to lead to violence. But at the same time, I think it is a theory which has at its base the desire to *order* man. I have been thinking about *rights* for several years., [I noted earlier that I believed I had no right to be a madman] what natural rights man has, what rights anyone has to write, to investigate, to theorize, to say anything at all about man's nature. It's certainly true that curiosity alone provides one right; the state of the world another, if one looks clearly at it. Nevertheless, I still see the genesis of Marxism as that of a *wish*, a single wish in the mind of Marx, probably sexual or otherwise arising from the way he was raised and interacted with his parents and the persons around him. I know my view seems completely reductionist, but I hold to it. I would go further to say that the impulse to know how matter works, i.e., the beginning of scientific discovery and knowledge, arises from a different kind of wish, a less dangerous one, a more humane one in keeping with the intelligence of those in whom it arises. It comes first out of a wish to *know* before the wish to *order* appears. The difference, to me, lies in the desire to order man on the one hand, and to order the world on the other. I must admit that my father wanted to order man to his satisfaction, and in wanting so, he created disorder in the family. His tragedy was that he had his own moral imperative but no means with which to carry it out. He could not step aside from the life he had, i.e., marrying, working, becoming a father. Circumstances drove him to immobility. We had that in common. I can only synthesize these ideas by concluding that if one thinks of himself as a thing or an it one still takes a chance on fate, on being a subject, on being recognized, no matter what qualities one possesses, no matter the political theories by which one lives. Perhaps thinking in geometric terms is a way of ordering man; whereas yearning is its opposite.

To have a fixed identity is to know you are going to die at any time.

***There is a way to put forth the question of why which preserves it as a question without losing its integrity as a scream. That was what I discovered with Dr. Gold.***

## *A Failed Experiment*

Toward the end of our time together, Dr. Gold posed a question to me that at the time I took at face value. He asked me if a triangle could have more than a total of 180 degrees. I thought it was odd that he would present me with a geometry question, but I went home and began to try to answer the question. I was able to answer it without looking it up, a triangle called a Riemannian triangle has three curved sides, with any two sides producing an angle greater than they would if the sides were straight. I presented my answer at our next session. He was pleased and responded as if he had expected me to find the right answer. But, looking back, his question may not have been merely a game; surely he had listened to me enough to understand the triangulation and the repetition I had been trying to work out almost since I had first come to see him, even if I had never explicitly stated it in a way that might have provided insight. He had taken my belief–that I thought in 2-dimensional terms, hence, my map–and turned it around to push it back to me, in a spatial frame of reference with which I was unfamiliar. If I were going to talk about mapping, i.e., to find out where I was latitudinally and longitudinally on earth, a two-dimensional system would never work. I needed a mathematics of curvature. The Euclidian system only works on flat surfaces; on the earth's curvature, another way is needed. As with the paradigm and the memory of my father and the tricycle, I had not used his question to expand my curiosity about it. [I noted earlier that it is possible to come to a completely wrong conclusion about a perception while the misperception takes one somewhere nevertheless.] Thus, I have spent my time working out a mental geometry which turns out to be the wrong scheme for my purposes! In the way of an awkward bumbler, though, I have by my efforts eliminated one framework and moved on to another. I am bumbling toward paradise!

The only way I had ever fit in the world was as part of a triangle, a son. Everywhere else, I was an outsider, a watcher. I had forgotten Korzybski's maxim soon after I learned it; I was not living on a map, but on the territory, the rocky, curved territory, which was constantly spinning through four-dimensional space.

I was the side of the triangle who watches the other two sides battle. They cannot come apart completely without destroying the triangle. But if it were a non-Euclidean triangle, it might bulge; it might even become a circle. ***If the triangle comes apart I will die! And yet, I have not died. The triangle may well become a circle; three persons can be a circle, no longer singular points!***

Dr. Gold dared me as I had dared him at the very beginning. The dream, which I wondered about for years, had things in it, yes, but the meaning of the dream was more direct: *I dare you to put me back together; I dare you to put my triangle back together; and then, I dare you put my world back together!* A fine way of saying *I'll come here but I won't cooperate (unless you trick me into it!).* Let me say that the content of the dream was meaningful, but it was used as a weapon, a defense. [Prove to me that I am the object of your desire; *establish me*!]. And Gold dared me: stand alone, apart from the triangle! *And the dream, which occurred soon after I began to talk to Dr. Gold, was, as all dreams are, a four-dimensional dream! Up/down, present time/past time, light/dark, child/adult.* A non-Euclidean dream that said "Forget the map, forget geometry; the life the dream describes is where you live, if only you would *see* it. In the end it was Dr. Gold who broke open the triangle, not me. That was his gift to me; it took me a long time to unwrap it. And yet, as I read and reread these notes, I see that what Dr. Gold said to me about my shallowness when not thinking of fucking, was precisely and tersely what needed to be said. Sex, sex and more sex and father love and father hatred and years of trying/not trying to escape the consequences of my own experiences by repressing any reflective thought of them. [The triangle was inside me; it was only the adoption of my family and its workings. A year after Dr. Gold's death, I had another dream that bore out this conclusion: [I have mentioned it before]:

*My parents were standing apart, shooting at each other. I stood aside, watching them fire.*

This was the first time I had ever put the lifelong conflict outside of myself. I was still an observer, but I was not part of the geometrical shape. I had unwrapped a gift that he had held for me; now he had returned it to me.

➤➤➤ ⬤ ◀◀◀

I borrowed the idea of becoming a thing from reading only the first pages and the last chapter of Heidegger's *What Is A Thing* and *I And Thou*, by Martin Buber. From the former I created my own definition: **a thing is any object to which attention may be drawn.** At first, I saw this definition as one that would include me in the world as an equal to all the other existent things. An unchanging identity. Later, I began to see that the definition had another possibility. When a child is born, his parents are things to which he pays attention, and the child, too, is a thing to which attention is paid. The definition then becomes an unconscious means of going back, to recapture that time when he was a thing to which attention was paid. Now he is an adult, but he carries within him a desire to be attended to which is finally acknowledged. It carries with it the possibility of peacefulness, of no longer struggling, of ownership. It is his! [The Marxist theory of natural man following natural laws drives me around in a circle, back to my father]. I have read that my actions may be only a way of sublimating the desires which I still have but cannot act on; and that any system, no matter how deeply one examines it, contains a limit beyond which one cannot go. But I have gone far enough for my purposes. I have had enough of "why".

Violence grows out of continual demands for the impossible.

*The repetition of the triangular unit has nothing to do with recreating the original unit, except insofar as has to do with reimagining my own neurosis developing at that early time. It is not about saving anyone or putting the family unit back together. That is not what I hoped to do. I may have just as easily wanted to recreate a violent scene, a tearing apart of the family which I may have either precipitated or enjoyed. If there was ever an Other in that triangle, a person in whom I saw myself as the object of another's desire, it wasn't there for very long. The giving up of the search for the Other at such an early age has repercussions forever. It is a denial of all one may know of one's self, and, ultimately, a denial of the unconscious itself. A denial of denial is the result. **[I am looking for a family that contains an Other]. The triangle itself is a myth which interposes itself between me and the Real. Its repetition continues to strengthen the myth at the cost of the Real. It increases the distance between the I and the Me. It also makes it difficult to love one person, because a third person is always sought. It is an attempt to be recognized (with mother beside me). I am looking for a triangle in which I can see myself reflected in the eyes of another as an object of desire!***

*I was not recognized by either parent. [Or by mother but not father]. Yet, I introjected them separately and as a unit]. The result was such that I became a conflict. How can I recognize myself if I've introjected parents who did not recognize me? I then repeatedly tried to overcome my father, not because he was, in my mind, always right, but because I was never right; I was a conflict. That was my being. I am still a conflict. That is my identity, a conflict! [My mother did recognize me, as did the second bully and Ericksen; but they did not intervene, and thus I did not apprehend their recognition at first. Thinking about the repetition allowed me to understand that, as neurotic as it was, it always included one person who did not have to be overcome].*

I *constructed* a triangular relation with the materials on hand: one was always right, the other recognized me.

What is possibility? Is it a quality of reality? It's independent of present facts, independent of any time but the present. It *accompanies* the present at every moment.

**The attempt at overcoming is an attempt to kill the original internal object which was never comforting! A repetitive attempt at murder of the object which has been introjected (or partly introjected).**

We do not consider how hard ghosts work. They toil in obscurity, but their work pushes through the surface of the membrane that separates them from our consciousness. We give them so little credit.

*I had always thought of myself as a watcher, but never as a noticer. Yet I see by the story I have presented that it is a history of what I noticed, that is, of things rather than people, [who are also things] a raincoat on a sill, a badge in the dirt, ashtrays, genitalia of both sexes. [And what I didn't notice]. If meaning lies in what we sense, rather than the objects we notice, then I have written a story about the things to which I have given meaning, as well as the persons with whom I interacted, and not, solely, about myself. I never understood what things meant, yet I sought meaning from them. I recall again seeing the Segal sculptures and wanting desperately to touch them and walking along the pavement needing to touch the solidity of the buildings I passed. Perhaps things were the Other from whom I sought recognition; secretly, unconsciously, I too must have wanted to be a thing. [Is this a way of behaving according to some natural law, which is the basis of Marxist theory, that is, another trap by which I continue to hold onto the introjection of a rejecting father, a way of being loved by a man already in his grave?]. Perhaps, but I have not lost my humanity; I have only used the concept to become equal to all things, human and nonhuman, taking the risk that I may never be recognized. By taking that risk, I become the equal of other humans.*

*As I read the episodic story I have created I notice that the language changes from one part to another. this change is noticeable in the part about Lara. I can see a yearning in it that is lacking in the rest of the story. I cannot say with any certainty what I was like at the time, but I have no doubt that my experience with her pierced the armor of myself, a piercing which was, no matter the end, thrilling. **It gave a name, a word, to what I had been experiencing for a long time and continued to experience; the word is yearning! And it gave sanction to the word, a human value which narrowed the distance between myself and every other human being.***

*The unraveling of the funeral shroud by Penelope is a metaphor for the unraveling of identity; or for the repetitive nature of the triangular image. The reason for the unraveling and the repetition is to ward off death. To **be** in the world is to risk death at every moment, because death is in the real world. The narrator works against himself. He continues to repeat behaviors in his desire to overcome his father; **that is, he wants to be the father in the family!** But he cannot. To be the father is to be in the world and is close to death, because the son wants to kill him! To be the son is equally close to death, for the father will kill him sooner or later. It is for this reason that sex, masturbation, looking at genitals, must be done in secret. It cannot be said that death was Penelope's desire, but in addition to unraveling the* *shroud each night, she was perhaps putting off the death of Odysseus and Laertes. It also may be that the narrator's wish to be the father in the family is a denial of his wish to kill his father. the question is: did Penelope wish the deaths of Odysseus and Laertes, and unconsciously act to deny that wish? The paradox here is that the son may wish the father to die in order to be the father himself, but if to be the father is to die, the son will die, too.*

***The idea of thingness as a way of stopping repetition [and time as well], is attractive;*** *it allows one to consider that he is subject to natural law, as are rocks, trees, flowers, animals. It appears to equal a man with all the things in the world, such that he may be attended to as they are, that is, by chance. Even if by chance, such attention removes his consciousness of his shame. If attention never comes he is still an equal. But considering one's self to be a consequence of the natural laws of nature places one squarely in the philosophy of Marx. If one has had a Communist father, who was a fascist in his views and his actions, then one is returning to the father, when for most of his adult life he has been trying to rid himself of the father within by the repetition and the Platonic friendship. One would be better off considering Martin Buber's 'I and Thou', wherein Buber writes that one can be a 'You' and an 'It' at the same time.* ***Buber's approach*** *lies close to the paradox which is what Winnicott says is* ***necessary to live in. I have come to live in paradox.***

➤➤➤ ⫷⫷⫷

*Dr. Gold, dead. Father, dead. Hart, gone. No one left to overcome, at least, no one who has the qualities I require for the process. No geometric formulae, no two-dimensional mathematics, no ape mask, certainly no map. No grand theory of my own behavior or how my mind works; no why. Every day for the rest of my life I will begin each day as a human and a thing [or an I and a you] to which attention might be paid, that is, the equal of all human beings. I expect it will be difficult. I may never be attended to. But waiting is also living! And yearning is permissible!*

*In my flat one evening I thought to call Dr. Gold to tell him I loved him. I did not call. The following day I told him I had wanted to call but had decided not to. "Why not?," he asked. "I thought I might cry." "Maybe I'd have cried too," he said.*

*And I was still sitting in that chair . . .*

On the old Jack Benny show, Benny was impersonating Ben Blue, an old Vaudevillian who did a magician—Eastern mystic impression during which he walked rapidly back and forth across the stage with his knees bent in a kind of hypnotic, trance—producing motion accompanied by snake—charmer music and which reminded one of Groucho. Blue always wore a long, multicolored robe of indeterminate design and a turban. He was America's conception of the East, and he personified and made fun of our idea of what the East was like in his very performance of his act.

In the skit, Benny was trying to get Dennis Day, his flimsy—minded singer, to step into and zipper up a supposedly bullet-proof canvas bag, at which Benny planned to fire several bullets from a pistol. Day, showing the wimpy fear and penchant for wordily excusing himself from exasperating situations for which he was well—known on the show, refused, and Benny, in a fit of put—on temper, agreed to get into the bag himself. He did so, zippered it up from the inside, shouted at Day to fire the gun, and calmly took the impact of the four bullets which Day cheerily fired. Benny leaped out of the bag to applause. The payoff came when Day examined the bag and did a double—take. *"Uh, Mr. Benny,"* he stammered, and Benny, exasperated because Day had been such a poor assistant, said (with that familiar disgusted expression of his over his shoulder) *"Now what, Dennis?!"* and Day replied, pointing to the bag, *"I thought you said this bag was bullet-proof."* . . . *"It is,"* said Benny, whereupon he picked up the bag and poked his fingers through several bullet holes, doing a slow turn to the audience, wearing an expression of *"Can you believe I did this?"* As Benny's fingers slipped through the bullet holes the studio audience roared, and it roared even louder as he felt his chest and pulled his wallet from his chest coat pocket. The wallet had four bullet holes in it, and inside the wallet paper bills were completely ruined. And then the roar became a tumult because, having set the audience up with his unmistakable expression, which told them—and me—that once again he had let himself become the fall guy for one of his bumbling cast members, his next line brought us all the crux of the matter, and left us no choice but to laugh to the point of hysteria. *"Why didn't you shoot at my head, for gosh sakes?!... You couldn't have shot at my head?!"*...

For all my looking, all my map-making, what had I seen? Flesh, beggars, smoke, the dappled bark of Sycamore trees in summer? The events I had experienced were as much of a conundrum as the question presented by Benny when he asked Dennis Day why he had not aimed at Benny's head. Hart had told me long ago that I was a Puritan, incapable of accepting my desires. That was why I had made my map out of those few things I seemed to have seen with clarity: the coat I placed so carefully on Zola's windowsill; the look on Lara's face when she saw I was staring at her breasts and not her face; the way Ericksen's pants cuffs always seemed just the right length; how a cigarette felt on a cold night, a sheriff's badge buried in an empty lot. I did not know what any of these things signified, yet they seemed to be a more complete history of a life than anything else I might have described. Perhaps they were all doors I was afraid to open. One day, on the way to visit my father in the hospital, I had sat on a bench in the bus terminal, smoking a cigarette. It occurred to me then that everything on earth and beyond it is just that: a thing. And I was a thing, too. I had begun by thinking of myself as an ape and had somehow found my humanity; and now that I was a thing I still retained that humanity. I took a drag on my cigarette and thought about it. I did not feel empty or sad; I felt clearheaded. I was a thing and that was that. [I was also a You]. Around me people rushed to catch buses and taxis while I sat with the same solidity and thingness as the bench under me, as the steel pillars holding up the terminal roof. I felt as if I had gained something rather than lost something. As I, too, got up to get on the bus to the hospital, I threw my cigarette in the gutter and watched the smoke rise, fascinated. I did not believe in epiphanies, but perhaps it was these small ones that made us all human. It did not matter what they were but that they occurred at all. I missed some things in P, but I was with them, too, because whatever qualities they possessed as things, why, I had those very qualities as well. I knew that and was content. I boarded the bus thinking I might know two things: that I was a thing-that was one; the other was about Lara-that she knew me, had known me from the beginning. It occurred to me that Dr. Gold might even have set up our brief romance; that was alright. I'd never have made a move otherwise. On the bus my thoughts turned to Hart, who was gone, now. I kept a clear vision of him, too, and it was pleasant. I imagined an empty block in Atlantic City, flattened by urban renewal and casino greed. The only structure still standing in the entire square was an old taproom, the kind that had a Ladies Entrance on the side. To get to it you had to tramp over mudpuddles and broken glass. And in that taproom sat Hart, the only patron, drinking Heaven Hill and smoking a Pall Mall while the sun went down. And he still spoke to me, though it was I who gave him the words, in our dialogue of love which had never really ended.

Between sips, still wearing his jeffcap pulled down over his forehead, he said to me, *"What have you learned?"*

*"Nothing,"* I replied.

*"Where is your territory?"*

*"Where all men live, in the core of their being."*

*"What about your map?"*

*"I have no need of it now."*

*"Are you an ape?,"* he asked.

*"Yes, but I need no mask to walk among men."*

*"And are you a thing, too?"*

*"Yes,"* I said. *"And it pleases me."*

Here Hart pauses. The bartender looks over to him to see if he wants another drink, but he merely smiles, still that maroon face breaking into a grin. *Christ!"* he says, *"You haven't developed any of us ... You didn't even give us our proper names!"*

*"I did what I could to love you. And, I had my reasons."*

*"And they were ...?"*

Now it was my turn to pause. I took a deep breath and suddenly Hart was gone, back to the world of big deals for restaurants that never come off, of girlfriends who could not even clean up cat shit ... [I am still arguing with him, debasing him, as I might debase my father for not making a living, failing in America, being unable to love me] And I am lying on the floor of my flat looking up at the ceiling, thinking that between the Sh'ma and my last breath, whenever it came, I would have just enough time to say the names I have given them, *the things themselves, not symbols*: Mother ... Father ... Hart ... Ericksen ... Gold ... Lara ... Zola ... Eleonor ... Tony ... Frank ...........

---

## *Commentary*

*If the preceding pages are, as Ericksen saw, my personal anti—Talmud, the notes below will serve as commentary. [None of them refer to a specific page; they are merely thoughts that occurred to me as I read my 'Talmud' again and again and again until it became merged into my blood, lungs and heart].*

*The father must die, and he must die in an arena. Around the arena are those elements comprising the swirl: shit, penises, vaginas, shame, rage, self-respect. And it is the arena also of the clown, the clown who in his costume believes he is hiding all the elements of that swirl. The clown chooses the arena because it is larger than the household, there is more room for combat, because the battle requires grandeur; blood will be spilled in front of the eyes of all those elements, which the clown is certain the elements possess. The clown has a secret, too; he is omnipotent and his emotions are as large as any ocean. How may I condemn a fantasy so huge if I have created it? A father and son may be miles apart or ten feet away, but they are always encircled by that arena.*

*Speculation is a substitution for achievement. Obsessive-compulsive behavior is also a substitution for achievement; it is work!*

*Any novel in which the narrator is a character is written on glass. If the glass continues to be opaque, he has written mud. If, in the process of writing, he manages to wipe away the cloudiness, he may create a mirror, at which he can stare. He may see a monster; he may see an ordinary fellow. Either has the possibility of being accurate. If he can withstand the accuracy, no matter the result, his work will have been worth doing.*

*After the father is slain or overcome, why do we not have pity on him? Is the slaying necessary because of some drive? If so, why does the drive destroy the pity? Is the slaying only a pushing away of love, because of the sexual element in the love? And what is the relation of the son to the father after the overcoming or the slaying? Certainly the father remains in the son's consciousness and unconscious. If the father is still alive, what then? Another self-overcoming might follow, but its success is doubtful. A son's love for his father is a duel between love and possession; this is not necessarily a sexual battle. The struggle itself challenges the connection between the two forces; if it is not settled, the son will never untangle those forces, and will push away love throughout his life.*

*The question 'why?' may be another heroic fantasy, as if seeking the Holy Grail. [An unconscious fantasy—a heroic quest!]. Job asked the same question!*

*Imagining what might have been, what could have been, is a way of learning what resources one does not have to pull forth in times of stress.*

*An image, a dream, a catharsis, a misuse of Euclidean geometry, if I had no answer to 'why?' I had something else: I had re- entered a labyrinth to which I had no desire to return. It was not thrilling, nor was it unpleasant. It was, above all, interesting. That was its most satisfying quality. Its value lay not in the possible selfishness it might produce in me, because my interest in it and its workings was, in a sense, a universal interest.*

*To watch someone becoming is the most thrilling experience one can have. Laing talks of experiencing another person's experiencing; Erikson speaks of actuality; I think of my experience with Lara as seeing her becoming! It is the experience of seeing, feeling the mutual benefit of two people being subjects, though they may have no awareness of their respective states. The raincoat Lara wore in my dream, which I saw as a symbol of her attempt to protect herself against tears at Dr. Gold's death, may have had another meaning: the tears may have been for her recognition that her becoming had ended prematurely. They were my tears as well.*

*Often I pick up a novel, open it to no particular page, and come across a paragraph that seems familiar though I have never read the novel. I recently read a short chapter in a Japanese novel that I realized was similar to the chapter I wrote about Lara. The writer was describing the act of sex; he used words I might have used— penis, testicles, wild, beast-sucking. He described his thoughts during lovemaking, his surprise, the mixture of desire and fear of becoming caught in some barely human web of relations and his awareness that the animal in him was overcoming his reason. On one hand, I was pleased at the thought that I might be a writer; I am considering the subjects writers consider; I am trying to make art—for no conscious reason. On the other hand, I begin to understand that I am in no way unique. The possibility of my saying something original is minimal. If I should discover something as I write it will be a surprise that I did not expect. At most I may tell myself that the other writer did not know what he would write until he wrote it and I am caught up in the same process. I am not him but I am in his universe and he is in mine. We are companions!*

*I was recently in a state of absentmindedness. An image came to mind: sucking at Dr. Gold's penis, then biting it. I did not shut it down, though I would have before the paradigm and the dream came into my conscious mind. Perhaps that patient of Gold who explained his free association to me prepared me for the image. But on this occasion I considered the image in another light, that of infancy, a desire to regress. If an infant suckles at its mother's breast, but also wants to bite that breast, I seemed to be considering a similar act with Dr. Gold's penis. That is, an infantile conception of the mother's breast had, in my mind, transformed into Dr. Gold's penis. It would not have been unusual for me at one time to bite my tongue upon the appearance of the image, that is, to hurt myself for allowing the image to appear, for it would have drawn me to consider my history of anger—at my father, my mother, and Dr. Gold. But somehow I was now able to consider the image in a different way, that is, first, as an expression of my desire to gain more satisfaction from our sessions, and to gain from the power I had invested in him, and second, as an indication that in my infancy, I had not been able to distinguish between a breast and a penis as a source of oral pleasure. I also had to consider the paradigm in a new way, not as an act of bringing mother and father together (though I am certain that at an early age that was an unspoken fantasy, having no language yet to express it to anyone, nor as a suicide by catalytic action. Rather, I may have simply wanted satisfaction from both parents, allowing, however, for the rear entry by my father as a punishment [or a present, given the paradigm). If I were going to penetrate my mother I'd have expected not only punishment but humiliation. [When I crush a thought by biting my tongue, am I seeking oral pleasure?]. One fact seems clear: I did not know the difference between a penis and a breast. Again I consider Dr. Gold's comment about my shallowness; he was correct. If I look again—closely—at my life in P it seems evident that everything I did, everything I saw, had one goal: to prove my gender. [I note that the patient who told me about sucking a horse has a part to play in the image]!*

*To be ashamed of shame, angry at one's anger, to experience one's experiencing, these are all of a piece. Apparently, I had been grounded for most of my life but did not know it. And I have made a botch of my question. The argument that has never ceased, between waiting and acting, between seeing and hiding, has always overwhelmed me. At most, I have approached the umbra that surrounds the deepest reaches of my mind, which has always wanted to breathe freely and to which I have paid so little attention. And yet, I cannot deny that there were a few events-more than a few, random and impulsive, signs of regeneration which were part of city life: meeting Lara, replacing the sheriff's badge, shouting "Avast, ye landlubbers!" on Dr. Gold's couch, those slight openings of a tightly shut 'mental apparatus'.*

*I became an adult without knowing how much danger I was in. I was afraid of my father; the struggle between he and mother had become a part of my personality. I was thus unprepared for the autosuggestion, which appeared often while I lived in P, that I ought to die. It was not a voice from outside of myself; it seemed to rise from my chest directly to my conscious mind. Of course I was full of self-reproach; I was angry without knowing that my anger had a degree of sadism. The fear of turning on myself was always present. I have learned over time that this fear likely existed from my earliest years; the paradigm is itself an indication that as a child I was, in fantasy, willing to die. It was fortunate that another autosuggestion appeared often: "You'll be alright! " Mother was speaking to me.*

*I cashed in my Bar Mitzvah savings bonds to pay Zola. At thirteen I was supposed to have become a man. I was now becoming a man again; I had not seen the connection.*

*My unconscious has been holding on with all its strength to my infancy and my childhood. All my life I have felt a child within me; I did not feel like a 'grownup' with any man older than I. But that childishness was misinterpreted; it was only the story of my first five years, filled with misconceptions, fantasies, misinterpretations of reality, yearning, desires, all of which led to a faulty template by which to interpret reality, that is, a mathematical template.*

*Consideration of one's self as a thing, or an it, has another consequence: it takes one out of myth into the realm of probabilities, that is, into fate. One may be desired; one may be ignored; but possibility is always present. Though growth always brings a separation of possibility and impossibility, with the latter viewed as a mature view, possibility has never disappeared. It may be recaptured.*

*Anyone who becomes an object choice for me will trigger the primitive process, i.e., sucking and biting. That is, they are not yet subjects. I wonder if Dr. Gold did not change in my mind to an object representative but remained an object toward whom my instinct was directed. I did not like myself, then, though and that attitude would have defended against object love. But unconsciously, the mechanics of it were working. Fear of a homosexual love object would also have made it difficult to use words to explain what I was feeling. There is also present here the failure to merge loving and hateful emotions, demonstrated by the image itself, which places the mechanism at an infantile, primitive level. I have always felt a child within me, but I never expected to find an infantile level of mental functioning. I consider the fear of speaking, now, because love of a man was the only way I had of framing it, whereas the image of sucking and biting was the way my unconscious was framing it, i.e., a primitive way of framing love had been more accurate than my conscious mind which was afraid to consider my relation to Gold in a homosexual way.*

*The initial consideration of thingness is defensive and infantile. It does not yet have the maturity of a philosophical point of view. Only later does it become an alternative way of being, because then it acknowledges that one can be an object and a subject at the same time, as can everyone else! It is an acknowledgement that other people exist as objects and subjects! It is an acknowledgment that one is willing to live with fate.*

*The question of self-hatred is difficult to parse, because the language we use to describe it is not well-defined. The self does not hate the self; a structural part of the mind is at war with another structural part. Self-hatred is thus an internal mind-struggle, with force and energy being expended. If only it did not have the force of law!*

*We think we were not recognized by our parents, but maybe we were. Maybe they saw that we were average at best; maybe they saw that we would never understand how their lives were frustrating and disappointing.*

*The word "why" takes on strength when one is a grownup experiencing a moment of child-thought. Many of our words, spoken as grownups, are co-authored by the child within us.*

*Dream: I walked along outside. I carried a folding table with my right hand. [Card table, cards, carrying fate in my hands. Residue: thinking about growth as acknowledging fate].*

*After reading Freud's essay on paricide: I need to revise my thoughts about the paradigm. It seems now to be a statement of fucking my mother and willing [or expecting] to be punished by my father by his fucking me in the ass, which would have been a great fear but would be a way of atoning for my intention. It leads me to think that the paradigm was a statement of my illness right from the start, but I did not know it. [I felt while reading Freud's essay a shiver of how strong my emotions could have been as a child. I had been thinking earlier that I have little empathy; I thought of myself as a 'demure iceberg' when I began seeing Dr.*

*Gold. It seems that the frozenness which applied itself to any emotional outburst of any sort affected my empathy as well. I have also to consider the possibility that I have thought about fucking for so long because I had to prove to myself that I had a penis; I had given myself to my father's punishment passively, and that may have been the source of my self-loathing (elf-loathing?). I pushed away that passive position every time I had sex. On the other hand, these thoughts make me wonder about the dream of a stele, which I believed was about mother. A stele is a hard tube, more like a penis than a vagina. Also, I might have enjoyed anal penetration.*

*A dream: I sat on the steps of our house. My father was to my left, leaning against the railing. There was a long empty space in front of our house that would allow two cars to park. [there was room for two egos now]. It was evening. I said to my father "If you played piano we could play together." He replied by looking at his calloused fingers, with a rueful expression on his face. He shook his head. He had accepted his history and his fate. We were on the steps of* my *house; I was still sitting, as a child might, but we were in relaxed postures. I offered him joint creativity, which he denied. It was too late for him to accept anything from me, but I offered it anyway.*

*Fear of the self, the weak, frightened self that will die rather than face the outside monsters who populate his child life. This is a life on the edge, with the thinnest membrane (if any) between the inner and outer life. That which frightens from the outside heightens the fear of what is inside. There is no place to stand except on that thin membrane. What kind of structure must this person create, to enable him to live, work, eat, breathe, create? He could not tell you, except in hindsight. Myths rise to meet demand, but, as with all products, they cost too much; nor do they need advertising to seduce us. We are already insatiable.*

*As far as my map is concerned, I have already met my goal. I live on that membrane between the inner and outer life, and both sides of it are dangerous. Where may I feel safe? The membrane itself is a tightrope and I have no balance. I have broken my ankle twice, had a bone graft, a skin graft; I limp when I am tired. I cannot "be in the world with both feet on the ground." That I quote from the Puer Papers demonstrates my desire to leap from the membrane into the sea of mythology.*

*It occurred to me that I am who I am because of the misperceptions I experienced in the first few years of my life. But then it also occurred to me that the opposite might equally be true: that my perceptions were accurate and left me helpless. The bits of information which rise into consciousness now provide clues into the environment in which I grew, but explanations are difficult; so many variables are involved which can be separated out only with difficulty [and assistance].*

*I've been thinking about my father and his anger and my anger. I need to put him now in the context of the cultural forces operating at the time of my childhood. I may have misperceived his anger as directed at me when he was probably distraught about the wave of anti-communist hatred in the country. I was a child during the Rosenbergs' trial, the Army-McCarthy hearings, all the HUAC testimony (my aunt and uncle were the subjects of some of that testimony), all the college professors losing their jobs, the Hollywood blacklist. He would have suffered through it all, without being able to do anything about it. My perception of his misery was accurate and painful, but I never had, nor could I have had, any context for it. My anger at him was, and remained, a child's anger. A question that has floated through my mind more than once has become relevant: that is, were my perceptions of the household mood inaccurate because I understood nothing of the cause of that mood, or, were my perceptions accurate though I was helpless to act? I cannot but think that my mother had no idea how to deal with my father's suffering. My fantasy of putting the family back together may have developed during this period. I do not discount my examination of the past in a psychological, even in a psychoanalytic perspective; there was distortion in the family. But it seems unfair to lay the blame for those palls of which I spoke earlier, smoke and anger, solely on my father.*

*I see several strains running through these notes. First, father love/hatred; second, a discovery of the strength of repression and the unconscious; third, repetition; fourth, a growth of understanding of the forces which affected my parents and me. What I do not see is an explanation of the strength of the anger with which I responded to these forces. I have unearthed the underlying history as best I could; I have reflected; I have understood my adoption of a destructive internal object and the long internal struggle to uncover it without dying. I have considered my history within the Freudian scheme and others (for which I make no apologies), yet I wonder whether my work has had only the effect of lessening my own suffering, though I may never understand how it began.*

*The fact of the catharsis being about an earlier event shows that the repression began earlier, perhaps by the third year. It may have begun when I was moving into the oedipal phase and prevented that phase from developing and then fading. The anger that was released locates a traumatic event during the first three years of my life.*

*Hatred had become a need of which I was loathe to rid myself.*

*Much has been written about children's fantasies and a child's early thinking about how sex is performed, genitals, birth by anus or mouth; but I wonder about children's accurate perceptions for which they have as yet no words, only feeling responses.*

*The dream is a birth dream, a birth into hell! It's a wish to be reborn! The escalator is the vaginal canal or the anus; the dream is an imagined rebirth, but not from actual birth; instead, birth at the age I am in the dream, i.e., somewhere between seven and ten. But why do I begin in a background of cleanliness to descend to a level of dirt [flat earth?]? Is that the age at which I wish my father dead—broken car parts? That is the age when I told mother 'I wish he were dead'! [the dream mixes rebirth with the childish belief that birth comes out of the anus].*

*I remembered the fantasy I had when I was considering analysis; I was lying on an operating table; the surgeon was standing over me, next to him was the nurse, both wearing masks, ready to cut off my balls, with monkeys running wild in the operating room. It occurred to me that I was afraid of both of them, i.e., mother and father. Perhaps it was the pair as a unit of whom I was afraid. They were going to unman me as a team. It recalls Herzog's theory of the parental unit as an internalized object, possibly a destructive one. I think now that internal objects oppose one another but they also cooperate. And monkeys are symbols of cosmic terror!*

*Everyone grows up with a mental structure which responds to any stimulus, whether pleasant or painful. But that structure has a logic to it which the sufferer does not understand; he does not know that it exists. I am not referring to the intentional part of mental disturbance, though it plays a role. what I am getting at is the logic of suffering. I have been reading <u>An Essay on Human Feeling</u>, by Langer. She discusses magic, ritual, sacrifice in primitive groups. It appears to me that there was a logic to these acts to which anthropologists did not pay sufficient attention.. I admit that whenever an idea occurs to me, I believe it is correct. Therefore, the first sentence in this paragraph may be an idea that has a logic to it of which I am unaware. It is only my awareness that differentiates me from the tribes which Langer wrote about. It is for this reason that I came to understand that how I thought was as important as what I thought. I have read much about fantasy; the content of fantasy certainly locates the age at which a fantasy arose and is an important developmental marker in therapy. But even fantasy has its own logic; it is defensive, yet the one fantasizing does not know that he is using logic when he fantasizes.*

*I did with my father what Dora did, but it was only a temporary act. When I blew up at him in the basement it was an immediate response, but when I told him to fuck off in my flat it was only an attempt to go back to the moment before something happened years ago to rewrite its history. The difference between the two acts is related to the question of how we think, not why, because the latter act did have the wrong logic behind it; it was not reflective. Retaliation is never reflective.*

*If "why" is a member of a community of words, then a scream originating in the body has no meaning yet. It needs those other words, as if it is not yet part of a sentence. That is why the need to ask 'how' becomes important. It is the way we put words before and after "why" to complete its meaning. [But events that occurred before I had words resist being comprehended with words].*

*I did not think to describe the sadism inherent in bullying. the boys on my street enjoyed seeing me cry and run away. When I bullied the boys my age, I had become a sadist, too, in order to strengthen my connection with them. I do not think I enjoyed my acts; nevertheless, an act is an act though its motive may be unknown to the actor.*

*I've said enough!*

*I consider the early memories, which were never completely buried, and what becomes etched in my consciousness is their concentration in my parents' bedroom or the bathroom of our apartment. I now see why my attempt to discover "why" was framed in the geometric form. I did not go far enough; I adopted the form but not the action that took place within its boundaries.*

*Most of the word pictures, the paradigm and my early memories have to do with the three erogenous zones. The sole catharsis was one of remembered anger, and it was incorrect as to the actual event. It was a lesson in repression but not the unconscious. The dream, while not overtly sexual, was a birth dream, and it contains images of cleanliness and filth. And, the overcoming of my father through Hart was not an overcoming; it was a wish to destroy a conflict. It might be considered as the expulsion*[28] *of a destructive object, but the method was illconceived. Thwarted love cannot be overcome, it can only be apprehended. Memories which rise from the unconscious may locate in time the beginning of an early crisis, but they are insufficient to explain the nature of it.*

*Swimming in the muck of infantility, where shit, genitals, breasts are the most important things in the world. A list of the word-pictures that have come from the lower depths of my mind demonstrates their importance:*

- *the paradigm*
- *the dream*
- *the smearing of shit*
- *the sucking and biting of Dr. Gold's penis*
- *the comparison of same with an infant at mother's breast*
- *the lifelong desire to see genitals*
- *the confusion and fantasy of infancy to four years old*
- *the hairy leg protruding from a blanket, with a greeting card next to the leg; an image of a teddy bear on the card [the drowned boy's leg?]*
- *a page from a book, very bright; a few lines at the top, a long footnote below [this novel?]*
- *the stele which I awoke and thought 'mother'*

*An image of ducks bobbing up and down on the cot next to my bed. I have never figured out whether this image came out of a dream, or something actually occurred in my bedroom during one of the cell meetings. Overcoats were thrown on that cot when the cell members arrived. I may have imagined two of them were having sex.*

---

28 And what does expulsion bring to mind but my memory of the potty. Is every bowel movement a flushing away of father?

*These images, which rose from the depths of my mind over a period of time, therapy and after, all have their place in infancy and the few years afterward. They demonstrate, certainly, the forces that drove me from the beginning of my life; they are directly connected to our bedrooms and the bathroom in our apartment. But they do not answer my original question: why? I now wonder if the answer to my question, despite the experiences I have recalled, my father's anger, my mother's inability to defend me, the bullies, is in the end nothing more than this: **something happened. And it happened before I had words.** I will never know what that event was. At most, I may be fortunate to consider the fact of an event. For my purposes, it may be sufficient to do so, for knowing that something happened is liberating.*

*A strong affect in a toddler may be traumatic. The abreaction, which was of an event prior to the one I believed it was, may have been the result of an earlier trauma which I cannot recall. One of the word pictures that arose afterward was (actually) not a picture but a quick memory: 'I saw it! I saw it!," spoken to my father. Was he shouting? How frightened was I?*

*Surprising that as I give father his due, mother begins to reappear. I recalled other acts of my mother in my childhood, warm milk at night, rubbing my calves with BenGay when my legs cramped, the game I played when I got up, by putting my books under the quilt and hiding under my bed waiting for her to come in and shake me awake.*

*I had thought once that internal conflicts could be separated into their component parts. Each side of the conflict might then be examined separately. When I began to think about my father as a communist, I began to consider the differences between he and I as different world views. I found Isaiah Berlin's thoughts insightful. Berlin wrote that communism seeks to order man, whereas I always sought to order the world in hopes that I might be able to live among men. I believe that Camus makes a similar point. I did not make a scholarly investigation, certainly, but my reading had the effect, I believe, of pulling apart, to a degree, the conflict which I had never understood and which had tortured me for years. I cannot say that his worldview produced the anger which I carried against him from my earliest years, but considering it loosened my grip on that conflict, that is, a component of it was torn away and I did not struggle to put it back.*

*The effort to separate father and mother may be only partly successful, but one consequence seems clear—the emergence of love for the parent who has been overshadowed. I have felt at times a powerful love for her appearing with clarity as I worked so hard to see my father as something more than an angry tyrant. That love, which had begun to appear as a symbol in the dream of the stele, began to take on physical being in the form of a longing for physical contact with her, an infant's desire, perhaps, but nevertheless a force. It was becoming clearer, too, that under the constant thinking about sex there lay a powerful longing for union, succor, comfort, all of which were beyond words.*

*In those states of ground, there is no past nor future, only a present which is timeless. I wonder if Hart and I, and our desire to stop time, was only a memory of a few instances of that state of which I speak. I had stepped out of time once; I do not know if Hart had.*

*It occurred to me tonight that I do not want to finish these notes, nor do I want anyone to read them. I noted earlier that it would undo me if I spoke to Hart and Ericksen about my desires, my illness; those words came back to me right away. I had spent the evening avoiding any revisions; I ate, smoked, drank coffee. Then, when I had the thought I just mentioned, it frightened me.*

*I found a sentence in my preparatory notes where I noted that analysts annotate what the patient says. I am not sure if I wrote it before I decided to annotate my novel or later. It may be another example of borrowing.*

*Finally, I found another sentence in those notes which excited me: "We speak ourselves into reality."*

*Again, a question: was the repetition an attempt at overcoming, or was it an attempt to create another family.*

*A list of Dr. Gold's remarks during our long therapy together:*
 *"When you're not thinking of fucking you're pretty shallow."*
 *If you're so angry, why don't you go out and punch the first person you see?"*
 *"When you shit on my rug you'll be cured."*
 *"They're just garden variety psychotics" [mother and father]*
 *[After calling him at midnight to say I was going to take a running leap onto the parking lot]; "Go out and get a quart of beer and come to my office in the morning."*
 *A list of my remarks:*

*"I don't like you!"*

*A thread: pulling the covers over my head is like pulling depression over one's mind. There is an intention as well as a fear. Suppose a child senses that his parents want him dead; is it not likely that many parents have thought they would be happier— or would separate—if they had no children? A child has no support for his fear except his parents; whether his senses are right or wrong, he cannot verify them.*

*Think of the id, the unconscious, the repository of desire, as a boxer sitting on a stool in his corner, who's been pummeled in the opening rounds, his face bloody, yet ready to leap off that stool, to run to the center of the ring, to beat his opponent as bloody as he is, while the referee, the ego, circles around the two fighters, pulling them out of clinches, ready to stop the fight if too much blood flows.*

*If objects are also symbols, then I am object and symbol. Is it as symbol that I may possibly become someone's subject?*

*The auto parts dream was a gift. It was an emptying of my bowels, and a rebirth, recreating the scene with me on the potty and my parents looking on, smiling. The dream message, and wish, was this: I give you my gift, I make you happy, look at my prowess, be my father and mother.*

*Writing is a reconstruction of the self.*

*The creation of a platonic friendship is a duplication of an internal conflict. Its genesis is an intention to recreate the latter in a less dangerous mode which one can control, up to a point.*

*I recall Lampedusa's remark that he didn't care if his work bored the reader. the statement could only have been made by a writer already secure in his literary position. That is, he had the right to be a madman.*

*I have brought forth two ghosts. Now, they are words. Love is shown only by the accuracy of description.*

*I began to look for examples of difficult father/son relationships. A book titled* Father and Son, *by Edmund Gosse was particularly relevant to me. Gosse was the child of parents whose religious beliefs were extremely strict. His mother died when he was a child, and he was then raised for the next several years by his father. The latter was a noted British scientist, who had tried to reconcile his religious pietism with the science which had allowed him to make discoveries of importance, but he foundered when he could not find a way to accommodate his certainty regarding Biblical history with his love of science and his intelligent comprehension that Darwinian theory was going to prevail. It seemed to me that I might consider my father as being in a similar position, unable to live comfortably with his unfaltering faith in Communism, on one hand, and his responsibilities to his family and neighbors, the latter of which required him to live, work and react to many people, including my mother's siblings, to whom he could never explain his yearnings. A certain arrogance made it difficult to live with the resultant conflict.*

*If the mind is one of the 'ten thousand things', and if words have the quality of sculpture, then what I tried to do is turn my mind this way and that to see it in a new way, a way I never considered though I looked at it for years; but not to transcend it!*

*If the story disappears when we use words to describe it, then what is left is only the scar which the story cannot reach. All that can be done is to describe the story.*

*I've written a book about a book and I fear that it is only another mask!*

*My story, my love object, my fetish.*

*It now occurs to me why I included some chapters, i.e., Lara, Zola, even the Screaming Woman. I acknowledged so little of Dr. Gold's comments; his comment about my being shallow when I wasn't thinking of fucking. In fact, during my time in P fucking was all I thought about, and it had nothing to do with desire. If I place the paradigm in front of my vision, I see that I was driven by a childish, almost infantile force; I was not to be denied sex! I have spent my life wanting the nipple; my parents had cigarettes; I smoked, too. **But I wanted the nipple! Over and over and over...***

*If the unconscious is a language then we want to hear what it has to say because the language it uses will tell us about the illness. That is, the illness appears in a form of language, words and how they are used. The use of the words indicates the type and form of the illness.*

*I always say of thoughts that they occur, as Wittgenstein said. The unconscious appears as an occurrence, always as a surprise. It is as if the attention of the conscious mind must be momentarily diverted, offering a bit of space for the unconscious to make its appearance.*

*If one says a word, 'rock' one is not speaking in symbolic language, because it describes a rock but not the symbolic meaning of 'rock. Its meaning is unclear. If Lacan says that the language of the unconscious is, in fact, a language, he is saying that any word the patient speaks is only symbolic if it has meaning beyond the word itself. One could describe analysis as listening for the symbolic meaning of words, with transference making it possible for more symbolic words to appear. In a sense analysis, for Lacan is a space where he, Wittgenstein, Freud and Levi-Strauss meet, with Chomsky adding pithy comments about the innate structures which provide the ability to learn language.*

*If ghosts are words, and words are persons, I may be a ghost in the mind of another. Putting aside for a minute the idea of desire and the Other, haven't I shown that I exist and the other person also exists?*

*The further work I speak of was, of course, a desire for achievement, but it was more than that, too. It was a desire to live truthfully, which, after years of therapy, I believed I had never done. I had only one model, Lara, but it was she who provided the template for that goal, though it had taken years to reach its beginning.*

*I was further encouraged by DeQuincey, who wrote in <u>Confessions Of An English Opium Eater</u>, that he "could not, without effort, constrain himself to the task of* *either recalling or constructing into a regular narrative the whole burthen of horrors which lies upon my brain."*[29]

*The television shows I watched with my parents were family comedies. The characters we viewed expressed their emotions, always in moderation and hardly ever in anger, for the most part. Only one of these shows, The Honeymooners, contained loud voices, arguments, disappointment in work and love, and a degree of hatred. Always, though, that show ended with husband and wife reconciled, the husband regretting his foolishness, the good friend still the good friend. As we watched, I lay on the floor while my parents sat behind me on our sofa. They sat apart, father at one end, mother at the other. I often turned around to see if they were laughing; if I heard no laughter, I turned around to see why they weren't laughing. The Honeymooners was to me the most realistic of all the shows we watched, but all of us, mother father, me, were frozen into immobility, physical and mental. It strikes me that I wanted to see emotion and laughter on the television; I saw it so seldom in our household, except for angry outbursts and sulking.*

*The story of the woman who screamed was about the attempt to negate reality or to destroy it because it cannot be overcome. I think it was also about words. I had been to Eleonor's house once, along with a woman I was seeing at the time. We sat around her kitchen table and each of us talked about what we wanted to do with our lives, as if we weren't already doing it. Eleonor wanted to be a scream therapist; my companion wanted to travel and to live in Europe. I said that all I wanted was to have an idea. The women laughed. My companion now lives in Europe; Eleonor became a scream therapist; her first patient killed people and is still in prison. I've had a few ideas which I tried to put into words. I had a scream inside me, too, but I looked for words to make into a sentence. Words!*

---

29  A terrible thought arises. I am and always have been a *collage*, made of quotes, scenes from movies, thoughts, paragraphs from novels, political theories, memories that are not my own. In other words, a manufactured person.

*When I spoke of reciprocal gift giving I was considering the concept of 'holding'. I mean that the analyst listens to words or the absence of words (which is also sound). He may have insights; he 'holds' those insights for the patient. Over a period of time he may give those insights back to the patient; this is interpretation. I mean to say that he holds insight on the patient's behalf. It's the courage of the analyst that may prevail.*

*It seems that all of my reading in every subject has had one aim: to answer the question "why" about my relation to my father. I have been reading <u>Sorel on violence</u>. He makes a point I have never considered, i.e., that Marxism is more than a theory, it is a call to action, to becoming through action, that is, reification. My father must have understood this idea but could not act on it. He had a wife, a son, work. Perhaps he chose to have a family as a way of avoiding action. What did he have left? Domestic tyranny. He and I are descended from a long line of Lithuanian rabbis; every generation of us has produced scholars, artists, scientists, but no revolutionaries. Were there constitutional factors which prevented him from taking part in more communist actions? Who can say? It is clear to me, however, that the conflict between theory and action could not be resolved. What remained was only a wish, more a conviction, that someday earth would be a paradise.*

*If I can live in suspension between love and hate, private peace and public activity, without the gravitational pull of the past, I might attain health.*

*When I described my platonic friendship with Hart, I spoke of it as taking in another person for the purpose of overcoming that person. I wonder now if, in calling Hart an other person, I meant an Other, a word I have come across many times in my reading but which has never seemed to me to have a consistent meaning. Perhaps I was actually arguing, with the goal of overcoming that Other, that is, what has always felt external to me.*

*The auto parts dream: the department store was deserted; it was night. The store was the absence of possibility in my adult life; the wish was to be small again, to have more possibilities. But to be small again was filled with broken parts. What is the counterwish? I could never put the parts back together; I knew nothing about cars. My father knew about cars but he was not in the dream (unless he was the broken parts). What had he done to be so broken? I went back to being small with an adult sense of what had been broken, but I only saw it, I did nothing about it. Why wasn't Dr. Gold in the dream? Did I expect him to fix it? Was there another wish? To become small in his presence so he could fix the past? Is there doubt in the dream along with the wish? That it could not be done, the store was empty. What does the store mean? A place with many things to buy, but it was empty at night. My time with him was dark; I expected it to be dark; he would not help me. I was comparing him to my father, saying you will not help me; I doubted I would be helped and may not have wanted to be helped, it would have been too painful. Dr. Gold's office is the department store. I want to be his only patient and his son. I show him my childhood, broken, covered with dirt (sexual ideas or urges). My father is in pieces; you must be my father (and get rid of your other children).*

*There is a difference between 'await' and 'wait'. A therapist awaits; he sees many possible outcomes.*

Composed in P, 1995–2021